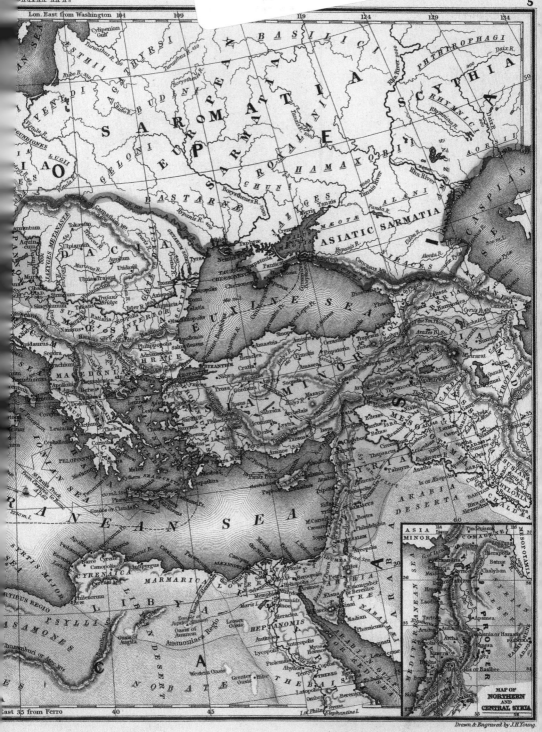

Drawn & Engraved by J.H.Young.

MAP OF
NORTHERN
AND
CENTRAL SYRIA

The Tortoise in Asia

To Francis and Penelope Chapman

The Tortoise in Asia

Tony Grey

British Library Cataloguing in Publication Data

The Tortoise in Asia

A catalogue entry for this book is available from the British Library

ISBN: 9780 86196 725 4 (Hardback edition)

Cover illustration: Detail from Hadrian's Column (Private Collection).

Published by
John Libbey Publishing Ltd, 3 Leicester Road, New Barnet, Herts EN5 5EW,
United Kingdom
e-mail: john.libbey@orange.fr; web site: www.johnlibbey.com

Distributed worldwide by **Indiana University Press**,
Herman B Wells Library – 350, 1320 E. 10th St., Bloomington, IN 47405, USA.
www.iupress.indiana.edu

Printed and bound in China by 1010 Printing International Ltd.

CHAPTER 1

*R*esting on pillows of morning air, a lone eagle stares at the ancient road of many-citied Syria. There's something strange below, beyond understanding, too big to eat. An exotic creature glistens and crawls in the early summer sun, like a gigantic bronze-clad caterpillar. With forty thousand mouths to feed, it gobbles up crops and herds, leaving little more than blight in its path. Local people are gaping in stunned apprehension; many scuttle into their farm houses to hide. The dreaded Roman army's on the march, in a massive troop movement that'll change the course of history.

Its head is a man, charming and well spoken, but notorious for sordid greed. His love of lucre could make Midas seem lacking in monetary spirit, or Croesus neglectful of wealth. Former triumvir and the richest man in Rome, Marcus Licinius Crassus is in the Roman province to launch an invasion of the affluent Parthian empire next door to the east. Through wealth and political manoeuvring he's procured the command of seven legions. It's the greatest success of his career, but only the penultimate step. Much more than this, even more than the expected spoils of war, are at stake. He's burning to become the number one citizen of Rome, *civis princeps*, never stops thinking about it. For that he must command an army that wins a glorious victory – on a par with what Scipio and his rival Pompey, not to mention the great Caesar, have achieved. Parthia is the place to do it, the successor to the Persian Empire of the Achaemids.

1

CHAPTER 1

At huge expense, he's paid for the army, bought his post in effect; so he owns it like a chattel; but he can't admit to thinking like that. He doesn't really own it; that's too outrageous a claim even for him to make. Private armies went out with the cruel Marius a long time ago. Anyway, it's a powerful instrument and he has the right to use it, a risky benefit admittedly for a man who has limited, albeit not negligible, experience as a commander.

He's prone to congratulate himself on being clever, exceptionally so, and much more focussed than the average successful man. Deep down though, he knows his real skill is in amassing wealth, using astute and often unconscionable means to do it. He's sensitive about this to the point of denial, not because of the dubious morality implicit, which is common anyway in Rome, but because he wants to tread the road to glory, a sublime path reserved exclusively to great military leaders, not plutocrats.

He feels the hot flush of glory already; why shouldn't he? He's in charge of the magnificent machine that brought glory to Pompey, the hero who must be upstaged. It can work wonders, as everybody knows. Prowess earned from the harsh discipline and novel tactical skills which moulded it provokes a dark shudder whenever it's on display abroad. There's nothing like it, never has been. Its unified and ordered structure, so different from the emotional rabble of other armies, forms an organic whole, a terrible colossus of preternatural power. He has it now; he alone can bend it to his will. With it he can satisfy that longing which drains all pleasure from his life, which stings his ego everyday with the pain that he's not number one, but could be, deserves to be, must be.

Soon he'll organise the Parthian army in a catacylysmic battle that'll pit West against East and decide the balance for years to come. He can't wait for it to begin.

The long serpentine line of might, of polished breastplate and helmet flashing in the harsh Asian light, dazzles the onlookers lining the road. It's like the time Apollo arrived in his guise of the sun at the ambrosial feast on Mount Olympus and stunned the gods into silence. The intruders radiate a self confidence that cowers all, not caring that it strays perilously close to the line that separates pride from hubris.

The road they're on is unique. It's by far the longest overland trading route in the world – stretching through Syria across Parthia and the Caspian Sea into the Central Asian steppes and man-eating deserts. It goes beyond the great mountain barrier which keeps hidden the strange people on the other side. Travellers tell stories of how eastern sands hide rich kingdoms of strange barbarians, and how it runs through them – a thoroughfare of mystery and romance which only wild imaginings can sense from this far west.

Like the sun and the moon it has a spirit, a personality – at times genial, at others cruel. The things that happen along it, often astonishing to the most jaded observer, seem to be steered by an invisible hand, yet it can be as unpredictable as the gods. In the Roman Empire it's simply referred to as the Caravan Road, and the safest way to travel on it is in convoys of long camel trains, for wild brigands constantly break its peace.

Today the great trade connector foresees that it, itself, will play a vital role in the curious chain of events soon to take place, happenings which are destined to resonate for centuries to come in the most unexpected section of its long pathway. Sometimes the part it will play in them will gladden its spirit and sometimes sadden it, but, happy or sad, the forces it facilitates will change the world.

In the first legion is a centurion with a curious habit. He's an avid reader of the Greek classics, brings them on campaign. His comrades josh him about it, but not too much; underneath they see him as down to earth really. They know they can rely on him in a difficult situation. He can be found late at night reading by the shaky flame of an oil lamp, sometimes crouching over an unrolled parchment of Plato's Phaedra, or Aristotle's Metaphysics, at other times the sayings of Zeno and the Stoics, or poetry. He knows the first part of the Odyssey by heart.

He's not a bookish type. Quite the contrary, although he finds the tomes interesting – especially the engrossing stories of spectacular deeds, of tragic flaws in great men, of uncompromising morality, of building strength in character, of the erratic role fate plays in the lives of men. Nevertheless, he admits the pleasure of reading them is not his main motive. His mother taught him that knowledge of the Classics is the key to social advancement – a talisman to influencing people of stature. Quotations from them buttress arguments, giving the speaker an aura of authority. A shallow reason perhaps, but he doesn't care; if it works, he's for it. Loot and plunder and the excitement of action are more important drivers, and above all, personal ambition. He is after all a soldier in an elite military force, not a school teacher or philosopher. Notwithstanding this, he can't help allowing some of the meaning of the literature to filter through his hardened exterior, sometimes to his discomfort, for often it contains wisdom that doesn't accommodate his compulsive desire to get ahead in the world.

In the camp outside a town whose name is not worth remembering, he's reading Plato's Republic – the part containing the allegory of the prisoners in the cave. Chained their entire lives facing a wall inside a cave, they see shadows cast by a fire outside of people carrying bundles. To them the shadows are reality for that is all they've ever seen. When they're released, they encounter the actual figures but refuse to believe they're real and that they've been living under an illusion. It takes a painful transition before they're disabused.

In the middle of reading it for the second time and wondering whether it applies to himself, a few comrades come over to his tent. They're in a good mood now the day's march is over.

> "Marcus, you at the books again? Too much of that reading stuff's bad for you. Relax. Come on out for a few drinks. Shit. I hear the girls around here are pretty friendly. They like Roman soldiers – especially ones with money, the greedy bitches ha ha ha. And the wine'll make your head spin."

> "Thanks Gaius; I don't feel like it tonight. You go; have a good time. I'll see you tomorrow."

They've seen him like this before and know better than to pester him.

So they leave him alone. Gaius can't help himself saying as he goes through the tent flap,

> "You'll be sorry when we tell you tomorrow about the great game we take down tonight. Ha ha ha."

It's not that going out drinking and chasing girls with friends isn't enjoyable. It is, clearly. But tonight he's in a sombre frame of mind – burdened with questions. He enjoys the fellowship and his good looks make him pretty successful with girls. Did he make the right decision to go on this expedition; was it based on a mistaken sense of reality – shadows on the wall? The letters start moving on the parchment as he loses concentration. It's pointless to continue, so he rolls it up and puts it in the box, and lets his mind go to what's really bothering him.

He could have joined Julius Caesar's invasion of Gaul when he mustered out of Pompey the Great's legions at Brundisium. Many think Caesar is the best general in Roman history, superior even to the divine Scipio, a match for Pompey, but he operates in the indigent North. There's a better chance for riches in the East; that's why he's here. But what about the new Commander in Chief? He's a lot different from Pompey, or Caesar. Can he really be counted on for the success everyone knows he's aching for?

Is it an illusion that Crassus is filling the role of a general, acting a part that's really not his to play? He's certainly not type cast for it. Will that spoil the expectation of riches? If it does, he's made a bad decision to come, possibly even a disastrous one.

Perhaps all that doesn't matter anyway; the Roman army can be counted on. It always wins. Besides, an illusion isn't necessarily bad in itself – can often be harmlessly pleasant. However sometimes it can sidetrack the logical flow of thought and seduce even worthwhile motivation into a perilous dance with fate.

He's thinking too much – time to go to bed. Maybe it would have been better if he had gone out with Gaius and the others – they always have a good time. But at least he'll be healthy in the morning while they're nursing hangovers.

og

Next day the army's on the march early, heading towards the fingers of the dawn which are slipping over the Road stirring up another hot day. Light splinters in the dust kicked up along the way cause eyes to squint and recovering heads to ache.

The morning banishes the doubts he had last night; its freshness brings out the positive. He's pleased with himself, a little cocky even, justifiably proud of his recent promotion to *pilus prior*; and why not. It's unusual for one so young, a few months shy of thirty, to be in charge of 600 men, a cohort. Since it's the largest tactical combat unit in the army, he'll have a certain independence of command.

He's on the way up. Eventually, if fortune maintains its smile, he'll become an eques, a knight, complete with an estate. It's not out of the question. Also, Crassus has begun to include him in strategic conferences. Why, the great man even comments on his talent for instant pattern recognition in the battlefield – an instinct everybody knows outstanding generals have. The Commander in Chief says he could become one. How complimentary is it when he's said to offer a new perspective, unspoiled by the conventional thinking so common in the High Command.

The opening battle, which he senses will be a decision point in history, is going to be his ultimate test.

As he marches, he looks at Owl's Head, his dagger; it's the one piece of equipment for which he has allowed himself a bit of indulgence. It was a curious little man, the master craftsman in Damascus who made it for him the last time he was in Syria, with Pompey's army – never stopped talking about his celebrated skills. How disgusted he was with the regular *pugio* issued by the Roman army; he could do so much better, make something that had a killing urge in itself, a spirit imparted by the elegance of his design. He was very persuasive. It's not hard to accept

6

when a weapon is personally made it has a magical quality, something that enhances a young man's belief he's immune to the risk of death.

When he had finished it he took forever to explain the technicalities behind how he had etched the silver hilt and the wide-leaf blade in their arabesque patterns, how he had decorated the scabbard with silver and gold bars, how he had inlaid an owl's head in gold on the pommel, and how carrying Athena's favourite bird would instil the goddess' martial spirit and some of her wisdom. The fellow charged a fortune – almost six month's wages, most of which had to be borrowed. But it was worth it.

Owl's Head always reminds him how important the dagger is to his style of fighting. He can still hear his old instructor, as loud – voiced as Stentorius, shouting at the new recruits to get in closer to their opponents, right up close, how that's the Roman way. The admonition was meant to overcome any natural inclination to stand back, but he often goes further; he can close so tight that it's hard to use his sword. That's where Owl's Head comes in. While he's proven he's above average in general weapons skills, he accepts he's not with the best. However, his reflexes are so quick he's lethal with the dagger, nobody faster. It's where speed is of the essence.

As the march gets under way, the uniform steps never wavering from the beat, slip into a sandal-crunching monotony. The Road compounds the Asian heat, so much more extreme than in Europe; maybe its stones are imposing a mischievous test of endurance. Every day is like this – hot and boring. Tedious though they are, the daily marches complement the training exercises to make the Roman soldier the fittest in the world, at least normally so.

No one likes the marches, but they must be endured. How else can infantry cover the vast overland distances? It's part of being a soldier, however humdrum. He looks for relief in day dreams – images of the booty that lies ahead, gold and silver in sacks of shining coins, gold goblets inlaid with precious stones, and polished silver plates, jewellery by the wagon load, heaps of glistering plunder which the cunning

Commander in Chief will extract from the opulent Parthian nobles, the richest people in the world. Try as they will, they'll never be able to hide it from the master wealth collector. As a *pilus prior* he'll get a handsome distribution, not a lion's share for that'll go to the legati and Crassus himself, but a leopard's portion, enough to make him rich.

A commotion erupts beside the Road; a donkey is bucking and braying. But it fails to divert the locals. They keep staring with wooden eyes at the shiny creature in a submissiveness that inflates his natural pride.

But not for long. Like most of the people who've arrived to watch, he too hails from the land. His late father comes to mind, the face like a rusty quince insinuating into his mind's eye. The old man is reminding him, as he always did, that the land is a member of the family, more than that, it's the *dominus familias*, the boss. The phrase won't go away; it's like a pesky moral tenet. Why should it? The army will never replace his formative attachment. Even his cognomen reflects it. Anyway, returning eventually to agriculture, hopefully as the owner of an estate, is not inconsistent with a soldier's lot – quite common in fact. It might just be lying in wait for his retirement from active service.

Through the hot simmer that bounces off the cobblestones in an eye – bending miasma, he sees the image of a ten year old boy. He's with his younger sister and mother in their wooden hut, the *pater familias* sitting amongst them on a rough-hewn chair, head bowed. It's a hot summer day, like today, and a short distance away one of their cows is calling in distress, possibly for a calf that's just died. Struggling for control, his father reveals the awful decision he's been forced to make.

Wetness trickles down his cheeks as he mumbles, almost too embarrassed to speak, about giving up their way of life. The *defensor familias* is powerless, unable to do what it's the essence of a man to do. By the time he's finished, the moisture is gone, leaving a salt track, gritty white against his sunburnt skin.

It was a day of pain stifled in silence when the family moved to a cheap district in Rome where the erstwhile farmer learned the blacksmith's trade. Money was never plentiful but enough for a decent, if largely self-taught eduction for the only boy in the family. It's remarkable that his mother encouraged learning, as she was illiterate. But she saw, more clearly than her husband, that education was the best way to advance for someone not born into the senatorial class. She pushed him hard – difficult for her sometimes, for it went against her gentle nature. However she believed that, like sugar in teeth, there's an acid in the sweetness of compassion which tends to dissolve strength in a boy. Nevertheless, as Danae did for Perseus, she gave him a sense of self worth, a faith that he was destined for an exceptional life.

It was tragic how the wrench tore a piece off his father's soul, how what remained was too reduced to allow for happiness, how city life turned out to be too different, too remote, how he could never feel the mellow connection there which is the essence of home, and how unsettling feelings would always disturb him, like the rumblings of Tryphon in the subterranean cave.

Being brought up in a stable, albeit simple home and rising in a career that'll lead to affluence most probably, he feels a tug of guilt that he can't identify fully with that depth of sadness. He was too young at the time to feel what his father felt, except vaguely, and now the thought of losing his home isn't something he really considers. He's always had one; these days it's in the army, a peripatetic one, but a home just the same. It gives him the emotional security everyone needs. Nevertheless it's impossible to forget that day – the only time he saw a grown man cry, an event shocking to the core. His Stoic background with its requirement to control feelings through disassociating emotion from pain seemed as-saulted. Later he understood that certain tragedies permit a different response.

The loss of the family land brings Crassus to mind, ironically the one man who must be impressed. Was he somehow implicated? He was among the most aggressive latifundia owners, those powerful men who drove down the price of agricultural produce by using slave labour from Rome's conquests. By squeezing the small farmers during those distressed times he added vast amounts to his domain – unconscionable behaviour in the extreme. Perhaps he's using some of those disgraceful gains to fund the Parthian campaign.

Is his presence here somehow condoning the outrage to his family? Should he be doing something about it?

There's no point thinking about the past; any suggestion that Crassus was involved specifically can't be proved one way or another. The man's presently the Commander in Chief and that's all there is to it. Besides he's showing kindness now and he's in a position where he's capable of helping or destroying careers, certainly his own. The man's an affable fellow, friendly to everyone, even says hello to people of low status, often calling them by name. It's difficult to imagine him in an evil role.

The clanking beast of war lumbers out of the Syrian plain into rough country framed by low lying mountains of smoky grey. A long shaky line, drawn like a child might, separates earth and sky. Heat smacks his face like the palm of an unseen hand.

Half focussed, he sees a man on the right hand edge of the Road in front of him walking in the same direction as the army – not beside it but on it. Dressed in simple Syrian clothing, he's bent over like an old man. A pole with a hanging bundle is on his shoulder. He wouldn't ordinarily notice except for the fact the soldiers ahead make way for him as they pass. They veer around him. He does himself. Later he asks why they all did that. No one knows why. They just did it, as if in response to some instinct.

A rise in the Road appears, a feature more common now. But this one's different. It looks down to a mighty river, wider than the Tiber, writhing over the landscape like a pregnant brown snake, fat and fertile. A Syrian scout says in perfect Latin,

> "The Euphrates – border with Parthia. It's dangerous these days. The currents are usually lazy but they're livelier now, what with the snow melt from the Armenian highlands."

This is it. The invasion's ready to begin. On the other side of the famous river, the march will take on a different character – more dangerous, more exciting. Discipline will tighten as they start to move through hostile territory. He looks down at the Road, almost feels like patting its stones for it'll take him to his destiny as if it were a beast of burden. He feels a certain affinity with the trusty track he's been on so long; it's like an ally, for once the water barrier is crossed it'll lead him and his comrades to a victory which promises to be Olympian. The Road will share in it, become more than an ally – a partner. An ideal one too, for he'll not have to share the spoils with it.

The army takes up rest positions under the trees by the bank. A human ribbon forms along the meander as the troops jostle to get close to the water. The air's sticky and clouded with blow flies. Since it's a sign of weakness to slap them off, they keep irritating at will; only reflex action prevents them from entering the men's eyes. His uniform tossed aside like the others, he wades into the water stripped down to his loin cloth. Thousands of chaotic white shapes spray onto the brown water, staying close to the shallow edge. The water's too cold for more than a quick dip, the current too fast for a proper swim, not that he has the skill anyway.

He lies down on his side, propped up on his elbow, letting the air cool him as he's drying. His childhood friend Gaius, who grew up in the same neighbourhood, comes over and sits on the grass, also stripped to his loin cloth; they all are. He's a crag of a man, big, blunt and square-faced. Unlike Marcus who is quite handsome, Gaius is too rough to be attractive to women, but he could lift a tree trunk heavy enough for three men, or smash into enemy soldiers like a battering ram breaching a fortress wall. He's the Ajax of the Roman army.

"What d'you think of this Gaius? Isn't it great – far cry from the marching huh? That dip sure beats the heat."

"Yeah it's all right. Nothing wrong with a break. But the men've slackened off – not good. Been like that for a while. Slipped off their peak. The Commander doesn't keep discipline up. Pompey would never allow it – no godamn ever."

"What are you worried about? They're still the best in the world."

11

CHAPTER 1

"No argument, but I don't like spending all that time booty hunting. Shit, we could pay for that when the battle starts. Too damn slack."

"Maybe, but you have got to admire the crafty way he requisitioned those men from Damascus and then let them off after they paid. He didn't want them anyway – useless idiots; just after the money. I know the locals hate us for it, but who cares."

"Yeah, but he don't keep the drills up. Look at what happened when he robbed the Jewish Temple – seemed like the whole damn army went on leave. Nobody did anything for weeks."

"I agree about that. Wrong to do it. Pompey never took their gold when he invaded Jerusalem. Had respect. Remember? We were both there. I'm glad Crassus didn't make us go with the squad. I don't know what I would have done."

"That's not the point – he shouldn't have wasted time."

"I know. I know. Look at those engineers. Aren't they terrific. No one can build like Romans."

Men with huge saws are cutting local trees into planks. Long, square – edged nails drive into newly planed boards. Rafts spring into life and are lashed together to make pontoons. A timber walkway is progressively nailed on top. Steadily and efficiently the structure moves across the rushing current. Its leading edge rolls towards the Parthian shore like the tip of a chameleon's tongue lunging towards its prey. Engineers overcome the impatient waters with technology which has no rival.

The scout attached to Marcus's cohort comes to the river's edge and says in a loud voice;

"We're going to cross near Zeugma. It's a small trading town a couple of kilometres away – almost three hundred years old. One of Alexander the Great's generals founded it. It's a stopping off point on the Caravan Road."

Marcus's heart quickens. Finally they're about to enter enemy territory. The interminable boredom will yield to the exitement of danger and action. Nothing's better. He'll have a chance once again to use his fighting skills, work with his comrades to smash the enemy. Owl's Head is ready to do its job.

"This is it Gaius. Don't worry about a little slackness. We're going to win just the same. This time we'll change history. Those barbarians'll sink below the tide of another Roman victory. They're too disorganised to be respected. No point in showing any mercy to them."

Showing no mercy is just a figure of speech. He doesn't think of himself as a cruel man. In fact he treats prisoners well and has never killed a man who's surrendered.

"I don't doubt we'll win. What'll we do afterwards?"

"Once we roll up Parthia I'm sure we'll push into Bactria and India. Crassus is ambitious and he'll have the troops to do it. Everyone knows he wants to be *civis princeps*. Probably the Parthian victory'll be enough for that but he'll go further. It's in his nature – he's greedy. We'll get past where Alexander went, past the Indus."

"What's the Indus?"

"It's a big river, a long way east. On the other side is where huge booty lies, even more than what the Parthians have. We'll really be wealthy, really rich. The Macedonians conquered the land where the Parthians are. Now it's our turn, but we'll go further. It'll be interesting to see what it's like that far east. But not as much as seeing the booty – ha ha ha."

He doesn't say he hopes to become a landowner of substance and be inducted into the *Ordo Equester*. What a climb that would be for the son of a farmer who lost his land.

CHAPTER 2

Orodes II, divine ruler of Parthia, king of Kings, Brother of the Sun and Moon, hasn't arrived yet. In the congress hall of his grand summer palace in the Zagros foothills, long-robed nobles and priests stand in little groups nervously chatting, awaiting the royal presence. Scouts are reporting the Roman army is at the Euphrates – a full scale invasion by the mightiest force in the world is under way and there's no strategy. Normality has changed overnight.

Torches in sooty brackets on the walls extract blackness from the dark, leaving a dim visibility. Usually the gloomy light enhances the majesty of the marble hall but today it doesn't; foreboding lurks in the corners like jackals in the night and impending catastrophe infects the air.

Four densely bearded soldiers with pikes and round shields stand rigid at the tall bronze – studded doors, massive enough to withstand a siege. Soft bonnets cover their long black hair which is tied in knots on top of their foreheads. The style looks like a battering ram. Outside, a huge stone lion reminds all who come of the glorious time when Cyrus the Great forged the Medes and Persians into the largest empire the world had known. These days the Parthians, of raw and lusty origin on the eastern steppes, are in power, having absorbed the cultivated ways of Persian civilization, or mostly so.

A priest separates himself from the little group of fellow clerics to shuffle over to where some nobles have gathered, and corners one he knows.

"My Lord Santruk, have you heard what's going on? What's the latest news? I've never seen people so worried. Everybody's talking about it at the Temple. We've got to mount a national resistance and do it fast."

"The situation's really bad Your Holiness. The Romans have a daunting army – tens of thousand of troops I hear. They've never lost a battle in our part of the world. Remember Pompey? Meanwhile we're bogged down in Seleucia. That rebellious brother of the King is dividing us just at the wrong time. I don't know what we can do."

"No defeatist talk my Lord."

"No sense putting our heads under a pillow."

The priest frowns and clasps his hands.

"This is a national emergency for goodness sake. Not the right time to be negative. At times like this that sort of talk doesn't do any good, just drains courage. Besides, if we appeal to Ahura Mazda, he'll save us."

"We need strong leadership in this world Your Holiness. Will the King give it?"

By now the hall is in uproar, everybody talking without listening and milling around, too agitated to stand still. Priests are loudly advocating warlike action, nobles trying to draw courage from their faith. Ahura Mazda is on everybody's lips. Nobody agrees on anything except the need for divine intervention. In the midst of it all, a sudden hush quells the chaos.

The Great King appears at the entrance. He's silhouetted against a brooding sky, sunlight struggling uncertainly with lumps of stygian clouds. He looks supernatural in the gloom, a threatening figure who can harness the power of nature at will. The fear of the moment is heightened by his dark presence which seems not only backed by the sky but invested with its might.

Wearing a half moon crown encrusted with rubies and emeralds, a star of diamonds on each side, Orodes stands in gravitas. After a moment, he proceeds slowly over the tribal carpets that lead to a dais of polished wood which supports his throne. It's made of lapis lazuli mined in the mountains of Bactria on the eastern border, worth more than gold. The blue mineral, with flecks like tiny stars, speaks of a sacred link to the life force of the sky.

The arms and legs are clad in gold leaf and lush, silk cushions soften the opulent stone. A window, cut high in the white marble wall, lets through a shaft of light when the sun breaks through the clouds, touching the royal seat like a celestial wand.

As the monarch passes by, the courtiers drop down progressively, like grass in a meadow bent by the wind, prostrating on the floor in his direction. He approaches the throne, and gravely turning, takes his seat, slave boys arranging his robes around his feet.

The Supreme Magus in turn sits on his high-backed wooden chair, intricately carved with symbols only the initiated would understand. He's lower down, off the dais. His tall conical hat points heavenward and the star – patterned shawl over his black and silver gown bespeaks astrological wisdom for which Zoroastrians are famous. A large gold clasp that gathers it indicates he's not entirely devoted to the ethereal.

Rising slowly, the rest of the assembly stands mute on either side of the carpet pathway.

The majestic solemnity of the occasion is somewhat blighted by the unimpressive figure of the King, now seen without his background, although no one would dare say it. Instead of a grand personage which many of his predecessors were, he's a pouty-lipped, podgy little man with a peevish voice, saved from insignificance only by his sumptuous robes. Everyone knows, however, he can be very cunning where his personal interests are involved, and vindictive, suddenly lashing out at an offender without warning and always with an exaggerated sense of slight. Prison, or worse, can be the consequence. The reaction he engenders is not respect, certainly not love, but caution.

"My Lords, you are gathered here with ourselves to consider the threat to our sacred homeland. We are informed that the Romans are at our frontier.

"Why isn't the Commander in Chief present? We've had to delay this conference for several days waiting for him. His emissary gave assurances he would be here by now and he hasn't come. We can't be kept waiting like this. It's so annoying."

As he slaps an over-fed hand on his thigh, thrusting his head up so violently his crown slips to one side, Surena appears at the doors.

The chief of the Parthian army is the second most powerful man in the realm, of royal lineage too, the one who placed the crown on the head of Orodes when the nobles and priests elected him king. But he's not the first; so he has to prostrate before the throne. He's of commanding presence, tall and handsome. Many say he's like the great Cyrus, whose uncommonly handsome looks alone demanded admiration. His soft, symmetrical face might be envied by women for themselves, except for the tightly sculpted black beard. But his beauty doesn't bespeak weakness, for he's a formidable warrior and brilliant tactician. Not at all a man stifled by modesty, his self confidence is so high that it's said he thinks he can dodge rain drops.

A deadly cruelty lurks beneath his skin, still smooth as he's just under thirty years of age. Unwilling to quell an arrogance fed full on his achievements, he has a contempt for Orodes which he finds difficult to disguise. In turn, the monarch feels diminished in his presence.

Noting the look of displeasure in the King, he says,

> "Noble Sire, I offer as many apologies as I have troops for being late. My reason, which I humbly ask Your Majesty to accept as an excuse, is that I had to stay in south Mesopotamia longer than expected. Your Majesty's brother put up a stubborn resistance. I have come to Ecbatana as soon as I could."

Never with an attention span longer than a child's, the King interrupts.

> "Yes, yes. But what success did you have?"

> "I am pleased to report that Seleucia and Babylon are in Your Majesty's hands and I have brought Mithridates here in chains. He is outside. As to be expected, he begs for clemency – remorseful for his foolish rebellion. He promises to be loyal from now on if your Majesty spares his life. The civil war is over Sire; the Kingdom is reunited. We are in a much stronger position now to turn back the Romans."

17

Controlled satisfaction spreads over Orodes' face – he has always hated his brother. Relieved murmurs fill the hall. He says in a reedy voice,

> "We're pleased with your work Commander. Our sad judgement is that Mithridates be put to death. It is not our wish but regrettably it must be done to ensure lasting order in our kingdom".

Dabbing his eye with a handkerchief, a gesture that produces a nod from the Supreme Magus, he says,

> "Though he is my brother, we must sacrifice him for the general good. See to it Surena."

As the Commander bows his head, a thrill rises up in him, so euphoric it almost overcomes his reason. For a delicious instant he thinks of doing it himself, with a bow string pulled tight around the neck deep into the skin, tongue flopping out as the death rattle begins. But that would be unseemly. Too bad, it'll have to be left to the professional executioner. He says.

> "That is a wise decision Sire, in keeping with the prudence Your Majesty is renowned for. I will carry out the execution without delay."

> "Good, Surena. Now what's your advice on how we are to deal with the invasion?"

> "Sire, while I have confidence we can defeat them, to do it we will need more troops. I humbly request Your Majesty to give me at least another five thousand, more if possible. With them and my secret strategy we will win, throw them back into Syria."

> "What secret strategy?"

> "I dare not disclose it Sire, even at this conference."

> "Come closer then and whisper it in our ear."

He hesitates, momentarily contemplating an excuse, for it's really too sensitive a matter to disclose to such an unreliable man, even if he is the monarch. However he thinks better of it and complies. Orodes smiles – more a crafty grimace than a smile.

> "Very ingenious Surena. But that would only apply if we go to war. Have all opportunities for diplomacy been exhausted? Maybe we could negotiate

a treaty. That would be better than chancing our arm. It would avoid the risk of defeat and, besides, save lives."

The Commander's face hardens, frustration rising like an attack of heartburn, searing his throat and constricting its air passage. Politeness struggles in his voice.

"Noble Sire, how can we deal with Crassus when he dismisses our emissaries without even a reply? The pig will not negotiate. I assure Your Majesty, the Romans are bent on conquest. It's their nature."

"There comes a time when war is the necessary next step in a dispute, and now is such a time. When that point arrives, the enemy senses cowardice in diplomatic overtures. They are emboldened by the contempt they feel when they are tried."

"I humbly advise that the only response is for Your Majesty to show the same resolve that your illustrious predecessor did years ago when he stopped the wild Hsiung-nu after they pushed into our territory."

Orodes winces and frowns to cover it up. He doesn't know much history but he knows that. The insult is clear, all the more as it highlights a weakness that he keeps wrapped in denial. But it would be undignified if not downright risky to argue the point with one so admired for valour, so he lets it pass. Anyway, he feels exhausted by these hard decisions. Why can't those tiresome Romans just leave him in peace? What has he ever done to deserve this? He's never fought them, never even threatened them.

He dislikes the unpleasantness of war, has no skill in battle, no interest at all in military strategy. He detests the arduous conditions on campaign, and having to deal with men so much stronger, men he knows will never respect him. Valour is not in his character, just not there. All he wants is a quiet life, self indulgent of course, but what's the use of being a monarch if he can't do what he wants? Being soft is not a sin, as long as he doesn't hurt anyone. Besides, plenty of people are that way. Let the warlike have their hardy ways; there're enough of them to keep the Kingdom safe. The moral capital the Parthians have built up over years of self denial is enough to allow for a little spending.

To skirt the risk of battle would be the most desirable strategy. But it's obvious that diplomacy has run its course. What makes matters worse though, is the ascendancy of Surena, a threat even more proximate than the Romans. That ambitious man placed the crown once; he's sure to want to put it on his own head next time. Having just subdued the rebellion, if he wins a great victory against the invaders his popularity could well shake the throne.

> "If it has to be war you have got to make do with the force you have. We need those men you requested for the autumn palace we are building. Why can't you defeat the Romans with your present strength?"

Surena is aghast. Not even his contempt for Orodes has prepared him for this. With fury bending his brow, he looks down at the floor, then around to the nobles and priests who're riveted in apprehension. After a silence of half a minute, he says in a stifled, quiet voice, both arms outstretched,

> "The Roman force is forty thousand, Sire. We have only ten thousand horse archers in the regular army plus a few thousand from the local satrap. The odds are overwhelming, especially given the reputation of the Roman army."

A hooded look falls over Orodes. It's useless to argue with the famous Commander. The plan his old friend and mentor, Versaces, suggested last week should be adopted. A nobleman with no independent power base and in need of royal favour after catastrophic losses on his estate, he can be trusted. Besides, he too is jealous of Surena for having superseded him as head of the army before he was ready to retire. If war's inevitable, then let Surena fight the Romans and lose.

Before the battle starts he'll go to Armenia with a second army commanded by Versaces to punish King Artavasdes for helping the Romans. It'll be an easy campaign and will remove any threat from the north. After his defeat, Artavasdes can be bribed to join forces with Versaces' army. Then, with Crassus' army weakened by the battle with Surena, the allies will either defeat the Romans or compel them to leave with threats from a position of strength. Surena can be blamed if he loses and executed. If he wins, another excuse will have to be found, but, given the likelihood of a Roman victory, that may not be necessary. It's best not to provide more troops.

He's about to announce this but before he can speak, the Supreme Magus, a white-bearded and pious scholar, whose hard eyes imply that any compassion he might possess is learned and not felt, enters the debate. He owes his office to a profound knowledge of the *Avesta* text.

> "Noble Sire, Ahura Mazda, the one god of the universe, commands us to combat Evil wherever it is found. It is here, now, in our ancestral land. Our holy prophet, Zoroaster, bless his name," (the assembly mumbles a repetition) "requires constant vigilance in the eternal struggle between Light and Darkness. These Romans, these devils who worship nothing more evolved than images of humans in the sky, come to our country as emissaries of the Evil One. They must be expelled at all costs.

> "We cannot endure foreign armies on our sacred soil, especially this one. No loss is too great for us to suffer in expelling them, no horror too cruel; death in this just struggle is a noble sacrifice that Ahura Mazda will reward at the time of judgement.

> "The Romans are disrespectful of our culture. They eat our crops and degrade our women. Their air of superiority and intention to dominate the world are an abomination. We must mount a holy war against these people who seek to pollute the purity of our ways. Sire, you must, in the name of the *Avesta,* give Commander Surena what he asks for."

As the nobles and priests nod their heads, Orodes shifts on his cushion and grimaces. The only sensible choice is to cave in; not a good time to brook opposition in the Court, especially since Mithridates' insurrection shows he doesn't have universal support.

> "All right, Surena, you shall have your five thousand. War it is. But see to it that you expel the hated invaders. We are tired of these discussions now; they bore us. You are all dismissed."

It would have been better if the King had volunteered more troops, but the outcome is acceptable – war will be declared and he has another five thousand men. More fruitless negotiations will be avoided and his hatred of the Romans, greater even than the old priest's, will be given full rein.

Hatred and its sibling, anger, are a constant in his psyche – flaring up especially whenever that feeble man on the throne comes to mind, when he, eminently more qualified and from a family just as exalted, is relegated to second place. Spiced with cruelty, they're nourishment for him, generating energy to excel in every competitive action. They justify a sense of entitlement and naturally lead to demands for obedience and hard work from others without any requirement for gratitude.

The feeling keeps him alert, ready to counter threats which can emerge at any time out of the toxic intrigues at Court. People however acknowledge that his patriotism is genuine, drives him to prodigious efforts on behalf of his fellow countrymen. He's a good man for war, more than good; he's one of the best generals the Parthians have ever produced. His restless personality suits mobile warfare, his specialty as the Parthians rely on cavalry not infantry. Provoking change and doing the unexpected are as natural to him as galloping is to a horse. And what exhilaration it is to catch the enemy wrong footed. A hungry lion can't spot and exploit a weakness more mercilessly. He enjoys a respect bordering on adulation from his troops, although nothing approaching affection. He's more a weapon than a human being.

The King rises suddenly and exits quickly through a door next to the throne, followed by the pages, struggling to keep up. There's no point being slow about it. What a relief the proceedings are over. He's ready for a break with his musicians and dancers, particularly that luscious one from the Zagros Mountains. Thankfully, the prospect of carnal pleasures for the rest of the day is enough to erase the distaste of having to deal with that obnoxious general. Some of the strong wine from Shiraz – maybe more than usual today, will help too.

Later he'll give the order to Versaces to get his troops ready for the Armenian invasion. It's a good plan, with the sort of deviousness that appeals to him, and ought to deal with the Surena threat, even if the dreadful man has a few more troops. On the way out he feels mellow again, mellow enough to think about what reward he should give Versaces for success. He can be generous when pleased, noted for it. It makes up, at least in part, for the less admirable aspects of his character.

As soon as Orodes departs, the nobles and priests file out of the hall through the massive front doors, calmed down now that a clear and credible strategy has been adopted. The Supreme Magus was good today, a hard man for a spiritual leader but strong in a crisis. The King looked wobbly until he brought religion into it. All have unbounded faith in Surena and his well trained troops, thankful he's there to save the nation so they don't have to rely on Orodes. Let the King have his harmless indulgences as long as order is kept under him and a competent military commander does the fighting.

Surena stays behind, not mixing with the others. He wants to be alone for a moment to collect his thoughts. The King's decision was satisfactory, even though it didn't go as far as he would like. But what a cretin! He was going to refuse any more troops until the old priest intervened, and for such a frivolous reason – building another palace while the country was being invaded! It was almost impossible to be civil to him. That such a man should be on the throne is a travesty. He himself should be there. The sense of injustice that he isn't boils his heart, heats an anger that he can't hold in. At the top of his voice, not caring who might hear, he shouts into the empty hall.

> "Why, just because he's king do I have to ignore his faults, suspend my judgement of his stupidity? Why do I have to extol virtues that don't exist? No virtues whatever are there, none, none, none."

He leaves in a foul humour and rides immediately to the army which is encamped outside the city. After calling the senior officers together, he gruffly orders them to incorporate the reinforcements. They've seen him in bad moods before so say nothing and merely go off to carry out the command. Secretly he's already made the selections, counting on getting the authority. Putting the finishing touches on that was the real reason why he was late for the conference.

☙

As soon as the new recruits are equipped, they link up with the main body. Fifteen thousand Parthians plus a few thousand allies begin the march towards Carrhae, a small town several days north east of the Euphrates as it approaches Armenia. It's not far from the Road. There,

23

he'll wait for Crassus, for he's sure the Roman general will continue his march east of the river. He has a plan to make certain of it.

The troops make fast progress since they're all skilled horsemen, trained to ride on the open grasslands since childhood, hardy and at one with their mounts. There's no infantry to slow them down. He rides by himself, deep in thought, working out, rejecting, working out again surprises to spring on the enemy. This is the biggest challenge of his career; he must not fail. The whole nation's survival rests on him, him alone, on his creativity, his ingenuity. To overcome this enemy, with its numerical superiority, he's got to be unpredictable, even quirky. He's up to it, no question – never known defeat. This will not be, determinably not be, the first one. Even so, though hard to admit and never to anyone else, the odds are against him.

As he always does for his campaigns, he brings two hundred chariots filled with concubines. Special agents are charged with scouring the Empire for the prettiest. Freshness is assured by continual replacement. The current favourite is Daka, a sloe-eyed beauty from Tabriz

Bringing so many on campaign is an indulgence politely ignored by the Supreme Magus and his entourage of priests which accompanies the army. The sacerdotal presence is required to convince the pious troops that Ahura Mazda is on their side. They need to be reminded that the single god is a far more powerful force than the disparate and often quarrelsome pantheon of the Romans. Besides, just before the battle, the priests will deliver the divine message that sacrifice of life in the name of the one true god will ensure a place in Paradise.

Given the dire circumstances they're in, the men can use a spiritual lift to animate to the fullest their natural desire to rid their homeland of the foreign infidels. These agents of the Evil One are reputed to be the best soldiers in the world; moreover they're more numerous. They'll test the power of Ahura Mazda as never before; it'll be a primal contest between Light and Dark.

At the end of the day's march, which accomplished a good part of the distance to Carrhae, he calls Sillaces, his Second in Command, to the headquarters tent.

> "Sillaces, here's the strategy. After we deploy the secret weapon, we'll hit them with a punch from the cataphracts. The Romans aren't used to heavy cavalry, probably never seen it before. Then we'll follow up with the light horse archers."

> "Yes, my Lord. Their manoeuvrability will make up for the enemy's greater numbers – plus of course your notable tactical skills, especially in territory you know well."

Surena nods.

> "It's critical though, that we fight on flat and open ground. If our cavalry get bottled up in trees or rough terrain, their infantry will cut us to pieces. In the open space we'll have the advantage. We must try everything to ensure that."

> "How will we do it my Lord?"

> "I've got an idea I'm working on. Leave it with me."

He dismisses Sillaces and calls for Daka to come to his personal tent. He plans dinner with her tonight. The day's ride has been hard and he's had a brain-wrenching time working out how to cope with the Romans. He needs a little relaxation. Before long, Daka appears at his sumptuously decorated tent, colourful silks draped from the apex and finely woven carpets covering the ground. A low table is set with a deep-cushioned couch opposite. Sleeping quarters are nearby, discretely closed off with a curtain.

> "Hello my dear. Come in. I've brought you a present."

> "Oh, what is it my Lord?"

He produces a solid gold pectoral, inlaid with stags fashioned from lapis lazuli, to be worn flat just under the neck.

> "Here, I bought it especially for you, as I know you love lapis. It comes from the main market in Seleucia. Remember, we were there for the civil war? I hope you like it. Come, sit down with me."

> "It's beautiful, the most beautiful necklace I've ever seen. You're really so

generous my Lord. I don't know what to say, except thank you, thank you, thank you."

She throws her arms around his neck and gives him a long kiss on the lips, and he smiles, for the first time today, the first time for many days. It's not the thing he normally does. In fact sometimes he looks a touch artificial when he does it. But not tonight.

He feels the cares fall away like a piece of silk slipping from a table as she tells him about her day – the bumpy ride in the chariot, the antics of the horses, the gossip of the other women, the heat, and, best of all her longing to see him. Her voice is beguiling, like a cascading mountain stream, sparkling in the sun.

He calls for wine and drinks with her. He feels comfortable, gruntled, as her open and affectionate attitude begins to penetrate his skin, so hardened by the demands of his character. Dinner comes and goes in a happy haze. She might well do for a bride, but no of course not; he must marry into a noble family.

The night passes in quiet pleasure and he feels refreshed in the morning. It's just as well for he'll have to spend the day's march completing the action plan he's been forming in his mind. One more day after this and he'll be close to Carrhae where he expects to meet his adversary.

CHAPTER 3

While the bridge crawls across the Euphrates, Marcus and Gaius Fulvius Aquila take a stroll to Zeugma. Never taken by education – uninterested in books, Gaius only ever wanted to join the army. He accepts that high rank is beyond him, content with being an ordinary centurion, practical and reliable. In the earthy twang of his youth, he often teases Marcus about his aspirations, especially the improved accent.

The two are life-long friends, unfazed by differences. Underneath, their values are the same, a moral linkage which allows each to admire the other's qualities. Gaius is stronger, Marcus quicker. The big man has more of an earthy attitude to life, uncomplicated by the disappointments attending ambition. He's a natural Stoic; Marcus works at it.

In a few minutes, another centurion in their cohort catches up with them, slightly out of breathe. Marcus says,

"Ave Quintus. You want to come with us for a drink?"

"Sure. I thought we were all going together."

Slightly embarrassed for leaving him behind, Marcus and Gaius mutter something friendly and non committal and Quintus joins them. He might have said something sarcastic but lets it pass.

When they get to the town they wander through unpaved streets full of bustling merchants, women too, but not many. Some people are on donkeys, others on camels laden with packing cases, but most are on foot, busy and loquacious. The atmosphere is organic, of braying and snorting and shouts, of sweat and animal droppings, of the touch of strange bodies brushing by in the moving crowd. Spicy cooking smells flow through the street like a light fog.

A large mud brick building with an open door stands out among the rest. They go through to a noisy quadrangle, with camels and donkeys hitched at one side, trade goods stacked beside them. A few gnarled trees snatch space for themselves and no grass intrudes upon the dried mud ground. It's a full service caravan inn, with sleeping quarters, stables and a dining room opening out onto the courtyard.

The Romans sit outside in the early summer sun and order a jug of wine and some water. Red appears. Marcus says "We Romans usually drink white wine, don't you have any?" The waiter says there's only local wine and it's red. "All right then, we'll take it".

Other customers are there. Their clothing styles mark the varied origins collected here by the Road. Clouds of meat- filled smoke belch out of the kitchen on one side. All the tables are full, the courtyard bursting with laughter and torrential conversation. The patrons are too engrossed with each other to notice the newly arrived overlords who're the only Romans in the place. But the Romans notice them, at least three attractive young women sitting together, locals probably. Marcus stares, knows he shouldn't but does anyway; they remind him of an incident years ago. Fortunately they're too involved in their conversation to catch him.

He had just returned to Rome from Syria with Gaius and Quintus to participate in Pompey's Triumph for the Eastern victories. They were celebrating in the Boar tavern.

The day was one of the most memorable in their lives, possibly the most. It was the only Triumph they'd been in. The atmosphere was euphoric. The whole of Rome was in the streets, excited with virtually religious fervour. Everyone but the marchers was dressed in pious white. They lined the Via Appia all the way to the Forum, like long thin clouds. People strained to see around the heads in front of them. Some were on the tips of their toes. No one wanted to miss the slightest detail.

Solemn magistrates and senators in their togas came first, striding the cobblestones and backed by trumpeters, their instruments winding into a G around their shoulders. Rolling cheers erupted as the booty wagons passed by, laden with captured armour and weapons, and, best of all, treasure – goblets, plates, vases, ewers, bowls of precious metal specially polished for the day, and mounds of gold and silver coins so brilliant they looked as if the sun had broken off a piece of its crown and tossed it down for the adornment of Rome. Downcast Eastern prisoners with tearful wives and children came next. After them, a group of soldiers carried paintings, holding them on high with upstretched arms. Artists had just finished making them to commemorate the most dramatic parts of the victories. Last of all came Imperator Pompey, the Triumphator himself, with red-painted face and crowned with a golden laurel. He was standing benignly in his chariot which was pulled by a team of elephants, a sign of the East. So intent on acknowledging the adulation of the crowd, with nodding head and broad smile whose energy never left his face, that he completely ignored the slave at his back who whispered repeatedly in his ear the customary *"memento homo"* – remember you are mortal.

Because the owner of the Boar could tell the three comrades were from Pompey's legions, he found a table for them even though the place was jam packed. Immediately a waiter bustled over with wine. Before long, the self congratulatory toasts repeated ad nauseam were taking effect. However, the revelry didn't prevent them from noticing a pretty young girl sit down at the next table. She was dressed to attract male attention. Soon, it seemed she was slipping discreet glances at Quintus. Or at least so he thought, but said he couldn't be sure. Suddenly he got up and appeared at her table with his wine cup.

Before long, Quintus brought her over. "This is Lucia" he announced. She was quite vivacious and self-assured, but in a pleasant way, aged around twenty. It was difficult not to look at the revealing tunic that spoke more compellingly than the voice. As time went on she became a little tipsy, and friendly – seemed to like the attention. And she was impressed by the stories of exploits in the East, grossly exaggerated of course, and the descriptions of the lavish gold and silver jewellery even the ordinary girls wear.

Soon she and Quintus slipped into a flirtatious phase, although still part of the general conversation, now somewhat coarsened by the wine. Eventually it got late and the tavern keeper announced in a loud voice it was time to drink up and leave. Quintus said

> "Let's buy a couple of jugs here and go over to your house Lucia. We promise to be quiet."

> "You don't have to be that quiet. My parents are staying with friends outside the city. They don't like Triumphs and their crowds. My father's an artisan; he makes shoes. We live over his workshop – not far from here."

At that, Marcus called for the bill and two amphorae of wine. The four brushed by talkative patrons reluctantly spilling out into the smooth-stoned street, palely illuminated by a half moon struggling with clouds.

They were completely inebriated by the time they got to Lucia's place, or at least the men were. She was fairly sozzled but steady. They entered the cobbler's shop, which was dark except for some timorous light coming in from the moon. They could just make out sandals in various states of repair neatly arranged on benches by the wall. Lucia lit a small oil lamp and led the way up roughly made wooden stairs that creaked all the way to a suite of small rooms. They went into what seemed to be the main room and Lucia lit two large lamps which stood on metal stands. There was running water in the room, a luxury which indicated the family was doing well.

The room was bare of all but a few pieces of furniture – a reclining bed, three rough-sawn chairs and a low table. Shadows flickered across the walls which seemed to be painted red. Nothing covered the wooden floor. Quintus sat on the bed, Marcus and Gaius on the chairs.

Marcus put the amphorae on the table and Lucia brought some earthenware cups. She sat down beside Quintus and everyone restarted the drinking campaign with raucous dedication.

All of a sudden, Quintus got up and took Lucia into the next room. Without those two, the party became quieter, lapsing into conversation about the Triumph. As Marcus was pouring another wine, Quintus called out in a thick voice;

> "Gaius, you're next. Come in", and appeared at the door, smiling. Lucia protested "No. No. I don't want that. What d'you think you're doing Quintus?"
>
> Quintus said, "It's all right Gaius. Don't worry. She won't mind." He took the cue and went into the bedroom. Screams came through the door, then muffled cries, and silence.
>
> Marcus said "Is this right, Quintus? She obviously doesn't want to do it with Gaius."

Just as Quintus was about to reply, the front door burst open and six men appeared, armed with daggers. The companions had no weapons as they had just been in the Triumph.

> "Tenement people; they must have heard her scream",

Marcus said, as he picked up a chair and crashed it over the head of the leader of the pack. His dagger fell on the floor and Marcus picked it up. He thrust it at the second man, gashing him in the arm and moved back quickly. Gaius came dashing out of the bedroom dishevelled and stood still at the doorway. For a moment all was motionless, an eerie hiatus as everyone took stock of the opposition, trying to work out the best move. Although the companions were outnumbered and had no weapons except for Marcus now, the tenants were wary as they would have known they were up against trained fighting men.

Suddenly Marcus leaped to the right and, wetting his fingers with saliva, doused one of the lamps on the table. He tried for the second but accidentally knocked it on the floor. It rolled over to the corner. Flames began to lick up the dry timber wall. The little blaze distracted the intruders. They knew only too well the terrible scourge that fire can be in the wooden tenements.

Before the tenants could react, the three ran out of the door, down the lightless stairs, across the little shop and into the street, slamming the door behind them. They sprinted around the corner and along the cobblestone street until they felt safe enough to slow down to a walk. The moon had sunk leaving the night mercifully dark and the revellers had left the streets. There was not much they could do except go home and meet the next day to discuss a way out of the mess they were in.

The three met outside the Temple of Castor and Pollux at noon, hung over and worried. They sat on the wide marble steps off to one side, out of the way of the streams of people coming to worship.

Marcus was feeling awkward for not trying to restrain Gaius. Partly it was because he didn't see clearly enough the seriousness of what was happening at the time and partly because of comrade solidarity. He was sharply mindful of the tradition of how soldiers fight primarily for their comrades, to support and be supported by them, to be seen favourably in their eyes, how this camaraderie forms the basis of honour, which Homer said, in the nearest the Greeks ever came to a religious book, is the essence of manhood, and how the highest decoration for valour is the *corona civica* – the crown of oak leaves which can only be won by saving the life of a comrade in battle.

> Clearly anxious, Gaius said "How could she not expect something like that would happen? Shit, she was in a tavern of loose women; she was dressed sexy; she invited all three of us back to her place. We were all drinking – she was too. It was obvious she liked the attention, enjoyed flirting. It wasn't only Quintus she flirted with. She did with you too Marcus, although not with me, I admit."
>
> "I agree", said Quintus. "I thought she was up for it with all of us. Plenty of girls like her would be. Some say no only to go along with it once it gets started. How were we supposed to know the difference?"

Marcus was perplexed by the ambiguity and felt uncomfortable, like they all did. It was easy to see that Lucia liked Quintus and was willing to have sex with him. That much was clear. It turned out that her consent stopped with him, but the atmosphere was set by that time. Expectations were aroused, fuelled by the wine. In a sense she was complicit. But still the consent wasn't there and that posed a problem. Something had to be done and done quickly.

> "Look, we have to stop her going to the authorities," Marcus said. "We're all in this together. If there's a trial we're done for. Those tenants will support her, give her a good character reference. Besides, they heard her scream. It won't just be her word against ours.
>
> Even if the sentences are light our careers will be over. We all know how seriously the army takes moral character and relations with the public. The only thing we can do is offer her money. And it has to be a lot."

The others agreed and pooled their resources. Next day Marcus appeared at the cobbler's shop, this time with Owl's Head hidden in his tunic. Fortunately, the fire had been put out before it destroyed the building. The door was locked. He knocked loudly and called out Lucia's name.

After several anxious minutes, he heard the scraping of a key. The door opened tentatively. Lucia recognised him and scowled, starting to close the door. Quickly he stepped in to keep it open.

> "Lucia, I'm very sorry for what happened last night. We're not bad men; we just got carried away with the wine. I know we can't rewind the threads, but I'm here to offer compensation and our apologies."
>
> "Why didn't Quintus come? Why did they send you?" she said with a sour look.
>
> "I don't know exactly. He sends his apologies too and says if you aren't too angry with him, he'll come by later."

This wasn't true but he said it anyway, a little red-faced.

> "In the meantime I'm to offer you this bag of denarii. I hope you'll not complain to the authorities."

She gasped at the amount, half the bonus Pompey awarded for the campaign and enough to set her up for life. Sullenly she accepted the heavy bag of coins, adding that she wanted him and the others to realize the deep hurt she felt, particularly for the callousness of Quintus, and the lack of respect all three had displayed. Marcus acknowledged it, his head lowered. He knew of course that she could go to the authorities anyway. But if she did, her acceptance of the compensation would most probably ensure they would take no action.

He left the tenement building with the sort of relief one experiences after falling into a well and being thrown a rope. He felt a rush of gratitude to Lucia, even affection. She could have ruined the careers of three men and didn't. The others felt the same way when he told them of their escape.

It's an experience Marcus never wants to go through again.

As he drains his earthenware cup, Gaius says, "This wine tastes like sandal sweat only good for getting drunk. Shit, we might as well do that. Life's getting pretty boring out here. All we do is march or wait around while Crassus adds up how much these people own. At least we could be doing field exercises."

"What do you think of him, Marcus?" Quintus says. "You must know him pretty well by now."

"Oh, he's all right, maybe not the most brilliant general. He's bright though, a logical thinker – pleasant to deal with. Never loses his temper. He'll listen to advice; even though he doesn't always take it. The big problem is he's spent most of his time in business and politics. He's confident though he can make the switch. To be fair, he should get there. Anyway, the good thing is he's greedy enough to collect lots of treasure, better at it than the career army types. We could get rich on it. Who'd object to that?"

"I'd rather have a good commander," says Gaius.

"I know that's ideal. But we can do with less. Our army's far better than anything the Parthians have. That'll more than compensate. After all, he's got good officers. They'll advise him".

He's made his decision, gone through all the pros and cons. However there's still a tugging doubt that it's a gamble, a toss of the dice. Maybe it adds too much to the normal risks of war. The thought is superfluous; what's done is done and cannot be undone. Besides, doubts belong to the night; in the day preponderance of evidence should overwhelm them.

"I hope the stupid donkey listens to them", Gaius says with a grunt and drains his cup, bringing it down in a thud with a hand like a boulder.

"So what if he doesn't; how could our army ever be beaten by a bunch of barbarians who fight in a mob? "

"I hope you're right Marcus. I'm just sick of waiting around while that greedy bastard grabs money. We should be out there thrashing those dung worms. Anyhow, shit, we haven't seen anything come our way yet."

"I know, but there's plenty of time. Everyone knows the best's in Parthia. It'll make what he's got now look like a pile of trash. He'll have to hand out our share. I'm confident, even though he'll keep more for himself than he should. He's on the stingy side, except where he wants to impress."

He's reluctant to talk too much about his Commander in Chief; it would be a bit unseemly. He has to admit that he's slipping under the influence of the plutocrat's financial success and alluring personality. He's not the richest man in Rome for nothing; he has technique. The almost friendly manner towards people as he filches their property is impressive. What disarming cleverness! He uses his patrician bearing to convince them that he's saving them from the crude avarice of the army's lower class officers who couldn't be expected to show the same consideration. He always leaves them with something, never takes it all.

Within the confines of the army, the sleek and round Crassus can be charming in an avuncular sort of way, always courteous and solicitous about the wellbeing of his officers. Prone to the enjoyment of praise himself, he offers it freely to others. Like Marcus but more learned, the Commander in Chief is schooled in Aristotelian thought, much admired in Rome. It helps him make rhetorical points in the Senate. The conversations in the evening Marcus has been having with him are enjoyable, and instructive. When enveloped in the wisdom of the great philosopher, Crassus shows a goodness of nature at variance with his reputation for avarice.

Feeling a wine-inspired generosity, Marcus invites the two black-bearded men at the next table over for a drink. They can speak struggle Latin.

"Where're you from?"

"From Zeugma; we Syrians. Just returned from trip across Parthia on Caravan Road. Three months."

"We know the Caravan Road. We've been on it through Syria. What's it like out in Parthia?"

"It's all right, mostly routine. Long rides with donkeys and camels. We stay at inns like this, but usually not as good. It's safe in Parthia because of army. They have to protect us. Whole economy depends on trade. King collects taxes from us."

"How does it all work?"

The merchant smiles, a little flattered at these feared overlords showing ignorance about such an important matter. Do they do nothing but march around and collect taxes?

"Buy goods here in Roman Empire like wool and linen textiles, bronze vessels, lamps, glassware. Gold, silver bullion most valuable. We carry to Margiana in East. Sell to other merchants. Buy Eastern goods. Carry back to Zeugma and sell in markets here. Those people take to Rome. We go on one section of Road only. No one goes all the way. Too long. Not know what it's like past great desert. We just know little bit from stories of Eastern traders."

"What stories?"

"Past Margiana country wild, no army protection. Weather bad – winter very cold, summer very hot; sand everywhere. Dune monsters come out of desert, carry people off track. Never seen again. Shapes come in shadows, go in flashes of light. Peer into your eyes, make you confess secrets – all you know, all you ought to know. Other spirits seem good, sing soft songs, melody beautiful as if it comes from heaven, make you happy; but lead you off to die in wilderness. Can never tell what will happen. Magic there. Caravan Road sends monsters and spirits; controls destiny. It the master.

"Dune pirates come out of desert haze on flying horses like storm. Wear fur clothes, like animals, have slanting eyes, fierce beards. Take cargo, leave no one alive, only bloody corpses with throats cut. Bodies disappear into sand after vultures eat. Risky out there. But profits big if you make it. Anyway, better business in Parthia -safer. Let others bring from Far East".

He has seen them in the Forum, extraordinary things – boxes with strange designs impregnated in their shiny coating, lapis lazuli as blue as pieces of open sky, fancy mirrors, and much else. No one seems to know where they come from or what kind of people make them. They fetch a high price though.

As the shadows of the afternoon lengthen, he gulps down his wine and abruptly interrupts the merchant.

"We have to go now. Good bye and thanks for the information. You're worthy subjects of Rome."

The merchants are surprised at the suddenness. Their culture allows more time for politeness. They mumble something to each other as the Romans walk off.

On the way back, Gaius says, "They seemed friendly enough."

"Sure, but they're still barbarians. Barbarians begin at the Hellespont. They're not up to much. I've never seen any I admire. Have you? They're born to be ruled by Rome.

We bring them *pax Romana*. I don't believe Parthia is as peaceful as that merchant claims. It'd be far better off under us.

And we get a quid quo pro – as we should. Listening to that merchant makes me realize how much better to get rich by force than trade. It's much nobler. There's nothing noble about bargaining and lugging goods all over the place and all the other things they do.

I say this advisedly, Gaius, as I admire our Commander in Chief who got his wealth, I know, from non military ways, even dubious ones. They say he seduced the chief Vestal Virgin to get her land, ha ha ha".

Gaius has heard his friend go on like this before and smiles. He often does it when he has a lot to drink. It's not that he's callous, only patriotic.

"Come on Marcus. Give us a lecture from those books you read."

Quintus chimes in, "I'm keen to hear it too Marcus. Ha ha ha".

"All right you two, you asked for it. Human progress is founded on military strength. Advances have always been on the shoulders of conquest. Look at Egypt, Persia, and Greece. Every one of them started with a military culture. Once they became strong enough civilization took root. But only then. They eventually declined because they failed to maintain their strength.

"Look at the spread of culture; it always follows power. When foreigners copy our way of life it's not because they really admire it. It's the power behind they want to be part of – even vicariously.

"We're lucky to be Romans. I've got no sympathy for Socrates' claim of being a citizen of the world. What's the point of that if we're superior? Anyway, how does that sit with patriotism, which the controversial fellow seemed to lack?"

"All right, all right" says Gaius. "Let's change the subject. How's Aurelia? Have you heard from her?"

"I've just got a letter. Haven't had a chance to read it yet. I'm amazed how good the postal system is, even here. The last one said she's well, still with her parents. Do you remember when she rescued that little dog hit by a chariot?

"Yes I do. You told me about it. Made a big impression on you."

"Well she mentioned it in the last letter. It's in good health now, living with her. We miss each other a lot. I haven't asked her to marry me yet but I might. I think she's willing to wait for me. But can't be sure. You know the temptations of pretty girls when their boyfriends are away."

"Sure. You'll be lucky if she hasn't found someone else by the time you get back".

"Thanks for the confidence my friend."

They laugh and clap each other on the back.

"We'd better speed up. We've been away a long time. It'll be time for the crossing."

☙

The finishing touches are being put on the bridge as they arrive. Hundreds of hammers driving in the last nails at different pitch break the silence of the place, sounding like frogs in a mating frenzy. At the river's edge a different sound joins the staccato, of flood water rushing past all obstacles in its way, over them, around them, under them – never to be frustrated for long.

Soon the order's given to commence the passage. Marcus and his men tread carefully over the pontoons. They're being jostled by the impetuous current, making it difficult to keep balance. Men stagger, grabbing hold of each other, some dropping their shields. The bridge is stout though; a tree trunk pulled out of its roots heads downstream and crashes up

38

against a pontoon. Failing to do any damage, it turns around slowly and dashes off down stream.

The troops are in full armour. It's a sunny June afternoon; fragrance of new leaves on a gentle breeze melds with the soporific hum of bees working endlessly in the flowers. Normally it would inspire a sense of well being, of comfort and security, but not today. Thoughts of battle blot it out. Marcus says to his optio nearby,

"It's a good time to give those barbarians a lesson in the art of war."

Just as he's almost at the other side, light vanishes completely. It's like being in a tent when a surprise wind blows through the entrance and snuffs out the lamps. He looks up in alarm. Rain clouds coming from nowhere have arrived while he wasn't looking and are rushing about like black chariots. Suddenly a bolt of lightning rips the darkness in a savage splash of beauty and screaming winds begin to assault the bridge like harpies.

He grabs the rope along the side and staggers forward on the rocking pontoons. The gale is heaving the clouds around like fragments of mountains. It's as though everything has fallen backwards into primordial chaos, where the gods are fighting the titans and the whole world breaks apart in their fury.

Waves rise as tall as horses, tossing white manes in deadly sympathy with the wind. Rain slashes down in whips stinging the eye and leaving pock marks on the surface of the water. Marcus is almost blinded. The raft in front starts to give way, its lashings tearing loose. Men frantically try to haul the ropes back into place but those closest to the water are swept overboard, eyes wild with terror as they're pulled down. Everyone's shouting, officers giving orders that make no sense. One man cries with arms outstretched, "We're doomed. O Neptune, save us." Another yells, "Call on Jupiter you fool. This isn't the sea."

Others shriek "This is an omen, this is an omen", repeating the phrase ad nauseam, overlapping each other in a chaotic chorus. Marcus tries in vain to get them to calm down. The men behind him bunch up in panic, adding to the instability of the bridge. Some rafts break away, dumping their terrified charges into the roiling brown stream.

The pontoon which Marcus is on holds, but only just, pulling and tearing at its sinews. As he stumbles, trying to get a better hold on the rope, a clutch of horses flashes by, frantically holding their heads above the water. They're neighing but can't be heard; only scared teeth show the poor animals are calling out to be saved. Some sink and rise only to sink again without trace. Among them his commanding officer's steed bravely fights the waves, its bridle catching whatever light there is, glistering gold against grey and black. Soon it's too far down stream to see, or in its watery grave.

Not normally superstitious, Marcus feels the cold hand of doom on his heart. Is there within nature's anger a law behind all laws, whose ultimate purpose is not for him to know, which today is somehow connected with the visceral misgivings about why he came to Parthia? Many in Rome oppose the war, spilling into the streets in protest. Parthia is a friendly nation and has done nothing to deserve the aggressive treatment. The real issue though is that it's blessed with riches that are the envy of the world. Crassus is after them, and so is he.

As the troops are sliding into despair, pleas for divine help the only hope, the storm clears as abruptly as it came. The clouds disappear and all is calm. It's as if an imperious hand has swept away the turbulence, giving permission to the elements to rest now they've delivered their sign.

ശ

With few fatal casualties, the host is now on Parthian soil. The invasion has formally begun. As the sun peeks out of the fleeing clouds, morbid feelings are put aside and pride returns. It was just a freakish prank of nature, Marcus thinks, no more than that. But still, it's not a good way to start.

Camp can now be set up near the grassy bank, close to a water supply. The storm has caused an annoying delay. As the task takes six hours, it'll be well into the night before it's finished. There's no way to shorten it.

The cluster of square, brown tents must be protected by earthen walls and a ditch, a requirement that takes time. Roman discipline allows no corners to be cut, ever.

As pitched roofed tents of oiled calf's skin begin to pop up in the usual linear pattern, Marcus slips away to sit under a tree to read the letter. It was right to wait until he can read it unrushed. It's from her – the faint perfume her signature. A touch of anxiety comes; her affection can't be taken for granted.

My beloved,

Your fingers will feel mine as you pick up this parchment for the ink still bears the imprint of my touch. I miss you so. How's the campaign going? When will you come home? I hold your letters close to me all the time to keep a connection that, alas, can only be spiritual at this stage. Please write more, at least one a day. I know you're busy but spare a thought for the one who loves you. Everything's so dull here without you and I'm lonely. Anyway life must go on.

I spend most of my days with my mother. Her sickness makes her bad tempered so I'm finding it difficult to look after her. No one knows what's wrong with her. It's a big worry. But anyway I know I must do my best to make her life as good as it can be. But sometimes it's hard.

I'm back playing the harp, but only by myself. It gives me comfort in those long days when you're not here. I think of the notes as little messengers that might go all the way to where you are. Well, must go now to mother who's calling me.

All my love, and write soon,

A

He reads and rereads, drifting into a reverie in the drowsiness of the moist heat. The river of civilization seems benign now; it has rediscovered peace. Such a short while ago it threatened to swallow his life. Aurelia's long black hair coiffed in the latest fashion hanging over her forehead curls into his mind's eye, and the image gradually extends to her broad and pretty face as a slightly impish smile creeps into her chestnut eyes.

That time he came home with wounds Aurelia was so sympathetic. But only until she realised they weren't serious. Then she showed a hardness admirable on one level but worrisome on another. They need to be weighed up – though impossible to calibrate. There's strength there but it may be difficult to live with depending on how it's wielded. On the whole though, it may be worth taking a chance. While he's holding the letter, an optio comes up to him and abruptly says,

"Sir, the Commander in Chief requires your attendance at seven tomorrow morning, sharp."

"Thank you Antonius. Tell him I'll be there."

The optio snaps to attention and salutes – right arm straight upward just above the shoulder, fingers flat against downward- facing palm. He spins around stiffly and marches off.

What's the old man want advice on now? The summons seems importunate. Some urgency's at hand.

CHAPTER 4

Gaius Cassius Longinus is sure to be there, the tall rope- muscled Quaestor and second in command. How could anyone like the man's cold and mineral personality? But you have to admire his quenched iron intellect, his uncanny ability to sense immediately the controlling ingredient in a muddle of facts, the main thing or critical combination that will determine an outcome. He knows instantly that it's a thorn in his paw that causes the lion's reactions while his colleagues still canvass other possibilities.

Although wary of him, Marcus reluctantly admires the man, keen to learn what makes him so successful. It seems that while his memory and cognitive ability are impressive, although not outstanding, he has an inexplicable additional element, something that can't be learned, which he brings to decision making. But, though present in military applications, that element is absent in others, in human relations for example.

Dressed in a white rust-fringed tunic fastened with the usual wide leather belt extending from below the rib cage to the abdomen, Marcus arrives at the praetorium, the command centre. Two exceptionally tall centurions, faces as still as stone, guard the tent's entrance. Close by is the flagpole that flies the colours of the army, hanging flaccidly, hot and lazy. An eagle sails high on the thermal currents keeping watch and the Road runs by, patiently waiting for information. It's within earshot.

Fattened with humidity from the river, the heat seems more sapping than in Europe. Despite this, the guards wear full uniform, festooned with

43

disk-shaped medals. They're formidable specimens. With bronze greaves on their shins, short coats of heavy chain mail and polished helmets with fanning plumes, they stand inert, like metal posts, but that's an illusion for they can move in an instant. A short, stubby sword – the gladius, hangs on their left side and their right hand holds a spear.

Crassus and Cassius, also dressed in rust-fringed tunics, are in a purse-lipped mood, not looking at each other. It's as though they are competitors at the games in Rome, or in Olympia. Senior officers, including the seven legion commanders, stand by, silently self conscious. A slave scuttles over with an amphora and fills earthenware cups with water. Nobody picks them up.

Manius Decius Cincinnatus, the commander of Marcus' legion, stares down at his foot, repeatedly smoothing the sand. Even Crassus' son, Publius, who commands the cavalry and is noted for his bellicose character, looks sheepish. Ineradicable flies, stimulated by the rising heat, keep everyone on edge and no breeze brings relief.

Irritated by his colleague's hectoring manner, Crassus stoops over a table with maps lying around like untidy thoughts, not saying anything. He overcomes his mood for a moment when he sees Marcus and straightens up. The frown on his face dissolves into the smile for which he's famous. It's in the form of a crescent moon lighting up his round face in a frankness which gives the impression that he's the nicest man in the world.

> "Marcus Velinius, I'm glad you're here. I want you to hear the discussion and let me have your views. You come from a fresh perspective."

Thin-faced Cassius also acknowledges his presence but with a detached air, just on the safe side of rudeness; he considers friendliness a waste of effort. Besides, a career soldier, he's particularly annoyed at having to argue with a superior whose military acumen he doesn't respect, whose battle experience is almost entirely lacking.

Marcus' nerves tighten. The atmosphere's like a summer storm forming up. Held for a while in unnatural stillness, the wind is waiting to leap into sudden fury armed with explosive rain as soon as the tension bursts.

Leaning forward on the map table with two hands, Crassus breaks the silence.

"Gaius Cassius, our scouts have been out there for days without seeing the enemy. The footprints they noticed that time pointed in the opposite direction. That signifies retreat. How could it mean anything else?

The sign's obvious; the Parthians are afraid of us. The logic's clear. We should go after them. Give them no time to rest. Hunt them down. Show them a touch of Roman spirit. Like Terentius said, *Fortes fortuna adiuvat* – fortune favours the bold."

Cassius' left eye twitches. In a tenor voice, nasal and rasping, he says,

"Marcus Licinius, it's always possible to lose a battle"

"But if we're bold we won't lose."

"Not the point. There's a right time for action and it's not now. Need more preparation. First, billet the men in the garrison towns along the river".

"What's the point of that? It'll just waste time."

"No it won't. We'll get intelligence. Don't know much about the Parthian army – a cavalry force, that's all. Got to find out more – their weapons, tactics, strength. Besides, the men need rest – regain condition. Battles are won by preparation, by knowing the enemy.

After that, march south to Babylon and Seleucia. Those people hate Parthians – were just in a civil war. Recruit them. Then bring the enemy to battle".

He shuffles the maps to find the one that shows southern Mesopotamia, pointing vigorously to the cities. "I don't agree", says Crassus, standing up stiffly, his voice gaining force, round and full, produced from the diaphragm like the best orators. Its volume expands like a boat's sail filling with wind.

"We must attack them without delay. Our troops aren't exhausted; they can still march and fight. By Jupiter, they can beat any enemy, certainly the Parthians. We know enough about them already. You're too timid. We'll have no trouble. You can be sure of that."

It's a curious argument, a case of role reversal. Cassius is a young man not much older than Marcus, his rotund commanding officer well over sixty and looking old for his age, grey hair receding into baldness, and sometimes clumsy. At the last rite of sacrifice, when the priest gave him the entrails they slipped out of his hand. One would think the impatience would belong to the younger man, caution to the older.

> "Commander, our troops are slack. No time for exercise because you had them confiscating wealth. Lost time in Hierapolis weighing treasure. Wasted more robbing the Jewish temple. All this instead of keeping our troops sharp. Got to correct that now."

> "How dare you imply I haven't maintained the discipline of our troops! There's no reason why they couldn't be deployed for a little time to extract treasure and still fight. I must remind you, Gaius Cassius, you, as well as the others, will benefit."

> "You're a better business man than a military commander."

> "That slur's completely unfounded. I led the army which defeated Spartacus when the slaves rebelled and the whole of Rome was terrified. I had six thousand of them crucified. Remember, their crosses lined the road from Capua to the gates of Rome. "

> "That victory was only against slaves."

Marcus knows the story. Pompey had a full Triumph for his exploits in the East – that was the one he was in, but Crassus received only an Ovatio. He was so jealous that he could scarcely be civil to Pompey even while sharing power in the Triumvirate.

After a pause that has the whole tent expecting an explosion, Cassius drops his voice, now worried he's pushed his Commander in Chief too far.

> "Marcus Licinius, if you insist on attacking now, don't do it across open country. Stay close to the river. It'll protect us against being surrounded. If you don't like that, engage through Armenia. The terrain's rugged there."

Marcus senses that the astute Cassius is probably right. What he advocates is standard military doctrine, even more important to apply in unfamiliar territory. He's correct to insist on avoiding open country which suits horses. The Romans have only four thousand cavalry, sufficient for tactical moves, but not enough to protect foot soldiers from the Parthians' numerous horse archers. They need the help of terrain. Crassus is being rash, impatient because of the time spent gathering plunder.

Things are getting intolerable. The two commanders are leading members of the senatorial class; they sit on an exalted platform. Instinctively Marcus edges himself behind a tent pole, as though imagining it can make him disappear. It's not just embarrassing; he's dreading the time when Crassus will ask for his advice, forcing him to take sides.

As Cassius' diplomatic gambit is having a mollifying effect on the Commander in Chief, one of the centurions pulls back the tent flap. He announces an Arab chieftain, Ariamnes. For some time the Arab's been lobbying Crassus for a chance to serve the Romans. Crassus has invited him today to give details. Perhaps in order to cool the heat of the debate, perhaps because he's running out of reasons, Crassus motions to let him in straight away.

Crouching with pendulous robes hiding his well fed frame, he minces forward. He stops at a respectful distance from Crassus, muttering poetical flattery. He reminds the assembly that he's been a friend of Rome for a long time, and his reliability has been recognised by the great Pompey.

An incipient sneer crawls across the narrow face of Cassius who's noted for scepticism at the most neutral of times. His superior is opaque.

"Imperator", the Arab says, using the Roman title of a commander in chief who has won a great victory. He knows Crassus longs for his men to call him that for his defeat of Spartacus. So far no one's obliged.

> "Why is it that, with the most feared army in the world, you're not hastening to the attack? It's well known that the Parthian leaders have made plans to flee north to the wastelands of Scythia with their goods and families if the only alternative is to fight you. Not only are they afraid, but there's confusion in the realm. The rebellion in southern Mesopotamia's just been put down. Now's the time to strike, while the Parthian forces are

regrouping. Besides, they'll gain confidence as they perceive your hesitation and become worthier opponents. I speak this as a friend of Rome who wishes you well."

Crassus says nothing, but waves him to continue.

"I'm willing to lead you by the most direct route to where the Parthians are skulking. You can corner them there, forcing a battle which you're sure to win. I know the country well. You can trust me; I've always been loyal to Rome. There can be no better reference than Pompey to prove that."

The Arab opens his arms in an expansive gesture to underline his sincerity and waits for a reply. An awkward silence follows. No one says a word. Cassius has no interest in asking questions or making comments and Crassus has nothing to add. Giving an embarrassed cough, Ariamnes mutters something about it being time to leave and goes out of the tent.

After the Arab departs, Crassus announces it's time to decide. He summarises the opposing positions, pointing out that he's verified Ariamnes' friendship with Pompey.

"Although I'm critical of Pompey on a number of counts, I'm well aware of his shrewdness. Any foreign friend of his would have to go through rigorous scrutiny. I'm satisfied Ariamnes can be trusted."

Turning to Marcus, he says, "Marcus Velinius you've heard the analysis. Before I make my decision, I'd appreciate your advice. Speak."

A quandary he dreaded, it's obvious the Commander in Chief wants to take up the Arab's offer, even though it may mean crossing open country. Cassius' approach is better. In business dealings Crassus is known for being decisive and brooking no opposition once he's made up his mind. He's usually right. Whether his sense of judgement can be transferred to the military sphere is being tested to the full today.

Marcus has heard of men who think if they're successful in one domain they'll succeed in another so long as it's similar, even if they have little or no experience in it. He's aware that in the transition the subtleties of the craft often elude them. Requirements in commerce are similar to those in the military, but they're not the same. What the High Command is facing now, with the annoying flies buzzing around, is a decision that could determine the campaign's outcome. And Crassus has probably got it wrong.

It's clear that the shrewd quaestor is not impressed by the Arab or his offer. His face is as hard as a skull. Nothing has changed his opinion. But he's finished speaking; he's delivered his advice, can say no more without being redundant, or offensive. He's like a judge who's given his findings; he's functus, any further statement being of no purport. It's now up to the young advisor.

His heart is pounding. The hot and muggy tent has so many eyes and they're all on him. He's alone, no one to tell him what to do, no time to think of consequences. The leadership of the Roman army is looking at him, staring even – worst of all the Commander in Chief. They're ready to convict him of folly if he founders and sentence him without mercy. A junior officer is dispensable. He feels his face go red and burst with sweat. His brain seizes up. He can't say anything; the others wait. The silence must end; he must get his tongue moving, the tongue that's sticking to the roof of his mouth; there's no way out. Tightening his stomach muscles into a knot, he pushes himself into speech.

> "Sir, the arguments put forward by Gaius Cassius Longinus are cogent and persuasive, and could lead to a favorable outcome. However, in this situation which is not clear cut, their prudence needs to be weighed against the imperative of aggressive action – what has always served our army well. I think on balance we should march straight for the Parthians, with Ariamnes as our guide. Pompey's reference is persuasive. The open country can be dealt with. Our tactical skills should be enough to overcome the enemy's cavalry. We win our battles with the infantry anyway."

How could he have said that? He doesn't believe a word. It feels like he was speaking as if apart from himself, the words coming from some outside source, only seemingly internal, as in a cave of echoes. But in reality, that was not the case. The ultimate source was deep within, the words involuntary, an atavistic response to the call of self-survival, of ambition. They emanated from a morally neutral place where instincts reign unchecked by thought. But as they hit the wall of consciousness their baseness is exposed. However, it's too late to take them back; they've been released.

On the battle field the tyranny of self preservation never rules him like this; he can discharge his duty whatever the cost or risk. His comrades think him brave – *acer in ferro* – sharp in iron. It's a different process there, however, less complicated, moderated by excitement, tradition, and training. It's certainly clearer; shirking would be instantly seen, unshielded by the cover of ambiguity or dissimulation. That's the merit of physical combat close to comrades; behaviour stands out like thunder in the silence.

> "Marcus Velinius, as always your advice is sound", Crassus says, a warm smile swelling his full-cheeked face. "It accords with my own instincts. I appreciate your forthrightness. We march tomorrow, due east with Ariamnes as our guide. We'll force that furtive Surena to taste the medicine of a Roman attack."

Would it have made any difference if he had given honest advice? Crassus seems to have made his decision and only wishes to go through the motions. But perhaps, speaking out forcefully might have stirred up Cassius to re-enter the fray, the two of them prevailing.

At least the decision is not certain to lead to disaster. It most probably won't. The fighting qualities of the Roman soldier should compensate for the poorer choice, despite the cost of additional casualties. But that cannot salve the wound to his conscience for it's beside the point. He's disobeyed the cardinal imperative of Stoic philosophy – make the right moral choice without regard to the consequences. Where would there be support for what he's just done? Not in the books he reads.

The conference is over. He and Cassius leave the praetorium without speaking. As the general is turning to go to his tent, Marcus moves to say something. If only he can open up the possibility of going back, this time arguing on the same side. Perhaps they can promote Cassius' compromise in attacking virtually immediately, with just a short delay so as to avoid open terrain. But no sound comes out; the hard lines on Cassius' face prevent it. He's offended the second in command. At least he can take comfort in the fact that it relates to the view he expressed, not the reason behind it. That, at least, hasn't been disclosed and never needs to be.

The portentous decision's been made – *alea iacta est* – the die is cast. It's observed by the Three Sisters who weave the fate of mortals. They alone can foretell who of the tens of thousands of Romans and Parthians soon to be embraced in battle will pass by Lethe's doomfull spring and forget their former lives.

Next day, in the early morning as the water birds come to drink, shouts of command shatter the peace along the banks of the river of civilization. Centurions put into action the decision to march east along the Road to find the elusive enemy, with Ariamnes navigating. The Romans would have left it if its Commander in Chief had followed Cassius' advice.

The Road is honoured that it's been chosen to carry the grand army into battle – better than being left out of the drama; perhaps it foresees that what it's to facilitate will lead to one of the most curious developments in its long life.

CHAPTER 5

Bearing the pride of Roman youth, hungry for battle, the Road leaves the silt-laden river and passes into grassy plains which are gently undulating and articulated with clumps of trees. Birds are singing and all is benign. It could almost be in Italy. The great connector is making the march easy, pleasant even, as if it's enticing the soldiers to the expected clash. And no wonder, for nothing in its history has been on the scale of what is to come. It lives for action. Whether it's in trade or violence is of no account.

The sound of the army on the march is prodigious. Squeaking and crunching of the baggage train's wheels, bronze armour rasping against itself, snorting animals, tread of man and horse, create a corridor of sound that extends the presence of the invaders wide into the countryside.

Soon the terrain changes, becomes drier and subsides into gnarled scrubland. Eventually it abandons vegetation altogether, sliding into sand like a shoreline ceding its domain to the sea. No birds are left to sing.

Anticipation is in the air; the whole army feels it; they'll soon find the enemy, pound them into submission. Excitement of battle is what they live for. The monotony that wastes so much of their lives will yield to the ecstasy that makes it all worthwhile. Young men need an outlet for the violence inherent in their nature; never more than when they're bored.

Marcus knows the others feel the same pumping heart as he when he imagines how he will bash his shield onto the enemy in front of him, knock him down and stab him with his gladius, or perhaps with Owl's Head, how the blood will spurt and the guts slip out like slimy snakes, how the controlled battle fury that dispels all fear will propel him to Achillean speed and agility, how the shouts of triumph and the cries of the wounded will split the air, louder even than the clash of metal on metal, and how he will chase the panicked foe until they are hunted down like wild animals and slaughtered or enslaved.

That's what happens when Romans go to war, and it's certain it'll happen again, this time in Parthia, close to where they are now. He'll have a chance to prove himself once again in the field and that'll expunge the guilt from giving self-interested advice to the Commander in Chief. The lapse will disappear without trace in the euphoria of victory.

But as they penetrate further into the sunburnt sands and thirst curls its bony fingers around their throats, doubts begin to form about where their guide is leading them. Several officers start muttering. Knowing the influence Marcus has, Cassius calls him aside.

> "I'm suspicious of that Arab. Been in the desert for days – no water. Parthians won't be in country like this. He must give us an explanation. If it's not convincing, we have to go to the Commander in Chief. I want your help."

Marcus says, "I agree", pleased that the senior officer seems to hold no grudge from the argument in the tent. They confront Ariamnes.

> "Yes, it's true that what we're marching through is rough," says the Arab. "But what d'you expect? You're not in lush Campania. This is Asia, not blessed with the green of Europe. Have you Romans gone soft, unable to endure what the Parthians can without complaint?
>
> Anyway, we've passed the worst. Hang on for a little while longer and we'll reach the Belikh River. The Parthians will be near it. However, I'm a little hurt that you doubt my navigation. Soon you'll see I'm right."

The Arab seems plausible; at any rate Marcus and Cassius aren't in a position to argue. A few more days will test his promise. They still have enough provisions to return by the same route so long as they make the decision by then.

Cassius decides not to go to the Commander and says so to Marcus. He's willing to put the doubts aside for the time being, but as would be expected of a man of his character, they will still animate his thoughts. The day is ending and it's time to make camp. The sceptical man will think some more about it overnight. He'll go to bed uneasy.

ᘓ

The small bronze oil lamp, which looks like a baby's shoe, casts a flickering light onto the brown leather walls of Marcus' tent. The worry about Ariamnes' reliability has dissolved into a pleasant sense of rightness about the decision he's just made. Usually finding it easy to make up his mind, he's taken a long time over this one. Love for Aurelia struggles with the pull of campaigning. To bring a wife into the rigours of the march and the risk of defeat seems unfair, especially to someone as refined as Aurelia. The alternative of long absences would create its own problems. Besides, how can someone as impecunious as he, expect Aurelia's upper middle class family to give consent?

However, the money issue should be resolved shortly. The Parthians will be defeated and Crassus will empty their cornucopia in a stream of plunder. Given the seniority of his new rank, he'll do well in the distribution. He'll have to negotiate the periods of absence, but that should be possible. Anyway, in a few years he could retire and buy a farm near Rome with his winnings. Her family would be impressed with his rise to the equestrian class, something his father would have considered unthinkable for someone of his social background.

The parchment crinkles on the table as he shifts it to write. He pauses at the marriage part. What if she rejects him? Her letters indicate he doesn't have much to fear, but expressions of affection, even love, aren't the same as willingness to marry. Practical considerations can intervene, especially when class is relevant. And Aurelia's rather haughty. Might she feel she would be stooping to marry a blacksmith's son?

54

There's such definiteness in putting something in writing. Ink provides a nondeniable record. Exposing his soul can't be explained away.

He makes the proposal, finishing the letter with a flourish of affection, and rolls it up. The postmaster will load it in his pouch in the morning. But it'll have to await the outcome of the battle. He goes to bed satisfied he's made the right decision and confident about the future. As he slides off to sleep, comfortable thoughts of home drift by, a new home for Aurelia and him, a traditional one in Rome, or, if things go well, outside in the country, but not too far away.

ભ

In the morning, Cassius decides to retain his silence, but reluctantly; he's ready to challenge the Arab unless his prediction comes true soon. Marcus too is concerned, but not as much as the hard-nosed Quaestor. Besides, he's somewhat invested in the unctuous navigator.

Three days later, as the Road rediscovers green, Crassus is pleased to inform the officers that the Belikh River is two days' march away and Ariamnes has gone to the Parthian camp as a Roman spy to mislead them about the strength and deployment of their foe. He appears jovial, his round face beaming confidence, which is just as well, for there were two strange occurrences in the morning.

Instead of the red garment Roman generals wear, he came out of his tent in a black robe. Why, nobody knows. He changed it as soon as he saw the reaction. Also, several standard bearers had trouble pulling up their eagle standards which were stuck in the ground. Marcus was near his cohort bearer as he tugged at the standard for several minutes to get it out; he needed some help for what should have been done by one man. Are these omens – if not a supernatural sign then at least something reflecting a sense of foreboding? There's no way of knowing, a source in itself of concern. It's best to put anxious thoughts aside and concentrate on the welcome news that the long and sterile prelude is soon to end.

Next morning, three Roman scouts ride up to the praetorium in a rush, bloody and dishevelled. Their horses are sweating and foam spills out of their mouths. People run over to grab the reins. Crassus comes out. While still mounted and bending over with three arrows in his back, the leader gasps, "Large Parthian patrol. Killed four of us. Saw army on other side of Belikh. Could see tents", and collapses on his horse.

A firm and delighted smile breaks out over Crassus' face,

> "The time has come. No more waiting. Sound the battle march". Almost as an afterthought he says "Look after the scouts."

Even Cassius manages a smile, like a skull, but still a smile of sorts.

ଔ

Soon the mighty instrument of war reaches a grassy plain emerging from the desert. The Belikh River is in the distance, a wavy silver slash flush with flood. Not a tree, not even a bush interrupts, nor undulation or declivity disturbs the perfect smoothness of the land.

Cassius moves close to the Commander in Chief,

> "Commander, we should deploy the troops in line and open the ranks to widen the front. Deter their cavalry from surrounding us."

> "I agree", says Crassus and gives the command.

It passes down the ranks to Marcus and the other centurions. After a few hundred metres another order comes, this time to marshal his cohort into its place in the hollow square, the traditional Roman formation that creates a front in every direction. What's going on up there?

The troops march across the flats, coming upon the little stream that's the Belikh River – a vision of the Elysian Fields. For days they've been persecuted by the baleful sun which has been baking them in their armour and sucking moisture from their throats. Perhaps it's supporting Parthia, angry that the peace of the land is to be broken. Even the Road has become discouraging lately, its surface converting to sharper stones and foot -burning heat. Is it telling them to go home, giving them a warning, a last chance to avert catastrophe?

Cassius approaches the Commander in Chief,

"Marcus Licinius, should halt here, make camp – send scouts out to see how the enemy will line up. Men need rest. Fight better in the morning."

Crassus barely hears, certainly doesn't listen. He's impatient for battle, for the victory that will see him lead Surena, followed by his defeated troops to Ecbatana, take possession of the Parthian king and his treasure. He can't wait for his return to Rome as an Imperator – there'll be no doubt about it this time. He'll receive a Triumph and become the *civis princeps* – the number one citizen.

"The men can eat and drink standing in their ranks. I'll allow one hour, no more. Then we march to battle."

Cassius stands still, sullen, saying nothing; the twitch in his left eye is the only thing that moves. After an awkward moment that seems longer than it is, he leaves to go back to his post.

The hour goes by slowly, the sense of time stretched by anticipation. But it eventually passes. The moment for battle has arrived. They're about to fight that afternoon, the 9th day of June, 53 BC. The wise and ancient Road will soon be charged with carrying the news of victory and defeat, and the tragic pool of blood spilled on the field close by.

☃

At the far end of the open space, Surena watches a dust cloud rising on the horizon. It's coming closer and closer, inexorably, like a huge rolling boulder. It holds to its path as if pushed by a divine source and is approaching the very place where it's wanted. The Parthian Commander smiles; he's pleased as much with himself as with what he sees. It confirms the deeply held belief in his judgement, a singular skill proven once again, this time in the most important challenge in his life.

"Noble Commander, you can see how well I've succeeded in enticing the Europeans onto the Carrhae plain as you wished", says the Arab who sits mounted beside Surena, also on his horse. The fidgety beasts sense the restlessness in the air, like chariot horses straining at the starting blocks in the hippodrome. Ariamnes is accompanied by his tribe, a group of irregular skirmishers. They've been with the Parthians all along.

57

Surena's face is painted, reds and blacks put on like a woman would, incongruous against his chiselled black beard. His hair is parted and hanging in the manner of the epicene Medes, not like his fierce warriors who tie theirs up on the forehead in a knot like the point of a battering ram. No one thinks to criticize him though, even in their thoughts, for he's ferocious and cunning in battle. It's his practice to paint his face like this on every military occasion.

He jerks his horse's head back as it tries to move forward.

"I can observe that for myself. Take your men and join the right wing."

Now that Ariamnes has fulfilled his purpose, he sees no point in wasting time with him. It's a huge relief to see the Romans fall for the treachery, for all depends on it. He's got no infantry, nothing but horse archers. The Romans can be assumed to count on the usual combination of cavalry and foot soldiers they see in Asia; he plans to do something different, unexpected. He places a thousand camels behind the front line, laden with spare arrows so his archers can reload without having to ride to the rear. He expects this to unsettle the Romans for Asian armies normally keep their ammunition in the baggage train, well behind, where it's safe from a collapse in the front line.

At the appropriate time he'll deploy the secret weapon, a device the Romans have never seen before.

ᗒ

Crassus' round face opens in a crescent moon smile. Confident in his role as Commander, an Imperator to be, he says to the officers around him, especially Cassius,

"Look at that. Surena's allowed us to manoeuvre with the sun at our back. I knew we were dealing with a second rate adversary."

Today the sky is without cover, its golden disc bursting with early summer vigour and aimed right at the Parthian lines. High above the armies, its light flashes off the wings of an eagle banking over a little life in the grass, preparing to swoop down to extinguish it.

The combatants are not on the Road but they're not far away, close enough for it to feel, at least dimly, the ground waves radiating from the mighty rumble of horses and men moving forward to engage each other in the great battle of East and West.

As the armies approach, a deep and hollow roar bursts from the Parthian ranks, like the roll of thunder or the bellowing of Tryphon in his underground cave. It's not the blare from conventional trumpets but the demonic rhythm of kettle drums. The Parthians have perfected the art, creating a sound that insinuates the dread of alien power into the ear, penetrating the emotional well where fear lurks, ready to rise up and quell the will.

In retaliation, Roman commanders shout orders for their curved horn trumpeters to bray louder as the square closes with the enemy, but they can't drown out the drums, nor match their unsettling effect. Marcus and the other officers aren't in the front ranks but in the hollow middle, their regular position; it affords a better view of the action, facilitating the giving of tactical commands. The Parthians are to be drawn into close combat where Roman discipline and tactics are the best in the world. The square formation is as solid as the earth.

Suddenly a wall of light leaps up from the Parthian side, as bright as the sun but a thousand times wider. It's the full length of the front side of the square. Before Marcus has a chance to blink, it hurls a salvo of rays like a storm of needles. Paralysis seizes him. It's more frightening than the drums. No one can fight blind. There's nothing more ineffectual than thrashing around without sight.

Something supernatural is happening. It's as if Jupiter himself is revealing his face to consume the Romans in a mortal blaze. The men lift their shields and stumble around aimlessly, ceasing to care about the enemy. They forget their discipline and let the line waver. The more credulous claim the gods must have abandoned them.

Recovering his sight, Marcus rushes to the front, shouting to the men around him, "It's only something that reflects the sun. There's nothing divine about it. Hold your shields up. Stand your ground."

Other centurions and their optios join in with angry commands. The troops begin to regain their composure. With squinting eyes they straighten up their ranks. But their confidence has been dented, something impossible to contemplate before the secret weapon came into play. They need the urgent reassurance of their officers, who themselves are shaken. Like them, Marcus has to drive his will to the sticking point to rally his men. He runs throughout the front line shouting encouragements, and insults to the waverers. The biggest problem is to debunk the superstition affecting many of his men.

Within minutes, a mass of cavalry explodes towards the square. A figure taller than the rest is in the lead. As the horsemen approach, they drop the cloaks covering their armour – Surena had ordered the disguise. They reveal themselves as the dreaded cataphracts, the heaviest armed cavalry in the world. These terrifying troops wield long lances and are protected by interlocking plates of Margianian steel. Their horses are armed too and look like weird metallic monsters. Their polished plates flash like sheets of lightning, amplifying the radiance of the wall.

They charge the square at full gallop, the shining wall blazing at their back. The metallic mass hits the square with a tremendous crash. But it holds fast. The disciplined rows give way slightly to absorb the energy of the charge as one does in catching a ball. The long lances of the attackers glance off the shields. The massive Roman barrier, several rows deep, dismays the horses, causing them to pull up and shy away despite the furious urgings of their riders. Confidence returns to the Romans.

They suddenly break the square and, with shields held up to protect their eyes, advance on the double into the faltering Parthians with shouts of triumph. Marcus and Gaius are at the front, thrusting their swords at the horsemen and bashing with their shields. But the armour of the cataphracts is impenetrable; they can't make headway against the monsters. Marcus drops his sword and grabs the end of an enemy lance, just before the tip. The rider holds tight, his horse bucking in fright. Marcus throws away his shield and yanks with both hands. The Parthian holds on with just one, reluctant to let go of his shield. With a piercing shout from the pit of his stomach, Marcus pulls him from his horse.

On the ground, the cataphract can't get off his back. He's like an overturned sheep heavy with fleece. As he wriggles in the dust, kicking in the air for leverage, Marcus finds a gap in his armour, just under his chin at the junction. He pulls out Owl's Head and rams it in; arterial blood spurts over the man's brightly polished breastplate. Marcus barely hears the hoarse gasp of death before he's off to try again, the fury of battle in his lungs. But suddenly the Parthians break off and retreat.

With the roar of thousands the Romans charge forward. Marcus is at the head of his cohort, sword in the air, shouting *"Ad victoriam, ad victoriam"*. Everyone takes up the cry, lusting for blood and triumph. But they only catch stragglers, the few who fail to get their horses moving fast enough. The rest disappear into the mystic wall. It shifts back, maintaining its distance from the charging Romans, gradually draining their energy. Marcus slows down. "It's useless. We'll never catch them. Stop. Get back into formation."

An uneasy quiet descends while the Romans dress into the square. Despite the frustration, they're buoyed by their tactical victory. Once again the highly trained infantry has proved its mettle against cavalry. Gaius cries out "Come on you dung worms. Next time we'll pull twice as many off your horses." The rest of the cohort joins in yelling insults at the enemy, highlighted with derisive laughter.

Surena pulls his cataphracts behind the shining wall. The attack was only a probe; it's time for his main strategy. He says to his second in command,

> "Take down the sheets Vardanes. They won't be needed any more – done their job. Did you see how the Romans staggered around? I knew they'd never seen silk before, ha ha ha".

He's right. The diaphanous cloth has travelled along the Road for years but never farther than Parthia. And its secret composition is still locked up far away in the East, past the great deserts and the mountain barrier.

As the wall of light comes down, the kettle drums, silent during the lull in the battle, start up again in full throated roar. Suddenly Gaius says, "Marcus, look over there". An undifferentiated mass, like a heap of debris, is rolling across the plain, blurred in a cloud of dust. In just a minute, the Romans recognise it as mounted men dressed in open–chested tunics and cloth trousers, forehead bands collecting their wild black hair. Recurved bows wave above their heads, arrow–stuffed quivers on their backs. The ground begins to rumble as they approach and the air fills with war cries in a strange language. The Romans are about to experience the huge torque of the composite bow. Layered with wood and bone it unleashes arrows with enormous penetrating power. It's a product of the East.

Suddenly they split in two and swarm past the square, shooting. Then they stop dividing and the remainder comes straight at Marcus' section, pulling their horses up to fire.

Passing the order from the High Command, Marcus says, "Form the Testudo". Immediately the troops close ranks and interlock their shields, the front row holding them upright and those behind horizontally. Bronze clashes on bronze. The army is transformed into a Testudo, a tortoise, its soft tissues protected by scales which form a carapace. Capable of standing its ground in the midst of mayhem, it requires the discipline and training only Romans have.

A cloud of arrows rises in a wide black arc, casting shade onto the armies fighting in the sun. In the dim light the projectiles hurtle down like pelting hail, thick and furious. Feathers whoosh through the air, and barbed iron heads hit bronze in chaotic pings. Some of the archers ride close enough to shoot in a straight trajectory, more deadly still. Again and again they fire, in a barrage without end. Inevitably the missiles find junctions in the Testudo – even Romans can't keep the scales from moving, however slightly. Man after man slumps down.

It's as if killer bees, angry that their hive has been disturbed, are in murderous swarm, intent on punishment. They get in everywhere, never stopping. No place is free from them. They'll never be content until their infuriator is stung to death.

> Marcus says "Hold firm with your shields. They'll run out of arrows. Barbarians always do. Once they do we'll fight hand to hand. That'll turn the tide."

But the arrows keep coming. It's as if they're from a magical source that has no limit. They never stop. Casualties are mounting; even the tiniest gaps between the Testudo's scales are penetrated and blood flows freely on the ground. Unless something's done soon, the carnage will weaken the army to the tipping point.

In desperation, Marcus decides to charge. With shouts of "*ad victoriam*" he leads his men into the barrage, shield in front. Before they can reach the enemy however, the archers turn their horses and retreat, twisting their bodies around to continue shooting at the advancing troops. After the battle the Romans call it the Parthian shot.

The charge peters out, arrows creating even more effect. Marcus orders his cohort to pull back and re-form the Testudo. He tries again, once more leading an assault against the retreating swarm; but that fails too, and again a charge, but to no avail. The highly mobile horse archers avoid contact. Roman skills can't be used; they're as useless as grasping at puffs of mist.

As more and more men collapse, doubt, the subverter of courage, infects the army. Paralysis takes hold. No more orders come down the line from the High Command. How can anyone continue to fight a foe that won't engage but kills at a distance?

Doubt morphs into despair – Marcus hears that the cavalry charge of Publius, Crassus' courageous son, has failed. It was the last chance for a break out. Nothing remains now but steady attrition and inevitable collapse.

The arrows keep coming. Some men try to yank them out only to have nerves and veins, even intestines drawn by the barbs. One screams that an arrow has gone through his foot pinning him to the ground; Quintus has his hand stuck to his shield. The darts have more penetrating power than the Romans are used to but it's the never ending quantity that's causing the trouble.

The terrible day comes to an end in a crescendo of suffering. It's as if the troops are standing naked in prison, the jailer thrashing them with a barbed lash. He keeps at it hour after hour with no compassion, oblivious to their pain.

As the western sun splits into horizontal fragments and merciful dusk spreads over the plain, the cloud of arrows thins out, subsides into single shots and ceases altogether. The victors disappear, leaving everything calm except for the groans of the Roman wounded. Even they fold quietly into the dark as their pain is dulled with time and the mortally injured slip into the silence of death. Squadrons of birds fly over, mute as if in sympathy, black shapes against the dimming sky. They're in their nightly migration to the safety of their nests. But some of them spy a meal for the morning.

Marcus flops down, stunned among the dead, wounded and silent others. No one has energy to bury the fallen. Even the stalwart Gaius is sitting listless on the ground, head bowed. Quintus is on his back propped up by one elbow, his torn hand across his chest, head hanging to one side. The impossible has occurred. No experience has prepared them for this. It's beyond comprehension. Today's disgrace blots out the glory from even their greatest achievements.

Covered in dust and blood, some his own, some the enemy's, Marcus wants to say something positive to his comrades, if only to lessen his own depression, but can't think of anything. Defeat ties his tongue. Only something banal could come out and that would do more harm than good. No other words are possible. The shock is even beyond black humour or escape into the absurd. It overwhelms the natural tendency to rationalise failure.

It might have been possible to take comfort in the fact they're not prisoners; the Parthians won the battle but they left the field and are known never to fight at night. However, the beaten troops are beyond thinking, capable only of nightmarish sleep on the open ground. It's to escape, not refresh, for few are that physically tired. Active fighting was impossible after the first few encounters. Casualties are so high the army will never again threaten the enemy. The only course to take now is to retreat to Syria.

଼

Encamped across the plain, the Parthians erupt in exuberance as the horse archers return, one after the other, dismount and join the triumphal feast that has spontaneously started. Casualties are few. Camp fires light up the plain in hundreds of blazing eyes as the victors rejoice with food and wine in the cooling night. They've a right to celebrate; they've won the most important victory in Parthian history; they've saved their country from the power of the West. It was a feat that seemed impossible when they saw the size of the Roman army. Everyone feels a hero, even on par with the Empire's ancestors, the soldiers in the legendary army of Cyrus the Great.

Surena is in his command tent with the senior commanders. Wooden tables accommodate fifty, their black beards soaked in wine. Within easy reach of their greasy fingers are piles of barbequed lamb and duck, flat loaves of bread, and rice. Earthen jugs are in motion, brimming with the best vintage of Shiraz. Slaves move in the uncertain light of oil lamps, keeping the noisy party supplied.

A thousand happy thoughts swirl in his head and like thermal currents in a summer morning lift him off the ground higher and higher into the sky. He touches heaven and feels at home. His face flushed, he stands up unsteadily with a silver goblet in his hand, filled so full that the wine spills in a sheet-like splash over the edge and down his tunic.

> "Here's to the greatest victory of all time. Today we've destroyed the pride of Rome, completely smashed it – and with a smaller force. I foresaw that getting them onto the flat ground was the key to victory. Wasting them with our arrows did the trick. The ammunition never ran out – putting it

behind the front line speeded up reloading like it was supposed to. Everything worked according to my plan.

"Rome will never be the same again. Never again will those foreign devils invade our land. We've made our Empire safe, impervious to attack. The might of our army is the greatest in the world. Nothing else comes close. We saw that today. Tomorrow we'll finish the rest of the rats off. I look forward to it – my personal pleasure. I'll lead a killing spree myself – I'll wipe them off the face of the earth, ha ha ha.

"Sillaces, send a message to the Roman commander. I give him one night to mourn his son. Then he must decide whether to surrender and walk to the King or be carried there."

Sillaces, a thick, rough-bearded man, almost as tall as Surena, but ugly and coarse, says,

"I'll see to it, my Lord. But to get Crassus alive we need to persuade him to negotiate; otherwise he may commit suicide. That's the Roman custom."

"Obviously. You don't need to tell me that. He'll be our greatest prize. But tonight just have one of our men with a loud voice approach the Roman camp. Shout the message across. We'll follow up in the morning."

A troupe of dancing girls from the Commander's harem, diaphanously erotic, weaves out in front of the revellers, accompanied by flutes. They're as gentle as the men are rough. A wave of silence overtakes the guests. They're entranced by the beauty and grace of the performers but each knows it's worth his life even to speak to one in private.

Music and the lithe movements transport the tipsy banqueters to a universe beyond the battle, a realm of inspiration. There, they sense with even greater clarity the brilliance of their victory, and more keenly enjoy the sweetness of its pleasure. Before the spectacle is finished though, Surena waves nonchalantly, impatient to get back to talking and boasting. The dancers glide off in an elegant curve like a rainbow fading in the distance. He says

"Ariamnes, as I told you, I would reward you if we won. Well we did, and I'm ready to give you a prize".

He produces a bag of coins from under the table and holds it up. The

Arab minces over with shining eyes and takes it with a bow, low and deep. A slight glistening appears on his nose. As he goes back to his seat he looks surreptitiously in the bag. But he sees silver, not gold. How could his grand service be so meagrely rewarded? Before he sits down he says,

> "Thank you my Lord; I'm much obliged. But forgive me for saying, I was thinking of a somewhat more valuable reward. I don't wish to overstate my contribution to the great victory, but enticing the Romans onto the open ground, as you yourself said, was the determining factor. Would it be possible for your Lordship to consider something more, particularly since I'll have to share with my tribe, who, as you know, fought valiantly on your side?"

Surena stands up, ramrod straight, red with fury.

> "You dog, you insult my generosity. I won't tolerate your insolence. Either you accept your reward with gratitude or you'll have your head cut off. Bring me my sword, Vardanes. I'll do it myself."

His eyes show the eagerness of the thought. The tent is suddenly silent. Ariamnes' mouth flies open. He doubles over in supplication, shaking so hard he can hardly maintain his balance. His voice quivers and sweat bursts through his skin.

> "My noble Lord, I humbly beg – forgiveness. My stupidity. Must've been the wine. Twisting my thoughts. What I said not what I meant. Deeply grateful for your generosity, heavenly generosity, heavenly, heavenly. Not even a king could be so generous. Will be grateful for all time. Never forget, never, never. Will extol your virtues among my tribe. Always be your loyal supporter – and ally. Always, always. Please, please, please forgive my awful transgression. I assure you, not meant. Not meant at all. Please."

> "All right Ariamnes. I accept your apology and acknowledge your gratitude. But see to it you keep your word."

While Ariamnes shuffles back to his seat Surena mutters to himself darkly. He calls over Maiphorres, one of his more villainous officers, a swarthy man with a sharp, bent nose and small eyes, and whispers in his ear.

Stupefied but relieved, Ariamnes carries on with the banquet. He has no choice. The reprieve could vanish at the slightest offence. Surena is well known for multiple eruptions when insulted. Even a tiny rudeness would cause one.

All he wants to do is to go home with his measly treasure but he's in a state of terror. So he stays on, speaking only when spoken to and then with little gusto. His tribal elders are embarrassed into silence. Virtually none of them speaks to the Parthians at the table and when they do, it's with uncomfortable restraint. No one else cares and soon they're ignored.

As the banquet progresses into the night, the guests become more fulsome in their praise of Surena, which he's happy to do nothing to discourage. While, if a vote were taken for who contributed most to the victory each would vote for himself, all would give second place to their Commander in Chief. And so he would get the accolade.

Any distaste for the man or fear of his cruelty has dissolved into adulation for his brilliance today and the euphoria of glory they share with him. He's the leader Ahura Mazda has sent to fight the pivotal battle between Good and Evil, Light and Darkness. It's the cosmic conflict which the *Avesta* foretells, the defining nature of life and the basis of morality. In the grand scheme of things it's irrelevant whether he's personally virtuous or not; he's the divine weapon that saved the nation. Nothing else matters.

Sillaces stands up with a cup in his hand and says,

> "Here's to our noble Lord. Your brilliant strategy and incomparable skills have led us to this day of glory. Admittedly the Arab performed a service but it was your strategy that caused the victory. You, Supreme Commander Surena, have the entire army of Parthia at your beck and call. We'll follow you anywhere, any time, against any foe."

All the officers leap to their feet with their cups on high and shout their commitment at the top of their voices. The din is enough to bulge the sides of the tent. Even Ariamnes' tribal officers have to stand and raise their cups, at least a bit, but their voices are weak.

The alacrity is pleasing of course, especially to a man of his ego hunger, but more important, it shows that the victory can be parleyed into a coup against the King. He's confident of that now. Although Orodes has his own army in Armenia, it could be won over. Even if not, the old retainer who commands it will be no match for the victor of Carrhae and his battle-hardened troops.

This is the time he's been waiting for. History's grand hinge now stands before him, oiled and ready to allow its door to swing open, revealing his illustrious destiny. He merely needs to give it a slight push. If he waits, the hinge will seize up and the door will stay shut. That'll mean he'll be ravaged for the rest of his life by the fires of unfulfilled ambition. No peace will quench the burning in his heart.

It's certain that he can subdue any military resistance the weak monarch is capable of mounting. But before he makes his move, he has work to do. He must take or destroy Crassus, for, as an oriental warrior, he's been brought up to believe that a commanding general is more than just a man in charge. He's the brain of the organism. Once he's removed, the body falls apart; it changes from an army to a mass of individuals who care only for their own lives.

CHAPTER 6

As night thickens and no leadership emerges from the Roman camp, everyone wonders what's happening at the top. The command structure has broken down. Marcus and the other officers are receiving no orders, no information, nothing. In a state of shock he goes in search of Crassus but can't find him. He comes across Cassius, looking more tense and gaunt than usual. It seems the man has some feelings after all.

> "Sir, where's the Commander in Chief? I've been sent by Legatus Cincinnatus to see what's going on."

> "Not here. Don't know where he is. Should look for him."

They've no idea where to look. Cassius says they should use an old hunting technique. If the lion is known to be somewhere not too far away, the tracker walks around the place he was last seen in widening circles. They do this, starting at the Command Post. After a few circuits they find him, alone. He's lying on the ground huddled in his cloak, shivering. He's looking so small, so shrunken. Even phlegmatic Cassius is jolted at the sight of the man who such a short time ago had the stature of a god. He asks for orders, for direction. Crassus can't reply; he just shakes.

Cassius says, his eye twitching,

> "Beyond help. Let him be. Still shocked at seeing the head of his son. Parthians rode by with it on a spear. He'll recover later. Doesn't matter

anyway; I'll take charge. Got to get the army out of here while still night. Parthians don't attack in the dark."

Cassius calls the centurions and legion commanders together for a conference, at least those not seriously wounded.

"Can't stay here; we'll be annihilated in the morning. Best chance's to slip away to Carrhae under cover of night. Wall will keep Parthians out for a while. Give us time to work out what to do next.

Leave anyone behind unable to make the march on foot."

Marcus considers challenging the order but thinks better of it. Cassius has made the right decision, tough though it is. They would all be jeopardised by the delay, including the incapacitated. It's too big a risk to take. If they're caught, everyone would suffer and the wounded would be no better off. There're too many to be put out of their misery so they'll just have to take their chances.

He accepts it's not a decision anyone would favour if they were among the unfortunates left behind, for when in extremis, hope, no matter how forlorn, trumps probability. And, like many hard decisions, its seemingly compelling objectiveness is tinged with the interests of the ones empowered to make it.

Comrades are in the fatal category, men he has feeling for. It's one thing to see a comrade die in battle; it's vastly different to leave him defenceless to an implacable enemy. He knows the hatred Parthian have for Romans. The order leaches out the glory from war, the heady feeling of dominance, leaving only a dry and numb realization of terrible waste, a waste that scars the soul. Blessed by the unbroken string of victories in the past, he hasn't had to encounter this before, and it deeply hurts. It's personal in a way that's shocking to the core.

Cassius gives the command to abandon camp and make for Carrhae. When it becomes apparent what's happening, the cries and curses of the wounded left behind flood the night air, now a messenger of grief to anyone who would hear. It carries the lamentations all the way to the Parthians. But the victors are too caught up in their celebrations to wonder about the plaintive sounds in the distance.

CHAPTER 6

Lucius Albius Aquila is one of the wounded to be left – from Marcus' cohort, a colleague from Pompey's campaign. He still has arrows sticking out of his side and neck, through gaps in his armour. The broken ends are blood-soaked stumps, too close to vital parts to remove. He stops crying out when he sees Marcus and for a few moments their eyes lock in silence.

A trusting appeal for help gleams in the wounded man's eyes, a return to innocence, like a small child might express to its mother when a fatal disease is making its final call. Marcus puts his hand gently on the man's shoulder, unable to speak, and moves on. This part of war is too contradictory. Comrades are meant to be helped, not abandoned to die, possibly in horrible agony at the titillation of a heartless enemy. For a moment he feels guilty at being the one to survive when it's but chance that separates him from his comrade's grisly fate. But there's no time for thought; the column of survivors must get going or everyone will die.

After the fall of evening, when a makeshift camp is made, with no attempt to defend it in the usual way, Marcus goes over to Cassius with a delegation of officers.

"Gaius Cassius, it's obvious Marcus Licinius is no longer able to lead us. The men have confidence in you and want you to take over command. You have the full backing of the army. Will you do it?"

"No. I will not. I've sworn an oath of loyalty to the Commander in Chief – like rest of you. I won't break it."

"We implore you, Gaius Cassius. All our hope of survival rests with you. He's finished, can't lead. Only you have the men's confidence. You've got the skills – he never had them. What few he did have are gone. What's an oath compared to the lives of the rest of the army? You're the only one that can get us out of this mess. We've got a chance with you, none with him. Besides, surely your oath would only apply while he's fit to lead. And clearly he's not. The gods surely would release you."

Other officers chime in noisily. After listening for a while with a stony face, his eye twitch its only expression, he raises his hand for silence and says.

"He'll recover – won't be in shock much longer. Be as fit to lead as before.

72

Give him time. Oath of allegiance is sacred. I won't break it. Go back to your posts and shut up."

Marcus and the others know it's pointless arguing with the strong-willed man. As always, he pushes the tenets of the Stoic philosophy further than most people would, not budging when he thinks an action is morally right. All they can do is obey the command. They're gallingly disappointed though, as Cassius is so clearly a better leader, always was.

Too bad the crisis has gone to waste. Ironically, the very capacity for logic and clarity of thought which could have helped has been turned in another direction. Cassius has chosen as the premise for his decision the sacredness of the oath of allegiance, a value which must take precedence over everything else, even survival, whose worth in this instance anyway is diminished by the shame of defeat. No rationalization is permitted.

Marcus has to admit to himself that his argument about the gods not insisting on obeying the oath is disingenuous. It would have substance only if the facts were supportive. They're not. The shrewd Quaestor expects Crassus to regain his faculties eventually, unsuited though they may be to solving the predicament they're in. It doesn't matter if his prediction is right or wrong, the important thing is that he's made it.

Taking over leadership now would therefore constitute a breach of oath. If later, Crassus should break down entirely, Cassius would be free to assume command, as he has just done, temporarily. In the meantime, he's rigorously applying the Stoic dictum of making the right moral choice without regard to the consequences. He knows this and was really hoping Cassius would bend his principles in the spirit of pragmatism. He wouldn't, and Marcus is not surprised. He wonders though what he would have done if he were in Cassius' position. He feels a touch of admiration for the man, and a bit of shame for himself because deep down he knows what he would have done.

∝

On the march, as the Second in Command predicted, Crassus recovers his composure enough to take charge. Under his unsteady command the sorry remnants of the army reach the safety of the town just before dawn.

CHAPTER 6

The journey is hard, undertaken at an uncomfortable pace, causing many of the walking wounded to collapse. They're left behind on the Road in a trail of human suffering, slumping into a distant and lonely death. The Road is sombre and not surprised to be claiming more trophies, for it knows the price of over confidence and arrogance. It brought these troops here, witnessed their attitude, and is ready to abandon them without compassion.

03

As the copper disc turns to yellow blister and lights up the low hills at the edge of the plain, Surena lurches out of his tent. He's been up all night drinking with his officers, make-up shoddy. Blinking at the sun and with Sillaces staggering out behind, he slurs his words.

"Get the men together. We ride into the Roman camp. Let's see how many are left."

"My Lord, what shall we do when we get there?"

"Slay them all; Ahura Mazda will be pleased. Let their bodies rot in the sun. That'll purify the vermin, ha ha ha."

Within minutes, sword flashing in the sun, he leads a cavalry charge across the plain and into the wounded Romans. They cry for mercy in pitiful pleas, unmindful of their status as soldiers of Rome. As many as can, twist their pain-wracked bodies onto their knees, their arms out-stretched; but the swords slice off their heads without compunction. Often the drunken cavalrymen make a mess of it, missing their targets or hitting them obliquely only to prolong the misery. They charge and go back to charge again. It takes several attempts to finish the job. Four thousand men die that day, their once healthy bodies stripped of clothing and armour, and left naked on the field. Not a scrap of dignity remains. Compassion has buried its face in rampant hatred.

All the Romans don't die in the massacre. A few survive, only just, a fortunate outcome for Surena. He orders an interrogation, and with promises of treating their wounds accompanied by threats, finds out where Crassus is heading. Satisfied they're telling the truth, he says to Sillaces in a thick voice,

> "Kill them. Assemble the rest of the army back at the camp; we march to Carrhae."

As the sated Parthians ride away, triumphant shouts fading over the soaking red plain, cruel-beaked vultures move in to claim their right. At first, one swoops to the ground, its large grey wings shuddering down as it waddles over to a corpse. And then another, spying the cue from a distance, flies over, itself signalling to a third further off. Soon a flock assembles in savage ecstasy around the fallen men, taking charge of their bodies like a butcher handling meat.

The dead lose possession of their mortal form, their identity, everything, to the heartless birds. They eat so much they're too heavy to take off and have to rest for a while on the deserted field. Other creatures, large and small, come to the feast, walking, crawling, flying. Before long the bones of the proud European warriors brought to Asia by the Road will be polished by the wind and mark the tragic spot with shards of white. Eventually their atoms will mingle with the earth, making permanent a macabre liaison of continents enabled by the great connector.

଼

Despite the defeat, the Roman army remains at large, though dramatically pared down. Like a wild animal wounded by the hunter, it's still dangerous and unpredictable, capable of rushing out of cover at any time to exact revenge. There'll be no security until it's killed or captured.

Before long the Parthians are surrounding Carrhae, calling on the Romans to surrender or be slaughtered. The town can't withstand a siege for long since the newcomers are swelling the population with too many extra mouths to feed, and fresh supplies are blocked. They have to do something soon, before the enemy brings up battering rams. Crassus calls the officers together.

> "We've got to break out during the night and make for Syria",

he says in a toneless voice devoid of energy. Gone are thoughts of glory, of becoming the number one citizen of Rome. No statue of him will stand in the forum to face down Pompey. If life remains at all, it's an existence only, self-respect flayed off like the skin of a buffalo after the hunt.

Cassius furrows his brows, his eye now twitching every time he speaks,

> "Yes, but should break into three groups. Take different routes. Better chance. You lead the largest, Marcus Licinius. Legatus Octavius and I'll take the others."

He's given up on Crassus. His chances are better on his own. By himself he should be able to outwit the Parthians, especially since they don't use the night. He doesn't think Crassus would be up to it. But his principles don't allow him to take over command of the whole army.

Crassus goes along with the plan without discussion. Just after midnight, under a moon that's still a sliver, the fugitives slip out of Carrhae quietly, past the sleeping Parthians who have failed to maintain a proper watch. Five thousand men go with Crassus in the direction of the Armenian hills. Marcus is with them. They're guided by one of the townspeople. Once again, the Commander in Chief has made an unfortunate selection; the guide leads them in a roundabout way not towards the hill country but into largely flat land.

Next day, the Parthians, who've been tipped off by sympathisers in the town, chase down Crassus' group and attack. He's been caught again in open ground. The deadly archers swarm around the hastily formed Testudo and start shooting. This time the end is certain; it's possible merely to stand helpless, eventually succumbing to the barbs. The thread the Three Sisters have cut is at its end.

ଔ

But that's not so. All of a sudden, Octavius, who was thought to have escaped, appears out of a nearby rise in the terrain and leads an infantry charge across the plain. The onslaught takes the Parthians from the side by surprise and forces them to move back in their usual manner. The reprieve allows Crassus' troops to retreat to one of the few wooded hills in the region. Octavius' contingent joins them. There, with the combined forces spread out over the top, Crassus gives the order to make a stand. But nothing happens. The Parthians, who're on lower ground, don't attack and the Romans don't dare. Stalemate grips both sides.

In the distance, two Parthian horsemen appear, riding across the plain, alone and unarmed. Crassus is alerted. They come up the hill and dismount. Speaking Latin, one says, with an attitude that seems almost friendly, certainly civil,

> "My Master, Surena, sends you his greetings. He admires the courage and prowess of your soldiers and sees no purpose in continuing the loss of life. He wants you to know that our King desires friendship with Rome. He proposes a peace conference to work out the details of a treaty. You will have to give up something but your army will be allowed to return to Syria so long as you abandon all territory east of the Euphrates."

The words of reprieve weave through the Romans like a heavenly melody, salving their wounds and softening their fears. Soon their ordeal will end. However, after the emissaries ride back down the hill, Crassus says to his officers and a large group of common soldiers nearby,

> "I'm suspicious of this. Why has Surena suddenly changed his attitude? He's always shown implacable determination until now. What's he thinking? Best to be cautious."

The troops will have none of this hesitation. Individuals, even centurions, call out demanding that he accept the offer. They hurl criticisms at him, like stones from the countryside. He's shouted down as he tries to argue that they should make for Syria via the Armenian hills where the trees and uneven ground will slow the Parthian horses to a walk. Finally he's absorbed Cassius' advice.

Men nearby the senior officers start clashing their swords against their shields. More take up the protest as the word spreads. Before long the staccato noise spreads across the hillock in a crescendo of dissonance that no voice can surmount, certainly not Crassus'. It's a warning even the most obstinate must heed. Crassus succumbs.

> "All right, all right. I hear what you say. I'll parley with them."

As the din subsides, he mutters that he's being undone by the subtlety of his enemy. The Parthian Commander is playing upon the minds of his men, their judgement blunted by his seductive pairing of fear and hope. A more charismatic leader, Julius Caesar, or, perish the thought, Pompey, could have held sway, but not him. That doesn't bear thinking about. Still, however, the remnant of the army is not an inconsiderable force. He can take comfort in that, a factor that might explain why Surena is offering to negotiate.

A meeting is arranged at noon. The day is hot, windless, and muggy. With Octavius and some of the other officers, Crassus descends the hill on foot to where it slumps into the plain. Marcus is among them, his limbs at the edge of action, determined to go down fighting if this is a trap. All are sweating in rivulets inside their armour, as much from nerves as from the heat. Crassus is in his red robe, stiff with apprehension. Everyone is armed except him.

The Roman party meets Surena and a small delegation of his officers. The Parthians are on horseback. Surena is carrying an unstrung bow ostentatiously in his right hand, and in full makeup, the red looking radiant in the sun. The two groups stop within a few metres of each other.

> "I embarrassed that you, supreme Roman general, on foot while I and my aides on horse",

says Surena in halting Latin. He's relaxed, full of confidence, on the cusp of arrogance. With a flourish he tosses his bow to an assistant.

> "It's the custom of Romans" says Crassus, quelling his surprise at the appearance of his adversary, "to attend conferences on foot, so there's no need for embarrassment."

Surena smiles condescendingly, as he holds his horse from moving.

> "As my King commands, I offer you retire to Syria. We will not harm as long as you leave all lands this side of Euphrates. Forever. I give you escort to river. You have to give me all treasure you took on campaign. I hear you took much riches from Syria.
>
> You come with me to sign treaty. Necessary to sign. Even after short time, memory of Romans loses touch with word."

Crassus gulps at the part about the treasure but his bargaining position is too weak to quibble. He accepts the proposition and orders horses to be brought.

"No need General. My King commanded me to give you this, his favourite horse. It has golden bit."

Two grooms come from behind the Parthian officers with the horse and bring it to Crassus. They help him mount, a little too forcefully for good manners. Once he's in the saddle, one of them hits the beast with a crop. As it starts to bolt, Octavius jumps forward to catch the bridle and a scuffle breaks out with the grooms. Octavius shoves one aside and tries to pull the horse up. The groom punches him in the face. Staggering backwards, but still on his feet, Octavius draws his sword and runs him through.

A conflagration erupts. It's as if someone threw dry kindling on a fire that has just died down. Its flames suddenly leap up, sharp tips piercing the air. Marcus draws his sword and stabs a Parthian in front of him but takes a blow on his breastplate that knocks him down, winded. One of the Parthian officers kills Octavius and the treacherous horse gallops off towards the Parthian lines with the Roman Commander frantically trying to manage it. Surena and his party quickly disappear across the plain.

ੴ

The Parthian commander has what he wants but must deal with the leaderless Romans. They're still dangerous. A thorough man, he'll take no chances; absolute elimination of the Roman threat is what he needs to complete the victory.

He sends another delegation to the Romans, offering fair treatment if they surrender. This, he accepts, is a bit presumptuous in view of the recent trick played on their Commander in Chief, but he gives it a try – better than taking casualties in a final battle. Anyway, a shrewd judge of character, he's confident the enemy no longer has the stomach for a fight.

Whether that's because their morale is shattered or because they've lost their head doesn't matter.

He's right. The Roman officers hold a brief conference and agree to accept the terms, for a wasted death is the only alternative. Quietness descends on the broken conquerors as the fateful decision takes hold and they prepare to face a future whose only certainty is disgrace and privation.

The dispirited legionaries begin trickling down the hill between the trees toward the Parthian lines in irregular rills, silently carrying the burden of their shame. Each has his own apprehension but says nothing. Marcus, Gaius and Quintus stay close to each other. No one suggested it; they just naturally drifted that way as if instinct propelled it. Everything is so disorganised there's no need for them to be with their units, which have dissolved anyway. Like everyone, their pace is slow and shambling, hindered by fear and the heat of the day that has reached a searing height. They barely notice the blow flies that land on their faces and crawl into their ears. Nor do they see the eagle circling high above them as they come onto the flat grassland. Their thoughts are narrow, their feelings inward.

The changing status is too weird to absorb. Captivity is something that has only ever occurred to others, never to them; it's beyond contemplation. How could it be, so outside the natural order? They're in the middle of a phase change, not yet prisoners, only about to be. It's like a larva in the process of becoming a moth; only the moth is destined to fly away. The transition has seized the present, freezing it in a state where it's neither freedom nor slavery. It can't be understood or felt.

Along with the others, Marcus walks towards captivity like an automaton, his legs moving as if bound to an outside force, his brain thickening like cream as it's churned into butter. Disbelief rubs against reality, producing a numbness that grips his entire body and prevents any thinking past what is necessary to move his feet in the direction of the enemy lines.

As the Romans are sullenly received into the Parthian ranks, their weapons and armour confiscated, a bonfire rages not far off at the bottom of a gentle rise that forms a rectangular hillock, like an outdoor altar. Its flames penetrate the sky in jagged stabs. Why do the Parthians find it necessary to compete with the heat of summer?

A commotion springs up among the captors. People mill around the hillock talking excitedly. Marcus is close enough to hear distinct words but doesn't understand the language. A tall and impressive man whom he recognizes as Surena is giving orders. He's standing near the fire gesticulating to the men in charge. Suddenly Crassus appears, bound hand and foot, dressed only in his tunic. Two burly men, their thick black hair tied forward in the Parthian knot, push him roughly up the hillock in stages.

His appearance is shocking. The round and pleasant face is now a slump-cheeked ·spectre with glassy eyes. He stoops and stumbles forward, shackles shortening his steps into the unsteady gait of an idiot. The guards force him onto a chair at the top of the hill. They tie his arms around his back and stand off a few paces, faces hard. The Roman is silent, features tense but unmoving; Stoic pride is all he has left. He has no idea what the Parthians will do to him. The most he could be hoping for is a quick death, but it's troubling that they're tying him to a chair in front of all to see. Why is that necessary?

From the direction of the bonfire, three macabre figures emerge close together, silent and deadly. Heavy black quilt bulks up their bodies to twice the human size. It covers their heads except for narrow slits for the eyes, which can't be seen. Two of them carry a long- handled stone ladle with something very hot inside – ragged clouds of smoke with a base of flame spew out. The trio appear inhuman, a three-headed monster. Without a sound it slowly glides up the hill like a fire-spitting dragon, intent on devouring its prey, helplessly trapped for its satisfaction. The cataphracts were less terrifying. Crasssus stares, motionless, transfixed, his eyes too terrified to blink. The monster stops directly in front of him, far enough away that its heat does no more than slightly singe his face. He barely feels it.

The prisoners are mesmerised. Even the Parthians are shocked speechless. The armies of thousands are as silent as the wispy clouds slowly sliding by overhead.

Out of the motionless crowd, Surena emerges and strides up the hillock, the magnificence of his pride on display. Standing beside Crassus but far enough from the heat, he says in Latin, projected loudly so that all the Romans can hear,

> "General Crassus, you have appetite for gold. Tried to steal ours. But no need. We give it to you. See how generous Parthians are."

In silence, he nods his head in a gesture scarcely noticeable. The part of the creature not holding the ladle, whose hooded eyes are fixed on Surena, suddenly jerks the Roman commander's head back, its gloved hand jammed under the nose – Crassus has little hair to take hold of. It forces the clenched mouth open with an instrument like the sacred mouth opener the Egyptians use when they perform the ceremony of the dead. The other hulks pour liquid metal, smoking and whitish yellow, into the mouth of the richest man of Rome. In sizzling climax, the gold fills his throat, some running down his chin, burning a channel. Within seconds it congeals and darkens to its normal colour. Crassus' head slumps to his chest, a large lump fixed inside.

A roar, tentative at first but building into tumult, erupts from the Parthians at the demise of the man who came to grab their country's wealth. The Romans are spellbound, the horror of their leader's death a presage of their future. In a black thought he can't help thinking, Marcus recalls the syllogism invented by someone seeking to praise the precious metal. Gold equals sun, sun equals love; therefore gold equals love. There's no love today, but only punishment for a love that lurked in the dark side of gold. That errant love blighted the virtues of an intelligent, cultivated and sometimes kindly man and led inexorably to his tragic end. Does his own fate also stalk in the shadows of that love?

"Cut off his head and his right hand.

"They'll be a fitting trophy for our King. Sillaces, take them to His Majesty with my compliments. The rest of us will go to Seleucia with the prisoners to celebrate."

It's best to enjoy his glory unpolluted by the King's presence. He has in mind a particular jubilation, one where he's the principal figure. It should be his occasion after all. That will take place in Seleucia, the rebellious city he brought back to the Parthian fold. The King will be far away to the north, in Armenia.

As he's turning to go back to his tent to prepare for the march, the gimlet-eyed Maiphorres sidles up to him and whispers,

"My Lord, it's done. The Arab had an unfortunate fall last night into a gully and hit his head on a rock. There was a brief investigation in the morning when he was found. It concluded the fall was an accident brought on by a night of heavy drinking. His people accepted the explanation."

"He deserved it. Where's the silver?"

"I've recovered it secretly. I put the word out it must have been stolen in the night."

"Put it in my tent".

The grisly ceremony over, the captives are forced into a column of march. The guards display an arrogance often seen in a people once inferior who're now on top. The Romans must endure insults shouted in recently acquired and badly pronounced Latin, and the humiliation of the cattle whip. They've no idea where they're going but the position of the sun indicates they're heading south, off the Road. It's disappointed to see them leave, but knows they'll be back.

The march is gloomy and hard, not of military precision but more like a straggling trek, each man on his own. Some fall behind and are whipped into catching up. Stripped of their weapons and armour which are now in the baggage train under guard, the prisoners are dressed only in their tunics. Gone is the shining glory of their march through Syria. And it's quieter, much quieter, the quiet of subjugation.

CHAPTER 6

Marcus barely notices the well watered grassland over-painted with bright summer flowers and graceful trees. The defeat has destroyed beauty. Beauty can't live in slavery. Only ugliness can. He looks around without focus as colour slinks away leaving only a grey and horrible abstraction of that tragedy-laden land.

Life has shut down, like a lamp doused into darkness. All that remains is an oily smoke around the wick which discloses that once there was a flame. His life has lost its substance; it's a bare remnant hanging off the past, hardly there at all, even in memory.

How long will leather sandals stand up to the sharpness of the unpaved road? Already he feels the wear. An extra pair is in his back pack. He's thrown out most of his clothes to lighten the load but has kept the picture of Aurelia. That would be the last thing to go.

What would she think of him now, a failed soldier? He's too ashamed to think of it. She's there in his mind though, fading in and out like a firefly on a hot summer's night. Maybe she would still love him. Certainly she would; she's loyal. Maybe not though, if her feeling for him is driven only by loyalty, and perhaps pity. Love could degrade to mere affection. Can love exist in the absence of respect? Could she still have that for him now? Maybe she wouldn't lose respect for him on the grounds that his shame is shared by the entire army. How would he know? It's all so sudden. Only a short time ago, a flash of time, any such thoughts would have been a ridiculous fantasy.

The flies are abominable, buzzing and crawling everywhere; perhaps they're congregating in expectation of a feed after the inevitable collapses, maybe his own. He gives them a desultory slap from time to time. There's no longer need to show indifference to the irritation.

The march carries on for days; two weeks pass by. For a while the captives get relief from the sun in the forest clumps on higher ground. While the canopies don't completely cover the path, they interrupt the cruellest shafts. Hunger grips them, and intolerable thirst. Their need generates scant sympathy from the guards. At the one mealtime each day, they're provided with a few sips of water and fed just sufficiently to sustain them for the march, like a herd of cattle only kept strong enough to make it to market. The most they get is thin gruel with bits of gristly lamb bobbing in grease, and thirst is like a fly that won't go away.

Every morning, as the sun peeks into the robin's egg sky, Surena goes for a ride along the straggly line. The prisoners are already on the march. In the full stretch of gallop he swings down in his saddle at random and lops off the head of any man who fails to duck or drop to the ground fast enough. It seems like a cruel ritual, a morbid combination of morning exercise and retribution. He always does ten, in mockery, the guards say, of the Roman custom of decimation. However the parallel is not exact; it isn't one in ten but a random killing that stops at ten for the day.

No one halts to bury the decapitated men, but only to strip them of their clothes. The dark –winged vultures accompanying the march, do the rest. Marcus says to one of the guards who speaks Latin,

"Why don't you bury them, or least bring them with us so their comrades can bury them at the end of the day? Don't you Parthians have any respect for humanity, even if these men are your enemies? Romans would not just leave our foes to rot without dignity".

"Zoroastrians don't bury the dead, we leave them on towers of silence. Their flesh is eaten by the birds. It's a purification; birds are the messengers of heaven. There're no high structures here, so we have to leave the bodies on the ground. True, we pay respect by collecting the bones and keeping them in a special place. But how can that be done for you people, out here?"

After several days on the pitiless trek, the outlines of a great city emerges out of the distance, its stone block walls indicating it's not as big as Rome, but perhaps not much smaller.

Surena orders a halt and calls his officers together in the shade.

"Ride on ahead", he says to Maiphorres, "and spread the word that Crassus is alive. Tell the people of Seleucia that we're bringing him and ten thousand Roman prisoners of war."

He gives instructions to Sillaces and the other senior officers how the celebration is to be conducted and orders the march to be restarted. He might have smiled or even laughed at the ludicrous nature of the event he was ordering, but, not a man imbued with a sense of humour, he keeps a straight face and none of the officers has the temerity of doing other than accepting the command is if it were perfectly normal.

ॐ

Before long, the prisoners are at the high stone gates of Seleucia. On Surena's orders, the guards pick out one of the soldiers near Marcus who has a face like a melon and could be taken for Crassus at a distance. They lead him away with impatient shoves.

The main street is lined with somewhat bemused local people who've been told by Parthian emissaries to expect a victory parade. They're required to attend, even though many have Roman sympathies. A spectacle is about to occur like none they have ever seen or are likely to see, something designed in the most malicious quarter of Surena's imagination.

The parade commences, unremarkably enough, with a group of Roman trumpeters pressed into service, long thin tubes winding into the form of a G around their shoulders, with flaring bell pressed against their heads. It's in mockery of a Roman Triumph.

Next comes a contingent of prisoners who are meant to represent a victorious Roman army, not horse mounted as in a normal Triumph, but on camels, signifying that they're better suited to be merchants of the Road than warriors. The bedraggled men are carrying bundles of rods and axes, the fasces borne by Tribunes which symbolise a Roman consul's authority. But these are different. Purses are hanging from the rods and blood-soaked heads severed by Surena in the morning are fixed to the tops of the axes.

The Crassus look – alike follows on a horse. Forced to respond whenever he's called Crassus, or Imperator, he's dressed in women's clothes, long powder blue robes of high Parthian fashion flowing over his mount. A group of bawdy female singers from Seleucia's demimonde walk behind gesticulating in derision and singing mocking songs about how cowardly and effeminate he is.

The rest of the prisoners stumble along on the cobblestone street, shamed and exhausted, consumed by dread of their future. Parthian guards prod those who don't keep up, black lashes arcing in the air when the prods don't work. Marcus is near enough to the front to see the grotesque figure on the horse. His stomach is wound in knots of humiliation at the sight. It would've been better if the man had committed suicide. How can it be that the conquerors of the world, soldiers favoured by the gods, have been brought so low that one of their number prefers such ignominy to its honourable alternative?

When the sarcastic Triumph ends, the Romans are herded together outside the city, awaiting the next stage of their fate. They're kept in the dark; when questioned, Latin speaking guards say they don't know what's in store for them, and they probably don't. Marcus thinks it unlikely that Surena will have them put to death; there're so many and it would be a waste. Using them somewhere as slaves would be more economical, but the man has shown such cruelty, anything can happen. Anxiety rises like bile from a sick stomach as nothing develops. No information, no commands, just silence and waiting. A few soldiers go mad, shouting irrationally, even trying to run away. They're lashed back into submission by the guards and settle down.

Hope, the only form of happiness in this world left to the prisoners, still animates most of the men, including Marcus. But it's the hope that accompanies those who're sentenced to death when the date of execution is some time off. It's not necessarily forlorn, but very thin, inadequate to dry the tears of the soul.

CHAPTER 7

In the Armenian foothills to the north, another weird ceremony is about to take place. The Parthian monarch has secured a truce with King Artavasdes of Armenia and is celebrating the wedding of his son to the sister of his new ally. It's being held in the well apportioned but not opulent Armenian palace. He's pleased that the first part of his strategy is working. No need for battle, Artavasdes was content with an alliance. Now there're two armies to deal with Surena, weakened as he's sure to be after the Romans have finished with him. Things are going well; he's got reason to celebrate, to drink with confidence alongside his new found friends.

As the bonhomie of the sumptuous feast is filling the grand hall to the ceiling, brute-faced Sillaces appears at the large bronze door and looks around for the Parthian King. A hush quells the partying mood as the big man strides through the tables to Orodes who is sitting next to his host. Standing several paces away, he bows low, holding something wrapped in cloth under his arm. Murmurings begin among the guests.

He straightens up slowly and with a flourish, removes the cloth and tosses the blood – congealed head of Crassus towards the feet of his King, its partly dissolved lips and teeth set in a grimace of horror. It rolls bumpily across the floor. The guests are transfixed. The movement gives the head a bizarre appearance of life, as if Crassus has shed his limbs and shrunk into a head and is about to speak, accuse his enemies of unnatural cruelty and lay an eternal curse upon the King. A lump of gold falls out, larger than the biggest nugget. It's bloodstained and tarnished with bits of charred flesh, but still recognizable as the precious metal. A gasp fills the room, and a horrified silence.

It takes a few moments but when the Parthians realise the identity of the grisly figure they erupt in joy, shouting and banging the tables. The Armenians congratulate them, more than ever convinced of the wisdom of their alliance. Sensing that Sillaces wants to speak, the King waves his hands to tamp down the noise. It continues to rock the hall, but eventually dies down as the happy guests obey the royal signal.

> "Your Majesty, we engaged the Roman army at Carrhae in a battle of the centuries. With the brilliant tactics of our esteemed Commander we smashed them to bits, killing twenty thousand and taking ten thousand prisoners. The remaining ten thousand have slunk back to Roman territory, broken and disorganised. Casualties on our side were light. It was an absolute victory. You have the head of the Roman general at your feet to prove it. The victory has shown our troops are the best in the world and Surena the greatest general. Nothing can stop us now".

Orodes is shattered. He sits there staring at the head of Crassus unable to say a word. It's just as well that the disappointment on his face is interpreted by all as shock at the macabre sight. He pulls himself together finally and looks at Sillaces. Artavasdes is stunned, mindful of the fate that could have been his if he had opposed these fierce people.

Standing up unsteadily, Orodes takes a slurp of wine and raises two fat and flaccid arms out wide. The goblet he's still holding shakes half of its contents onto the table. One of the Parthians titters, stops immediately as prudence takes hold.

> "You bring great news Sillaces. This victory is a fitting tribute to the fighting spirit of our nation. We always knew that with the aid of Ahura Mazda". The Parthians in the hall mumble "Bless his name". "We would defeat the Forces of Darkness. And at last it has happened. Parthia is safe and now a nation as powerful as Rome. The Romans can have the West; we have the East. We shall rule Asia in peace and prosperity, with our Armenian allies enjoying our beneficence." Artavasdes nods in approval and gives a wan smile.

As he speaks, a sharp pain rises from the pit of his stomach and spreads up his chest into his arms, weighing them down and making his gestures leaden and awkward. It's the toxic fear of Surena infecting his blood stream again. This time it's worse. He staggers a bit and recovers, the pain subsiding, but not the anxiety. The glory of the victory will elevate his rival to a status impossible to cope with. And it's obvious his army was not weakened by the battle as his friend Versaces predicted.

The Versaces plan has to be abandoned. It'll never work now; Surena is invincible. Besides, something other than a military solution would always be more appealing to his epicene nature. He must think of a new strategy, subterranean and devious. Something comes to mind, something he had been thinking about before he adopted the Versaces plan. While it's put into place, smiles are the best reaction to Surena's achievement. No one must know his hidden thoughts about the great victory.

> "Sillaces, go immediately to your Commander in Chief and give him our personal congratulations. Tell him to come to Carrhae as soon as possible with the prisoners. We'll meet him there in ten days. We wish to see them in person."

With that, he dismisses Sillaces with a flick of his hand and returns to socializing, but with little enthusiasm. All the rest are in such a jolly mood they don't notice the change. The pudgy face is darker now and seems disoriented. His eyes are hooded and heavy with thought. Somehow the effects of the wine have suddenly disappeared; he's alert and steady now.

The festivities carry on with Orodes in a distracted mood, uncommonly lacking in urge for pleasures of the flesh – showing no interest in the offers of delights from his hosts. He leaves the hall before the rest, telling his courtiers he's tired and wants to be by himself. They're a little bemused but are used to the King's aberrant behaviour. He barely says goodbye to Artavasdes, making him wonder about the manners of his new ally.

Rising the next day earlier than his courtiers had ever seen, Orodes is on the road to Carrhae. The night before he had ordered an early start. He takes with him the five thousand troops he had brought to intimidate the Armenian king.

ප

Outside Seleucia a couple of days later, Surena gives orders for the Romans to move, to march north. As the guards prod them forward, a huge relief arises in the men, as if a warm blanket is spread over them while lying naked in bed on a frosty night. They will not be killed, at least not yet.

The fast courier system of the Parthians, based on relays of fresh horses and made famous by their Achaemid predecessors, brought the King's message quickly. Determined to meet the royal deadline, Surena pushes the speed of the march – too fast for some of the Romans to keep up. Uninhibited by pity, he permits no laxness to subvert the objective. When the lash fails, the swords get rid of the impediments. No time is wasted. He makes it on the day the King ordered.

At the main gate of the town that will forever be remembered for the worst defeat of Rome since Hannibal crossed the Alps, the two leading men of the Parthian Empire meet. Orodes' troops are outside the walls, Surena's army and their sorry captives inside. What an opportunity. The wheel of fortune that carried him to victory at Carrhae is still active, still turning in his favour. It may eventually turn past the happy zone, but not today, not when the blush of success is still on his cheek. Orodes has made a mistake coming here, exposing himself to the full might of the invincible Commander.

The King proclaims that it would be best to hold their discussion in private, away from the crowded town, at a little distance along the Road. Surena sees no reason to quibble.

In a shady copse just off the Road where the land rises in a gentle wooded slope before it levels off in the distance, the two men dismount and smile at each other. They're somewhat stiff but cordial enough. Their retainers stand a little way off, dismounted too. The men mingle and speak of the victory, congratulate each other; all are in a good mood. The Empire is united and at peace, more powerful than it's ever been. No one could possibly divine the disruptive thoughts the Empire's two most important men are holding within.

Orodes feels he must begin.

"Nowhere in history has Parthia won such a victory. It'll rumble down the memory of time like the rolling rhythm of the kettle drum, never to be silenced. Thanks to your achievement, the balance of power has shifted East. You've remade the map of the world. We wish to congratulate you in person and command you to name your reward. You may have anything you wish."

Surena's dislike of the man fades into pleasure at the compliment. Not even someone as cynical as he can remain unmoved by the praise of a monarch.

"Your Majesty, I thank you for your gracious words, but I must remind myself that the glory is to be shared by the men who fought that day. They excelled in their duty, a feat that was rewarded by the favour of Ahura Mazda.

"Your Majesty's generosity has taken me by surprise. I beg for a little time to think of what I'd like for the reward Your Majesty so kindly speaks of.

"Now, we must decide what to do with the Roman prisoners. There're about ten thousand. Is it your Majesty's wish that they be killed or spared?"

"It would be a pity to waste them. They're skilful soldiers, despite their defeat. Send them to Margiana as slaves. There they can help guard our eastern frontier. Best if they're far away.

"You can go back to Carrhae now. We've had enough conversation. We'll stay here for a while. We've brought our falconer. He claims there're some trophy specimens in these hills."

"Thank you Sire. I wish Your Majesty good hunting. I will prepare a banquet for tonight."

"Yes. Do that."

The Road takes the famous warrior and his small retinue towards the town at a comfortable pace. Like him, it feels pleased, proud to host a conference between such noble men. The effects of the flattery worn off, Surena concludes that the King realizes he's in a weak position. That's why he offered that reward. It could be huge. He'd be embarrassed to refuse any request, whatever it is. He's trying to buy him off.

It doesn't really matter; the only worthwhile reward is the kingdom. That can only be had by force. Now is the time, when the King and his retainers are exposed. They'll be no match for the victors of Carrhae, flush with loyalty to their Commander. Only a pretext is needed. Something can be worked out. The senior officers must be persuaded to cooperate – an easy task. Then key nobles and priests will have to be brought onside – they'll follow the army. Much needs to be done, and quickly, before Orodes leaves Carrhae. Allies must be recruited without delay.

As he's musing in the gently rolling woodlands, the hot air completely still, a cluster of horsemen bursts out of the trees ahead, brandishing swords. They're Parthians. But not from his army. Not looking friendly. It's an ambush. Must be that damned king. No time to prepare. He's heavily outnumbered. How can that be? The sneaky bastard has outmanoeuvred him, him the great warrior.

Fortunately they have their swords. And they're mounted. He took the bold step of appearing before the King armed, confident he would get away with it, given the glory of his victory and the monarch's weakness.

The attackers ride hard at his troops and slash down two men who're a few paces in front. He shouts to the others to defend themselves. "Head for the trees. They're assassins", and charges off, closely followed by his comrades. His reaction was so quick it caught the attackers by surprise. But soon they recover and gallop off in pursuit. They catch up when their quarry is slowed down by fallen trees. A fierce combat begins in which no quarter is given, no time for prisoners.

Surrounded now, he parries the long blade of the man in front of him and cuts him down. His sword dispatches three more in quick succession, causing the assassins to pull back in fear. He feels confident he'll prevail. His history of success, his unshakable faith in himself give him energy, afford him superhuman strength. He'll beat off this scurrilous attempt by that podgy cretin.

He and his men kill a few more, their long swords flailing like a farmer threshing grain, and push back the assassins. Their leader shouts at them to regroup yelling insults at their timidity. As they retreat, Surena and his remaining men take off into the forest. Chastened by their lack of success, the assassins charge after them through the trees. The forest becomes thicker and allows them to catch up. Surena has to turn and face them. For a while the fight is even; his efforts inspire his men, combine with their terror to produce more commitment than the hired killers can muster. Just one great surge may be enough. But they can't do it; the enemy's superior numbers are overwhelming. His men start falling one after the other, until he's left fighting alone.

He's still on his horse, so fierce a warrior that his enemies show reluctance to attack. Nevertheless, at the furious urging of their leader, they eventually unhorse him. Several jump off their horses and try to knock him down with their shields.

They can't subdue the leonine man who's lost his sword and is now fighting with his dagger, stabbing two men and lunging at a third. The assassins hang back in indecision. He knows they won't kill him with their swords. Because he's from an exalted family they would be under orders not to spill his blood.

Then, suddenly four men charge from different directions, and before he can beat them off, grab him around the waist and wrestle him to the ground in a mighty struggle, kicking the dagger out of his hand. Another pulls a bow string around his neck. A monstrous roar leaps out of his throat as he's choked, cursing the King to hell, and then a dry gurgle, which diminishes slowly into death, but not before the strangler has to tighten the string three times. Twice he thought he had killed his man only to see him recover.

ରଓ

As the falcon lands on his gloved hand with a small bird in its mouth, Orodes sees the leader of the assassins riding up, dishevelled and panting.

"Your Majesty, Surena is dead. I've never seen a man fight so hard. But we were able to subdue him with the bow string. I lost a lot of my men though."

"Excellent news. Well done. You'll be handsomely rewarded, particularly if you and your men promise never to speak of today's events. Your life will depend on silence. So will theirs. Even a whisper will be fatal. Remember that. Only I will report the tragedy that befell the esteemed Surena."

All the same he plans to put them all to death as soon as possible, just to make sure. He pulls the bird out of the falcon's mouth, tosses it on the ground and hands the splendid hunter over to a servant to put the hood on.

"We must go back to Carrhae right away."

The heartily relieved King and his entourage ride back along the Road at a steady pace. It has another story of treachery to add to its archives. No need to rush. What a relief that now his blood can run through his veins no longer inflamed by the fear and anxiety that never left him in peace.

When they reach Carrhae he calls a conference of the nobles and priests in the Great Hall of the fortress. All stand; he sits.

"We have grave news to report. While we were conversing with Commander Surena outside Carrhae, a contingent of his troops charged out of the woods and attacked us and our retinue. As soon as the assault began, Surena joined in. We could see immediately that the ambush was part of a plot to usurp the throne.

"Fortunately our men were able to subdue the conspirators and kill them all, including, we're sorry to say, our illustrious Commander in Chief. We've brought his body back for a proper funeral.

"We must now inform the two armies here and explain Surena's treason to them. What makes it even more despicable and what saddens us the most is the fact that we offered him a reward of whatever he wanted for his victory over the Romans.

"It's tragic that this great hero who saved our Kingdom should have such a fate".

He pulls out his handkerchief and dabs his eyes and sits down forlornly.

The High priest nods his head and folds his hands in front of his gown.

"Your Majesty has been most fortuitously preserved by the grace of Ahura Mazda, bless his name." All mumble a repetition.

"And the nation has been spared the baleful presence of Evil through another civil war. Lord Surena was a gifted man, a great warrior who won the most important victory in Parthia's history. But, as the report of Your Majesty indicates, he failed to control the ambition his undoubted talents evoked in him.

He was tempted to excess by high achievement, a failing of many gifted men. The extent of this sin is measured by the enormity of his crime. His attack on Your Majesty was a breach of the sacredness that surrounds the throne, the divine unifying element that gives order to our nation. In doing that, he committed an act engineered by Evil, which Ahura Mazda, bless his name (all mumble again), justly punished through Your Majesty's hand. We must all unite behind the throne and move forward to enjoy the enhanced position our nation now enjoys after the defeat of the Forces of Darkness."

The nobles and priests nod their heads in agreement; there's no alternative. Some may doubt the King's version of events, but there's no evidence that he wasn't telling the truth. Besides he's the monarch, too exalted to be challenged in public. True, Surena's troops will have to measure their loyalty to their Commander against having to fight their brothers. But he's just a memory now. Expedience prevails as nobody wants another civil war. Orodes is satisfied he'll get away with the murder. But all are not as happy as he.

CHAPTER 8

Next day, the Parthian guards order the prisoners out of Carrhae onto the Road in the direction of the awakening sun. Everyone wonders who will fall victim to the brutality of the morning. All prepare to dive quickly to the ground, hopefully into a gully. But as the sun emerges from the pale blue, the usual signal for the dreaded horseman to arrive, he doesn't appear.

News of Surena's fate winds through the straggly line. A ragged cheer breaks out from the tired Romans in stages, as word of the deliverance passes along the Road, whose flatter stones here seem to indicate its relief too. Marcus says to Gaius that Epicurus had a point when he said pleasure is the absence of pain. The big man merely grunts.

Even the Parthians seem pleased, for while admiring his talents, many of them suffered from his dark side. They have a new commander for the march, a junior officer, noted for harshness but not savagery. And so the prisoners know they will live today, unless sickness or unhealed wounds claim their due. It's a blessing, even when measured against their journey into slavery.

From time to time they pass by local people walking short distances, farmers sometimes, sometimes just villagers on donkeys. They share the Road with them, easily moving around them as they're not marching in column as before. Marcus doesn't know why but his eyes fall on a lone man a few paces in front of him dressed in a tunic, head covered by a dusty red cap that gathers his hair in the Parthian fashion. He's walking slowly, wearily, as if he has a long way to go. He's carrying a bundle over his shoulder and is leaning forward. It's not possible to get a look at his face because his head is turned the other way as Marcus walks past.

The guards don't say where the trek is heading; but it's always east, fatally lengthening the distance from Roman territory. As the days fall by like sand slipping into the next chamber of the hour glass, inexorably and without distinction, the terrain leaves its trees behind and dries out into seared fields. Then it yields to steppe country of paltry scrub; sparse grass takes over, spreading its flatness into a wilderness that has no boundaries, except a horizon blurred in dusty haze. The sun, *sol invictus*, is in a wicked mood, devoid of pity for the struggling unfortunates. No cover shields them from its baleful shafts. Even the Road has lost sympathy, its stones magnifying the heat in cruel alliance. It seems it's punishing them for their defeat, or perhaps for their hubris.

Each step pulls a little more at the hope Marcus has allowed himself to hold. No chance of escape exists, for even if he and a few comrades were able to elude the guards, the huge and hostile country would ensure their recapture and certain death. While there's some possibility of a high level truce which might permit repatriation, it's dauntingly remote. Too much enmity separates the two nations.

The epic struggle of Odysseus comes to mind, carrying a hint of guilt. He recalls the hero's sacred duty to return home – the Greek tradition and his own. Must he follow it? Yes of course; he's been brought up to it. But only if circumstances permit. While Poseidon frustrated the determined Greek a number of times, whipping up the sea to drive him off course and a series of monsters sought to detain him, it was not an impossible task. This one would be. It's normal for the sense of duty to dissolve in the face of a superior force. Maybe he's rationalizing again, not like Cassius would think.

Gaius is walking beside him, grimly silent. He hasn't said anything for hours.

Marcus has to mention what's on his mind.

"I wonder if my last letter to Aurelia got out."

"Marcus, you have to be realistic. The only hope is if Cassius' group escaped, and that's not likely. If the letter had any chance it would've been with his contingent."

"Yes I know. He's still in charge of logistics. In a way it's probably better for her not to get it. Or would it? If she got it, at least she would know my true intentions. But it might create a false hope. If she hears nothing she would be freer to find someone else."

"My friend, you'll have to forget her. Some one'll tell her about the defeat. She'll wait a while for stragglers to come home and find out you're not among them. Then give up hope."

"I know, but as long as there's some chance of getting home, even if it's remote, that's hard to do."

There's no point in continuing the conversation. They trudge on in silence, retreating into their own thoughts. A wave of self pity breaks over him no matter how hard he tries to resist it. Why was he chosen to suffer this degradation? Who chose it for him? Was it a force activated by the choices he made, or does he bear no responsibility- a victim of uncaring chance? Why did the gods who are supposed to protect Rome permit it? Nothing has prepared him for this.

Briefly, he looks over at Gaius' impassive face. His friend doesn't seem to have the same or even similar thoughts. He just accepts his fate like a true Stoic without questioning it.

The books that used to while away the weary hours of night are no longer of interest. Perhaps they contain some answers but what difference do they make? He husbands them though; at least their presence offers a kind of connection. Fortunately the Parthians don't think they're worth stealing.

Of late he has retreated more and more into himself, downwards in a vortex, farther and farther from the horizon marking the boundary with the outside world. Down there, a cold fog of lethargy seeps in and stifles any movement except aimless drifting.

Nothing is worthwhile; self worth is an illusion – shadows on the wall trapped in the past. To an equal and opposite degree, erstwhile pride has morphed into self loathing. His summons to destiny has vanished like a vision faded; it's become an unreadable parchment, all meaning dying in blurred ink. Positive thoughts of the past or the future have abandoned him, escaped into the terrible vastness of the steppe. He's locked in a negative mentality of the present which constrains his freedom as much as the guards.

He can't think of change, even for the better, though he knows Democritus showed that everything changes; nothing stays the same; you can't step into the same river twice.

A paradox bedevils him – if he's worth nothing, is nothing, why is it that all he can think of is himself. How can something that doesn't exist be so consuming? *Ex nihilo nihil fit* -out of nothing, nothing comes. If there's nothing left, no Aurelia, no home, no family, no prospects, no self, why not end life now, right here on the callous Road? At least it would have the elegance of demonstrating the ultimate futility of it all.

That evening when the others have gone to bed, he wanders off into the steppe. It seems lonelier at night, devoid of life, a place where death would feel at home. He takes out Owls Head, looks for a full minute at the lethal beauty of its silver damascene; the pale star light picks it out. He holds it with both hands. His arms stretch out. The tip is pointed to his belly. One thrust and he'll be at peace. The nothing will return to nothing, where it belongs.

Why doesn't he do it? Cowardice isn't the reason; his bravery is proven. Perhaps there's something deep in the vortex that's an antidote. It can't be the hope of repatriation; that's become too slight to matter. No, it must be something else, something beyond consciousness, a hidden device of nature that whispers denial to the negative.

He puts Owl's Head away and returns to the camp. He has a restless sleep and wakes up jaded. His sense of failure is compounded by last night's brush with his reluctant dagger.

All that can be done is to march in leaden sullenness with the rest of the unfortunates. The Road is as hard hearted as its stony path. It's leaving Roman territory behind, steadily moving away from civilization and humbling its habitat as it penetrates the fearsome unknown. Human settlements are further and further apart. Towns and villages become smaller and poorer as the bedraggled throng heads east.

Soon the parsimonious Road offers only dry and sun-blasted steppe which stretches out in a vast beige wilderness, struggling to support even camel thorn. The Romans are constantly beaten to walk faster, their strength compromised by the meagreness of the meals they get once a day at the end of the march. The smell of putrefaction poisons the air as some of the wounds progress to the mortal stage.

Marcus is beginning to smell it around Quintus, who's looking pale these days and has lost his vigour.

"Quintus, how's that wounded hand?"

"It's turned bad. I didn't want to say anything – thought it would heal by itself. But it's not going to. Blood poison's set in. Spreading. I know the symptoms Marcus. I'm done for."

Marcus doesn't know what to think. Quintus would never say a thing like that unless it was serious, very serious.

"Quintus, you shouldn't keep walking. I'll arrange to put you in one of the wagons."

"No. It's too late. I'll keep going as long as I can and then just sit down. It's the fortune of war."

Marcus puts his friend's arm around his shoulder and grips his good hand. With his other hand he holds his belt. For a while he's able to help him walk fast enough to avoid the attention of the guards. But soon his weight begins to pull as his legs buckle. There's nothing for it but to carry him piggyback. While there's still life he must do what he can. Fortunately the guards call a rest halt. Marcus looks at the eyes of his comrade. He's gone.

Telling one of the men to look after him, Marcus goes to see his legion legatus.

"Manius Decius, Centurion Quintus Tullius has just died – only a few minutes ago. We must bury him. Can you persuade the Parthian Commander to allow it, maybe as an exception? We can carry him until the end of the march today and bury him then."

"I've been to see the Commander of the March about the burial policy – several times. He won't budge – must have orders not to allow us to bury our dead. They're being vindictive."

"He was a close friend. I can't just leave him for the vultures."

"Nothing more I can do. I'm sorry. I know it's appalling but that's it."

Marcus goes back to Quintus and calls his officers and a few of the others together.

"I'm not ready to let Quintus rot out here. It's an outrage that the Parthians won't let him be buried. I propose that our cohort refuse to get up when the guards order a restart until we're allowed to bury him. This is not an order but I'll do it even if I'm the only one. Who's with me?"

Everyone agrees without hesitation. Word is passed down the line to the others in the cohort. When the rest period is over, they all refuse to get up. The guards are furious, prodding and hitting them with the cattle whip. But nobody budges. A guard officer comes up to Marcus,

"You, you're the commander of this section. Order your men back on the march."

Marcus says nothing, only stares defiantly into the distance. *Alea iacta est.*

"What's the matter with you?"

"One of our officers has just died. We want to carry him to the end of the march today and bury him. It's only civilized that we be allowed to do it."

"You know the policy. No burying. Now get up and order your men to move out."

Marcus sits still, silent. The officer comes over and cuffs him across the face, then orders a guard to give him ten strokes of the lash. This produces no action. Then another ten. Marcus' back runs rivulets of blood but still no obedience. He doesn't care. Life's hardly worth living out here anyway.

The officer's frustrated. After a moment's hesitation, he disappears to go to the Commander of the March, leaving the guards to kick Marcus a few times until he tips over on the ground, barely conscious.

The Commander is in a quandary. He can't just leave the stubborn Romans behind, or kill them; they're too many. His orders are to bring the prisoners to Margiana as slaves to do important work. They're all needed, except for unavoidable losses. He'll be held responsible if the expected number doesn't arrive.

He's a pragmatic man, not particularly driven by hatred, and he's in a remote area, far from headquarters. Besides, the burial policy was instituted by Surena, and he's dead. Why is it vital to keep it now without exception? It's more important to complete the march with the full complement. Without giving reasons, he abruptly orders the guard officer to allow the burial so long as it doesn't slow the march. This means it has to be done at the end of the day, on the time of the Romans, and by them.

When the guard officer announces the decision, the entire cohort gives out a cheer. Marcus is helped up and is able to walk, but only with the support of two comrades. They make it to the end of the day, just, for he's near collapse. It's just as well he's as strong as he is.

That night he leads a small group of men who knew Quintus well in the sad job of burying their comrade. He can barely walk but insists on taking part. They carry the corpse to a few metres off the Road, dig a shallow grave and bury him with a denarius in his mouth.

After the burial Marcus moves to be by himself. He's grateful for the chance of standing up for Quintus when it would have been expedient to let him rot on the steppe. The virtue in it gives him some pleasure but he knows it shouldn't be exaggerated. It really wasn't much of a challenge despite the beating that had to follow; Quintus was a close friend and the code of comradeship demanded action. Besides, the effects of the beating are temporary. It's much worthier to do something outside the circle of friends and family, such as give honest advice at a critical moment. The lapse in the Command tent can't be assuaged just by what happened here. Today was close and personal; in the tent removed and objective, a different and, in a sense, a harder test. An opportunity needs to come for him to pass that type of trial. If it doesn't, the guilt that's obsessing him will never be expunged.

The next two days he rides in a wagon. Gaius has bribed the baggage train guard with a couple of denarii, which he has hidden in his belt, not to notice. Gradually Marcus recovers his strength and rejoins his comrades on the march, which carries on day after day in boring monotony, pushing further into the desiccated east.

Sometimes they pass caravans travelling in the direction of Carrhae with goods from far away. Lines of imperious camels, heads in the air, lope by in relaxed strides with wooden crates hanging off their sides. They're roped one after the other, like a string of pearls. The beasts seem contemptuous. Merchants in garments matching the dust ride them without a word. In some cases donkeys do the carrying, their shorter steps requiring more energy. They seem tireless though, albeit less regal.

Other camel trains come out of the horizon's haze ahead, their general shape emerging shakily, pass the alien soldiers by and disappear in the distance, silent and exotic. The prisoners have to move to the side of the track to let them by. Sometimes one from the west catches up and slides by at a faster pace. On occasion a halt is ordered so the Parthians can catch up with the news.

A guard who's just been talking to one of the merchants says;

> "You might like to know that your general Cassius has escaped to Syria with his men. We tried to catch him but he got away. He's a tricky fellow."

Does that mean the letter got through?

It's no surprise to hear of Cassius' success. If anyone could escape it would be that clever and calculating man. Without doubt, once he gets home, his abilities will ensure a career that'll influence the world. The thought gives a moment of vicarious pleasure, but then stirs up painful memories. Why the choice of Crassus over Cassius, Crassus over Caesar? Why the tendency to let expediency crunch principle? Cassius didn't allow it, and he survives, a free man who's returned home, like Odysseus.

It's tempting to become the sole point of concern, the centre of the tragic narrative. There, personal actions perform an exaggerated role. His choice in the tent could not have caused the disaster; Crassus was bound to make the fatal decision anyway despite his corrupt advice. But like it or not, he was part of the decision, however minor his role in it, however minimal his influence could have been.

Sometimes small things, in themselves of trivial account, can set off a chain reaction if the circumstances are right, that builds to create a major effect. Could his counsel, if it had been honest, have produced a different result ultimately, in a similar manner? For instance, could it have energised Cassius to some extent as the next step in the chain?

This line of reasoning only aggravates his guilt, which even without the enhancement, is heavy enough. In a morbid symmetry, it matches the enormity of the tragedy that followed. Fate has taken note and meted out a horrific punishment for being an agent in the catastrophe. Subtly, though he's dimly aware of it, the reasoning fallacy of *post hoc ergo propter hoc* has taken over – after that, because of that. He must resist it or go mad.

It's useless to stew over past actions – against the teaching of the Stoics. The present is what really matters, and the future. Face the dragon which fate has sent as best he can and don't worry about the consequences. Gaius does.

Every night the same dream arrives. In the distance a black spot appears and grows bigger and bigger. As it gets closer, it differentiates into a flock of eagles. They swoop over him in an arc, black against a grey sky. Screeching in fury, their beaks open wide, impatient to devour their prey. Talons drop down, sharp as the arrows that ripped apart the Testudo at Carrhae. They're going for his liver, seat of the life force. Just before the touching point he wakes up, blanket soaked in sweat. In half sleep he looks for them but they've vanished. It takes an hour before he can fall asleep again. What makes them worse is that they're a form of the Eumenides, the demonic avengers of wrongful deeds. They'll never leave him alone until placated, a requirement he has no idea how to satisfy.

扣

One morning he wakes up to a cold mist tumbling across the steppe and collecting in a grey shroud outside his tent. The summer has formally ceded it domain to autumn. For some time now darkness has been squeezing the day at both ends. The Parthians don't change the routine though; the march lasts the same number of hours. There's a vast distance to cover before reaching Margiana, the wild eastern boundary of their Empire. Most of them have never been that far east; they rely on Sogdian guides. Navigation is no trivial exercise for often tracks or even roads go off in different directions obscuring the true path. It's as if the Road takes fiendish delight in leading unwary travellers astray. Is it just being frivolous or is it sending out a coded message? The journey so far has shown there's counsel in its stones, however hard to interpret

Marcus strays a little away from his comrades in the pre dawn dark. He strolls towards a brazier which casts an unsteady light into the black background to reveal two Parthian guards sitting beside its warmth, eating breakfast. It's a pleasure never afforded the Romans. The guards let him approach, even say good morning in Parthian. He's learned a few words and understands. The loaves of bread they have are mesmerizing, flat and freshly fragrant. The Romans never get bread, only watery gruel, and then have to wait the entire day to receive it. They're always at the portal of starvation, kept just alive by the cunning provisioners who've worked out the minimum rations needed to prevent them from collapsing.

One of the guards silently offers a loaf, a whole loaf, as precious as a brick of gold. Without a word he shoves it under his tunic – someone might see. Embarrassed at the lack of civility, from him a man of civilization, he thanks his enemy in Parthian, adding a few superlatives.

As he walks away into the gloom, a mist of tears forms with realization of the irony in what has happened: the first kindness since the battle, from an implacable enemy, whose country he came to despoil. Gratitude springs from his heart – real thankfulness, a sensation he's never felt as deeply before. Self absorptive pride had always kept it shallow whenever he felt it was appropriate to show it. For a moment, the virtue embedded in the full feeling pulls him out of himself to connect with something outside, something spiritual, and it feels good. It's not without reason that it's said that gratitude is the parent of all virtues.

What if the situation were reversed? Would a Parthian soldier be wandering off with Marcus' loaf of bread? Or would that comfortable Roman contempt for inferiors hold fast? That attitude – once so vital to self esteem, now seems absurd.

Defeat at Carrhae has crushed his sense of superiority but it hasn't eliminated his xenophobia. But he feels it's on the way to doing that. The little act of humanity of the Parthian has crossed the cultural barrier and revealed a commonality, a universality, not apparent to him before. It tends to unpick the illusion he's been labouring under the whole of his life. The shock of fortune's reversal in the presence of kindness has opened his mind to see a new reality, or at least dimly so.

The foggy darkness of the hour offers a chance for concealment – an opportunity to devour the treasure unobserved. But the generosity of the Parthian rules out such behaviour. Some must be given away. There're too many Romans; a choice must be made, including how much to keep. The noblest thing would be to give it all. But keeping some won't make an appreciable difference. Anyway, being there to receive it gives the best title.

He breaks the loaf into three equal parts, carefully saving the crumbs that fall off. He gives two to the first prisoners encountered then moves away. The sublime moment of eating is to be enjoyed quietly, alone. As the first morsel slowly dissolves in his mouth, the aroma and the crumbly taste exclude everything else. Nothing is as important as this. Then the image of the whole loaf appears in his mind's eye – the round, flat, beautiful loaf, with a diameter the span of a hand. With emotion and reason allied at the deepest level, the form of the loaf arises in his mind, a Platonic revelation of the ideal. Ineluctably, something outside himself touches his soul, something real, and it feels good. It's the first time he's felt good since the catastrophe.

🙰

On the Road, ever capricious like the gods, time passes by the cycles of the moon and Odyssean hope lets go at long last. In a way it's a relief for it looses a tension that has only added frustration to helplessness. An illusory dimension has been removed, opening the way to accepting a new existence. That may be so, but he has little will yet to try for it. Inertia hems him in, undermines positive thought. All along however, the kindness of the Parthian guard acts as a safety net to his depression, saving it from sinking further.

The sun's heat gradually flees the steppe and temperatures drop to below freezing at night, seldom warming up past it even at noon. Sometimes wisps of tiny snow flakes hardened in the wind sprinkle down from leaden skies like winding gossamer. It takes hours just to cover the frozen ground with a thin sheet, which the wind soon tears apart. The colder weather takes a toll on the weaker prisoners, those once strong men now undermined by wounds or sickness contracted along the Road.

The symptoms are sadly obvious. Vacant stares in opaque eyes show the will has lost its energy and the mind has given up. The number of men slumping down, impervious to the lash, increases each day as the knives in the wind slash their lifeline. It turns out that the permission to bury Quintus was an exception. The policy itself hasn't changed. Sporadic attempts have been made to force it but they've faded with exhaustion. Even Marcus has given up. The animus behind the successful push for Quintus can't be kept up.

The dead soldiers are left on the side of the road, discarded like rubbish tossed out after the daily meal. There should be more food now for the rest, but the Parthians keep the rations the same.

Grey winged scavengers which have been following the troupe in relays like merchants on the Road, wait politely until the last soldier has passed by and flop upon the bodies before they stiffen into lumps. Everyone is too exhausted to do more than note the loss. The cruel march is an acid, extracting humanity like leaching gold from a heap of rock and leaving nothing but tailings behind.

The trudge merges with the monotony of the steppe. Time slides into the distance they're covering and both seem as one. No one really cares. They just keep on walking, if they can, fixing on the present. Their past is a blighted memory and their future too terrible to contemplate.

Despite the severing of links, from time to time Aurelia's face appears in the morning mist, and sometimes on the wind when it blows across the steppe. It seems to be mournfully motioning him to come back, in a gesture of love that can no longer be. Occasionally there seems a touch of reproach in the beautiful eyes and Odysseus comes to mind.

The days pass through the savagery of winter into its later stages where frost seldom appears and then only in the early morning. It's best not to think of it as spring for that would bring to mind images of new life, something too unsettling.

The desolate column eventually comes to a barren land, all sand, where not even scrub or straggly grass adds the temerity of life. The guards say it's the great Black Desert. Ahead, a plethora of tracks snakes through the endless dunes, some subsiding into oblivion, others going in the right direction. It's almost impossible to tell which is which. The Road claims them all. At this stage it's a trickster, mischievously tempting the unwary into perdition.

It's also a cruel hunter, festooned with trophies of dead men. Romans are not the only ones; it's been awarded countless others, some from violent attacks, others from the callousness of the waterless domain that lies on either side. The promise of wealth can be counted on to produce many more over the years to come.

Just as it seems the dunes will last forever, the landform changes – full vegetation arrives with a sudden demarked edge, as sharp as a phase change. In its midst, a system of water courses spreads its tentacles like a shiny octopus, twisting and turning as it moves across the land. Mud brick buildings of a major city appear, interspersed with trees whose bare branches scratch the sky in dormant life.

The men, exhausted though they are, quicken their pace as they see the water, and break into a run. At last they'll be able to throw off the thirst demon. The guards can't stop the rush towards the shallow and not exactly wholesome stream. So eager are they to drink that they swallow almost as much silt as water. Spring coldness pains their throats as they gulp without restraint. Some become sick within minutes, but all are relieved.

The guards allow them to take their fill. Tired themselves, they loll around on the coarse grass. Marcus says to the one who speaks Latin, "What's this place?"

> "It's Margiana, big caravan town. Farthest east of Parthian Empire. Frontier with Sogdiana. You Romans stay here rest of your lives. You here to help our garrison protect frontier. Don't think you have lazy life, just waiting around for attack. Ha ha ha. When you're not on guard duty you work on wall we're building to surround town."

This is the final degradation, for little skill is required, just a strong back and the fortitude to withstand harsh working conditions and the lash. He has seen how Romans build their roads and bridges. So little regard for health and safety that the spectre of death stalks the workers every day. Can he expect any better treatment?

So this is how the rest of life will be spent, in a distant hinterland where half civilized barbarians interact with people even more feral. A slave forever – a tool that can be discarded when it's no longer sharp enough or if it's too difficult to wield. The most arbitrary commands must be obeyed and all civilized scepticism stifled in a servile acceptance of the masters' whims.

Former life afforded an identity and self esteem, indeed an exalted one. It was nourished by the connection with home and a sophisticated culture. Now those are gone. There's no home here and probably never will be, and Roman culture is not appreciated, nor even known. A vignette of his father's sad figure flashes up. How much more fundamental is his deracination than his father's! Identity must be rethought entirely, much more profoundly than the stubborn farmer did, or should have done. Unless that can be accomplished somehow, it'll be impossible to convert mere existence into a life, and he'll be condemned to unrelieved misery for the rest of his days.

og

However, the situation turns out to be better than expected. The Parthians realize they're a long way from the super heated centre of the Empire where hatred of Rome has the rawness of immediacy. Everyone knows that Margiana is too far from the borders of the Roman Empire to permit serious thoughts of an escape West and no one would be expected to test the unknown East. So security is comfortably lax. The Romans are allowed to take possession of their armour and weapons; they're needed for their job as frontier guards. And the rich soil of the oasis produces so much food that there's no need to scrimp on diet, even for slaves.

At present, no threat from the East disturbs the peace, so military activity is reduced to desultory patrols and exercises. Marcus' cohort, now shrunk to a hundred and fifty, is still intact as a unit.

He calls his men together one day after their guard duty is over. In a voice strong enough to cover up his depressed state of mind, he says,

> "Men, we don't have enough to do out here. Besides, if we aren't careful our skills will decline. I don't care what the others in the army do – they don't do anything but what the Parthians order. We're going to exercise hard– for two hours a day, starting now.
>
> "I want everyone to make a wooden sword for himself. We'll use them for practice. Divide into two groups for a skirmish. I'll be joining you – so watch out. Tomorrow we'll concentrate on shield manoeuvres."

There're a few groans but Gaius quietens them down with a stern call to pride and they all go off looking for pieces of wood in the oasis, leaving Marcus alone in his thoughts.

111

It's some consolation that the boredom at Margiana has a tendency at times to dull the soul's anguish, and activity helps, but never for long. Nothing can salve the abject humiliation of slavery. The bathos of that is intolerable – for him, a man used to the pride that springs from superiority. It bores into him every day and toxic anger and frustration pour into the holes until he's ready to explode. The reality of slavery is with him always like a chronic disease sharp with pain. The line he knows by heart from the Odyssey rubs it in. "Zeus, the Old Thunderer, robs a man of half his virtue the day the yoke clamps around his neck."

Just today a guard came over to him with an arrogant expression on his face. Standing about three metres away, he said "Bring that rock over here", and moved another five metres away. When he brought the rock, the guard said, with a superior smile, "Now put it back." He couldn't stand the insult and threw the rock at the guard's feet. This brought a savage slash with the whip and a kick in the groin.

Everyday the Parthian guards find some new insult to throw at him and his comrades, whether it's verbal or a stroke of the lash, whether provoked or not. He must find a way to escape or he'll go mad. But that's impossible, stuck out here surrounded by enemies and terrain as danger-ous as a hungry lion.

Religion fails to offer solace, for its tenets, as many people are thinking these days, are too difficult to accept. But that doesn't mean the spiritual dimension doesn't exist; it's just that another way will have to be found to activate it. In a small measure, the way the loaf of bread lifted him out of himself for a moment was a rudimentary step. Nevertheless, the sea of lethargy that presses in retards the process from going further and anger interrupts his thoughts. Besides there's no one to help; in this he's on his own. However, while it still takes too much effort to read, of late he finds comfort in picking up the books at the end of the day, just to hold for a moment.

Wandering at random through the camp at the edge of the oasis, he encounters Gaius.

"Ave Marcus, you look lost. What's the matter?"

"Nothing much. Just thinking. Let's go to my tent to get out of the cold."

They sit down inside on makeshift wooden stools. Marcus lights the brazier but they keep their thick winter cloaks on.

"What do you think of the men's morale? I mean the men in our cohort."

"Not bad. Shit, they're depressed but stubborn. They're trying to survive. It's hell being slaves. Nothing worse. They talk of escape all the time. Useless though. The daily exercises you make them do are good for them. What d'you think?"

"I agree. It's against the natural of things for Romans to be slaves. Anything's better than that. They're angry though at Crassus, blame him for the disaster."

Gaius' eyes suddenly flare.

"So do I. The man's an idiot. I can't believe he led us onto that plain. The silly goat should've known. He got what he deserved."

"That's right. Should never have left the business world. Too fixated on his own way of doing things – couldn't put himself in the other man's shoes, underestimated the enemy, saw no ability there. It's very Roman though, don't you think?

"Maybe it is but can't do anything about it now. All we can do is endure. Take each day as it comes and get through it. It's not much of a life but no worse than death."

"The biggest mistake was going into Parthia in the first place. I know we went for booty, but maybe that isn't a good enough reason. Besides, it's a bad decision to invade another country without being really sure of winning."

"Are you getting soft Marcus? What difference does it make? We're here, slaves, and that's all there is to it."

"No, I'm not. I just believe it's worthwhile to think about these things sometimes. It doesn't mean I don't have the toughness to survive like the rest of us."

"All right. All right. Don't get upset. No offence."

They chat on for a while and Gaius goes off to his own tent, Marcus thinking about his friend. He's a good man, reliable and uncomplicated.

113

He doesn't think too much and can't even read properly, but seems to cope with adversity well – doesn't complain when fortune turns its wheel against him, but takes it as it comes. That's the Stoic way and he practises it better than many who study philosophy, including himself. And he was right to prefer a good commander to a good booty hunter. Would he have stood up to Crassus in the tent?

☙

The retreat of the frost makes way for the next stage of captivity – building the fortification walls around the city. Since ancient times people in this part of the world have used mud bricks for permanent structures. The technique is simple but ideal for the climate where rain is as scarce as the gratitude of kings.

It's easy to learn how to make the little rectangular wooden boxes, fill them with mud and straw, wet enough to expel the air, and smooth the tops with a trowel, then to set them in rows for drying in the sun which shines more than three hundred days a year. After a short time and a little tap, the rock hard bricks fall out of the mould and are ready to be laid. Before long each man is making hundreds a day. Under supervision, the Romans are soon able to lay them, keeping the rows straight – at least when they try.

But they don't always try. Surreptitiously some men slip half- made bricks into the wall or deliberately make crooked rows. They're punished when the Parthian foremen catch them – beaten for minor offences and thrown into the dungeon for more serious ones. Still the subversion goes on.

The Parthian construction manager takes Marcus aside to complain. He's upset and worried that unless more co-operation is achieved, the fortress will not only miss the schedule deadline he has promised the local satrap but may turn out to be unstable. Threats of harsher punishment are shouted – maiming and even execution. Marcus says he'll speak to the men. In fact, although he doesn't mention it, he also is concerned, for he doesn't agree with their attitude.

He calls the men together next morning before the work begins.

"Some of you have the attitude of not caring how well we build this wall. I've even seen sabotage. I understand that. We're slaves so why should we care how we build it. We don't benefit – they do.

"But that's not the right attitude for Romans. We're the civilised people – not them. We should show we're capable of excellence – not for them but for ourselves. If we can fight well we can build well too.

"I want you all to do as good a job as you are capable of. We should build the best wall possible. Then we can be proud of our work, and because of that we can be proud of ourselves. If we do it, in our hearts we won't be slaves. That's the benefit. We don't need to feel guilty if it helps the enemy. What we do out here makes no difference to Rome – too far away. We do it for ourselves. Besides, the wall could protect us too.

"Any man found shirking or doing a sloppy job will be put on report. The optios will be looking out for it. It's a matter of military discipline – Roman not Parthian."

Marcus' initiative is taken up by the commanders of the other cohorts who also call their men together and, despite some mumbling, they accept the order and lift the quality of their work. The wall begins to show its form, strong and thick, nut brown against an aquamarine sky. Over the weary months it gradually crawls around the city – a barrier against the wildness of the East. Towers for archers emerge at strategic intervals, adding symmetry to the creation.

The labour is not onerous. The Parthian bosses don't want to exert themselves particularly, so the working day usually ends in the early afternoon. The worst effect is boredom, and, of course, humiliation; though pride in the construction allows for some self esteem. The construction manager asks Marcus to pass on his congratulations to the men. He doesn't bother to do it; they're not doing it for him or the Parthians.

The tedium dries up the sap of life, leaving only a wilted husk at the end of the day. Everybody longs for respite in sleep. And that, for Marcus, the screeching eagles are prone to interrupt. Months drift by like pieces of driftwood on a sluggish river and it's now late summer, one and a half years since they arrived at Margiana. They're still building the wall and still in slavery, getting used to it, or some are. Not Marcus though – never will.

The Parthians maintain a desultory role count at the beginning of the day but generally allow free movement into the town for the officers once the work is finished. They assume their charges are unlikely to escape; there's nowhere to go. The desert surrounding Margiana would soon swallow them up.

ᘓ

The chaotic and spirited markets on the inside of the wall are an attraction, almost like a theatrical performance – a pageant of shape and sound and colour. By now Marcus has learned enough Parthian to hold a conversation. He's taken the trouble to pick up some of the related Sogdian language too because it's the lingua franca of the Road immediately to the east. It bespeaks a brilliant culture – its country said to be the second of the good lands Ahura Mazda established when he created the Earth and divided everything into Good and Evil.

The Sogdians he's met so far are friendly – a race of merchants who're reckoned to be the most astute traders in the world. The other day he saw two of them bargaining. When he came by them again two hours later, they were still at it, offering imaginative and persuasive reasons to support their positions. The issue was but a trivial advantage in the price.

The Parthians, who don't particularly like them, acknowledge that years of profitable trade have smoothed the wildness of their original character into a sophistication that ranges freely into philosophy, fine cuisine and art.

They admit that Sogdian knowledge of medicine and science combines with a refined strain of Zoroastrian thought to create a renown for wisdom that resounds throughout Asia, penetrating cities as diverse as Babylon, Damascus and Jerusalem. Sogdian magi are frequent travellers on the Road, always willing to engage in conversations with strangers about the meaning of life. They've learned the secrets of the stars and can read the fate of humans in the patterns they form. Sogdian music is considered the most beguiling anywhere along the Road.

He's recently found himself part of a disparate group of merchants and other travellers who congregate late in the afternoon. Sometimes magi join them, spectacular in their long flowing robes and tall conical hats, decorated with crescent moons and stars. He's welcome though everyone knows he's a slave; all are humane enough to ignore it. The condition is commonplace in these parts. However, that an officer of the Roman army, renowned as conquerors even this far East, has fallen into that state is a novelty worthy of attention.

They meet at the Margiana caravan inn for refreshment and conversation. Here one seldom drinks wine. If it's consumed at all, it's always cut with water and drunk sparingly. Though the composition of the assembly constantly changes as people come and go, there's always a core who know each other. Set in the heart of the buzzing population centre close to the market, it resonates with the throb of visitors from distant lands who come along the Road. Everyone looks to the Margiana as a clearing house for news and the exchange of ideas. No subject is taboo, even religion, which, despite a diversity ranging from the sceptical to the pious, everyone treats on a basis of tolerance.

Today's gathering was particularly interesting – Marcus hardly said a word, just listened. A magus in full religious garb, complete with conical hat, who's a frequent visitor to the Margiana, had a long and intricate conversation with a leading caravan merchant. The subjects they discussed ranged from commerce and various types of goods, to a mathematical means of estimating their quantities without individually counting them, to philosophy, music and art. Even warfare was a topic.

That night the day's conversation stays in his mind keeping him from going to sleep. After a while he dozes off, but suddenly he sits up, startled as if someone had prodded him with a sharp stick. It's not the Eumendides though. Instead, a thought as clear as a shooting star has come to him. It shouldn't be amazing at all, rather absurd in a way that it is, but the sense of superiority he's grown up with has been such a block to perception. These Sogdians he's been meeting with are remarkable, really impressive; their knowledge of the world and its workings, their cultivated ways are clearly admirable, even, though awkward to admit, to some extent awe – inspiring. There's real merit on display here; he can learn from it – as long as he has an open mind. It's not an easy thing to do when he's been so sure of what constitutes the only civilization.

At first he was visiting the Margiana tavern just to have some company, slumming it among barbarians, because there was nobody else around except his comrades, and he wanted to broaden his acquaintances. But the demonstration of expertise today, which puts into sharper focus what's been seeping into his view for some time, perhaps subconsciously, requires a change in how he looks at non Romans. Perhaps it's the need to adapt in these strange circumstances, perhaps it's because he's so far away from home, perhaps something else, but whatever the reason, tonight he's passed through a portal into a new state of mind.

The next day he hurries to the Margiana after work, expecting a continuation of yesterday's discussion. But that's not to be; the magus isn't there; something more pressing to talk about has come up. One of the merchants, a Parthian, says

> "Last week someone tried to poison King Orodes. He was at a banquet – you know how he loves his food – and somehow poisoned meat got past the tasters. He fell violently sick on the spot and had to be taken away immediately. Miraculously he didn't die and began to recover in the morning. Obviously the poisoner botched it – probably didn't put enough in."

> "Who would do such a thing?" says one of the others.

> "Just a minute; there's more. After sundown, while he was in his bed sleeping, an assassin snuck into the room. Got past the guards who must have been bribed and strangled him with a bow string.

> "It's thought that Phraates, one of his sons, was behind it. He's ambitious enough. Support was building for some time against the King. His effete habits were offending many of the nobles after Surena's death. They complained about the lack of a strong military leader. Maybe the great general's clan also had something to do with it. No doubt they had a motive. They never believed the King's story of how their kinsman died.

118

"Good riddance I say. Everyone's been worried that with Surena dead, Parthia's vulnerable – without a good commander any longer. Orodes was weak and useless in war – only good at intrigue.

"Fortunately, the speculation is that the succession will probably be settled without a civil war. Orodes' faction is not strong enough and there's nobody else to challenge Phraates. In any event we're too far east to be affected even if there is one.

"My Roman friend, the battle of Carrhae has cast a curse on both our countries. The Caravan Road is spreading it far and wide like a disease. It'll cause trouble for a long time to come."

While the news elicits some interest, what they talk about next is far more compelling. Orodes and concerns about succession in the Parthian Empire are far away, but something is starting to happen right here, near this part of the Road, something that could change their lives.

CHAPTER 9

Lushan, a flamboyant Sogdian merchant just arrived with his caravan, is holding forth in front of an attentive audience. He's got them spellbound. A picture of what Romans think of the East, he's a vision of colour and panache. His silk tunic, as blue as lapis, is open to mid chest and gathered by a silver- studded belt. Pearls trim the edges of the garment. Still strange to Marcus, the fabric seems like the surface of a pool, capturing the light and freeing it. He's embarrassed as he's caught staring at it – mesmerized by its beauty and the memory of its battle role.

The Sogdian has a narrow black moustache, drawn above his lip as if by an artist's crayon. Its precision suggests more personal grooming than could ever be contemplated by a Roman, even if moustaches were in fashion. He's wearing a conical hat, shorter than the type worn by the magi, with silver plaques at the bottom. Loose yellow trousers are stuffed into sharp-toed boots that rise almost to the knee. His well modulated voice is pleasantly refined. Opulence and sophistication seep out of every pore.

> "There will be a lot of trouble on the border soon I am sorry to say. Worse than anything in Parthia. Political waves in the East are building up to a crest that threatens to break over the Caravan Road. A deluge could come at any time.
>
> The King of Sogdiana wants to push back the Wu-Sun who have been harassing our people for years from the East. He has entered into a risky alliance of convenience —"

One of the merchants interrupts,

"Not with Jir-Jir of the Hsiung-nu surely?"

"Yes, with him. I know it is dangerous, but what choice does he have? The Hsiung-nu have defeated the Wu-Sun before. They are traditional enemies, even though they speak the same language and look like each other. We made a treaty with Jir-Jir and sent him three thousand camels and a lot of our horses from Fergana, you know, the ones that gallop so fast they sweat blood. Hopefully that and the subsidy we pay will persuade him to keep to the bargain."

Marcus is intrigued. A flicker of an idea begins to form in the bottom of his brain, stone cold for so long. But first he needs more information.

"Tell us more of what's going on".

"We Sogdians are a commercial people, peaceful and rich. The Caravan Road has blessed us with trading opportunities and we concentrate on these, not fighting battles. Art and science and cultivated living are imperatives for us, not soldiering. We are no longer trained in war like the nomadic tribes around us, the Wu-Sun for instance. They are constantly raiding us, swooping out of the desert like a foul sand storm into our cities, stealing our goods and raping our women. Our section of the Caravan Road is no longer safe. There is a danger it will actually be cut. You can imagine what that would do to our commerce."

The other merchants gasp. That's what their class has always feared. It's forever been a frightful possibility since the Road was opened up and cleared of the wild Hsiung-nu. Cutting the Road would bring ruination to not only the caravaners but to all the people for huge distances around who rely indirectly on the income from it.

Lushan continues, "We are sick of it but can't stand up to them. So we need Jir-Jir – he is the tribal leader, called a Sharnyu by the way. It means Son of Heaven."

Marcus asks about the Hsiung-nu. Lushan says, "They are a fierce nomadic people who dominate the Eastern steppe which the Caravan Road runs through. They are traditional enemies of the Han who live to the south east, past the great mountain barrier."

He explains how the Han are a good deal more sophisticated than the nomads, how they look similar but speak a completely unrelated language, how they have a legendary empire that extends to the great eastern ocean, how they have sent their armies against the Hsiung-nu to open up the Caravan Road, how people say the Road actually begins at their capital city far away in the east, and how nobody he knows has ever been there.

The others at the table point out that the Hsiung-nu can't be trusted, that they're essentially raiders who prey on the sedentary affluent. If the region is stirred up business will suffer. Marcus barely listens to the voices, now a babble as the merchants interrupt and talk over each other. He's never seen them so excited. They all parade the horrors of warfare boiling over into Parthia and interrupting the flow of commerce. Everyone of them is staring at the face of financial catastrophe.

As the group breaks up, he takes the Sogdian aside and says, "Can I speak to you confidentially about a sensitive subject?"

Lushan nods.

"Do you think there's any chance the chief of the – how do you pronounce it?"

"Shoong noo"

"… Would he hire a few Roman soldiers as mercenaries?"

"Yes there is every chance. When he was on his way to Sogdiana a cold snap hit his tribe and wiped many of them out. I'm sure he would welcome some reinforcements. The King is paying him well so he has money. What do you have in mind?"

"I'm in charge of a cohort – a hundred and fifty men. I'm sure they'd follow me in an escape if we had somewhere to go. We can't go back to Rome; it's too far. But Sogdiana is a separate country and if we joined the Hsiung-nu, the Parthians wouldn't dare try to recapture us. I don't know what life would be like out there but it would have to be better than here. At least we'd be free. And there'd be action – beats the boredom we suffer from now.

"Would you be willing to help? My men and I have been able to hide some money – Roman currency. Is it of any use to you?"

Always with an open mind when there's a chance of making money, the merchant's eyes light up.

> "Yes it would be. I can have it exchanged on the western part of the Caravan Road, but you need to appreciate there would be a significant exchange loss that far from Roman territory. So your denarii will not be worth as much as you might expect".

> "That's all right. I understand."

After a short negotiation they agree upon a sum. No chance of losing Lushan's interest should be taken by being difficult. Besides, Marcus is too excited by the prospects to waste time bargaining, and it's not a worthy thing anyway in his opinion.

Virtually all of the money saved will have to be used. What an end to his get – rich campaign! Not only did the expected plunder never materialize, but now he has to spend what little wealth he has to buy his freedom, an asset he had before in abundance.

> "I will have to find a way to speak to Jir-Jir personally since he will make this sort of decision himself. Right now he and his tribe are in the steppe north of Samarkand. That is our largest city. You will have to give me half the fee up front and take the risk that I will not be successful. If I fail, you will save the other half".

There's no choice. He must take the chance. Of course the merchant could take the money and disappear, but, judging by the respect the others show him he's a man of good repute. In any event the prospect of earning the other half would be an incentive to keep to the bargain. Another risk is that Lushan could return from Jir-Jir full of good news which he could say justifies a price increase. But all opportunities to extract more money can't be avoided. In any event, the potential reward of escape outweighs monetary considerations.

> Lushan says "We have to wait until my caravan is ready to head back to Samarkand. I have to hire armed guards. It's too dangerous to go alone or in a small party. Desert bandits would pick us off like sheep in wolf territory. I don't even know how to wield a sword – ha ha ha. But I can pay others to do that. I suggest we meet again in three days. Make sure you bring the cash."

Excitement burns off the fog of depression as Marcus returns to camp. He calls together the officers of his cohort in a secret meeting at his tent after dark and explains the plan.

> "For this to work, it can only apply to a small number of men – our own cohort, nobody else. Don't tell even the others in our cohort until I give the word.

> "I hope to conclude the arrangements with Lushan within a week. We'll have to put up all the money ourselves for now but we can get the rest to do the second payment. Gaius, you work out a fair arrangement. I've asked Lushan to get the Hsiung-nu to send a contingent to meet us on the Caravan Road at a discreet distance from Margiana, if we can do the deal".

His comrades have not been so lively since the capture. It's like seeing colour return to the cheeks of a dying patient. A hopeless condition has been reversed by a miracle.

> "This is great, Marcus, Gaius says. "The money's no problem. Nobody'll care. We've got to get out of here, that's all. The main thing is to keep everything secret. Let's give the bastards a surprise, ha ha ha."

The men are keen to organize the details. Suggestions and counter suggestions keep the discussion going well into the night. Nobody wants to go to bed.

Expectation and tension, almost too much to bear, dominate the days until the meeting with Lushan. They meet outside the Margiana inn. Marcus suggests they go for a walk nearby in the wooded parkland bordering one of the delta's arms. Flocks of long-billed egrets are taking refuge from the sun in the trees, standing motionless on the branches like white lilies. Too hot to care, they're unperturbed by the strolling con-spirators.

> "I have good news," Lushan says. "The caravan leaves tomorrow and I can be in Samarkand in three weeks. From there I can ride to Jir-Jir's camp in a couple days. There is a Hsiung-nu officer in the Sharnyu's's army I met at the palace of the Sogdian King. He was in charge of the negotiations for the military aid. I am confident that he will pave the way for me to meet Jir-Jir. I arranged a personally lucrative trade deal for him while he was there. Have you brought the money?"

Marcus hands over three small sacks of coins. Lushan takes them with a gracious bow, not looking inside.

"Don't you want to inspect the money?"

"It is unnecessary. I trust you. Besides you are too intelligent to cheat me at the beginning of our grand enterprise, which can only be successful if we work together. I will contact you when I return. We will meet at the same place.

"Make sure that you are ready to leave quickly as the Sharnyu is an impatient man. If he has made up his mind to take you and your men on, he will insist you come over immediately. He might change his mind if you are later than he expects. Then you will really be in a fix.

"You will have to find a way to bring your military equipment. The Hsiung-nu won't have weapons for foot soldiers like you. They are cavalry people".

He nods; the requirement is obvious. He gives Lushan the Roman salute and heads back to camp, his heart thumping so hard it lifts his tunic.

The estimated period of time passes wearily and stretches into lateness that has everyone on edge. Tempers are stoked up and hard to control; petty comments seem to take on an importance they shouldn't.

The plans are laid, rehearsed ad nauseam. There's nothing more to be done. The conspirators try to quell their anxiety by reminding each other that time estimates involving the Road are always imprecise and Lushan might be detained at the Sharnyu's court for longer than expected. Marcus allows no negative talk.

His anxiety builds though, and as it's descending into despair, one of the guards, a Sogdian, approaches him as he's on his hands and knees making mud bricks. Ensuring that nobody is watching, he leans over and says in Sogdian,

"Your friend has arrived. He wants to see you when you finish work."

Showing no sign of a jumping heart, Marcus looks up, nods slowly and goes back to work. It's hard to wait for the remainder of the working day; hard to concentrate fully on his trivial task. As soon as possible he goes to the parkland beside the water.

Lushan greets him effusively with a hug, his short conical hat slipping sideways. A broad smile pulls his pencil moustache to its full width.

"My friend, I have been successful in pressing your case. Jir-Jir is willing to hire you and your men. He says, though, you will have to prove yourselves. If he judges you not up to the mark he will sell you all to the slave traders on the Caravan Road. He is a man without mercy, so be warned."

"Thank you Lushan. I'm very grateful for your efforts. I'm sure Roman fighting skills will satisfy even the most demanding Hsiung-nu. Did you discuss the terms of our engagement?"

"I mentioned the subject but the Sharnyu said it must wait until you arrive and prove what you are capable of. You will have to take the chance. However, he is a shrewd man and, although extremely tough, will want you satisfied. On the other hand he is known to be capricious and given to bouts of temper, particularly when stoked up by drink. Are you willing to go ahead with this? To be fair, I cannot guarantee what will happen to you once you are in his power."

Venturing so far into the unknown East and joining up with savage men are at the extreme end of the risk spectrum. Their culture would be as far removed from Roman norms as war from peace. He could be leading his men from misery into catastrophe, even death. However, his officers all agreed that the prospect of freedom so outshines other choices that even to consider them would be cowardly. There's not a man who hasn't suffered the pain of humiliation to the core. Any risk is worth taking to get rid of that. As is so often the case when desire for change is extreme, hope is energised to minimise the fear of consequences.

The walk with Lushan among the quiet trees is exhilarating. He feels the caress of the goddess *Libertas* for the first time since Carrhae. True, he's still a slave, but her touch of freedom can be subtle, expressed in simply making a choice. And he's done that. His life force, drained so completely after that fateful battle, is coming back, flowing warmly through his veins and restoring his confidence.

"Of course we'll go ahead. We're committed. Assuming we can get onto the Caravan Road in the night, what then?"

"As you requested, the Sharnyu will send a detachment to meet you on the

Caravan Road at a landmark I will give you. It is a half day's march from Margiana. The Hsiung-nu don't want to encounter a Parthian patrol if it can be avoided. They will bring spare horses for your men to ride. That will speed up the journey to their camp. It is just as well you will be going soon because Jir-Jir has decided to take his tribe to the Talass River on the other side of the Jaxartes, a long way east"

"Most of my men have never ridden a horse".

"They will just have to learn on the spot. Anyway, as long as the horses don't go faster than a trot, they should cope."

It doesn't take much thought for Marcus to realise the critical time is the first twenty –four hours. It's vital that they get as much of a head start as possible before the Parthians realize what's happened.

"That seems fine. We'll work to that plan. What's the next step?"

"I will send a fast riding emissary to tell Jir-Jir of your decision. We will have to take the chance he will get through. I know a man who will do it for money – not much since he is a daredevil. He loves risks – any chance to prove himself.

"The Sharnyu will send his escort to you as soon as he is informed. This will mean you should time your escape for two weeks from now. I will give you a more precise date next week. Just be ready."

It's easy to like this sophisticated man, with his genuine friendliness. Surprising really, to find resonance in a foreign voice. Who would have thought a year or so ago, of counting a barbarian as a friend? It takes some getting used to. But somehow it seems natural now.

"That's excellent. I'll come back just before the escape with the rest of the money. Let's keep in contact."

ଔ

Everything seems to be propitious for the escape, but there's one obstacle. While Parthian security is lax, it's not non existent. At night, squads of four soldiers patrol the perimeter of the camp at intervals.

One must be taken out, but silently, so none of its members can give the alarm. He's ascertained that if that's done, a sufficient gap would open up to allow the cohort to slip through unobserved and head for the Road. He details Gaius and two others to join him for the job.

They spend the time before the appointed day training how to get close to the guards without creating suspicion and how to kill them in the dark with no sound. Footwork is important; they must maintain their balance at all times, feet directly under shoulders, taking small steps to get into position. Movement must be quick and smooth so as to avoid a scuffle. Speed is essential, with the number of separate motions required to get to the throat kept to the minimum. Any clumsiness will give the targets a chance to cry out.

Marcus will lead the mission, for the responsibility can't be delegated. One slip and the whole enterprise will fail. It's vital that it run without a hitch. All in the little task force are keen to practise, even until they're sick of it, and beyond, until there's no danger of a mistake.

Time passes and merges into a heart throbbing present, the day before the planned escape. All along, tension has been building up. Freedom's in the air, but so is the risk of failure. Despite the practice, something unforeseeable can intervene. Killing four men without setting off an alarm is no trivial matter; the human factor is often unpredictable. And after silencing the targeted squad, the others could somehow be alerted, even though they'll be some distance away. One hundred and fifty Romans will be there also, in the dark, moving through the gap. They must be silent too. Fortunately Roman discipline will help, but nothing is certain.

Marcus and the others in the task force spread the word to the rest of the cohort. They've left it to the last minute for security. As it's not prudent to call a meeting, they visit the men's tents individually, starting just before bedtime so they don't miss anyone. There're twenty tents in their section of the camp, normally with eight men each but in some cases fewer. Each takes five tents. As they go around, they encounter enthusiasm – sometime whoops of joy, even though a few men express a little concern, mainly about details. They're easily answered.

Gaius however, runs into trouble. One of the men, Trebonius, is quite outspoken, complaining it's too risky, that if they're caught they'll be executed. He's so forceful that some of the men in his tent get wobbly and begin to agree with him. Gaius calls Marcus over who says;

> "What's the matter with you Trebonius? You're the only one in the entire cohort that doesn't have the guts to go for freedom. Do you prefer slavery you piece of shit? Pick yourself up; be a man. If you don't show some spine I'm going to run you through."

As he puts his hand on Owl's Head, Trebonius steps back and drops his head in shame.

> "All right, all right Sir. I agree. I was only pointing out the risks anyway. Count me in."

Gaius has rarely seen Marcus so angry. The tongue lashing stops the rot; all is now settled. Everyone supports the escape. *Alea iacta est.* Tense and alert, few will sleep that night. They quietly pack their belongings. The Parthians never come into the camp so, for the time being, they're safe from discovery.

The Romans are guards; it's normal for them to keep their armour and weapons. They're obliged to leave their tents behind for fear of alerting the Parthians by striking them (besides they're too bulky), but they can take what they need as soldiers, except their throwing spears, their pila, which are too unwieldy.

Next day, everybody goes about their business as usual, building the wall; the only difference is that nobody feels like speaking, but that isn't enough to create suspicion. Besides they're only one cohort in an army of prisoners. No other Romans know about the plan. They'll be as surprised as the Parthians, maybe a little envious. The day goes by with intolerable slowness but finally the sun drops down. The men are in their tents awaiting the signal.

As soon as the evening dies into night, the task force saunters towards the edge of the camp. They're dressed in their tunics. Daggers are hidden in the folds. Marcus has Owl's Head. Their armour is stored in the dark nearby. They move towards the nearest Parthian squad, trying to appear casual.

CHAPTER 9

The guards have congregated around a brazier, as the late summer night is cold. They should be on patrol but, predictably, they prefer the warmth and conversation. Besides, nothing ever seems to happen during these long nights. An important uncertainty in the plan has been avoided. Marcus has counted on them being together – they always are, but there might have been an exception.

The Romans sidle up to the Parthians, who remain sitting, and begin a casual conversation. Nothing seems abnormal; often Romans fraternize with their keepers. But suddenly, Marcus recognises one of them; he's the man who gave him the loaf of bread. How can he kill him, the one whose kindness rescued him from despair?

The plan is that once he scratches his head they all attack, each taking out the guard nearest him. If he weakens, fails to give the signal and leads his comrades back to the camp for another attempt, or even moves to another patrol squad, the escape will be jeopardised, possibly fatally. Once momentum is lost it'll be impossible to regain. The Hsiung-nu won't wait around for ever. If the cohort doesn't escape tonight, chances are he and his comrades will lapse back into slavery and stay there. And it'll be his fault.

He can just kill the man as planned. No one would know, and his comrades would applaud his action. After all, he's responsible for one hundred and forty-nine men. That should outweigh the life of a single enemy, even a kind one. Slowly he moves close and scratches his head. His comrades leap forward, quickly get behind the Parthians they have marked, and shut their mouths with one hand. With the other they slit their throats before they have a chance to utter a sound, and quietly let them down on the ground.

At the same time, Marcus slips behind his Parthian and jams a straightened hand under his chin. With the other crossways in support, he yanks the man back in a choke against his hip. No sound can come out, none except a subdued gurgle. Holding him tight, he orders his comrades to rip off some fabric to fill the man's mouth. As soon as he's gagged he loosens the choke – just as the man is turning white and limp.

"Tie him up with your belts, we're bringing him with us"

Gaius says in a tense whisper, "Are you crazy? Why are you sparing him? If we take him he might escape, alert the others. It's safer to kill him, damn it. Are you getting soft Marcus? What's the matter with you?"

"I don't care what you think Gaius. This man did me a favour. We're not killing him. He comes with us to the meeting point. Then he can walk back. If it's a risk it's a trivial one. I take personal responsibility for it."

As soon as the Parthian is secured, Marcus gives the signal for the mass movement – a short wave of the arm. Instantly it's passed around the camp. As the men are emerging from their tents, Trebonius tells his bunk mates he's changed his mind and decided to stay, repeating his fears. This is reported to Marcus who comes over immediately. He pulls the man aside by the front of his tunic and draws Owl's Head, pointing it at his throat.

'Trebonius, I'll kill you on the spot if you don't come with us."

That's enough to pull the reluctant legionary into line and the crisis fades. It would too dangerous to let him stay. For whatever reason – perhaps to ingratiate himself with his captors, he could give the escape away.

The cohort quietly slips out of the camp and into the darkened trees. As always it's a clear night, but the moon has not risen yet; besides it will a small one, on the wane. All is calm. No Parthians seem to notice. An escape is the last thing they expect – the desert has always deterred it before.

That night a hundred and fifty fully armed Roman soldiers and a Parthian slink through the darkness and disappear into the desert. The waning moon is up too late and too weak to give them away. Outside the oasis they look like a stain spreading haphazardly on to the landscape which is wanly lit by stars.

They make good time and reach the Road by midnight. Using the North Star as their guide, they have no trouble finding it. Marcus orders a roll call as they emerge onto the roadway. All are present, even Trebonius. There's no sign of their Parthian masters.

It's too soon to feel liberation. At any time horsemen could appear out of the trees and run them down, even at night, for the Parthians could overcome their reluctance if they discover the escape.

The pace picks up now they're on smoother surface and the distance from the camp widens satisfactorily. Marcus pushes the men to the heavy breathing point. The Road embraces the vulnerable soldiers, its smooth path helping them. It likes the drama, pleased to play a role in support of men it's grown to favour.

There's still no sign of the Parthians, but their swift horses could easily make up for a late start. The last thing they need is another encounter with the penetrating missiles.

As pale blue light rises from the horizon to swallow the stars, a dust cloud appears in the distance. It's moving towards them at pace. The men let out a cheer as the forms of horse archers materialise on the Road. There're about twenty, ahead of a herd of horses. They stop a few metres away as if they hit a wall. Marcus has never seen such control. Man and beast move as one creature, totally coordinated. A single brain seems to animate both. Roman cavalry is capable but nothing like this; even the Parthians weren't that good. The newcomers look supernatural.

He thinks back to the centaurs of the classical Greeks – torso rising out of the horse's back, one brain, one creature, a human horse. It could well have been that in ancient times a few Greeks encountered these unique people and brought back the story as myth. Arrow stuffed quivers cling to their backs and short, recurved bows of wood and bone are slung over their shoulders. Their oblique narrow eyes and high flat cheekbones as immovable as sculpture are like nothing the Romans have seen before – unreadably implacable. They're the strangest people imaginable– could be the invention of some myth.

In the front is Lushan, riding well but not like the others. He dismounts and embraces Marcus.

"What a happy meeting! Our plan has gone better than expected. You are safe. Even if the Parthians catch up they will not attack now that you have a Hsiung-nu escort. They wouldn't dare commit an act of war against Jir-Jir.

"Marcus Velinius Agricola I would like to introduce you to Jiyu the commander of the escort and a close comrade of the Sharnyu. He will take us to him."

The Hsiung-nu commander, remaining on his horse which is completely still, motions a greeting without a smile.

"Thank you Lushan. You've done a brilliant job. What'll you do now?"

"I will accompany you to the Sharnyu's camp. It is not far from Samarkand. I have some business there. It is my birthplace. I will return to Margiana after that with my caravan".

"That's good. You can interpret for us." Marcus says to his comrades,

"Bring the Parthian over."

He gives him a couple of denarii, his last but one, and says in broken Parthian,

"You go back home now. Sorry for this. Good luck."

The man turns without a word and starts the long walk back along the Road.

Horses are brought. Most of the Romans need a lesson. The Hsiung-nu, who've been forewarned of this, patiently show the novices how to mount and dismount, how to guide the horse with the reins, how to sit and hold on with their thighs. The instruction, done without language, is pretty rudimentary and stops short of the cantering stage, let alone the gallop. But it's enough for the purpose. It seems bizarre that the best horsemen in the world are taking the time to teach a bunch of beginners. It's not easy, for they naturally assume too much knowledge in the Romans. But they've been well briefed. They find it's amusing to encounter people so ignorant of something as fundamental as riding. To them it's unimaginable. But they don't show any emotion.

As soon as Jiyu has decided the Romans have had enough instruction, he signals the start of the long trek to Samarkand. The cohort falls unsteadily into line. Marcus is in front, just managing his difficult horse.

CHAPTER 9

How are they ever going to be able to fit in with these people who're so unusual? He wonders what the leader they're about to meet is like. Tonight's escape has shuffled him through another portal into the unknown, another domain too different to imagine; like the one he's just been in it's sure to be fraught with danger and challenge. But however it turns out he'll be free.

CHAPTER 10

The Hsiung-nu seem to be showing a concern for the safety of the Romans above what might be expected. Of course it's in their interests to have the potential mercenaries arrive intact but they could just leave them to their own devices along the way and defend them only if an attack materializes. Instead, Jiyu has split his escort so that it protects the Romans in both front and rear. Just what they're protecting them from isn't clear. Perhaps it's the Parthians who might catch up once they notice the escape but that's not likely now that so much time has passed. It's certainly not the peaceful Sogdians, nor the usual marauders of the Road; it's the Hsiung-nu themselves who're the bandits. Anyway, it's refreshing to see Roman soldiers valued again – something not evident for such a long time.

Jiyu rides in front by himself, silent and aloof. Just behind are Marcus and Lushan. The merchant is riding competently and is as voluble as ever. As the sun comes up he says;

"We are entering the fearsome Red Desert, home of cobras. Tell your men to be on their guard. These snakes can be very aggressive. Sometimes they even spit their venom. They are liable to slither into the camp looking for food and warmth, even sliding into the bedclothes. Check them every night before you get in. Stamping around usually gets rid of them. Be careful. Their bite out here in the desert will mean certain death".

The going is mercifully smooth as the landscape is reasonably flat – a boon for the novices. Though exhaustingly sandy it's not entirely without vegetation. A threadbare carpet of camel thorn stretches into the distance

135

and passes under the horizon through a dusty portal. Pale green saksaul bushes, like small weeping willows, grow along the sides of the Road, and little purple tamarisk flowers. A few wild camels are chewing, imperious heads in the air. They fix the intruders with a contemptuous stare while their lower jaws slowly rotate in a shallow ellipse. Perhaps it's that they feel superior to the horses, but likely to humans also.

The cloud-free sun glares at the travellers, but it no longer causes them discomfort. Indeed all it can manage is to warm up the day to a pleasant temperature by ten o'clock. The troupe moves along steadily. The newly recruited horsemen are doing reasonably well, even though they're getting sore. It hasn't taken long for their untrained thighs and buttocks to be rubbed raw. No respite is given as Jiyu wants to maintain the pace. Besides he has scant sympathy for sedentary types. The Romans don't complain; they're used to hardship and are happy anyway to be slaves no more, despite the risks that lie ahead.

In a few days they see the silver flash of a mighty river carving its channel through the sands, leaving a calling mark of vegetation along its sides. Lushan raises his voice to demand attention.

> "This is the famed Oxus, one of the two great rivers of Sogdiana. Its origin lies hidden in the roof of the world far to the south. It is where Alexander the Great tracked down Bessus the assassin of the Persian monarch and killed him because he had killed a king. The massive water flow of the noble river travels north to feed the cold and mighty Aral Sea, which stands by itself in the desert, alone and majestic".

So that's the mystical Oxus; he's heard of it, every Roman schoolboy has. It's always been seen as so distant, so far way from the Mediterranean, at the extreme end of the world, where strange things happen and magical creatures live. It would never have been discovered if the great conqueror hadn't led his unbeatable phalanxes so far. And now he's here, but not in a victorious army, just as a mercenary, lucky to have a job – only so long as he can convince his employer that he and his comrades are worthy of their hire.

They cross where a shoal rises, a point traditionally used by travellers. On the other side, the Road follows the meander for a while, sometimes venturing north. However, it turns east as it leaves the river into land which is the last link to the world he knows. Even the most learned European geographers are ignorant of anything past the mighty river. All there may be on the eastern side lurks in a mysterious void, a knowledge blank that permits only wild and fanciful speculation. An attack of loneliness grips him, a feeling of being removed entirely from his world, a final break. But there's excitement too, a sense of adventure; it's almost a privilege to be venturing into this unknown hinterland. He loses concentration for a moment and lets the reins go slack. His horse rears up, intent on throwing him off. Lushan grabs the reins and settles it down. "Thanks Lushan. Just as well you know how to ride."

In a few minutes Lushan raises his arm in excitement.

> "Bukhara is ahead, the great trading hub of the Caravan Road. We are making very good time. We will stay there for a day to rest and restock on supplies. I have arranged it with Jiyu. Besides, you should see the sights. I will take you around."

On approaching the metropolis it's easy to see why Lushan is so proud of it. The desert stops as if in reverence in front of a vast fortress built into a wall that runs around the city. It's the highest structure he's ever seen, looming as large as a square-topped mountain, all made of mud brick. The amount of back -breaking labour to build something that tall would have been prodigious, even for the gods. It rises in a brown textured mass out of the grass-studded sand and articulates its height against the clear sky. Crenellated turrets linking with each other on high create an elegance that ties the whole structure together. Its unity of design and scale speak of the highest architectural skill.

Jiyu and Lushan lead the troupe through the majestic stone gate set at the bottom of the wall. Suddenly they're engulfed in the cheerful chaos of a Sogdian city. Nothing is orderly; everything is tangled like a garden grown to weed. There's a happy confusion in the loud voices often springing into laughter, in the erratic movement of sweaty people, donkey carts and camels lumbering among the crowd.

Still mounted, they walk their horses down the main street, cobblestones worn smooth by centuries of feet. It's a relief from the Road, which out here often challenges travellers with sharp stones pushing through the sand. Brazen stares indicate the Romans are a curious sight. They're of course familiar with the Hsiung-nu. The Sogdian men are dressed like Lushan, although more economically. The women, who are rarer, are in bright colour too, their long dresses inspired by the rainbow. Ever present silk weaves throughout the throng like a whispering breeze.

Jiyu allows everyone to dismount and wander at their own pace through the markets. The Romans and the Hsiung-nu mix. At first some of them make an attempt to communicate with each other in sign language and laughter but soon give up. No one has money to buy anything but that doesn't deaden their enjoyment of looking at the wares or the ardour of the merchants trying to make a sale.

Lushan takes Marcus over to one of the pools where the city gets its water. They're strewn all over, like shiny buttons on a green garment. In the protection of bending trees, it's still and deep, a sanctuary of cleanness in the dusty and sweaty city of trade. Its surface is like a silver sheet, gleaming and unsullied.

> "Purity is an important ideal in the Zoroastrian faith. It is celebrated in many forms. Fire is the main one. The sacred pool is another.
>
> "See those giant storks resting in the branches of the trees over there, the ones lining the pond?
>
> "They fly here from Egypt every year. Men of wisdom claim that in ancient times they brought the learning of the Pharaohs to Sogdiana. That is why our culture is renowned all along the Caravan Road. You can see their nests near the top of the canopies."

ೞ

Next day the travellers are back on the Road, heading through the Red Desert. Green-spiked karagach, about two spans high, invades the desolation in small clumps. At times the sand has a red ochre tinge. The colour tends to relieve the bleak and endless expanse. Suddenly Marcus sees a creature scuttle in the sand. On closer look he recognises a small tortoise about a span long. No doubt it has strayed a bit far from the leafy greens of the Bukhara oasis.

After a week of monotony, a mountain range rises in the distance, capped in snow. The troupe moves up and onto a wind-swept mesa with an open field of view. In front of them a great city carves a turreted profile into the sky. It leaves the desert suddenly, within an explosion of vegetation. Lushan announces that it's the legendary Samarkand.

Lushan pulls his horse closer to Marcus.

> "The sages of the past always claimed that after a long journey through the desert seeing Samarkand washes away all melancholy and worry. It gives people a sense of purification that puts them in a state of mellow content-ment. And when they go through the gate they feel uplifted by the many gardens that bless the city. You should know that the Zoroastrian concept of eternal paradise is based on the garden."

He can see the point, despite the exaggeration of the Sogdian patriot. He's getting used to his flamboyance – even starting to enjoy it.

They approach the daunting walls, built thick with mud brick and rammed earth. Not even the savviest enemy could knock them down. They pass under the big stone lintel of the main gate into a bustling throng even larger than in Bukhara. Samarkand is the capital of Sogdiana and the royal residence.

The loquacious merchant can't contain his pride.

> "Samarkand is the jewel box of the Caravan Road. Its wealth and culture have attracted visitors for centuries. And conquerors too. It was here that Alexander the Great married Roxanne, the Sogdian princess he won at the battle of the Sogdian Rock. That was nearby – in that direction. She was the only woman he ever truly loved".

What might have been with Aurelia?

Everyone dismounts, leaving their horses in the care of a few Hsiung-nu so they can walk through the town. As they amble along the main street, crowded and set in cobblestone, they smell a complex and beguiling aroma. It turns out it's from the spice market. Lushan claims it's the largest in Sogdiana, possibly the world. Waist high stands of mud brick fifty paces long are arranged in rows. On them, sacks with turned down tops and brimming with multi-hued spices sit touching each other. A few of them are slumping, in danger of spilling their contents. Lushan recites their names – coriander, rosemary, thyme, mint, basil, saffron, cloves, and cumin.

Women in long dresses with zigzag patterns of bright yellow, green, blue, and red are sitting behind the stands taking money and packing goods into the shoppers' baskets. They're garrulous and giggly. Indeed all the people in the market, the men too, are unreservedly friendly. It's a happy place, where commerce playfully joins with socializing.

They pass into the fruit area, where silver-grey peach kernels are sold. Looking like limestone gravel, they're piled in elbow-high heaps, giving off a white dust which covers the saleswomen. Customers are eating them as nuts as they shop. Figs wrapped in vine leaves, mounds of red and green grapes, apples, peaches and plums crowd the sides of their stands. A magus in tall, conical hat and flowing robes, pale blue with gold stars, picks up a fig. With one hand he puts it in his mouth, with the other he holds a roll of parchment, a look of quiet contentment on his face.

Next in line, plump lettuces, onions, tomatoes, cucumbers, squash and eggplant crowd the stands. Sweet smelling dried grass to be used for incense is on a stand nearby. Beside it, in the shade, men are stacking melons, some palely beige, others striated green. A man throws one from a donkey cart to his workmate on the ground in an elegant arc. He places it neatly on the pile. Lushan says that all the produce has been brought fresh this morning from the oasis farmland.

Before they leave the food markets they go past the meat section. Men in blood-stained tunics are butchering, slicing pieces off large carcasses of sheep and quartered camels hanging from hooks, complete with heads. Nearby, meat is being cooked over braziers to eat on the spot. Smoke billows over wooden tables, spreading the cooking smells, which are spiced with cumin, garlic and cloves.

Tinkers and blacksmiths hammer out a form of chaotic music in the next section. Remarkably, the blacksmiths use the same technique Marcus has seen in his father. The high-pitched staccato spreads to where the rare fabrics are sold – the silks. The Romans are amazed. They're like sheets of mist imprinted with the rainbow and their smoothness seems as subtle as poetry. They speak of luxury and sophistication. It seems a wonder why no one has brought them to Rome. Perhaps, after Carrhae someone will.

But the most enthralling is the jewellery quarter. Unlike the rest of the market, it has proper shops – built from mud brick set side by side in a long row. Armed guards slouch around outside. He's never imagined a display of wealth like this. It's a treasure only the gods could amass. Long gold chains hang like bunches of grapes on the walls; clusters of rubies, emeralds, diamonds and sapphires are set in rings, brooches, bracelets and necklaces. Sometimes they're piled loose in heaps. They seem even more opulent like this.

The money tumbles into the coffers of these mercantile people like ripe apples falling on a windy day. What are the Hsiung-nu allies thinking as they see all this affluence? Although they're in this part of the world to protect the Sogdians from the rapacious Wu-Sun, they're rough nomads just like them.

He knows the meeting of the poor and strong with the rich and soft is often incendiary. How long will Jir-Jir hold to the alliance once the Wu-Sun are beaten off? It's possible to imagine his warriors riding through the market place, slashing the heads off the merchants and sweeping the saleswomen onto their horses, or at least the younger ones, and taking them off into the desert for violation and abandonment.

He drops back out of earshot of Lushan to speak to Gaius.

"I hope our new employers don't turn on the Sogdians and make us fight them. They seem a friendly people – a lot more civilized than these nomads we're joining up with."

"What does it matter who we fight for as long as we're free?"

"Yes, I guess. But I still wouldn't like it – wouldn't seem right to fight for a backward tribe against these civilised people. I like the Sogdians. Never thought cities like the ones we went through existed. They're really impressive. And what about their men of wisdom?"

"Marcus, you worry too much. Are you getting seduced by these barbarians? Shit, that's not what you used to sound like."

"Maybe I just see things I never saw before. Besides Lushan's a friend. We wouldn't be here without him. One thing's certain. If the Hsiung-nu do turn against them, we've got to look after him. We owe him that."

"All right. I agree. But let's leave it at that. We've got to look after ourselves. That's number one. Don't get soft."

"I'm not getting soft, Gaius. Anyway, we probably won't get recruited against them. Changing the subject, the big thing now is to impress the Hsiung-nu leader when we get to his camp."

"That's right. Stay focussed on that Marcus"

The troupe continues walking along the cobblestone street, stared at by the locals but left alone by the city officials. At the eastern gate everyone mounts his horse and passes through undisturbed, onto the Road.

Soon the riding soreness, given respite in the city, starts up again, but the Romans have no option but to endure it. Jiyu is not willing to accord stops. He does once though. As a caravan comes alongside from the east, he orders a halt and talks to the lead caravaner. At a guttural signal the camels lurch down on their haunches, their crates dangling near the ground.

"What are you carrying?" Marcus says to one of the merchants.

"Medicine herbs to Margiana – rhubarb, cinnamon and ephedra."

He's seen rhubarb in Rome – a rare product used as a digestive. Cinnamon too – for combating diarrhea, toothache and colds.

"What's ephedra?"

"It comes from a plant in the hills. Usually it's diluted – for respiratory problems. However some of the Magi take it in full strength because it alters the mind. It helps them get close to Ahura Mazda. There they can truly see his wisdom. Do you want to try some?"

"All right."

The merchant hands over a small packet of brown powder.

"Eat it."

For a while nothing happens. Then other worldly feelings come over him – wave after wave. He becomes dizzy and the desert begins to move, folding into the sky and out again, and the tamarisk bushes crawl towards him. It's not unpleasant, quite good in fact, suggestive of an extraordinary advance in perception – he sees the Platonic form in everything around him as never before. His mind leaps out of his brain and embraces the forms in a metaphysical connection that lifts his spirit to a new height. But it doesn't last.

Suddenly the blazing sun sheds a flock of black birds, expelling them as if they were enjoying its brightness for longer than they should. They swoop down, beaks and talons as sharp as Parthian arrow heads. He turns away, ducking in fright and tries to fend them off, but they keep coming, relentless and savage. They're more vivid than in the dreams. In their flapping wings is Aurelia's face, scornful and reproachful, coming closer and closer until it envelops his head and disappears only to reappear in front. He sees himself bound to a mast, screaming at the ear-plugged sailors to untie him so he can swim to the seductive singing on the shore.

The merchant hurries over to give him water, helping him to sit down.

"Don't worry. You've just had a bad reaction. It'll be all right in a few minutes."

He recovers slowly and laughs off the experience.

Jiyu gives orders to restart the march and they pass by the caravan, leaving it in the shimmering haze. They go off the Road into wasteland un-marked by tracks. It's amazing how he knows the way. No one says a word; the Hsiung-nu have said virtually nothing since Margiana, except for a short while in the market and that of course was unintelligible. They seem to take on the taciturn nature of their leader, unlike Lushan who talks all the time. Much of what he says makes sense though and he's always willing to answer questions. One comes to mind.

"Lushan, what's the Hsiung-nu society like?"

"It's tribal, with a sharnyu as the head. Sometimes the tribes come together in a federation with the most powerful sharnyu at the top. That's when they are most dangerous. Jir- Jir is only the head of his own tribe. Right now there is no federation.

"They are ferocious most of the time, but they have a spiritual side – in touch with nature and its spirits. The spirits can be beneficent or harmful. It depends on whether they are propitiated or not. Even though the sharnyu is all powerful he must show respect to the shaman – like a high priest. He is the one who conducts religious ceremonies. Whenever the tribe is about to begin something important, the shaman performs sacrifices to the ancestors, also to heaven and earth and the spirits of the steppe".

A herd of wild camels shambles among the thorn bushes just off the Road, quiet and insouciant. They're different from the beasts further west. This type has two humps, rising out of their backs like sand dunes with a space in between. It's as if their design was derived from the landscape. Lushan says,

"They are from Bactria, the mountainous country to the south – a breed common out here."

The camels are unimportant; it's the meeting with the Sharnyu that matters. Anxiety is building up. If it goes wrong, things could be far worse than the Parthian captivity. How should the barbarian be approached? How can he be impressed? Any mistake could be fatal – Lushan said he's unpredictable.

Weird imaginings are fruitless. All the Romans need to do is demonstrate their martial skills. That's what they're there for. To steel his nerves he recites under his breath, like a prayer, the three moral building blocks, *virtus* -self discipline, *pietas* – respect, and *fides* – faithfulness to an engagement. Above, an eagle circles with unmoving wings, looking for little lives hiding in the karagach.

Any doubt he might have had about Jiyu's sense of direction dissolves as an array of circular white tents appears. They're set up along the bank of a mighty river, tinged with green, which Lushan says is the Jaxartes – the other Sogdian river that feeds the northern sea. He points to the bank and says

144

"Not far from here, Alexander the Great built a city called Alexandria Eschata – Alexandria the farthest, because it was the furthest east of all the cities he founded. Mothers out here still name their children after him, although the pronunciation has drifted from the original Greek. Sometimes it is Iskander."

The tents are strange – of white felt, not brown leather of the Roman type, and round, not square. Horizontal bands near the top hold the fabric onto frames which are made from tree branches. The structure is adapted to the extreme cold that'll settle in soon like the embrace of death. Felt insulates against the temperature and the ferocious steppe winds slip around the sides.

Women and children are scattered outside, unselfconsciously staring at the weird people in their strange uniforms. All are silenced by the sight. They've never seen anything like it.

Jiyu leads the troupe through them to a master tent several times the size of the others. In front is an artificial pool. Lushan says

"That pool you see there is in imitation of one that is famous in Hsiung-nu culture. In the far distant past a dragon fell from heaven into it. The dragon is worshipped out here."

"How do you know so much Lushan?"

"I don't think I know any more than anyone else in my country."

They go around the pool and stop at the entrance of the tent. Several men with faces like round granite suddenly appear, arrow-stuffed quivers on their backs. Jiyu dismounts and they take his horse. After a brief consultation, he waves at the Romans to get off their horses, then motions to Marcus and Lushan to come with him. The fateful meeting is about to begin.

CHAPTER 11

Two expressionless soldiers stand outside the entrance of the tent, armed with long swords and composite bows. They guide Marcus and Lushan through the flap. A slight stoop is necessary, to put visitors in an inferior position. Their eyes take a while to adjust to the dim light inside. Brightly coloured carpets cover the raw ground, overlapping each other to the walls – soft under foot. Some are of thick felt, articulated with animal and abstract designs and others, more refined, are tightly woven and thin, like the ones sold in the Bukhara markets.

In the middle of the tent the Sharnyu sits on a rough wooden chair with arm rests. A guard on either side stands rigid with a vertical banner attached to a spear. The banners have different patterns and colours, presumably belonging to distinct regiments. Marcus has never seen their like before. Flags are always set to flap horizontally not to cling up and down the pole. Body odour fills the tent like smoke and almost causes him to gag. It's as strong as the stink of a boar's carcass in the second day; but it's not a smell of death. Life, sweaty and energetic and disdainful of creature comforts produces it. The foul air projects the savage reputation of these men he's seeking to join and gives fair warning of the risk he's taking.

The atmosphere is dark, silent and menacing. The shades of the after life must be like this and Pluto just as impassive as the figure in front of him. He's in the power of darkness, utterly exposed. As in the myths, strength of character is his only means of survival. He tells himself to concentrate, to ignore the threats that surround him like demons in a dream.

He looks at the Sharnyu and tries not to stare. What's noticeable is not his small, black beard trimmed just below the lower lip to highlight a moustache which curves down to his chin. Nor the nose that spreads to his high cheek bones. It's his eyes.

They're hot, like obsidian fresh from the volcano. Shining splinters explode from narrow slits, sourced from something terrible inside. Everything else is still, including the rest of his warriors, presumably officers, who're filling the tent, the ones further away fading ominously into the shadows. They're all motionless and silent like the Sharnyu. It's as if they're a collection of black granite statues, the eyes of their leader the only living force.

The eternity of a minute goes by and nothing happens. He has to do something to break the tension. In a few steps taken as firmly as he can, he approaches the Sharnyu but not so close as to be disrespectful, leaving Lushan in the background. Looking straight at the igneous eyes, he says in Sogdian,

"Sir, my name is Marcus Velinius Agricola and I'm a Roman soldier. I've come to offer the services of my cohort of a hundred and fifty men, skilled in warfare".

Jir-Jir sits straight-backed, a golden hilted dagger hanging across his flat belly. His neck is stiff, chin high, jutting out like a small shovel. It's the haughtiness of the warrior who always wins, who never doubts the certainty of victory. After a silence calculated to diminish the supplicant's confidence, he says, also in Sogdian, "Yes, I know. You were sent for."

Marcus shifts his feet – the only sign of nerves.

"What would you like us to do, Sir?"

"You're big men, taller than ours. But are you strong?"

"You can find that out for yourself. Give us a test."

Jir-Jir leans back and nods slowly, a shadow of a smile crawling into his horseshoe moustache. He fingers his dagger, maybe a distraction, maybe an unconscious gesture to show the foreigner he's in his power. He's never seen a Roman soldier before – the breastplate, the greaves are strange. Facially, Sogdians look similar but he assumes they're different, a lot softer.

> "All right. Let's see if you can string a Hsiung-nu bow. I'll send for you in the morning and you can demonstrate your strength. If you pass the trial, I'll use you and your men as part of my army. If you fail, I'll still use you. But in the next battle you will fight the enemy first, before we come in. Your deaths will amuse my troops.
>
> "We're here to fight the Wu-Sun. I'm going to manoeuvre them into battle in a couple of weeks. You'll be part of that. Jiyu will take you and your men to your tents. I expect you outside my tent tomorrow morning."

He stands up, seeming much shorter than the man in the chair. But his broad raw-boned shoulders and barrel chest show he would a tough adversary in hand to hand combat. Shoes don't lift his height for he wears soft soled skin boots with round toes. Coming half way up his shins, they have an elliptical pattern in light blue on the sides. His stature exaggerates the size of his head, or perhaps it's the large round fur hat he wears.

Jiyu comes over and leads Marcus and Lushan out of the tent, mercifully away from the noxious smell. He gently steers them to walk out backwards, as he does himself. Outside the tent the air is clear and fresh and the light hurts the eye. He motions to the rest of the Romans to follow and takes them all over to a group of round white tents on the outer edge of the camp. Marcus and Gaius are to have their own while the rest have to share. Lushan looks worried.

> "Marcus, you have to learn how to string the bow. It is not easy. Strength is required but there is a trick to it. You must use the time until tomorrow to practice. Jir-Jir is testing you as much for adaptability as for strength. I will get someone to teach you".

At their new quarters the Romans gather around Marcus to hear the news. Like some of the others, Trebonius is concerned.

> "Watch out Marcus Velinius. Jir-Jir might be setting you up. Maybe he's got no respect for foot soldiers since his people are cavalry – just wants you

to fail so he's got an excuse to send us out front like he said. Might want to see us cut down like wild beasts in a hunt. How do we know what he's thinking?"

"Maybe so, but I've got to try, got no choice. No choice is the same as the best choice."

"Yes you have. You could just refuse and tell him we don't fight with bows. It's too big a risk. If you fail we'll be all doomed."

"No that's the coward's way out. I can do it. It's important we impress him. You don't balk at a challenge with the strong. You take it up."

Most of the men agree that he has to try; certainly Gaius does, but all are worried. In a way it's like the ancient way of determining a conflict – a champion tested in single combat while the troops stand by. Everything depends on it – life or death for all.

Lushan has spoken to Jiyu and he he's agreed to teach Marcus the art of stringing the bow. They spend the rest of the day at the lesson. The prospect of imminent death concentrates his mind. Time and time again he tries it. As Lushan warned, it's not easy. The technique requires agility and co-ordination as well as strong arms. Soon his arms are screaming like harpies but he continues.

He tries to pace himself, stopping from time to time to recover his strength. The sun passes overhead and sinks towards the steppe and he's still at it. Gradually the clumsiness smooths down and the times the string spills out of the slot become fewer. By the time darkness arrives he feels he can do it; but doubt remains. A sudden attack of nerves in front of the man who can decide life or death could unsettle him. It's still a technique he's just learned, not one he feels comfortable with.

Next morning, just after the sun has climbed out of the horizon, Lushan arrives to collect him. He's been up for an hour practising.

They walk to Jir-Jir's tent and meet him and Jiyu outside the pool which is flashing sunlight as if it's drawing attention to the event about to occur. The Sharnyu doesn't acknowledge their presence, nor does Jiyu. They stand silent, examining him, legs slightly apart in perfect balance. It's the beginning of an unseasonably hot day, a hark- back to summer. A throng of the Sharnyu's people are there to see the spectacle; the Roman contingent stands in square formation, apart and tense.

The Hsiung-nu banners shudder nonchalantly against their poles in a slow breeze, adding colour to the white tents and gnarled vegetation. Marcus says good morning in Sogdian. Jir-Jir doesn't reply but tosses him an unstrung bow. The string jumps in the air forming a rat's tail, but stays connected.

"String it. You have until I count to five."

The pressure is enormous. Burdened with the fate of his comrades, the task is like pushing a huge boulder up a hill. One slip and it'll roll back and crush him like a beetle. He must focus all his faculties, precisely following the instructions of his teacher. If he bungles, he'll do himself a serious injury as the bow will whip from the pressure, possibly gauging out an eye with the string. But that would be the least of his problems. He'll get no second chance; Jir-Jir will fail him unless he strings it with no mistakes. Death is sure to follow failure. Being sent into battle while the Hsiung-nu troops watch will ensure that.

He catches the bow and places it upright on the ground, his foot as a chock. He slides the string up past the horn-plated belly and toward the recurved end, toughened with strips of laminated bone that make the apparatus strong and stiff. In a mighty pull with one arm he bends the bow and slips the loop into its slot. He does it in one elegant motion, like a move in a dance. The Romans cheer as he holds it high for all to see. He's well within the time limit.

Jir-Jir smiles, eyebrows rising to open up his face for the first time.

"All right, you succeeded. But we shall see how well you fight. Come with me."

Together with a small entourage, they walk towards the edge of the camp. Jir-Jir moves with his knees slightly flexed and legs apart in a rolling gait on the balls of his feet. It gives him stability and the capacity to spring into action suddenly in any direction. In a way it's like a gorilla walks but more balanced and smoother. Alertness seems to inform every movement. He could be expected to attack or defend in a split second, before anyone could land a blow. No enemy could surprise him, even from behind. There'd be no doubt as to the outcome if one tried.

"My scouts tell me that the Wu-Sun are forming up a few days march away. They expect us to attack. Which of course is what we intend to do. We've got them where we want sooner than I expected. Now, you and your men – give me the bow."

He grabs it and in a curved flash pulls an arrow from the quiver on his back. With a fluid movement that allows virtually no time to aim, he slots it into position and shoots. Everyone is silent.

Marcus looks in the direction of the arrow and sees a hare stumble and fall about fifty paces away in the scrub. They walk towards it and a warrior picks it up by the arrow to show the Sharnyu. Shot through the heart just behind the forequarters, the animal is dead.

"If I had missed I would've blamed you for not stringing the bow properly. Then you would've been in trouble."

He throws back his stiff neck and laughs to the sky. The retainers join in and Marcus feels accepted.

In a few steps they come across a recently flattened piece of ground with no vegetation. On it are marks which seem to represent two armies facing each other, with lines coming out of the one on the right indicating the direction of attack. The map, elaborated with little flags, is so neatly drawn it could be a work of art.

Jir-Jir points to the contingent behind the attackers' right wing.

"Here's where you and your men will be positioned".

"I want your men to be ready to march tomorrow morning. They must be on horseback. Can they do that?"

"By now they can, but they'll be much slower than you people."

"I know that. Nobody is as fast as us. I'll give you guides so you won't get lost. You can catch up to us later at the battle site."

It's a relief to see that when Jir-Jir referred to fighting he meant against the Wu-Sun and not another test. Also good that his cohort won't lead

151

the attack but will be used as a reserve to be committed later. It'll give them a chance to see how these strange people operate in battle.

CHAPTER 12

Jir-Jir leads an eight thousand strong force out of the camp in full panoply. Drums bouncing on the sides of the horses begin the growl of war and regimental banners flash colour onto the steppe. The Romans are on foot in the rear, carrying two standards, one for each century, a sober contrast with the flamboyance of their new comrades. An enterprising man has made them out of found objects.

It's an odd combination – a barbarian army of horse archers leading the most sophisticated infantry in the world. But Marcus doesn't think it shameful as once he would. He and his comrades are free and that's what counts. Besides, proving the merits of the Roman way to the sceptical Sharnyu is a welcome challenge. The pressure is heavier though than in a normal battle where victory solves all. They can be part of a winning event but still fall short of the standards this unpredictable character requires.

It's just as well that he had the men keep up their skills in the daily practice at Margiana. It was really done for morale boosting but today its effect in the battle could be decisive. He looks at his men steadfastly marching as they used to and feels confidence return – good to be at battle again. The cohort's like a slack sail without wind tighten up from a new breeze and become full and strong. Today he'll wipe the slate clean after the ignominy of Carrhae, or die in the attempt. He has no doubt the others feel the same.

The Romans soon fall behind. After five days on the march, they catch up. The centaurs of the steppes take less than half that time to reach the site. Jir-Jir had his troops ride all night, every night. They slept on their horses. It's something they often do, a feat worthy of respect – another example of merit in people east of the Hellespont. It's something he's finding himself less and less reluctant to see, a factor that's making him question his earlier cast of mind, possibly reverse it.

The speed of the Hsiung-nu march has taken the Wu-sun by surprise. Their slow reaction permitted Jir-Jir to manoeuvre his army onto high ground overlooking them.

His position established, Jir-Jir ordered his troops to rest, allowing the Romans to catch up and join them. Opposite, on lower ground, the round white tents of the Wu-Sun spread out like mushrooms across the steppe. As darkness falls, their small brazier fires light up like stars coming out one by one. All is quiet, except for sporadic voices, thin and hollow in the distance, oddly peaceable. Notwithstanding the calm, the periodic breaks in the silence warn there're unseen enemies out there that must be faced in the morning.

Jir-Jir sends for Marcus.

> "Tomorrow we'll line up in three sections. I want you and your force behind the right wing as part of the reserves. It's my intention to overpower their left after the first charge and turn it. You'll be part of that. Fight well and you'll be rewarded. Fail and I'll make sure you and your comrades are meat for the vultures. They're always hungry out here – ha ha ha."

"You'll see how well Roman infantry performs. You can depend on it."

For all the bravado countering the Sharnyu's banter, he's under no illusion about how testing the encounter will be tomorrow. He's never seen the Wu-Sun in battle before and the composite bow he knows they have will be as daunting as what he saw on the field of Carrhae. How they'll use it is yet to be seen; it'll be formidable that's certain. The Testudo will have to be tight. Gone is the confidence he used to have about winning battles against barbarians. It seems so long ago that he thought like that. Still, he hasn't forgotten how to concentrate, how to block out insinuating doubt, how to deluge fear in the storm of battle passion. And how vital the morale of his troops is. He knows the fears of his men tonight, fears born of the unknown, the great exaggerator. Some are beginning to bend to negative talk.

He goes from tent to tent calling them brothers, friends and countrymen. Showing not a scintilla of fear or doubt, he reminds them of their skills and abilities – the best in the world. He gives praise to individual commanders, engendering confidence in the others.

"All you have to do is fight as well as you know how. Remember your tactics and follow your officers. Do that and we'll earn a permanent place in Jir-Jir's army. Above all, be aggressive. Take the fight to the enemy.

"It's good we'll have the Hsiung-nu as allies. Jir-Jir's impressive. He's beaten the Wu-Sun before – and he's clearly got the drop on them. Getting the high ground was a master stroke. Look at the discipline and stamina of his troops marching all night. We've got to show we're as good as them in a fight. We can do it."

He looks everyone in the eye and the confidence he exudes thaws cold.

All the same, it's difficult to sleep tonight. But at least the anxieties of the coming challenge block out the Eumenides for once, when at last he falls asleep.

Next day, while the copper disc struggles to rise from a thin bed of clouds, the big drums start up. Both sides try as hard as they can to outdo the other. The thumping pierces the air with insistent rhythm, deep and base, full of portent and confidence. Suddenly a tumultuous roar breaks out of the high ground. A mass movement of horses and shouting men thunders down and across the steppe. It's like a giant stain spreading over the landscape in splotches. Reds, greens, blues, and yellows of regimental banners flutter vertically beside the straining horses. He orders the Testudo to form. Holds it back out of range. The first salvo of enemy arrows flies into the charging horsemen. A few of them fall but the main body surges towards the lower ground intact.

On Jir-Jir's command given in Sogdian he orders the Testudo to move forward at a slow pace. High speed arrows hiss through the air. They hit it like a sheet of black hail, rattling the bronze shields. The formation holds firm. Its scales are intact. The waves of missiles aren't as thick as they were at Carrhae; the Wu-Sun are concentrating more on the Hsiung-nu charge.

Inexorable, oblivious to danger, the Testudo lumbers over the flat ground. It's like a primordial monster hankering after its prey. Arrows ping off of its carapace and do little harm. Abruptly it halts behind the front line. The horsemen are starting to fight with swords, still mounted. They've exhausted their ammunition. No more arrows to worry about. He orders his men to collapse the Testudo. They form the square and wait, ready to charge at the command. It's frustrating not to be part of the action but he must obey orders.

Despite thirty minutes of intense combat, the wings of both sides remain stable. They show no sign of bending. In the centre, the Wu-Sun are making some headway. It's not much but noticeable. He's starting to fear the worst. If the line cracks he and his cohort will be on the defensive. They might even be deluged by a panicky swarm of fleeing men, jostled and unable to fight as they should. He'll be denied the chance to prove Roman worth. Is another disaster looming?

Just as the bend in the centre is reaching its breaking point, Jir-Jir gives the order for the Romans to attack. In a mass they charge the left wing of the enemy. They bump into horse and man with their shields and lock them into close action. That's where their gladii are supreme. Unlike them, the Hsiung-nu and Wu-Sun have long swords. They fight with a slashing motion. The Romans easily parry their swings with their large shields. Up close the short gladius has the advantage.

He's in front, thrusting upwards at the mounted men and bashing with his shield. Gaius comes up beside him, overpowering all before him in a killing spree. The rest of the cohort press behind, yelling battle cries. The assault causes the enemy to bunch up. They're unable to move their horses out of the way of the converging infantry. Their legendary riding prowess is inhibited. There's not enough room. The Roman skills are beginning to have effect. Wu-Sun casualties mount; the gladius finds its mark. It's more manoeuvrable than the long sword, more responsive to quick reflexes. The sharp blade easily slides through the leather that passes for armour in this part of the world for most of the troops.

The spurting blood and cries of dying men ignite his battle fury, lain dormant since the great defeat. He's a Roman soldier once again. He's *acer in ferro* in the thick of battle. He's winning again. Like his comrades, he loves hand to hand combat. It's what they're best at. It's nobler than killing at a distance with arrows.

The cohort's charge propels him right up close to the enemy. Even the gladius is difficult to wield now. Marcus pulls out Owl's Head and drags a man off his horse onto the ground. He drives it through his face into his brain. Owl's Head has had its first taste of blood on the steppe.

As the Wu-Sun in front of the Romans show signs of weakening, a surging weight of cavalry comes up from behind. The Sharnyu flashes by, swinging his sword, lopping off heads and arms, a thrashing demon cutting a swath through the enemy line. He and his tribal guard are smashing into the enemy like a flash flood hitting a town. The violence of its flow subdues every obstacle and overwhelms all in its way.

The Wu-Sun wing falls back; the Romans rush forward yelling "*ad victoriam, ad victoriam*". With Gaius beside him, Marcus shouts his men on as the mass in front begins to turn. Once the retreat starts it picks up momentum. It's like a wind change evolving into a storm. The invading wind starts slowly, gradually picks up speed and becomes a raging gale. The wing collapses, exposing the centre's flank and drawing in the foe. Flights of Hsiung-nu cavalry rush past on the right and get behind. Faced with the assault, the main body curls up like a dying leaf in autumn. Inevitably the enemy loses confidence; panic takes hold and rout explodes.

The Romans are on the double now and charge with their allies into the mass of trapped horsemen. They're like a hammer striking the anvil. He's amazed to see how similar it is to the strategy adopted by Alexander the Great in all his battles. The Wu-Sun army breaks down completely. All cohesion disappears. As the fighting stops, crowds of prisoners are disarmed and herded into a limp throng.

The Romans suffered a few casualties – five killed and twice that many wounded. Every death is regrettable, but under the circumstances, the loss is not too heavy, and the wounded are expected to recover. It's an unambiguous victory. Although only achieved in the company of barbarians, it's still a victory. Some at least of Carrhae's shame has been scrubbed clean.

Gaius, still out of breath, finds Marcus.

"Trebonius is among the dead. He fought well but was overwhelmed in the action."

"I'm sorry to hear it. What an irony. He would still be alive if we had listened to him in Margiana."

"Marcus, it was the right decision for him to come with us. Death on the battlefield is better than a life in slavery. He did his duty. That's what counts."

"Yes. I agree. There's no doubt about that. Come, we must bury our dead and do it in the Roman fashion. They helped restore our honour. It's a debt we owe them."

ଔ

After the burial ceremony, Marcus joins Jir-Jir, sitting beside him as his special guest at the victory banquet in the Sharnyu's tent. Marcus is on the left, facing north, the place of honour in Hsiung-nu tradition. Tables had been quickly set up to accommodate them and thirty senior officers. Braziers provide light and heat as the autumn evening, no longer flirting with summer, cools into night. Jir-Jir is in thunderous voice, fuelled by drink.

"Roman, you and your men fought well today. You've earned your keep. Our army will have a place for you. Tomorrow I'll send Jiyu to say what your wages will be. You'll be happy for I'm a generous man. Here's a reward for today."

In a grand gesture, he gives him a leather bag, heavy and clinking. Marcus puts it on the floor out of sight between his legs and mumbles thanks as he bends down. Before he can say something appropriate Jir-Jir slaps the table.

"Have some drink, Roman."

He hands him a bronze goblet full of off-white and foul smelling liquid. Marcus nearly gags as the sour odour billows up. It's worse than the body sweat in the tent, which, fortunately, he's getting used to. He takes a deep gulp and maintains a straight face. The liquor sears his throat. At least it's better than the smell. Right away, he swallows another; Jir-Jir smiles and nods approval.

The Sharnyu drinks from a silver-coated skull of an enemy chieftain. The handles are two stags facing each other. He drains it to the last drop and slams it down on the table. The cup next to him leaps up and spills its contents over his neighbour's tunic. The victim merely laughs, pats it down and calls for more drink.

"What is this stuff?" he whispers to Lushan who's siting on his other side.

"It's fermented mare's milk – what they drink out here."

Slaves bring wooden platters heaped with mutton, beef, and goat cut up into little pieces and stuck on metal skewers. They strew loaves of coarse bread over the table, a solid structure made of planks, crude product from the local trees. The cooking, over a wood fire, is done inside the tent which has an opening at the top to let the smoke out. Notwithstanding that, the air soon becomes a fug. But nobody seems to mind.

The diners eat with their fingers, wiping them from time to time on the table or on their rough woollen tunics. Lushan has brought a cloth which he keeps surreptitiously under the table on his knees. As the drink takes hold, the reluctance of the Hsiung-nu to speak vanishes into a raucous din. They all talk at once, interrupted only by uproarious laughter. Occasionally groups break out into song which spreads around the tent. People bang the tables with their fists and slap each other on the back. The wild energy makes Roman parties look funereal.

Jir-Jir leans back in his chair with his goblet.

"I like you Roman. We'll get on. I saw the way you and your men fought today, very disciplined. You'll have to teach my people some of that. Only I don't think they will learn – ha, ha, ha."

Marcus has passed the stage where taste and smell are relevant. He picks up his goblet and says with a slur nobody would notice,

> "Thank you Sir. We worked well with your troops today – tough warriors, very skilful riders. We'll enjoy it here. You Hsiung-nu are very hospitable.

> "I'd like to say that I appreciate what my friend Lushan has done. Without him we wouldn't have gotten together."

Lushan is visibly pleased.

Jir–Jir holds his goblet up in an expansive gesture.

> "That's right. Lushan you deserve a reward too. You're my friend. Here, take this."

Lushan accepts the bag with a bow. It's smaller than Marcus', but he's not disturbed by that. In a few minutes, they quietly open their bags. Marcus is surprised to see his is full of large gold coins. He's never seen any this big except in Samarkand at the jewellery market. Even there most were much smaller. Their lustre is powerful enough to catch the uncertain light in the tent and flash it into his eyes. It's much more than he expected. For a moment he feels rich. What a stroke of luck he's linked up with a man with access to the Sogdian King's wealth and one who's so generous – a good deal more than Crassus. The alliance could well be even more lucrative as time goes on, particularly when news of the Wu-Sun's defeat reaches Samarkand.

As Jir-Jir takes another gulp from his silver goblet, one of the officers sidles up to him quietly, head bowed. He receives a bag and, bent over, slinks back to his place. Some time after, another comes up surreptitiously and shuffles back with a bag. Throughout the evening, Jir-Jir hands out bags of varying sizes. There's always a period between approaches, as nobody wants to appear eager. Everyone is pleased with the Sharnyu's generosity.

Suddenly there's a commotion at the entrance. Guards force three men forward and push their heads down in front of the Sharnyu. When the noise settles down, he turns to Marcus with a stern look.

160

"I have to pass sentence on these men. What's the punishment in the Roman army for cowardice in the face of the enemy?"

"It depends on the circumstances. The most severe is death but there're other less drastic ones."

"It's reported that they didn't show enough aggression in the attack. What would you do with them?"

"That's not as bad as desertion or real cowardice. I would just demote them if they have rank or, if they don't, put them in prison for a few days."

Jir–Jir points a finger at the men.

"Tie them to a tree and shoot them"

As they're led out in silence, Jir-Jir picks up his goblet and drinks, his sternness melting into a half smile.

"You see, Roman, we're tougher than you. We Hsiung-nu don't tolerate anything but the utmost bravery. Aggression is everything. That's why we always win battles."

Before Marcus has a chance to reply, although he doesn't know what to say, five musicians come out. Taking their place on the floor in the ample space between the Sharnyu's table and the others they start playing. Their instruments are flutes and awkwardly bent string contraptions which they pluck. The sound is completely drowned out by the revellers who pay not the slightest attention to it. Then, a small group of dancing girls, exotically pretty, emerges from the entrance. The drunks become quiet, showing instant respect.

The music can now be heard. Its soft and beguiling sound completely changes the atmosphere. It's now a sphere of peace. Beauty has entered the tent and war departed. Lushan whispers to Marcus.

"The Hsiung-nu are very musical. It's a basic part of their culture. They got the flute they are playing from us and passed it on to the Han. Those are the people on the other side of the great mountain barrier. It is an essential part of the Han music – usually played along with the stringed instruments they pluck."

Suddenly the whole table breaks into a slow song, deep and mellow, its simple melody moving in and out of resolution in sombre waves. Large tears role down the cheeks of the singers, possibly the most feared warriors in the world. Jir-Jir sings along with them, his goblet in the air and his eyes closed. He sways from side to side with the others as the song transports them all into a state of sentimental camaraderie.

The young girls, dressed in purple gowns with golden silk overlays, move forward in fluttering steps. Gold bands with dangling silver medallions surround their foreheads like a beautiful frame and necklaces of gold plaques with ruby inlays spread to their shoulders.

They move slowly forward and back, and gracefully twirl around with elegant movements of head and arms. Their hidden feet propel them so smoothly they seem to glide over the carpets. From time to time they look up sideways to expose the whites of their eyes in a gesture of innocence. They're skilfully made up, the outlines of their lips and eyes sharply clean and differentiated. Marcus can't help but stare. Their gentle and precise movements are so completely opposite to the clumsiness of the warriors at the table.

The performance is well received but, sensibly, doesn't last long, the entertainers leaving on their own timing. The revellers have a short attention span and want to get back to serious drinking. The jollification is accompanied from time to time by resonant singing in slow, soulful songs. The whole table joins in, the participants bending from side to side in unison with goblets spilling and nobody noticing. Woollen tunics are soaked and the carpets wet.

Jir-Jir is in an expansive mood.

> "Now we've defeated the Wu-Sun I'm taking my tribe east. Closer to our traditional lands. You and your Romans will come with us. There'll always be fighting to be done. You won't get bored ha ha ha."

> "Where are we going?"

> "The Talass river. You probably don't know where that is. No matter. It's east of here. The Sogdian King has granted us rich grazing land around it. I'm going to build a permanent residence there. We leave in a couple of weeks. Be ready".

It doesn't make any difference where they're going; they're so far from home now. Besides, the Sharnyu's generosity is a pleasant surprise and the atmosphere in the tent tends to quell any thoughts that might stir up worry. Being part of a victory again boosts his mood, as does the potency of the liquor. And the Sharnyu promised him some female company tonight – one of the dancers, as a special reward.

The raucous camaraderie pushes the hour well past midnight and still no one is showing any sign of slackening. At last, the Sharnyu rises and says in a slurred but loud voice that it's time to go to bed. The guests depart, leaving a colossal mess behind and a smell that would frighten a satyr.

Marcus leads his reward by the hand out of the tent into the night air. Its cool clarity hits him like a slap in the face. They stand still for a few moments looking at the moon, new like his life now. Slaves can be heard bustling around cleaning up inside. A little squeal emerges from the sleeping quarters and a short time later, snores.

CHAPTER 13

A week later Lushan appears at Marcus' tent.

"My good friend, I have come to say goodbye. I am off to Samarkand. Jir-Jir has given me an escort. I am very pleased that you have found a place with him and the Hsiung-nu. Your life will be so much better than under the Parthian yoke."

This is a moment that had to come. As Lushan speaks, nostalgia begins to tug at him. The chances of meeting again are as unlikely as the steppe avoiding the coming freeze. The Sogdian is the first non Roman friend he's made. He'll miss him. He's grown used to his expansive manner and sentimental attitudes – so unlike the Stoic approach but engrossing all the same. In a way Lushan has been a teacher, one who has sympathetically led him to at least a partial understanding of the world outside the Roman imperium. He's shown him how to see things from the perspective of another culture, a perception seldom experienced by Romans and never before by him.

"Lushan, I've been honoured to know you. Who can tell, maybe our paths will cross in the future. I hope so. Anyway, best of luck in your endeavours. You deserve it. You've been a good friend to me and my comrades."

"I too feel honoured Marcus Velinius to be your friend. Hopefully we will meet again. The Hsiung-nu are nomads and even though Jir-Jir says he wants to build a permanent home, it is likely he and the tribe will still wander – maybe even to Samarkand. I am often there, as you know. It is my base. If you can come, please get in touch. I would love to see you again. You would be welcome in my home any time."

164

As the farewells are creating embarrassing blushes, a ruckus starts not far away. They go over. Outside the Sharnyu's tent, people are gathering round, talking excitedly and gesticulating at a four camel baggage train. Jir-Jir comes out and orders the drivers to unload the beasts. At a guttural command, they slump down, awkward and bad tempered, allowing the metal- strapped chests on their sides to be taken off. A driver opens one.

A gasp of amazement seizes the onlookers as a heap of gold coins is uncovered, glistering and luxuriant, as opulent as the Sogdian empire that produced them.

Jir-Jir strides over, bends down and digs his hands in, a smile softening his warrior face. Again and again he washes himself in it up to his arms, sometimes tossing glances over to the other chests. The head of the Sogdian King on the coins seems to nod its approval and beckon him to dig deeper. The riches would have impressed even Crassus and gone a long way to reaching his monetary objectives for the campaign.

The gold is a cruel reminder of the choices Marcus made. He's here because he wanted wealth. While he's reasonably paid as a mercenary and did well after the battle with the WuSun, he'll never get rich. His feeling of opulence at the banquet was suffused in drink. Yes, what he's seeing in these chests is impressive but virtually all the bounty will go to others. His standing is much lower than it was in Crassus' army so he'll get proportionately less. He isn't in a position to complain, to insist on more even though there's so much. He's like Tantalus, standing under a tree and reaching for the fruit only to have the branches rise out of his grasp every time he tries to pick it.

In any case, out here in the wild steppe, there's nothing to spend on and certainly no estate to boost his social status.

Jir-Jir looks up at the crowd who're fascinated by the size of the tribute and salivating about their share. Noticing Marcus, he says;

> "It's just as well for the King that he paid us what he promised. We could've taken all this by force, and more. Maybe in the future we should anyway, ha ha ha ... Jiyu, strike the camp tomorrow after the journey ceremony.

We're off to the Talass River. Roman, you and your men will come with us."

He orders the camel drivers to store the chests and walks away, leaving his tribesmen still marvelling.

Marcus and Lushan give each other a final hug and say goodbye, Lushan using more words. The Sogdian turns to mount his horse and trots off back to civilization with his escort. Marcus suddenly feels lonely; he's lost touch again with civilization, albeit not his own but one which he's grown to appreciate.

೮౩

As the sun is about to breach the horizon and the cold morning air blows quietly across the steppe, the entire tribe gathers in front of the Sharnyu's pool. All are in respectful silence. Not a person moves. The Romans are there too, their attendance required.

Jir-Jir comes out of his tent, wearing a tall crown of two circles, one on top of the other, surmounted by an eagle, all of gold. He's accompanied by the tribal Shaman who's dressed in a long white robe of tightly spun wool.

They proceed in measured steps around the pool to an altar of rough wood. It sits on a rise in the sand in front of the congregation. Four men are standing by with tall drums on the ground. Jir-Jir moves back, allowing the Shaman to approach the altar alone.

The tribal gathering is as quiet as the sand, motionless; the children don't fidget. It's as if they're all blending into the steppe, at one with its spirit. Their benign faces show that they've allowed their vanity to submit to its power as a small child does to its parent. In return they receive its benevolence which envelops them like a warm blanket on a winter's night. It will keep them safe and guard them from evil as they take their long journey.

Quietly the drums start up, the beat slow and muted, inexorable like it was in battle but now gentle and peaceful. The Shaman spreads his arms to the sky and intones an invocation with a strong and musical voice, the drums adding foundation. Someone tells Marcus that he's imploring the mother goddess of the sky, who lives in the great Dome of Heaven, to bless their journey and bring fortune to their new home, and that he's acknowledging the ancestors of the tribe and the spirits of the steppe, seeking their support. The prayer lasts a few minutes and when it's over, two assistants, also in white robes, lead several sheep through the silent crowd and hold one, struggling, on the altar.

With a deft motion, the Shaman slits its throat, blood splashing over his white garment and onto the ground. The rest of the sheep follow one by one, noisily giving up their lives. The drums are still beating, although their sound is louder as they give emphasis to the sacrifice. They're insistent, forceful, now carrying overtones of war and the dreadful punishment the spirits of the steppe can exact if they're not propitiated.

After an interval in the proceedings, the drums now returning to their quieter tone, a soldier brings a snow white horse up to the altar and holds it still by the bridle. Jir-Jir moves forward, the Shaman stepping back. The Sharnyu spreads his arms upward and murmurs a quiet incantation, his face serene, eyes closed, all fierceness gone. He looks almost gentle. The crowd is still, heads bowed.

By this time Marcus knows how important the horse is to the Hsiung-nu, that the human soul is a wind horse, the spiritual power that steers the lives of men. No wonder horse and man are at one like centaurs. The beast is not sacrificed; sometimes horses are but not today. It just stands there docilely, from time to time shifting its legs and switching its tail at the flies. Perhaps it feels the reverence in which it's held.

He's moved by the ceremony, somehow becoming part of it involuntarily even though he doesn't understand what's being said. It's created a mood of calm in him, even mellowness. Certainly it has in others, judging by the faces in the crowd. It's as if the people have moved out of themselves to feel near a higher power present at the ceremony and through that connection become closer to each other for the moment.

The contrast with the normal fierceness of these horse archers is remarkable. But even more startling is the similarity with Roman religion after one penetrates the superstructure of ritual. Of course he sees them very different in many respects, certainly in style. At a fundamental level however, they both seem to express a reverence for the heavens above and the moral law within.

He's struck most of all by the stark disparity between the spiritual sincerity evident in these people, even Jir-Jir, and the lack of it in Rome, so sophisticated and cynical. The sincerity and the connection it stimulates with a force superior to the mundane are producing a strangely liberating effect on him. It's freeing him from the shackles of self absorption, a relief which he now realises is an antidote to the depression which so often grips him. Maybe that liberation is the main purpose of religion and it doesn't matter what type it is so long as it accomplishes that end.

The sacrifice over, the whole tribe participates in a feast of roasted sheep, the Romans included. The spirits are propitiated and none ignored. Everybody is in high spirits and particularly friendly, even to the Romans. They can start their trek to their new home now with confidence.

ಣ

Soon the entire Hsiung-nu tribe is in its nomadic mode. Thousands of families plus a hundred and fifty Roman soldiers head towards the Road, a couple of days away. A vast herd of sheep and cattle stumble along setting the pace, slowing the horses down to a leisurely walk. The colourful mass reaches the Jaxartes, crosses at a low point and enters the daunting steppe. There they meet the Road which is waiting for them, eager to take them on its back again, especially the Romans whom it seems to have adopted as a client. Marcus is getting used to it, feeling a warm connection with it. True, it brought him to the disaster of Carrhae but it also introduced him to adventures and education that he would never have had otherwise. It's easy to think of it as a mentor of sorts.

They head north – east into a gnarled scrub wilderness devoid of any human presence. Only an eagle sailing on high seems able to penetrate this far. The animals have barely enough to eat from the sparse vegetation, a threadbare carpet on the sand. It's getting thinner as the journey progresses. Everything goes smoothly though, as would be expected of people who're following their natural way of life. At least the novice riders can easily keep the pace. Anyway they're becoming more expert, although they have no hope of ever being as skillful as the centaurs who teach them.

They pass through oases, somehow appearing just when the leather water bags need replenishing. The navigational expertise of the Hsiung-nu is impressive, as is their affinity with nature. They know from evidence too subtle for others to see where the elusive springs are.

Marcus is riding beside Jir-Jir who's showing interest in Roman technology. Tales of the glory of Rome, its civilization and power, slide off his back like arrows bouncing off stone, but more concrete things capture his attention. Unashamed of the technical limits of his people, the Sharnyu says,

> "Can you suggest ways to help us build my town? We're not used to building anything – don't know how to work with bricks. Not part of our culture."

Jir-Jir appears almost childlike in his question, his tone quiet, all fierceness gone; even his chin is no longer jutting out. Unshakable confidence in his warrior culture allows him to admit without embarrassment to lack of technological knowledge. It can be bought or taken. It's superficial.

> "If you're thinking about a permanent residence, you need to consider protection. My comrades and I can work with your men to build earthworks to surround the town like we do in the Roman army. We know how to make mud bricks for a wall and lay them straight. Also I recommend a wooden palisade, like we normally have. We build them around our camps."

Weeks on the trek accompany autumn's journey into winter, a cold and windy challenge to the Romans who're still not used to the rigours of the steppe in full frost. Not so with the Hsiung-nu who relish the clear cold days.

They give the Romans furs to wear. By now their worn out sandals have been discarded and they're wearing the round- toed boots of the Hsiung-nu. As in the summer, the sun is virtually always with them, but now aloof and tepid. Infrequently clouds appear and toss meagre snow flurries into the wind.

They go off the Road onto a subsidiary track, leading due east, until they come to wide grasslands, squashed by winter but promising lush growth in the spring. A narrow river of ice runs through them into the distance. Jir-Jir orders a stop and gestures to Marcus who's riding close by.

> "This is the Talass River. I'm going to build here. There's plenty of water and the grazing's rich for the cattle and sheep. As soon as we set up camp we'll start. You'll help us."

> "We have to wait till spring, Sir. The ground's too hard for digging now."

> "All right, if you say so. We'll stay in the camp until then, but no unnecessary delay. I'll be watching."

> "There won't be I assure you. We want to get it done as much as you do. It'll be our home too".

Jir-Jir jerks his head back and laughs.

> "It's good to have you Romans with us. You're useful"

ೞ

Once the spring has loosened the earth and the ice thaws to water, the project starts. Mud bricks can be made now. Marcus takes charge, not that he's an engineer; he's there by default. The Sharnyu was not exaggerating when he spoke of his people's capabilities. They truly have no experience with permanent structures, even simple earthen fortifications.

Jir-Jir is happy to leave everything to the Romans, merely supplying unskilled labour, which is on the lazy side of motivation. Marcus has the Hsiung-nu make shovels from the plentiful oasis wood. Not much good for digging, at least they can be used to shift dug soil into the wicker baskets the women make. The Romans still have their metal spades – an essential part of their equipment.

First they dig a ditch around the town in the Roman fashion – a square. The excavated material creates a ramp next to it, extending into a mud brick wall with a tower and gate at each side. With the wood of the oasis they construct a double palisade in front of the wall. It's made of thin trunks and branches set upright against each other, placed closely enough to stop arrows. The whole enterprise is finished in six months, well before the winter frost arrives. The Hsiung-nu and the Romans are now installed in a permanent residence; but they still live in tents.

Marcus and Gaius go on an inspection tour – like a commissioning. Marcus says

"I think we did a pretty good job, not perfect but good enough. It's no Bukhara – couldn't stand up to a big attack, but at least it would delay the enemy for a while. I'm not surprised the Hsiung-nu are pleased.

By the way, have you noticed a change in Jir-Jir recently? He was always full of himself but now, with all his success, he seems down right arrogant. Maybe it's because no one criticises him. He's out of touch with what he's supposed to be doing here".

"What d'you mean?"

"Samarkand merchants tell me he's been sending out raiding parties to pillage the Sogdian towns. They're meant to be allies. Extracts tribute from the whole of Fergana, when the King already pays him. Pushes the people past any sensible limit. He's worse than Crassus.

"Thank Jupiter he hasn't ordered us to help him. I like the Sogdians. Anyway we should stay on good terms with them in case we have a falling out. He's an unpredictable character. Cruel too; he's been allowing his men to kill and rape all over the country. Although, I have to say, other Hsiung-nu chiefs do the same."

"I've noticed. The Sogdian King's spoiled him. He's getting greedy. You're right Marcus – like Crassus. I don't trust him."

"I don't either. He needs us though, at least for a while. Doesn't have enough of his own troops. We'd better be on our guard in case he does something stupid. He can be likeable though at times, and he's been really generous to us. Anyway, I'll see you at dinner."

Negative feelings are intruding again. Marcus doesn't want his friend to know; better put up a positive front. The pleasure of freedom is sustaining to a certain degree but its first flush has dissipated. The euphoric end of slavery felt on the Road is only a distant memory now. As time wears on, this alien place where life is so primitive becomes more and more depressing. It could never be a home. And how is it possible to go anywhere else? The nightmares still haunt; the vicious birds attack without mercy. He can never get a decent sleep.

The Hsiung-nu culture is too unevolved to allow real friendships to form. Comrades are around but the conversation is not the same as with the senior officers, Crassus particularly, who're long gone. The building of the town provided a certain distraction; action always defeats morbid thoughts. But it's over now. Nothing remains but waiting for military action that hasn't come for a while. What purpose there is consists merely of earning some money, not that there's much for the mercenaries. Anyway, what use is it on the steppe?

It's hard to avoid slipping back to that melancholy state where outside connections are lost and there's little point in life. Aurelia is gone and no prospects exist for someone else, not that he's ready in any case. Somehow her picture is missing – probably fell out of his pack when the Romans were moved to the other side of town. He searched for it in vain.

One of Jir-Jir's men who can speak a little Sogdian comes to his tent and says through the opening,

"The Sharnyu summons you."

He comes out immediately and goes to the command tent. Jir-Jir is seated serenely on his wooden chair flanked by his officers. In front are four men who look like the Hsiung-nu but are dressed differently. They have tunics and trousers of dark blue silk with strange patterns and wear small black caps. Long thin beards hang from their chins. They're speaking a language he's never heard. While he doesn't understand the Hsiung-nu tongue he's picked up its cadence and a few words. What he's hearing is completely different. Not a syllable is similar. Jir-Jir seems to be able to speak it though.

The Sharnyu nods at him but gives no indication what he should do, so he merely stands near the entrance. One of the visitors, who seems to be the chief, makes a long speech and the Sharnyu nods his head passively. An exchange follows, the Sharnyu barely saying anything and looking unimpressed. Progressively the chief's voice becomes louder and more insistent. Apparently he's demanding something the Sharnyu is not willing to give. After a climactic passage, he points his finger at Jir-Jir, his voice now shrill with anger.

Jir-Jir's expression suddenly darkens, his eyes narrow and his head jerks forward, chin jutting out. He shouts at the visitors and raises his arm, palm towards them to command silence. It produces no result; they're all talking now, in loud voices and gesticulating wildly.

Jir-Jir leaps up, eyes blazing like lava flowing from a volcano, and shouts a command. Six of his men move forward and seize the visitors around the neck, forcing an arm behind their back and jamming it up until it almost breaks. Terrified into silence, they're bundled out of the tent. As they pass Marcus he sees black patterns painted on their faces.

Jir-Jir motions for him to come forward, his expression still fierce.

"Roman, are the fortifications completed?"

"Yes Sir. They are. They're strong enough to beat off an attack – even withstand a siege as long as the enemy don't have engines. Who were those people?"

"They're emissaries from the Han Emperor. His armies are becoming more and more aggressive. They're pushing our tribes further west. We always used to beat them and raid their lands from the north. That's why they built that big wall. It's to keep us out. You've never seen it but it's huge, very tall and long. But now they've got better weapons and are more difficult to defeat. However I'm not afraid of them."

"What did they want that made you so angry?"

"They were demanding that I return the corpse of a major of their Palace Guard I had executed last year. The Emperor sent him to negotiate a new treaty. Wanted too much so I had to show who's boss of the steppe. The arrogant weasels, they're lucky I didn't have them killed too. I'm just expelling them."

"Why do they have those black markings on their faces?"

"It's our custom to have envoys surrender their credentials and have their faces painted before they enter a Sharnyu's tent.

"The Han are sure to march against us after their envoys return. It's a long way for them to come though; so their army won't be that large. However, I've broken with the King of Sogdiana, so there could be some danger from the Sogdians too, although they're useless in battle. I had his daughter killed, the one he sent me for a wife.

"Too bad, she was good looking, ha ha ha. I did it to make the split clear. I don't need him any more. I'm powerful enough now to collect tribute from the Sogdians direct, the rich weaklings. That gives me much more than the King ever paid."

"How do you plan to deal with the Han army?"

"I will let them attack us. We will defend behind the fortifications and sally out. They had better be strong, Roman. You and your men will be under attack too. Don't expect any quarter from the Han."

"Don't worry Sir. The walls are thick and the palisade'll be hard for them to get over."

Marcus has no idea of the fighting capabilities of the Han or their numbers but doesn't want to be equivocal in front of the Sharnyu. Besides, what he's seen so far of the Hsiung-nu in battle gives him assurance.

"They will take a while to get here – have to get over the mountains. But get your men ready anyway."

He comes over and puts an arm around Marcus' shoulder.

"Roman, you and I are comrades now. I look forward to seeing your men fight again. Together we will smash the Han like we did the Wusun. You'll see, ha ha ha."

The prospect of action is exhilarating, spiced by the expectation of facing an unknown enemy. And what a relief it'll not be against the Sogdians. Marcus' faith in Roman fighting ability has returned, but without the erstwhile arrogance that sometimes strayed into hubris. And it's good to have the confidence of the Sharnyu. He leaves the tent in an upbeat mood and goes to share the news with his comrades.

CHAPTER 14

Far away from Sogdiana, on the eastern portion of the Road and past the great mountain barrier is a lonely outpost in the wilderness. It's built of mud brick in a low lying oasis on the northern reaches of the Taklamakan desert. In that region, every few kilometres, rammed earth beacon towers, four and a half metres high, rise out of the sands and extend like a necklace all the way to the frontier of the Han Kingdom. Whenever danger breaks out, each tower signals to the next – wood fires at night, black smoke from wolf dung in the day. Arduously collected from the wilds, the dung produces a colour not only aesthetically pleasing but distinguishable from normal fires.

Inside the multi-towered fortress, a hastily called meeting is in progress between Gan Yen-xu, the Protector -General of the Western Region and Chief Commandant of Cavalry and his second in command, Colonel Chen Tang who's in charge of military operations. Both are relatively young, Gan a few years older than Chen but still in the vigorous part of middle age. The Emperor knows of the hardships facing anyone in the wild west, so remote from civilization that only the hardiest can cope.

The climate at Gaochang is difficult enough in winter but next to impossible in summer. Heat, glancing off the Flaming Mountains bordering the oasis, is hot enough to cook without a fire. It's now autumn, the season that's meant to tame the heat; but here it reduces it only by a few degrees.

The garrison town is there to discourage the Hsiung-nu from raiding the

Road. Although the Confucian scholars in the capital at Chang-an consider the trade it facilitates to be somewhat parasitical, the more pragmatic Emperor considers it a significant benefit, worth protecting.

As this is a private conference, it's held in an ante room just off the main hall. Although small, the room has high ceilings supported by wide, rough-hewn beams. A window at eye level looks out onto the central courtyard which is paved in cobblestones, sun-drenched and empty. The occupants of the fortress are all inside the thick walls trying to avoid the heat. It's said that the only way to be comfortable is to lie in a cold bath. At least the water from the underground aquifers is protected from the savagery of the sun.

The two leaders are dressed in floor-length robes of dark silk, with compendious sleeves that hide their hands, and sometimes other things less benign. The generous folds of the garments give the wearers an air of serenity, of calm haughtiness that requires no effort to impress. The smooth comfort of the silk speaks of the sophisticated pleasures that only a highly evolved civilization can bring. Especially important are the flat-topped, round hats with sable tassels which are believed to provide a cultivated appearance, far superior to that of the barbaric Hsiung-nu who're content with wild fur hats.

They sit opposite each other cross-legged on silk rugs patterned in sinuous dragons of gold on an azure background. Their wide garments spread across the floor in equilateral triangles, solid and stable. A female slave serves tea on short rectangular tables of red lacquer, one for each. Gan has had the leaves specially brought from Chang-an where the beverage is drunk, although not with any great popularity. It's really for the avant garde. Two male slaves in dark cotton tunics try to cool the air with silken fans, largely in vain.

At least there're no flies, thinks Chen who comes from the East. A product of the military establishment, he's thin and angular, of a somewhat choleric and impatient disposition, not at all interested in philosophy or literature – too pragmatic for that. He takes a noisy sip of tea, clear with nothing added, and says,

"The envoys we sent to Jir-Jir have returned. He treated them with insolence – unforgivable. It's an insult to the Emperor. They report that his tribe is permanently established at the Talass River. Now they're in a position to raid the Caravan Road. Already he's sent out a party to attack one of our caravans. We can't let this continue. Also it looks as if he's spread his power into Dayuan so he can interrupt our supply of heavenly horses. This demands an immediate military response."

Gan takes time to reply, gravely nodding his head, which is round and full-faced, in the manner his countrymen deem propitious for wisdom and power. He has a kindly and reflective demeanour, suggesting a life experience beyond what could be expected from a man whose beard is not yet grey.

"Yes, I agree with you, but we need to ask permission from the Emperor before we send an expedition. The mandarins have made it very clear that His Majesty is cautious about military entanglements, especially with the Hsiung-nu."

"Protector-General, if we do that it there'll be no end of delays. You know how bureaucratic the Palace is. Also, those skinflints in Chang-an will never approve the expenditure. We must act now or Jir-Jir will consolidate his power. If that happens he'll cut the Caravan Road, just like his ancestors did. You know how difficult it was for Wu-di to open it up. And also how important the trade is. We can't allow the work of a hundred years to be undone just because we wait for the eunuchs to make up their minds."

"Colonel, I appreciate the danger just as much as you do, but the issue has a diplomatic dimension as well as a military one. If we attack Jir-Jir without the Emperor's knowledge, let alone approval, we do so in ignorance of any arrangements he may have made with the Hsiung-nu in general, with neighbouring tribes for instance. Besides, we need the protection of authority in case we run into difficulties with Jir-Jir. He is a formidable warrior and he may have allies now. I know that will mean delays, but even if he moves against the Caravan Road it will not be too late to roll him back, or even destroy him. Caution is the wiser course here. Any rash action, no matter how enticing it seems at first instance, will be regretted. We must seek approval first."

Chen, feeling the anger boiling his head, says, "We are so far from Chang-an, the Court will never …".

Gan's face begins to go white and he doubles over in pain, knocking over the precious celadon vase on his table.

"What's the matter, Protector-General?"

"I don't know. I feel sick in the stomach. Please, let's end the discussion. I need to lie down."

જી

Over the next few hours, Gan's condition worsens. He's wracked with vomiting and severe stomach pains. Chen visits his bedroom to check on him.

"Protector-General, how're you feeling? What does the doctor say?"

"I feel terrible. Whatever this is makes me very weak. Too weak to move, can't even think straight. The doctor has given me some tiger powder and ginger. He thinks it's a bad case of stomach poisoning but can't be sure. If he's right I should be better in a few days. In the meantime you take over command."

As Chen leaves the room he wrestles with the issue of the Hsiung-nu. The Protector-General is advocating the conventional approach, the safe way which could not be criticised. But the waste of time is intolerable. Gan's incapacity affords an opportunity. He must seize it now, whatever the risk. So, he does something almost unimagineable, out of character for a Han official. Only remoteness from central authority makes it possible.

He goes to his room alone; not even a slave is around. Shutting the door, he walks over to his red lacquer writing table, low and wide, and sits down quietly, cross-legged on the floor, thinking for a moment. Reaching into a box nearby, he takes out an array of flat, thin bamboo slips and carefully places it on the table. The slips are tied in parallel with two horizontal lines of hemp string threaded through holes drilled in the bamboo. It's the common writing material employed in this remote area which is too rough for parchment.

He selects a brush from a clutch in a cylindrical pot. It's his favourite, the one with a centre of stiff wolf hair inside a belly of soft goat. The tip is sharp and the belly holds a generous amount of ink. He picks up his ink stick, of pressed pine soot, and grinds it slowly on a black stone carved with dragons. The shavings pile up in the hollow. Adding a few drops of water, just enough to make the ink flow smoothly but not so much that it bleeds, he's ready to start. However he sits quietly for a minute, eyes closed. Training by expert calligraphers requires him to be deliberate, unrushed.

With back upright and face impassive, he dips the brush into the ink and rolls it to a point on the ink stone. Holding it comfortably at right angles to the bamboo slip he begins to write a letter, the characters flowing rhythmically down from the top in free and confident strokes. It commands himself to lead an expedition against the Hsiung-nu at the Talass River and recruit auxiliaries from the vassal states in the Western Region. He signs it "Han Di" (Emperor of the Han). When he has finished he lets the ink dry and calls in his second in command.

> "We've received an order from the Emperor that must be communicated immediately. Here it is. You are to take it around personally to all the officers above middle rank; also the heads of the vassal states. You can get the list from Major Li."

The man salutes and departs with the document. Chen gives a sigh of finality and tries to quell the anxieties that are rushing around in his head about the enormity of what he's just done.

ख

The doctor's diagnosis is correct and Gan recovers in a few days. He hears of the order and is furious. He knows it's a forgery. That such a command arrived just when he was sick is simply not credible. He summons Chen to the anteroom.

> "What have you done? You know it's a capital offence to forge a document in the Emperor's name. It's an act of treason. There's nothing worse. How could you do such an insane thing? You must stop the mobilization right away. Send out a countermand. With luck, maybe the forgery will go unnoticed."

Chen is relieved that Gan doesn't accuse him of poisoning. He didn't do it but the circumstances could look suspicious.

> "Protector-General, it's too late. The order's been circulated. It could only be revoked by another forgery. Any countermanding would be so odd – would make things a lot worse. It would be sure to be reported. Anyway,

I'm sure somebody's already informed Chang-an. I'm sorry to say we're both involved here. Our best way forward is to attack the Hsiung-nu and win a glorious victory. We can do it. In the glow of that we'll be forgiven and rewarded. Have faith Sir, you'll see it'll turn out all right."

"You should have consulted me, Colonel. You've put both of us at great personal risk by your impetuous action."

An uncomfortable silence fouls the air while neither knows what to say. Chen respects his superior, believing him to be a well-intentioned man, although he doesn't admire his indecisiveness. It seems he always has to be pushed into a decision. It would have been impossible to persuade him to support the mobilization without going through the tortuous approval process. Anyway, he doesn't want to exacerbate the situation, and he has what he wants.

Gan also wants peace. They're both in a remote and isolated outpost, in charge of completely different domains – him the political, Chen the military; it's best to get along. Besides, he has confidence in Chen's expertise, notwithstanding his volatility in other matters. Maybe Chen is right; they could win glory and be forgiven.

"I suppose the die is cast. At least I agreed with you that it's in the interests of the State to meet the Hsiung-nu threat. I would've preferred the safer course of getting the Emperor's permission, but obviously that's not possible now. All right, we mount the expedition. Get ready. I'll go with you.

"But we have to do something to cover ourselves. At least dampen the enormity of what's been done. We must send a letter to the Emperor – build the case for the action we're taking as a dire necessity. Also we must admit the forgery and the mobilisation of imperial troops without authority. If we confess it might make it easier to forgive us, assuming we win the battle. If we lose, it goes without saying we'll both be executed no matter what."

"Yes. I agree. I'll draft it for your approval and we'll both sign. The vassal troops will arrive the day after tomorrow. Our own force will be ready then so we can begin the march. I suggest we divide our army for the expedition. You and I can lead the bulk of the troops along the northern route. The rest can take the southern.

I'm so sorry I offended you, Protector-General. I apologize. I'm sure the expedition will be a success and end in glory for both of us. The Emperor is certain to be so pleased he'll forgive us and give us a big reward. You'll see."

"I accept your apology Colonel. I know you did what you thought was right. I'm not used to taking that much risk. Anyway, let's hope you're right and we win a great victory. It's life or death for both of us."

ɷ

In the hot and flaccid morning, as the sun fires up the Flaming Mountains, forty thousand troops of disparate nationalities march out of the sandy marshalling fields at Gaochang. The Han army is swollen to several times its normal size by vassal forces arriving the night before. It's like a river in flood when individual streams flow across the land to join the main course, threatening to deluge everything in its way. While the core of the army is composed of experienced Han soldiers, who double as farmers when not on military duty, most of the numbers are made up from subordinate Hsiung-nu and Sogdian populations – sixteen states in all.

The grand army feeds slowly onto the Road like a file of ants moving towards a spill of honey – inexorable, unstoppable. Multi-hued banners splash colour haphazardly onto the land like a drunken painter might, and the bronze hubcaps of the chariots flash in the sun. Gan and Chen have their own – comfortable seats on wooden wheels drawn by four horses. Flat lacquer roofs like tortoise carapaces shield against the skin – darkening sun. Scions of the ruling class, they don't wish to be identified with tillers of the soil. Soon they pass the first beacon tower, standing proud in the desert, no smoke rising from its top.

Gan has insisted on bringing a staff of envoys educated in Chang-an. They're to assist in establishing trade relations with the states around the Talass river in the event of success. Their leader is Kang Guiren, a Confucian scholar who speaks fluent Sogdian. He's a graduate of the Imperial University founded a century ago by Emperor Wu, an elite institution focussed on literature and philosophy, gated by an exacting national examination. Only the top minds get in.

Kang is a mild mannered man who has a way with people, friendly and modest, with an easy laugh. Slated for high office, he agreed to be assigned to the Far West Protectorate for a stint in order to gain broader life experience. It's a career move favoured in Chang-an. He's older than the others, his beard sprinkled with the salt of middle age.

The two forces navigate around the fearsome Taklamakan desert, one taking the northern route, the other the southern. They're both part of the Road and each offers it an opportunity to acquire trophies of whitened bones; sometimes they lie in the scouring sun for long periods of time awaiting the quixotic sands to blow over them, uncover them and blow over them again.

The arms of the Road converge at an oasis town that looks up to the vast mountain range which has kept the Han peoples separate from the rest of humanity throughout history. They've passed several beacon towers, but none had smoke, not that they expected any. After a few days rest, the combined army begins the daunting task of passing over the peaks, their dense snow caps defeating the sun even at the hottest time of year. While a few unfortunates are lost to the precipices, it reaches the other side.

The host swarms down off the western slopes and marches through medium dense woodlands. There the Road takes the visitors north-west, deep into steppe country and then to the wide grasslands of Fergana (called Dayuan by the Han), the ancient Sogdian breeding grounds of the heavenly horses. Access to these magnificent steeds, so much superior for war than the undersized Han ponies, was the main reason Emperor Wu opened up the Road.

In Fergana, which is just a couple of weeks' march east of Samarkand, they're welcomed by the local Sogdian population, disaffected by Jir-Jir's rapaciousness. Gan and Chen hold a conference to decide on how best to take advantage of the situation. They call in Kang, who can be counted on for giving wise advice, particularly in unfamiliar circumstances. He says,

"I think now is a propitious time to negotiate a treaty of trade and friendship with them. Through commerce that benefits them as well as us we can gain influence and gradually make them dependent on us over time. We must act now; any delay could waste their good will. With your permission, Protector-General, I'll arrange contact with their leaders.

"We'll need some time for this, which is just as well. It's important to remember we're on a punitive expedition. Confucius said that punishments ought to be carried out in winter. If you win a victory against Jir-Jir and the Hsiung-nu a month or so later, the Emperor will consider it more glorious. Besides the troops could use some rest after the arduous passage over the mountains."

Gan looks to Chen who nods his head so slightly it would be necessary to pay strict attention to notice it. Anything that can be done to increase the chance of winning the Emperor's favour is imperative given the perilous situation they're in with the Court, something of course the sagacious Kang doesn't know about. Gan says,

"That's sound advice Kang. We'll adopt it".

Negotiations are successfully concluded with the Sogdians as the first snows of winter arrive. The expeditionary force starts up again. The Road takes them through the grass plains into the endless steppe, cold – blasted by winds uninterrupted in their sweep. Although more or less accustomed to it now, the men who're from the clement East still feel the wind chill bore through their quilted coats and rattle their bones. The Sogdians are happy to guide them to the outskirts of the oasis where Jir-Jir's town borders the newly frozen Talass River. There they stop to rest and prepare for battle.

Ƀ

Word gets through to the Hsiung-nu that they're about to be attacked but they're slow to react. They've been hearing rumours for some time that the Han army is on the march against them. However, as horizontal flags with ox tail tassels streaming off the ends appear in the distance through the trees that fringe the oasis, the town jumps to action. The Han take up positions outside where dense vegetation meets the open steppe. Jir-Jir calls an emergency conference of the senior commanders.

183

Marcus attends, with a translator. The Sharnyu is tense but deliberate, his igneous eyes flashing will power, but unusually mixed with a tinge of doubt, something Marcus has never seen before. The man never seemed capable of anxiety.

> "Jiyu, see to it our best archers are on the towers. As soon as the enemy attacks, our main force will sally out. Forget about their allies; shoot at the Han. Roman, take your men to the eastern gate and follow our assault. Get ready. We don't have much time."

Pandemonium is breaking out around them. Men are rushing all over the town shouting, archers mounting the battlements, horsemen getting into position behind the gates. Pots of scalding oil and man-crushing boulders are being lifted to the top of the towers. Horses are neighing in fear at the confusion and all the women have disappeared inside their tents. Marcus clambers up the inner steps of the eastern tower, pushing past the porters to get to the highest point.

What he sees is shocking. There seems no end to the troops swarming around the town. Spears are standing up in thickets. Cavalry officers in long capes covering the rear of the horses are marshalling their forces in the thousands. The fields are crammed with manoeuvring regiments, their clothing varied. Multi coloured flags, some of them with strange, curvilinear markings, flap impatiently like a stand of young poplars. Two gigantic drums set up sideways, as big as wagons, thunder out bass notes with a mind-numbing beat. Marcus looks to Gaius who's joined him on the tower.

> "Gaius, look how many of them there are. If they can fight at all, we're doomed. Our only hope is to stick together and ride it out. Defence is the right strategy. Jir-Jir has bitten off more than he can chew."

They go down the winding steps and join their comrades who are assembling inside the eastern gate behind the cavalry.

> "I estimate the enemy outnumber us at least five to one. They've been reinforced by a lot of Sogdians Jir-Jir's offended. Also, other Hsiung-nu tribes who don't like him. Clearly he wasn't expecting that big a force.
>
> "Remember we're only mercenaries. We get paid to fight but that doesn't mean we have to go down in a hopeless situation. Our best strategy is to

stay on the defensive. Let Jir-Jir's troops take the brunt of the battle. Keep your ranks tight in the Testudo and move cautiously. No charging. Look after yourselves and your comrades, and we'll come out of this all right."

It's just as well he's speaking Latin, for the defeatism would offend his employers to the core if they knew what he's saying. He doesn't like taking this line but it's the only sensible thing to do for mercenaries under the circumstances.

As he finishes, the first salvo of arrows flies over the walls like a sheet of knives. In the interval before the next one, Hsiung-nu horsemen thunder out of the gate brandishing their long swords. The Romans march behind at slow pace in the Testudo formation. Outside on the plain furious fighting swirls in front of them as the Hsiung-nu sally out in strength from the other gates. They're like a turbulent river debouching into the sea, driving its current into the open water, but soon getting swallowed up.

Before they can engage, the Romans are confronted with a new weapon, one they had never heard of, much less seen. It shoots short, thick arrows with greater penetrating power than even the Parthian arsenal. They pierce shields as if they were made of paper. The only consolation is that the assault is not sustained. Marcus shouts an order.

"Retreat to the walls. Keep your formation. Move".

They manage the manoeuvre before any deaths occur, but several men are wounded by the strange missiles. They fall back just in time. The air thickens with black spines but they fall on the attacking Hsiung-nu.

The battle is going badly for Jir-Jir. His troops are being overwhelmed by the sheer numbers of the Han, despite the famous Hsiung-nu ferocity which inflicts heavy casualties on the besiegers. The town is now completely surrounded. Jir-Jir and his body guard retreat behind the walls. Others follow him chaotically, slashing at the enemy as they fall back. Clouds of arrows fly over the walls into the troops inside who desperately try to parry them with their shields. Their only chance against the short arrows is to turn their shields slightly to cause them to glance off.

The Han start shooting flaming arrows at the palisade, setting it alight at several points. The fires join up and for a while the town is encircled in a blaze. Once the flames die down the attackers break through and run at the wall with shouts of triumph. A mass of Han soldiers clamber up and spread over the wall like a dark blanket. The town itself is weakly defended now as most of Jir-Jir's forces are engaged on the plain. The oil and boulders strip off some of the intrepid soldiers, but nothing can stop the human tide mounting the fortress; its momentum overwhelms all obstacles like an angry sea. The palisade is no help; it's now burned and breached.

As the besiegers threaten to surround the Romans, who are on the plain close to the walls, Marcus orders the square formation. Seamlessly the Testudo changes form, its scales receding out of sight, and collapses into a shape that confronts the enemy on all sides. The Romans engage with the first of the attackers, using their shields as a battering ram, their gladii held out front, but not moving forward. After a few minutes of incon-clusive fighting, the Han leave the prickly force, too small anyway to be a strategic threat, and charge off to the main body of the defenders.

Nothing can save the town now. The fortifications are not holding – the pressure of numbers is too great. They were never designed for such a force. The Hsiung-nu who're not yet overrun are still fighting though; their leader is alive and hasn't ordered a surrender. Besides, it's in their nature. They're like wild beasts cornered by the hunter, desiring only to kill their tormentor, or die trying.

For a few minutes Jir-Jir can be seen on top of the northern tower shouting orders and firing arrows. He has several women with him, concubines and servants. They're gallantly wielding bows beside him like Amazons. One by one they slump down, hit by incoming fire. The Sharnyu staggers as he takes an arrow in the thigh but he retains his balance and continues to shoot. The Han archers have spotted him as the chief and concentrate their fire in a deadly cloud. Suddenly he disappears from sight down the steps followed by the last of his Amazons. Marcus is seized with sympathy; for all his faults he's a gallant and formidable warrior. Now he's doomed.

The Han and their allies charge through the northern gate en masse and spill into the town in a wild killing spree. Almost nobody is left alive. Women and children are pulled out of their hiding and slaughtered. No time is taken even for rape. The carnage is colossal. Among the chaos, a victorious yelling splits the air, overwhelming the general noise of battle. A Han soldier stands on top of the tower holding the Sharnyu's head on a spear.

The sight speeds up the inevitable; the Hsiung-nu army disintegrates into individuals and the battle is over. The Romans are left standing on the plain, the enemy no longer showing any sign of attacking them.

There's only one order Marcus can give.

"Stand still. We wait to see what happens."

CHAPTER 15

The wooden palisade, its entire length set alight by the flaming arrows, is receding into charred stumps, and the town that was to be Jir-Jir's permanent residence is slumping into a shapeless mound that will soon be abandoned to oblivion. A senior officer comes up to the Han Commander in Chief and says,

> "Colonel Chen, during the battle we saw something curious outside the gate on the eastern side of the town. It seemed like a giant creature covered in fish scales. When we looked closer, it was a group of soldiers with round eyes like Sogdians but in uniforms we've never seen before. They're there now. I counted them. There're a hundred and forty-five.

> "During the battle they showed a lot of discipline, holding their formation stubbornly against our attacks. They may look odd but they're impressive soldiers, and big, taller than our men."

The officer leads Chen and other senior commanders over to the Romans. A detachment including Gan and Kang goes with them. The legionaries are silent and still, holding their shields with the bottoms on the ground and their swords pointing down. They're passive but ready to defend themselves. They expect to die and intend to charge a high price for their lives. It's what honour demands.

The Han soldiers stop a few metres away and stare. No one says a word. Both sides merely stand in silence, studying each other. They're like walls of sandstone on opposite sides of a river, in each other's presence but utterly separate. Arabesques of smoke curl up from the dying palisade.

With no idea of the language these strange people speak, the Romans can do nothing but wait. Kang takes a chance that the foreigners can understand Sogdian. He speaks to Marcus who's standing in front of the square, head high.

"Who are you people? Where do you come from? What are you doing here?

"We're soldiers from a great city in the west, far away. After a battle in Parthia – the other side of Sogdiana, we were taken prisoner. We escaped to Samarkand – joined Jir-Jir's tribe as mercenaries. I'm the commander. My name's Marcus Velinius Agricola."

Kang translates into Han what Marcus says. Assuming the Romans would not understand, Chen speaks in his own language.

"Protector-General, these men fought bravely. They're skilled soldiers. They come from far away so they probably don't have loyalty to the Hsiung-nu. They're only mercenaries. I think we should enlist them."

"I agree. Killing them would be a waste. We might as well try them out. If they're no good or start to cause trouble we can always sell them into slavery. They're not that many."

Chen speaks directly to Marcus, his tone hard and sharp, incomprehensible words coming out in staccato, like a stabbing sword. Kang translates into Sogdian,

"My officers tell me you're brave soldiers and fought well. Since you stopped fighting before we captured you, officially you're not prisoners. Therefore we can give you a dignified choice. You can join the Han army as auxiliaries. Because you're foreigners you'll be treated as mercenaries. The alternative is for you to be slaves. What's your decision?"

With no need to consult his comrades, Marcus says "We accept your offer. Mercenaries get paid. How much are you willing to pay?"

"Yes, you'll be paid. The amount will depend on how well you perform. In our culture we expect service first, before any discussion of reward. Show us what you can do and we'll decide on your compensation. We're not raiders like the Hsiung-nu so don't expect as much as Jir-Jir paid you."

"That's all right. We're not greedy. We know how to prove ourselves. When you see how much use we can be, you may feel generous. Where will you take us? You people don't seem to be from around here."

"We'll travel back east to the frontier of our kingdom, over the mountains and past the desert. But we'll not go yet. It's necessary to stay here until the spring thaw. The mountains are impassable in winter. Keep to yourselves until we're ready to leave. We'll give you food."

Chen gives the order that the Romans are not to be molested. With that the Han party turns and leaves the bemused mercenaries standing alone. They go back into the smoking ruins of the town to collect their belongings, passing rampaging troops running, looting and shouting, and throwing lighted torches into anything that burns.

The Romans save most of their tents. To make up the deficiency, they salvage felt from the Hsiung-nu's tents still intact. What's left of Jir-Jir's tribe, and that's not much, has fled into the steppe, except for prisoners who have been rounded up for transport to slavery. The Road will take them to the Chang-an markets.

Marcus sees a soldier in a Sogdian uniform carrying the strange weapon he saw in the battle.

"What's that weapon? How does it work?"

"It's a crossbow. Yun, come over here and explain how the cross bow works."

The Han soldier cannot speak Sogdian so his friend translates.

"It's more powerful than the ordinary bow. We invented it. It depends on a special trigger mechanism which allows the bow to be made much stiffer. The thrust is increased several times. We reduced the length of the arrow and made it thicker."

Marcus is ready to accept another instance of merit. These strange people who look so different must have a certain base of culture to invent such a formidable weapon.

"Thank you. It's very impressive. We've got nothing like that where I come from. I wonder when we'll get it."

ଔ

As they wait out the bitter winter months, Marcus and Kang are often seen together. The Confucian is keen to know about the odd and distant civilization whose soldiers have come such a long way. Marcus of course has no choice but to be interviewed at Kang's pleasure. It's enjoyable though, not a prisoner's interrogation but an opportunity to speak of a whole range of subjects where no harm to the interests of Rome is possible. He's proud of his culture and is happy to talk about it. Besides it offers a certain connection, however ephemeral, with the home he's been forced to leave. For a moment he's there in spirit talking about things that give it life.

They meet in the scholar's tent, at least once a day. Kang is content to spend hours satisfying a curiosity that seems to have no limit. The questions he asks are always in a quiet and respectful tone. A scribe is present, sitting alertly in the corner taking notes. The language of the conversation is Sogdian, so Kang has to translate for the scribe. Sometimes the poor man's face tightens as he struggles to keep up, his brush jerking in an uncharacteristic rush.

He's writing on parchment at Kang's instruction because the amount of information is too great for the more cumbersome bamboo slips. The scrolls are put into a special box after each interview and properly marked. It'll all be useful once the scholar returns to Chang-an. The Palace, maybe even the Emperor, will be interested. It's important to know about remote countries, especially one as powerful as this one seems to be. Maybe one day in the future actual contact will be made.

The tent's interior is lined with silk drapes of blue phoenixes on white which curve around the walls. Red lacquer boxes sit open on the ground, stuffed with rolls of parchment showing angular markings that Marcus takes for a type of script. Three braziers keep the cold's savagery at bay. It's comfortably warm inside.

Small tables for serving tea are on silk rugs woven with striding tigers. The strange beverage is served in small lacquer-ware cups, decorated with stylized flowers. It's an acquired taste but quite pleasant – producing a relaxing effect and stimulating conversation without the gross effects of wine.

Kang is confident and unruffled, always sitting with his hands in his silk sleeves. The folds are like billowing clouds. Surprisingly, the edges carry a pattern that's very like the key motif so common in Greek tradition. Where did that come from? Did Alexander's army bring it to the Sogdians who passed it along the Silk Road or was it invented independently? Kang doesn't know.

In a few weeks it seems appropriate to ask Kang about his own culture. So probing and charged with insight are the questions he's been asking about Rome that his answers should be revealing. Each question seems to have a background of profound knowledge of the human condition, its good points and bad. And all are suffused with a degree of humility and sense of wonder. To think of Kang as a sage is not outlandish. It's surprising to encounter someone like this. He might even be considered the equivalent of a Greek philosopher. He's seen nothing like him in Rome. Marcus has been reading again. Each night he unrolls different authors and stays up late. His interest is recharged by these meetings but also he wants to be prepared to discuss ideas with this unusual man.

As to be expected, Kang speaks about completely different traditions and customs – the Han monarchical form of government with its rigid conventional court, the intricate rules of interpersonal behaviour for example. But there's one aspect that takes Marcus off guard.

He's curious about how the Han society enforces order;

"What's the role the law in your country plays in ensuring appropriate behaviour?"

"We have laws of course; every society must, and we enforce them where necessary. But we're instructed by the saying of Confucius, our great Master: *If a man is correct in his own person, then there will be obedience without orders being given.*"

"But that's similar to what Democritus in our tradition asserted – *The persuasion of reason is a stronger inducement to virtue than law.*

"Does Confucius deal with the human tendency to go to extremes?"

"Certainly. His grandson wrote it down in one of the books of the Four Classics which every educated person must study. When the passions attain due measure and degree, that's harmony, or the moral order, which is the universal law in the world. It's called the Doctrine of the Mean."

"We have that too. The Greeks have an inscription on the temple at their main religious site saying "Nothing in excess" Aristotle took it up in his work, calling it the Golden Mean. He said a virtue is the midway point between two extremes."

It's an astonishing similarity of ideas, something impossible to have foreseen. Could there really be such sophistication so far from Rome? The thought is jolting. It's difficult to decide whether the resemblance diminishes the importance of Graeco – Roman civilization or whether it's a fascinating addition to it.

Since the escape, merit in foreigners is becoming progressively obvious. It can no longer be denied. Kang, particularly is worthy of respect. The realization is so much at variance with Roman attitudes that it's embarrassing to admit. It's confronting. But out here, far past the Hellespont, after so many misfortunes, thick-skinned pride has peeled away, allowing observation to inform opinion, uncomfortable though that may be. But not that uncomfortable; it's possible to feel interest, even admiration in what's encountered. It's a weird experience, but exciting – an adventure into the unknown, with more to come. Kang's revelation is like the harvest on one section of a farm; it'll undoubtedly be followed by others.

Marcus begins to speak faster, eager to hear more about the cultural connections. He stumbles over words and has to slow down. His Sogdian is reasonable but not completely fluent. In his agitation he knocks over his cup, spilling tea over the table. A slave quickly moves over to wipe it up. He's embarrassed and begins to apologise for his clumsiness but Kang interrupts him saying there's no need. Encouraged by the warmth of the man, he says,

"In your culture what is the most important instruction of all?"

"When asked if there's a single word for guiding behaviour, the Master replied it is '*shu*', reciprocity. Most people think he meant you should not impose on others what you yourself do not desire."

"We have that too. Isocrates said it, almost word for word. That's the foundation of our ethics. All morality stems from that and the law is meant to reflect it in a formal sense."

How can it be? It's impossible for someone this far from Rome to speak these thoughts; they're Greek. Kang acknowledges that he knows nothing of Mediterranean civilization yet he has just quoted three of the most important moral tenets of Graeco-Roman society – in almost exactly the same terms. They're in the books Marcus carries. Every educated Roman knows them. Even more impressive, the insights were produced by one philosopher; Western culture required several.

Kang gives the impression of one who actually lives the philosophy he speaks. Unlike Crassus who could quote at length and discuss with intelligence but then ignore most of it in the life he led.

Kang quotes another aphorism, this one cutting, all the more so because it's also what the Stoics hold.

"Faced with what is right, to leave it undone shows a lack of courage."

Marcus passes no comment on this one. His failure on that count is why the Eumenides pursue him, He doesn't want to go there with a comparative stranger, no matter how sympathetic.

As more discussions while away the weary hours between winter and the time for departure, the sense of alienation begins to fade, like the wound's pain in the healing process. There seems the possibility of a social connection with these people, not to be exaggerated of course, but still real. Living with them may not be as strange as first appeared, at least at the level where values lie. That could be built on over time to create positive relationships, even permanent ones. It'll not be easy; the greatest difficulty will be how to determine whom to trust. The telltale behaviour necessary for discernment must be learned because, as in all societies, it's often culture specific, based on conventions unknown to foreigners. In some cases it'll be easy though; the signs will be so basic that even a foreigner can understand them. Kang seems to be an example.

The conversation drifts into differences between people. Marcus admits that Romans are taught not to respect other nations, particularly those east of the Hellespont.

> "We call people who're not Greek or Roman barbari, which implies they're rough and uncultivated. The origin comes from when the Greeks first encountered people who spoke a foreign language. To them it sounded childish, like ba ba ba. I hope you're not offended."

> "No, I'm not. It's understandable. We Han feel superior too, especially to the Hsiung-nu. Throughout the years we've called our country the Middle Kingdom because we consider it to be the centre of the world. The borders we have with others are merely to differentiate those who have not yet acquired our culture. We expect in time they will learn it and become part of us. In the meantime they're benighted. If they're willing to learn we offer respect; if they are not we withhold it.

> "However that's not the full story. The Master teaches that men are close to one another by nature. They diverge as a result of repeated practice".

> "Does that refer only to people the Han have encountered or can it cover all people, even those you don't know exist?"

> "Without question, all people."

While the meaning of this is sinking in – so unroman a concept, the first case of a dissimilarity, Kang suggests they have a meeting with the Protector-General and the Colonel. Yesterday he picked up on something Marcus said about Roman military custom. The High Command has expressed an interest in it.

Marcus feels a pang of expectation when Kang mentions this. It'll be a good opportunity to strike up a rapport at top level. It's important to do this in order to ensure the best conditions for his cohort. If they stay down at a junior level they're more likely to be mistreated. At this stage it's impossible to guess just what the Han have in mind for them. In the case of the Hsiung-nu, Jir-Jir needed some extra troops and the Romans could play a useful role; the Han are so numerous this factor might not apply. Anyway, after his discussion today he feels confident he'll make a reasonably good impression. He looks forward to the meeting.

CHAPTER 16

On the way over to the Headquarters tent Kang asks Marcus to explain to his superiors the Roman custom for celebrating a victory. When they enter the grand structure, as large as Jir-Jir's he introduces him. Gan says;

"Yes I remember you. What have you got to say?"

"Kang Guiren asked me to tell you what happens if Romans win a big battle. If we do that, the commander is awarded what we call a Triumph. He's allowed to march his entire army through the city to a sacred hill on top of the forum – our market place. Along the way the troops carry pictures of the victory and the crowd applauds."

"Protector – General", Kang says, "This is what I was telling you about. Wouldn't it be worthwhile to have an artist paint pictures of our victory and send them to the Emperor?"

"What an excellent idea," Chen says. "It would impress the Court and help persuade the Emperor to pardon us. Nobody has ever done this sort of thing before."

Somewhat sceptical, Gan says, "Do we have an artist who can do it?"

"Yes we do", says Kang. "He's very talented and would do a good job. He could start right away. Should be finished by the time we start our journey back."

"Will the Emperor really be interested in a picture? He might think we concocted it like we did with the bogus order. It could get us into even more trouble."

Chen takes two steps towards Gan, his hands coming out of his sleeves.

"Protector General, everyone in the Palace will believe the picture is genuine. Why shouldn't they? It'll be accompanied by a detailed report. The report will verify it. We'll send senior officers to Chang-an who're beyond reproof to deliver it – at the highest level. The picture will add drama. There's no doubt the Emperor will be impressed. He'll love to actually see what the Far West is like. We must do it."

"All right, if you insist. I hope you're right. Tell the artist to come immediately with his equipment. And request the mercenary officer to stay here and help him with his side of the story."

Within minutes Xi Bingwen arrives with brushes and a scroll of parchment. With wild grey hair and sloppy clothes, thin and slightly stooping, he looks as unmilitary as it's possible to be. The poor man is a little out of breath, nervous, and without the slightest idea of what's expected of him. A slave brings over a table. Chan says;

"Xi Bingwen, you are to record our glorious victory in a painting. We will send it to the Emperor so he can appreciate our exploits more easily. Mercenary, would you please tell the artist how pictures are set out in a – what do you call it? Yes, a victory parade."

Marcus suggests that scenes of the battle be portrayed in separate paintings. Gan and Chen settle on the eight most prominent phases. Tentative and apologetic, Xi Bingwen asks permission to start out with rough sketches which he can expand later into proper paintings on silk cloth. That's agreed and he begins with the first scene to see if he has understood the instructions. It's clear from the few lines he draws that he has. Gan tells him to go ahead, aided by witnesses of the battle, including Marcus.

ᘓ

In a month, Xi Bingwen brings his finished work to Gan's tent for a viewing. He's taken special care for he knows he'll be punished if his painting is not up to Court standard. He had to go through several scrolls of silk to get it right. A mistake on silk can't be rubbed out.

Kneeling on the floor, he unfolds the first scene from a continuous roll encompassing all eight pictures, each separated by a wide border. Everybody gathers round, the Han with their hands in their sleeves looking pensive. All are impressed, Marcus included, even though the style is unfamiliar to him. Kang, who has studied art in Chang-an, says,

> "It's an excellent piece of work. Vitality resonates in the texture and fluidity of the brush strokes, as required in the proper style. The shape and line of the forms correspond closely with what's depicted. The colours are eminently suitable and the varied tones give a depth that draws the viewer in. I like the subtle layering. The most important thing is that it expresses the spirit of what he's painting. All in all it gives the right impression of the battle."

The painting is surprisingly detailed, showing individual Han soldiers manoeuvring outside the town and coloured banners flying from the turrets. Hsiung-nu warriors are on the wall, fully armed and shooting downwards. But it's the part near the gate that attracts the most attention. There, the Roman soldiers are standing in Testudo formation, their shields raised, alone and distinct from the others swarming around the battlements and the plains.

Through this work of art, which even Marcus, who has little interest in painting, thinks is superb, the Roman presence among these mysterious people is certified, given legitimacy, even permanence. The painting's silk is durable. It'll be seen by the supreme ruler, the Son of Heaven, probably kept in the Palace archives for ever. The Han must have archives; Rome does and these people seem just as sophisticated.

Like the Road, the painting forms a connection across the world, linking two civilizations so remote from each other that they exist in total isolation, like different planets. The artistic linkage will have a certain degree of longevity, if not immortality, for the Roman presence captured in paint will be studied by Han officials and scholars at the highest level, not only in this but also in future generations. They'll learn of the adventure that brought Roman legionaries so far from their home. Unknown publicly in their own country, they'll have a significance in a major foreign land, a place they've never seen but which they've been told has a capital city bigger than Bukhara and Samarkand combined. He's pleased by the thought. Out here so far away from home, in a situation that may take him even further away, the little touch of Rome made permanent in these foreign lands gives a certain solace to the pain of his deracination.

So far Gan has said nothing. He's content to let Colonel Chen run the conference for it's his idea that's being put into operation. Gradually though he's becoming more confident that the painting will do some good after all. Chen likes it but not all of it.

"That part there looks like the scales of a giant fish, Chen says. "It's an amazing sight but odd. Should we leave it in? It doesn't really contribute to the glory of our victory. And the eunuchs at the Court might think it's unrealistic."

If Marcus had understood the language he would have been dismayed.

"Yes, I think we should have it in, definitely." Kang says. "It adds to the authenticity of the record. Besides, the Emperor will be curious about it. It'll fuel his interest. I think in fact it'll create more praise for our achievement because it shows what strange challenges we had to face in penetrating so far into the unknown."

After some discussion, Chen relents and agrees to let it stay. Gan supports the decision. It's just as well because Xi Bingwen has gone to a lot of trouble and silk doesn't allow for any changes to be made. He would have to start all over again.

Much relieved but showing no emotion, Xi Bingwen unrolls the next scene. Han soldiers are holding crossbows. The lethal weapons are drawn to the full and aimed at the Hsiung-nu horsemen charging at them. They retreat to the wall. Again it's well received. The third scene however produces another spike in Marcus' interest. With drums beating, the Han surround the town. On top of the earthen wall the artist has painted a double wooden palisade. All of this is faithfully recorded, leaving no doubt that the fortification is Roman.

The rest of the silk scroll is rolled out to the approbation of the Han officials. In the remaining scenes the painting shows the investing of the town, the shooting of the Amazons on the tower and the beheading of the Sharnyu, all to the great credit of the attackers.

"This is good", Chen says, nodding his head. "We must send it to the

Emperor immediately, together with a full report. I'm sure he'll be impressed."

He asks Kang to translate into Sogdian.

"That was a good idea you… what's your name again?"

"Marcus Velinius Agricola"

"That's too hard to pronounce. What shall we call you?"

"You can just call me Marcus."

"That was a worthwhile idea you came up with. Thank you."

oȝ

The spring is sufficiently advanced for Chen to order the troops back onto the Road to tackle the great mountain barrier. Naturally he consults with Gan but only out of courtesy since it's a military matter. Gan, who's trying to keep his anxiety under control about what the Emperor's reaction will be, agrees it's best to get back to the fortress as soon as possible. Fear of the worst eats at his heart every day and he has difficulty sleeping. Visions of his execution come virtually every night. What will become of his family who'll have to live in disgrace for the rest of their lives and in poverty after all his wealth is stripped away by the state? He marvels at Chen's apparent lack of concern – takes some comfort from it.

The army is smaller now. The contingents from the vassal states on the western side of the big divide have gone home. Good progress is made, uninterrupted by Hsiung-nu raiders, for the victory has pacified the region, at least for now.

Marcus considers it worth trying to learn the language of his new employers. Hsiung-nu was too much of an effort for the rewards, but these people are more interesting, and language is the best entry into a culture. Kang is willing to help – and does what he can as a tutor but the task is daunting. No books exist so Marcus has to pick up words and grammar orally, bit by bit. There's not the slightest similarity with Latin; even Sogdian is closer. And the tonal requirements scramble his brain.

Anyway, with little else to do on the march, he persists. Ever of generous disposition, Kang praises his efforts. Eventually he learns enough to speak at a rudimentary level. It impresses Gan with whom he is striking up a rapport. He sees him as a gentle character and naturally friendly. Chen is more difficult; he seems a bit xenophobic, correct but distant. He would be a dangerous man to cross. It wouldn't be easy to have a discussion with him that contained even a scintilla of disagreement.

The other Romans are learning the language too; they know it's likely their engagement with the Han will be long term, probably for ever, so it's worth the effort. They didn't have to bother with Hsiung-nu since the few words of Sogdian they had picked up were good enough to get along. Here, no one except Kang knows any Sogdian.

The Road takes the home comers through the wild steppe again. For a while the direction is southward but then turns east. The potential boredom of the trek dissolves into the task of learning the difficult language and discovering more about the culture imbedded in it. Conversations with Kang, and sometimes with Gan, shed the layers, one by one, of preconceived notions about people outside the Roman imperium. It's not a comfortable process for one with strong prejudices, but evidence is a powerful opinion changer. Anyway, there's no doubt that his fate will be played out among these people. Better get used to it – become competent to live with it. That means effort, starting with the language.

Despite the challenge, it's a relief to come upon a civilized society – even such an unusual one. It generates energy for the task of making a life in it – maybe also tackling the art of happiness, which appears so remote now. Socrates seems to make the attainment of it a moral imperative, distinctly possible if it's worked at. The inference is that life is only unhappy because of moral failure. Unhappiness can therefore be a badge of shame; he's wearing it. Perhaps that's a bit harsh. The defeat at Carrhae was enough to make anyone unhappy. Even Socrates would allow for overwhelmingly adverse circumstances to have a determining effect. But in this case those circumstances have imbedded in them his failure of moral courage and that muddies the waters.

The battle is in the past; so is the slavery. There's an opportunity now to reassess life, see it in a more positive light. The wheel of fortune continues to revolve for him, sometimes into negative space, sometimes positive. The wise Solon was right to advise no one can be judged happy until their death – so ironic to think about it, for he gave the advice to King Croesus, the richest man in the world at the time, a man who, like Crassus, had a prosperous life but a dismal end at the hand of a military commander from the same country as Surena's.

What he can't get out of his mind is his moral lapse in the tent, can't separate it from the defeat no matter how much his reason tells him it would probably not have had anything more than a trivial effect. It magnifies the other times he failed to stand up for what was right. Even little cases come to mind, of minimal importance singly, but they add up. The Eumenides only visit him at night, but an underlying impression of their presence stays with him in the day, almost every day. It makes laughing seem awkward, even at jokes, for laughing is a release from guilt, something he's not entitled to.

The army marches towards the great mountain chain that Kang says has separated the Han nation from the rest of the world since before time. It's a barrier that all attempt with apprehension, and many fail to cross.

As the desiccated land yields to grass, puffy white shapes appear on the blue horizon. Soon they emerge as mountains, their peaks so high they host permanent snow. Marcus has only heard about the Alps, never seen them. Are they equally majestic or as dangerous? As the Road approaches the grassy lower slopes leading to the pass they must cross, he steels himself for the deprivations that Hannibal's troops had to suffer.

CHAPTER 17

The weather is clear and warm as the troops wind through the dense forest that hugs the lower slope. As they ascend, the trees grow at steeper and steeper angles, and conifers start to appear. It's really a walk at first but after several hours it becomes a climb, though not requiring skill. The temperature is noticeably dropping. They're coming close to the clouds which glide over the peaks in white and grey shapes, like ships. They tease the eye, covering everything then opening up patches of empyreal blue. A rainbow from a recent shower shines in the distance.

Little white flowers peek out of the underbrush. And large blossoms in clusters of brilliant reds, mauves and pinks on trees with twisted branches paint blocks of colour on the mountainside and in the valleys below. Monkeys sit in the taller trees and gossip about the strange intruders who have no right to come into their abode.

It's a relief from the grimness of the steppe. Here everything has a green presence, green in all shades and textures, moist and luxuriant green. It's hard; it's soft, sometimes threatening in its impenetrable mass, other times seductive and mysterious. Like siblings, its forms compete with each other for attention. At altitude, dwarf bamboo plants in pale green appear and eventually give way to the darkness of conifers. Meadows like lawns are revealed without warning, so smooth they could have been scythed by human hand. Sometimes they surround tumbling streams which carve the host rock as if with a white knife and crash in misting cascades. Often they're flat like balconies in the sky. On one of these the Romans spend their first night.

Next day's climb shatters any complacency that might have tempted a few during the journey so far. In three hours Marcus is above the snow line, bracing against icy winds that knife through his clothing into his bones and slap hard against his forehead. Within minutes it starts to ache furiously. He has to put his hand up to protect it; so does everybody else. The Road disintegrates into a miserly track, as if it has lost interest in the climbers, content to let them struggle along in lonely single file.

Little clouds, more like patches of mist, dart around at eye level like incoherent thoughts. An eagle glides among them, eyes on the lookout, its moving head a contrast with its wings. He looks into its eyes, so cold and menacing they seem like spear points. It sails on by and fades from sight around a peak, then reappears and disappears again. For a moment he thinks of the army standards and the times as a boy he and his friends climbed the hills of Rome looking for nests of the noble bird but not finding any. Then an image of the Eumenides emerges out of the cold air and he bends his head further against the wind.

Further up, the troupe enters the world of full cloud. It's not dense, but shifting in intensity, transforming the landscape into a magical state, where objects appear and dissolve as they're observed. Mysterious forces and strange happenings are possible here, even a passage to Hades for the unwary. Stark dead trees, like shape monsters, scratch at the vaporous air and disappear. Large shaggy brown creatures emerge out of the mist, vanish and suddenly reappear in different positions on the slope as if in a magician's trick. He's told their tails are used as tassels for the dreaded banners of the Hsiung-nu.

The Road has become part of the mountain's form, its rocky track here fully integrated with the peril of the heights. It winds tortuously up the face and stares across the lethal void to snow capped peaks that look like serpents' teeth. At this altitude the path shrinks to a precarious shelf, cut into the cliff. The Road is challenging the climbers to go into the jaws of doom, just as the Alps dared Hannibal's troops. He and his comrades have no choice but to take it up without flinching for they must impress their new employers. Nothing is as important as that.

Snow is blowing in the wind and covering the path in a slippery film. The temperature has dropped to a skin-shrinking low. Not a man is without fear of falling into the void that waits in silence like a giant predator. The soft falling snow blends with cloud to wrap a blindfold around the men, reducing visibility to fuzzy shapes. They're ordered to hold hands and move cautiously, small step by small step. Each expects a sudden pull from his neighbour at any time. There's just enough width for the wagons and chariots, but only just. Sometimes they have to be eased around sharp bends with ropes.

Marcus' breath starts to come in short gasps, driving shards of pain into his lungs. A strange headache breaks out, different from what's caused by the wind, and much worse. The pain wracks his entire skull. It's difficult to hold concentration, avoid the pull of the void that calls to him like Sirens on the shore. Several of his comrades are vomiting, doubled over in pain. So are many of the Han. He's never experienced anything like this before. However, the fear of the unknown at least is relieved when one of the Han says it's just mountain sickness that'll go away once they descend.

Suddenly, a horrifying shriek breaks out behind him. It's followed by others and an ugly crashing sound. He turns to see the outlines of a wagon and three Han soldiers bumping down the face. The cries of the doomed men echo down the slopes and into the valley, diminish and fold into the wind. The spirit of the mountain has claimed its due. And the Road is complicit.

Everyone stops. They're immediately risk averse, brave men terrified. The deaths are starker than usual, more foreboding in this other-worldly environment. It's as if they shouldn't be there, as if they're being punished for being out of place by a malevolent force that's protecting its forbidden domain. But in a minute or so, officers bark orders and the trek starts up again. Painful hours pass as the struggle with the mountain pushes the limits of endurance further than he thought possible.

As he climbs higher, the visibility opens up. The snow belt thickens into deep powder, stretching smooth and pure up the mountain slope, its contours shaped in clean curves by subtle shadows. Sheets of bright sunlight bounce off its crystals like the silk at Carrhae forcing him to look down where the snow is broken. It's harder to walk now as his feet sink in up to his knees. It's worse for the men ahead who have to walk in virgin powder up to their waists. If the climb weren't so arduous, if the venture into the unknown weren't so disquieting, he would have marvelled at the beautiful whiteness which wraps the mountain like a wedding dress. The fresh snow creates its own universe, a place of purity and innocence, but lurking within it unseen, is the constant threat of a sudden avalanche or a fall through a corniche.

Soon the clouds close in again and visibility drops to nil. At the front of his cohort he reaches the top of the pass but has to be told it's not just another ledge; the cloud masks everything. It's a huge relief to get there without Roman casualties – a few close calls but not even a minor injury. Now he and his comrades can start the descent. However it proves more difficult than the climb in many ways, although thinking of the finish line is a consolation. The withering headache fades with the lower altitude, but his thighs and knees are on fire and the cold is still wracking. Finally he and the others reach the warm grass of the lower slopes. On the flats, the first of the Han troops are marshalling, commands and regimental banners filling the air. It's pleasant there; the warmth brings his cold – shrunken skin back to normal. The passage now is just a memory of challenge, justifying a sense of pride and repeated telling with embellishment.

Once all the men have reached the flats and have rested a while, Colonel Chen orders the march to start up. After an hour or so, Marcus catches up with Kang who says,

> "That was a very successful crossing. Too bad about the wagon accident, but we had minimal casualties really given the risks. You might be interested to know we call that range the Roof of the World. People go up there for a spiritual experience. Its remoteness allows the mind to roam free from the strictures of everyday living. In our land we have many

mountains and they're the inspiration of poetry and calligraphy, our greatest art form."

CB

The Road soon loses its green mantle to the grip of the desert. Marcus is used to it now, able to see more in it. If he bends down to look at the sand closely he can see that it's made up of tiny stones, a splendid array of individual shapes in various colours – reds, blues, magentas, yellows, whites. They're like jewellery in microcosm, secretly beautiful in their own right. It just takes patience to see them, something most people aren't willing to muster. Little lizards dash around in the sun, camouflaged against the stony sand which appears beige even from a short distance.

In a few days they reach an oasis where the Road changes into a parkland of poplar trees, their leaves scintillating in the breeze like silver coins. Marcus asks Kang about the town built here.

"It's called Kashi, famous for its weekly markets, where thousands of people from all around come to shop. It's the furthest west we've extended our power. Although we go on punitive expeditions, we have no permanent interest on the other side of the mountains. The locals are a branch of the Hsiung-nu although some are Sogdians. A few, mixed. They're in a tributary alliance with us. Not an easy one though; it's always at a breaking point. As you can imagine we don't get on terribly well".

Townsfolk line the thoroughfare as the army marches past, staring at the Romans as if they're watching a freak show. It's mid day and the sweet spicy smell of roasting meat is in the air. But sight of the bizarre cooking on the side of the road squelches the appetite of even the hungriest Roman. Sheep heads are bubbling in murky water, thick wet steam rising from the pot. A sweaty cook pulls one out, tosses it on a wooden block and hacks it two with a small axe. One thwack and the two halves fall outwards. He throws one on a metal plate; it lands with a splash of fluid. The customer takes it over to a rickety wooden table and eagerly demolishes its steaming eyes, brains and cheeks.

Past the sheep heads, vendors are selling small birds in cages. They're singing so loudly they can be heard above the clatter of the soldiers and the babble of the locals. Perhaps it's a song of protest, or maybe they've transcended their condition. Anyway the Romans no longer have to think of themselves as captives.

> "That's the song of the nightingale," Kang says. "Its sweet voice has captivated the Han people since before time, especially emperors. The contrast between the beauty of its sound and the plainness of its brown body is a common theme in poetry."

Nearby a scruffy man with one eye is selling dogs, strange little animals Marcus has never seen before. They're beige with wrinkly black faces squashed flat, unlike the long snouted variety in Rome. Their eyes are striking – large, black, and bulging, giving them a trusting air. All are animated, jumping up in their cages and wagging their tails which are curled in a tight spiral. He asks Kang about them.

> "They're a special breed that goes back centuries. They were bred to be chunky, with flat muzzles. It gives them trouble breathing sometimes. Emperors favour them because they have such appealing personalities– friendly and whimsical. And they're good watchdogs, totally fearless. Even though they're too small to survive in a fight with big animals they will attack anything. Here they're sold for the table."

To be both a pet and a food seems a contradiction – a disturbing one.

> "I'd like to buy one, but for a pet. I know we must keep going but could you arrange that for me somehow? I'll repay you when I get paid."

> "Yes, of course. We're marching slowly. Don't worry about repaying. It won't be much."

Kang speaks to someone who disappears into the crowd and brings back a male – just past the puppy stage. He's animated, squirming around as he's being carried, trying to get down.

> "What shall I call him? What's a good local name?"

> "Well, Ting Ting might be all right. You'll have to carry him until we stop for the day. That'll be soon, when we're outside the town. Then he can travel in one of the wagons."

Marcus says as he picks up the little dog. Ting Ting settles down in his arms, wagging his curly tail, and seems content – at least willing to be carried now. Within a few steps he feels a warm wetness spread over his bare arms.

☙

The Road leads the troops out of Kashi into the desert. Soon they come to a small oasis where they set up camp for the night. He keeps Ting Ting with him as the tents are pitched and gives him his first feed – raw sheep meat meant to be cooked for the army. It disappears in a few seconds. That night he sleeps in his new master's tent.

Next day he puts his little friend in the baggage train and joins the rest of the cohort. In a short time the Road comes to mountains striking due east. Wrinkled drainage channels give them a personality of benign old age. The Road continues parallel, keeping watch, perhaps in awe of their wisdom so much more ancient than its own.

Marcus' language is improving and he's now able to hold a conversation with Kang without too much Sogdian.

"Can you tell me about this place?"

"That range is the Heavenly Mountains. It'll be with us all the way to Gaochang, like a guardian. We're passing through the Taklamakan, the most dreaded desert in the world. Countless people have died in it. The name means 'If you go in you never get out'. People say stone demons emerge out of it and eat caravans whole. The Emperor sent troops in once and the stone demons ate them all.

"Sand storms blow up without warning and cover everything. They completely change the landscape so you'll lose your bearings unless you're an expert. It's said there're hundreds of rich cities, full of gold and precious jewels buried out there. Treasure hunters have been searching for years. So far they haven't found any, but they keep trying."

They continue to march together, discussing the wild terrain, so removed from the comforts of Rome and Chang-an. It's the remotest place he's ever been in and the strangest, far from any human presence whatsoever, a land entirely of itself, an entity with its own rules. On their left the Heavenly Mountains are their chaperone, stern and constant. Reddish bedding, with white patches and green inclusions lies in wavy layers across vertical wrinkles. Soft dust in the air covers them in a subtle gauze. During a lull in the conversation, he lets his vision slip out of focus, allowing faces to appear on the slopes, their eyes narrow and cheekbones high.

Further down the sides, outliers take on supernatural forms that come alive in the shifting haze as reference points disappear. At the base of one a giant dragon sleeps on the sand ready to devour any traveller who wakes it. He knows the Hsiung-nu worship the dragon; so do the Han. It's a creature of power and authority.

On the flat ground that stretches to the right as far as the eye can see, salt pans and isolated tufts of camel thorn form a ragged pattern on the stony sand. The Road is taking them into an otherworldly place, a retreat for ascetics. Its severity beckons the mind towards the sacred and liberates it from mundane distraction. Here it's possible to go through a portal into a state entirely divorced from conventional life. Perhaps it's the Road's spiritual home, a place where it takes travellers so they can begin to understand the meaning of its mission.

Kang points out that the Road is now passing across lands never fully subdued by the Han armies, lands where death and destruction can suddenly swirl around caravans like quixotic gusts of desert wind. It's no wonder that tales of sand demons and other magical figures have been animating the imagination of caravaners for years. Marcus is intrigued by something he's just noticed.

"What is that tall thin structure just off the Road to the left?"

"That's a beacon tower, made from rammed earth. It's part of an early warning system. We've built a chain of them from here to the borders of our Kingdom. They're the scariest buildings this side of the Great Mountains. When the smoke comes out of them, it means the Hsiung-nu are about to attack. Those devils are a constant threat to caravans, also settlements. They can come out of the haze at any time – leave no one alive, unless they're on a slaving raid. However, our army is too big to attack, so don't worry. They'll leave us alone"

"It looks impressive. We have nothing like this where I come from. How does the system work?"

"Whenever a threat breaks out, each tower signals to the next one – wood fires at night, black smoke from wolf dung in the day. The dung – it's quite a chore to collect it, produces a colour different from normal fires, so there's no confusion when that smoke is seen. It means danger pure and simple."

The troops have to go over a subsidiary range striking outwards from the Heavenly Mountains. The Road winds through a pass down to a river and onto a wide plain. Its surface is sculpted in sand waves whipped up by the wind. Jagged shores edge it and sandstone cones rise up like islands. It looks like a vast inland sea enclosing random landforms. Not a scrap of vegetation intrudes on its lifeless form.

While the Road is crossing the sculpted plain, little puffs of dust begin to dart around like unruly smoke. Wind start to suck up particles and swirl them, first slowly, then faster, in a torque like a spinning top. Kang says

"We have to take cover. Wrap yourself in what ever you can find and stay close to the ground."

The wind builds to a shriek and darkness descends over the desert; new waves form on its surface. They're in motion now but soon they'll stabilize and change the terrain once again. Visibility plunges to blizzard level. Dust particles so fine they invade the pores come in endless blasts. Marcus pulls his tunic over his head and lies down curled up in a ball. Though uncomfortable, flying dust stinging his exposed flesh like wasps, it's nothing like the tornado at Carrhae. Three hours and then slowly it subsides into a thin orange shield which the sun eventually pushes through. Brown lumps on the sand begin to stir and men emerge as from a chrysalis. Ting Ting is safe in the baggage train. Marcus feels guilty that he didn't go back to look after him, but there was no time. He does now and finds the poor little dog terrified but unharmed; fortunately someone had covered him during the storm. The locals call it a Black Hurricane.

❧

The march starts up again.

One by one, oases come and go, each struggling to survive in the grim

Taklamakan. They're like knots unevenly tied in a long string. There would be no crossing without them. It's just as well that whoever is navigating knows which track to follow. The Road is in its mischievous mood, leaving false clues to lead the unwary to perdition. Since time before reckoning its heartless fraud has claimed many victims, desperate men walking into endless wastes, their hopes becoming more and more frantic until thirst overwhelms them and they lie down to die in the cruel sand. Spurious paths are not the only delusions. Shimmering blue sheets on the distant sand near the horizon beckon the visitors, promising life – giving water only to fade into nothing on approach.

Suddenly a frisson spreads through the troops like the stirring of poplar leaves. A black plume is rising from the beacon tower just ahead, straight as a pole. A halt is called and the leaders hurry to Colonel Chen's chariot. Kang brings Marcus over. The commander of the beacon tower is summoned.

"Commander," Chen says, "Which direction did the signal that set your's off come from?"

"Due west, sir."

"That settles it. Other Hsiung-nu tribes have heard what happened at the Talass River. They're probably heading to Gaochang. With us away, the fortress is weakly defended. The dogs have always wanted to eliminate that thorn in their side. If we have to we'll send the cavalry on ahead but we'll need the infantry if we're going to chase them off."

Order a march at the quickest pace," he says to his second in command.

"They'll be a lot faster than us, probably ride all night. At least we're ahead, impossible to know by how much. And they'll have to go out of their way to pass us by – won't want to run into us. If we make good time we have a chance of getting there soon enough. The fortress should be able to hold out for at least ten days."

Gan is horrified. "My wife and daughter are there. We must make it."

Despite the arguments in the past and their contrasting personalities, he's relieved that Colonel Chen is here. There's a time when aggressiveness is worth more than his kind of mildness and it's now. But he's still hideously worried, struck silent by the enormity of the peril. He always knew the dangers of the West but until now they were not as immediate, or personal. All he can do is remain silent, leaving everything to Chen, and hope. It's hard to keep his apprehension under control, especially as he has no role to play in the drama to distract him.

Gan is not the only one worried; most of the army have families at the threatened outpost. The anxiety pushes everyone to a heart-thumping focus on getting there before it's too late. The foot soldiers pick up pace, more than they, even the officers, think possible. Although they're not particularly concerned, the Romans have to keep up. Fortunately their condition allows it, uncomfortable though it is.

Marcus wonders if they'll they meet any familiar Hsiung-nu faces, any of the old crowd. There was never a lot in common – but they were the ones who provided that first taste of freedom. Odd, this life as a mercenary, switching sides. Not like being in a national army. Anyway the remnants of Jir-Jir's force may not be part of this group. He hopes so. A soldier working for hire doesn't have a choice but he has a preference.

Chen demands an even faster march. Without demur, the men push their speed past what they've ever dreamed of, like athletes in the finals of the games at Olympia where pride of city state rests on their performance – only more so, as the lives of their loved ones are at stake. Determination is overcoming pain, leaving it behind without a thought. It's still a race they can win; they just have to arrive before the fortress is overwhelmed. Much depends on the tenacity of the small force there, but, as everyone knows, it can't hold out for long. Each beacon tower they pass has a black plume. Thoughts of the savagery that'll take place if they're late scream in their brains. Although Kang has no family in the West, his natural empathy shines through. It's reflected in his subdued demeanour, quiet and tense, facial muscles unmoving.

While Marcus and his cohort are understandably disengaged from the anxiety, they can't help but notice the grimness in the faces of their new comrades. They too feel the tension in the air as the march quickens.

CHAPTER 17

cs

The army descends into a widespread depression that concentrates the heat like the pit ovens people use out here. But the pace doesn't slacken. On the left, the Flaming Mountains appear. Anxiety linked to hope rises like an ocean swell as the rammed earth walls of Gaochang come into view. Yak tail banners are moving jerkily on the horizon. The Hsiung-nu are surrounding the town; they're probing to find a weakness to breach. But they haven't found one yet, although the battering rams have partly dislodged sections of the wall. The garrison is holding out, but under extreme duress.

Marcus can see Han soldiers on the top of the walls pouring hot oil and boulders onto the attackers and shooting them with crossbows, but they're being thinned out with salvos of arrows shot from below. Men are tumbling down in clusters. The reinforcements have arrived in time, but only just.

Chen has decided on a plan of attack while they marched, mounted scouts having gone ahead and reported on the disposition of the enemy. He orders a halt and calls the commanders together. Marcus is required to attend. The Romans are to support the Han infantry on the right wing. There's to be no retreat under any circumstances. Every man must fight to the death.

As the relief army approaches, some of the Hsiung-nu react, but the main force is slow to abandon the siege. They're like flies feeding off a carcass, reluctant to leave even in the face of danger. Eventually though, they turn away from the town and confront the Han as their cavalry charges towards them across the hot plain. Most have already discharged their arrows so only a small hail of missiles descends on the Han. The besiegers draw their swords and a melee of slashing and shouting erupts across the plain.

The allied infantry begins its attack, swarming across the stony sand into the oasis. Marcus leads his men in the Testudo formation, a battering ram smashing into the enemy cavalry. Arrows bounce off the scales like hail. The horses shy away from what seems to them a giant monster. Nearby Han soldiers are amazed by the sight. So are the Hsiung-nu, who fall back momentarily. They think something supernatural is attacking them, a colossal monster with a hundred feet. They recover though as soon as they make out the individual soldiers, but still retreat.

Romans call the formation a Testudo, their word for tortoise, because the interlocking shields look like the scales that form the creatures carapace. It lumbers over the land like a tortoise, slowly and exorably, its shell designed to protect it against predators.

Fierce hand to hand fighting swirls around the fortress, neither side prevailing. Collapsing the Testudo, the Romans cut their way forward with thrusting gladius and push the enemy back. The Han cross bows begin to have effect and the Hsiung-nu take heavy casualties. But they have a lot of fight left in them. Still mounted, they swing their long swords at close range with animalistic fury. Their resolution stops the Roman advance.

Marcus is at the front of the cohort with Gaius beside him. They carve a salient into the enemy mass and the Romans begin to make progress again. In the heavy fighting, three Hsiung-nu gang up on Marcus, separating him from his comrades. He fends them off but one of them lands a blow on his helmet knocking him out temporarily. He falls to the ground and while he's recovering his senses the Hsiung-nu move in to finish him off, their horses stamping impatiently. His shield dropped, he rolls over on the ground and uses his short gladius to parry the slashing swords coming at him from all sides. Desperately trying to save himself he fears he's done for. All he can do is keep rolling, present a moving target until finally someone gets him.

Gaius sees his friend through the chaos. He rushes over and, standing over him, smashes the first Hsiung-nu's horse with his shield with such force that the animal is stunned. The blow, which only Gaius could deliver, causes its rider to lean over, almost breaking the bond between horse and man. Seizing the vulnerability, the Roman runs him through.

He does the same to a second. Marcus gets up, pulls the third one off his horse and stabs him with Owl's Head.

"Thanks Gaius" Marcus yells and runs back to the fray.

After three hours, about as long as soldiers can fight at peak form, especially in this heat, the tide turns and the Hsiung-nu begin to flee. Most escape around the back of the fortress and gallop off into the desert, yak tail standards sinking into the sandy horizon. It's a complete victory and Gaochang is spared. But everyone knows what a close call it was. A few more days on the Road would have sealed the fate of the town and all the families in it. The uncertainty is likely to have titillated the heartless Communicator.

As the Romans trickle back towards the place where their camp is to be set up, Marcus seeks out his saviour.

"Gaius my friend, thanks for what you did out there. You saved my life. I owe you. If we were back in Roman territory you would get the corona civica for that. No doubt. Absolutely no doubt. Here you just get my thanks – for ever."

He gives the big man a long hug.

"Marcus you would have done the same for me. You don't owe me anything. Life-long friends don't owe each other. Let's have a drink."

"Good idea. I need it."

They take a swig of the Hsiung-nu poison from a leather pouch Gaius has carried with him. The strong liquor hits their throats in a pleasant jolt.

Ↄ

The next day, Chen summons Marcus to the fortress. When he arrives he's led to the great hall; its mud brick walls and high ceiling give some respite from the heat. Outside it's intolerable. To conserve the cool, the windows are small, letting in only a miserly amount of light. No one wants to add the heat of torches so the hall is sombrely dark.

Gan, Chen and Kang are there, sitting cross-legged in silken splendour on a polished wooden dais at one end of the rectangular room. Gan is in the middle on a slightly raised rostrum. Military banners flank the dais like poplar stands. The hall is full of people, all silent and impassive, sitting cross-legged on the stone floor. A space of at least five paces separates the dignitaries from the audience. Gan gives Marcus a slight nod which seems friendly and a sentry takes him down one side.

After several rows, he sees women, presumably wives and daughters. They're sitting about a third of the way back. One particularly is noticeable – a pretty girl who seems around twenty. In a few steps he gets a good look at her, more like a stare. It seems she notices him; perhaps there's a suggestion of friendliness. Probably it's just his imagination.

She's sitting in the row behind the one he's is led to, beside an older woman, probably her mother. Several rows are taken by women. The rest of the hall is occupied by about two hundred officers. There's no indication what the occasion is, but undoubtedly it's important.

After a silence long enough to be eerie, Gan begins to speak, announcing that this is to celebrate the great victory at the Talass River and the saving of Gaochang.

> "It's also to honour the courage of our soldiers. As the representative of the Emperor in the Far Western Commanderie, I'm authorised to award honours for bravery and will do so today."

A number of men come up one by one to receive awards. Marcus hears his name called. Somewhat bemused he walks up to Gan.

> "You and your men were observed to fight well in the action at Gaochang. I'm pleased to declare that henceforth you'll be officially integrated into our army. You Romans will be given permanent residence here and appropriate accommodation as soon as it's built. In the meantime you'll continue to live in your tents".

Kang seems pleased, Chen inscrutable.

Marcus mumbles a thankyou and returns to his seat, looking at the girl again but trying not to be obvious, which of course he is.

After the awards ceremony has concluded, a name is called out and a soldier comes forward, looking dejected. Chen says

"Wu-Jiang, it's been reported that at the Battle of Gaochang, you showed cowardice in the face of the enemy. You turned and tried to run away. This is particularly disgraceful since we were trying to save our families. For that you'll be punished with ten years' imprisonment."

Marcus remembers Wu-Jiang who was in a unit fighting alongside the Romans, in fact got to know him a bit afterwards. The report is wrong. There must be some mistake.

Before Chen has finished his criticism, Marcus leaps up as if stung by a wasp and quickly walks to the front.

"That's a false report, Colonel Chen, completely false. I was there at the time and saw Wu-Jiang. He did fall back with some of his men, that's true. But it was only a feint to draw the Hsiung-nu in. As soon as they were extended, he attacked with great courage and routed them. Instead of being condemned he should be given an award for bravery."

Chen's face tightens and his long sleeves twitch. He says in a loud voice, almost a shout,

"How dare you interfere with our proceedings. This has nothing to do with you. You're a foreigner. Be silent and sit down or you'll get into trouble. Wu-Jiang must be punished for what he did and that's all there is to it."

"But Colonel Chen, the report you're basing your decision on is wrong. The facts don't support it. I don't know why someone would say such a thing. I can only suspect there was a personal motive behind it. Anyway Wu-Jiang is not a coward. He's a brave man."

"Be quiet"

"I cannot just stand by and see an innocent man condemned. I implore you to at least order a formal investigation into the case. Give Wu-Jiang a chance to defend himself, bring forward witnesses who saw what happened. I'm one. There's a great injustice being done here."

"You've gone too far, mercenary. I'm satisfied with the verdict. It's not your place to question it. You're a foreigner, foreign, foreign, foreign," he says jabbing a finger that suddenly jumps out of his sleeve like a striking snake. "You've insulted the Empire. Cheng – Jing, arrest this man."

Marcus is stunned. Like a puddle of winter water in a flash freeze, he's suddenly changed his state – once again. Just a few words did it, words which he need not have spoken. Or was there a necessity standing in wait for the time to act? However fast the reversal happened, its cause lay in the past, in his wounded soul. He takes a deep breath and stands tall. As two soldiers lead him down stone stairs to the dungeon he feels strong and clean, as if he has just completed a healthy exercise and washed in the Pierian spring.

CHAPTER 18

H e's pushed roughly into a small lightless cell. Nothing is in it except a bucket in the corner, no bed, no chairs, just a blank mud brick enclosure with no windows. The door slams shut with a harsh rattle and a key scrapes in the lock. He's been deprived of his liberty before but never locked up. On one level it's frightening, being alone in the dark with no idea for how long – people grow blind without light after a while, but on another, its horror is assuaged by the events in the hall. His sprits soar out of the cell as he savours the one thought that comes to him over and over again. He's done what was needed to placate the Eumenides. Now he can breathe without a clamp on his heart. Deep down at the spiritual level he feels a new sense of freedom. He doesn't care about his incarceration. It's sure not to last long; something will happen to release him.

The night passes well, though he has difficulty sleeping on the stone floor. The torturing birds don't appear. While the tormentors didn't come every night, the threat was never absent. This time is different; he knows they'll leave him in peace now.

When he wakes up, the warden comes to move him to another cell – doubtless at the behest of Kang. At least now there's a small window, simple but reasonably comfortable bedding, a small wooden chair, and visitors. Gaius is the first, bringing his books. And with him is Ting Ting. As soon as he puts him down, the little dog rushes around Marcus wagging his curly tail and making squeaking sounds. The warden brings in some straw and tosses it in a corner. He seems a bit friendlier than he was last night. Gaius says;

"Marcus, we're doing all we can to get you released. Not much we can do though. I spoke to Kang. He's sympathetic. That damn colonel's an idiot. Shit, he should know we need you if we're expected to fight for them."

"Thanks for that Gaius. I want you take charge of the cohort until I get out of here. Be sure to keep the men busy. I don't know when they'll release me, but I can't see it's in their interests to keep me in forever."

"By the way Marcus, why did you have to antagonise him like that? So what if one of their men gets falsely accused. We don't owe them anything."

"I felt I had to do it, as simple as that."

"All right, your decision, but it seems odd to me. Anyway, we'll do all we can to get you out of here."

He hears the scratching of a key and the clank of the door opening. Ting Ting barks furiously and runs to the door. Kang appears. Gaius says hello and leaves.

"I'm very sorry for this, Marcus. Colonel Chen's hot tempered and rash sometimes. I've looked into the Wu-Jiang affair. You're right. He was unjustly accused. There was somebody out to get him. He played to Chen's prejudices. He's an extreme nationalist, despises everyone but the Han.

"Wu-Jiang comes from the minority nation in the south west. He's spoken out for the rights of his people sometimes, perhaps a little too forcefully. Chen doesn't like that. You know we have a lot of minorities in our country. Relations with them aren't always easy."

"It's good of you to come, Kang. I appreciate it. What d'you think can be done?"

"It's a difficult situation. Colonel Chen has taken a stand – can't back down without losing face. You must understand face is very important in our culture. It's how we're judged.

"It's a good thing that the Protector-General is a wiser man. He can take a broader view. But unfortunately we must let some time go by, work quietly in the background for a while. It wouldn't be prudent to push things yet. In time the issue won't be as sharp. Maybe some pretext can be found to get you out. Then Colonel Chen won't appear to change his mind."

"How much time?"

"I don't know. We'll have to wait and see. I'll try to get the Protector-General to review the case, but he won't cross his Deputy. Especially since he's such a strong- willed character. The way Colonel Chen put it in the Great Hall was that your intervention was a type of treason. That's very serious. Clearly he overstated it but that impression is still in the minds of the people who were there. Time is needed to dull the memory, allow an adjustment in perception. I'm afraid you'll just have to be patient."

"All right. I've got no choice. I still have my books to keep me occupied. And Ting Ting. Why was what I said taken so badly?"

"You shocked Colonel Chen when you spoke to him like that. He's second in command – a man of authority. In our culture it's disrespectful to confront authority directly. An indirect approach, through an intermediary, would have been expected if you had something to say. You must realize how seriously we take the need to obey the rituals of behaviour – what Confucius called 'li'.

"At first, Colonel Chen might have ignored your breach of etiquette because you're a foreigner. But when you persisted, as if you considered yourself his equal, it cracked his patience. His reaction was aggravated by his dislike of anything foreign. He's a fervent patriot who wants to maintain our traditional culture. He won't tolerate any attitudes from abroad that might sully its purity. He fully believes that the Han are the superior race, with others in diminishing status the further they are from us."

"I consider him unwise at times, and so does the Protector-General, but he's a competent military man. Very shrewd and calculating – a good man for war, but not talented in the ways of peace."

"Will you visit me from time to time?"

"Of course I will, my friend. In the meantime I'll do all I can. The way forward is to persuade the Protector General to influence Colonel Chen. However he's very cautious, concerned about ensuring he's supported. He won't want to upset the Colonel."

The jailer comes in and says there're two other visitors outside, waiting, very important ones. Kang says it's time for him to leave. As soon as he departs, two women appear. One of them is the girl, the other older – probably a governess.

"I was at the Great Hall yesterday and saw what happened, "says the girl. "I'm upset that Colonel Chen treated you so badly. My father has always taught me that the most important moral quality is benevolence, as we call it. As a foreigner you may not understand, but trying to help someone in trouble is part of it. You shouldn't be punished for what you did."

"Who's your father?"

"He's the Protector-General."

"Oh … I'm honoured that you should take an interest in my case. It's very kind of you. What's your name?"

"Meilin. I've heard yours, but it's hard to pronounce"

"You can just call me by my first name, Marcus. That should be easy."

She smiles at that and he does too. They speak for a while, until her companion, a jolly-faced woman as round as a rice bowl, says it's time to leave.

"Thank you for coming. Is it too much to ask if you'll come again?"

"Yes, I will" she says and goes out the clanking door.

This is overwhelming. Meilin has the grace and beauty of a goddess. Her face is as smooth as the silk dress she wears. True, the disparity of their positions encourages that conclusion, but even so, she's exceptional. Somehow, her presence takes away the sting of prison.

It's hard not to feel regret that so suddenly she's replacing Aurelia, and a touch of disloyalty. But how is it possible to keep Aurelia foremost in mind when there's no chance of getting back to Rome? Even Odysseus wouldn't make it home under these circumstances.

Meeting her banishes the loneliness of confinement. Not that it's solitary, for Ting Ting is there – even sleeping at the bottom of the bed. There's a bond now. At first it was based on food, but it's grown beyond that. He's sure of it.

"She's very pretty don't you think Ting Ting? There's a deep humanity there too – must be. Why else would she have come?"

Ting Ting sits patiently, listening to him speak, from time to time cocking his head to show he's paying attention. His large bulbous eyes look up, glistening in innocence.

ଔ

Meilin and the rotund woman climb up the dark stone steps to the ground floor of the fortress. They go down a wide corridor with small windows, past the Great Hall and up another flight of steps to Meilin's bed chamber. It's in a suite of rooms in the southern tower reserved for the Protector-General and his family. With a sigh of relief as if she's just been through a challenging but exhilarating experience, Meilin throws herself backwards onto the bed, arms outstretched. Sitting down beside her, the woman says "Meilin, I think you're a little intrigued by that foreigner."

"Oh, I don't know Ping. Maybe I am a bit. He's good looking and his eyes seem kind. Did you notice how he looks after that little dog? He's so good to him, even has him on his lap some times. They seem to have a very close relationship. I can't imagine any of Colonel Chen's soldiers showing so much affection for a dog.

"But it's really the unrighteousness. I just can't see why Colonel Chen was so harsh. We aren't cruel people, like the Hsiumg nu. We're supposed to be civilized."

"Be careful Meilin. Colonel Chen's a powerful man – won't tolerate criticism. Besides it's not good for you to be seen with a foreign man."

"I know Ping. But I can't always do what those boring Palace people say. Besides, what if that soldier wasn't a coward? Was falsely accused like the foreigner says. Wouldn't that be terrible? It's not because I really care about the foreigner as an individual; I hardly know him. I'm only interested in the principle. Why shouldn't I? I'm my father's daughter."

"You always were headstrong. I know you want to do the right thing but being idealistic can get you into trouble. Be prudent."

"Will you support me Ping? You always have. I want to see him again. Find out more about his background. Why he spoke out against Colonel Chen so I can go to Father for help. What do you say?"

"Of course, my dear. You know you can count on me, always. We'll go in secret. No one must know. I'll bribe the prison guard not to say anything."

"Thank you Ping. You're so kind." She rushes over and hugs her.

ↃↃ

Meilin and Ping come to the jail cell the next day. Marcus has the warden bring chairs in for them.

"Why did you stick up for Wu-Jiang? He's not part of your army."

"I did it because I saw him in the battle and knew he was a brave man, not the coward they said he was. It doesn't matter that he's not part of my army as you say. He's still a soldier, a sort of comrade in a way since we were both fighting on the same side."

"I see. You actually saw him on the battlefield?

"Yes I did. My cohort, sorry my comrades, and I were close by and could see everything."

"Where do you and your comrades come from? I have never seen people like you before – nobody here has… "

"We come from far away to the west, on the other side of the great mountain barrier. From a great city called Rome. It's a very rich city; the women wear elegant clothes and have lots of jewellery. We were in a battle and got taken prisoner. After a while we escaped and went along the great Caravan Road. We became mercenaries for the Hsiung-nu". Meilin gasps, her eyes opening wide. "We had to, had no choice. But afterwards, we joined up with your father's army and that's how we got here."

"Why does Kang like you so much? He seems a good friend of yours."

"I don't know. We do get along well. He's an impressive scholar; I too am interested in literature and philosophy although he's much more learned in his than I am in mine."

"What are those scrolls at the end of the bed?

"They are the classics of my tradition. I read them from time to time. They keep me in touch with my culture."

"Oh. You can read then?

"Yes. But not in Han"

She laughs and says it's time to go.

♋

Meilin comes often, soon every day, and she and Marcus talk about things that people who want to get to know each other do. Their conversations are becoming more and more personal. One day she arrives without Ping and that seems a watershed. The governess never comes to the cell again. She stays outside, ready to fend off the unwanted.

Weeks pass by with no sign of release. It's been two months since his arrest but Marcus is not depressed. On the contrary, Meilin's visits are enough to make life worthwhile. Little Ting Ting, the books and thoughts about her keep him entertained when she's not there. Besides Gaius and some other officers come frequently and keep him abreast of what's going on in the cohort. Kang comes too.

His relationship with Meilin evolves. Her feelings have progressed past the stage of moral indignation. She's intrigued by the exotic world he leads her into when he speaks of his background and the great western city with its sophisticated ways. She's always had an enquiring mind, even adventurous. And he seems to combine a natural self assurance and strength with a certain warmth – not bad looking either, even though very different from what she's used to.

With him there was never any need to evolve. He fell in love from the beginning. It was easy; she's very attractive – her face, though obviously different, has the symmetry that underlies all things beautiful. Eventually the two speed evolution merges and both declare their affection, he unreservedly, she with some caution.

One afternoon after a visit, as Meilin and Ping walk up the stone steps, she whispers that she wants to say something in the strictest confidence. When they get to the little room outside her bed chamber, she says

> "Ping I think I'm falling in love with that Roman. He says he loves me and I believe him. What am I to do?"

> "Oh my poor child. This is going to be fraught with difficulties. I'm happy

226

for you all the same. It's a gift to find someone you can truly love. I wish I had been so lucky. "

"He's asked me to marry him. Do you think that's possible?"

"Your father's going to be a problem. I know he's a kindly man but he has aspirations to go to Lanzhou and maybe one day even to Chang-an. How can he be seen with a daughter married to a foreigner, especially one so unusual? I don't know what to say."

"That's all right. I don't expect you to say anything. It's a relief just to know you're sympathetic. Anyway we have to get him released first. I spoke with Kang Guiren the other day and told him about us. He was surprised. Why wouldn't he be? But, like you he was sympathetic. He likes Marcus and is trying his best to help him. I hope he'll be an ally when I speak to Father about us."

"What would Marcus do once you're married?

"He commands a brigade of troops that even Colonel Chen says is valuable. Besides, Kang Guiren thinks he's highly intelligent and would make a good adviser. I think he'll find a place."

"Where would you live? Would you follow your father to his next posting?"

"I don't want to go to either of those capital cities he talks about. It's too busy there. I love the country, and the tranquillity. I've spent my whole life out here with nature. I'd hate to be cooped up in that stifling society with all the rules. How could I get along with those women who've been brought up there? They'd never accept me. I'd always be trying to prove myself and they'd be laughing behind my back. No, if he goes, I'll stay here where I belong."

⌇

One day Kang arrives with Meilin. This is unusual. They've never come together before. Kang says,

"Meilin has spoken to her father and I have too. We think it's a propitious time to do something about your case. He and Colonel Chen have just been notified that the Emperor is so pleased with the victory over the Hsiung-nu that he's forgiven them.

"Even better, he's made the Protector-General a full Marquis and Colonel Chen a Marquis of the Imperial Domain. That's a lesser title but still important. Both have been awarded incomes of three hundred households. They'll also receive a hundred catties of gold each. It's a life changing event.

227

Colonel Chen will be in a good mood. This could be just the thing we need to get him to see your case differently."

"Marcus, my father has decided to hold a hearing into your case. Kang Guiren has graciously agreed to represent you if you wish."

"Thank you Kang. I certainly would. When's the hearing?"

"In a week. We've got just enough time to round up witnesses. It'll go better for you if we can prove that Wu-Jiang was not a coward."

"I'll speak to Gaius and see if any of our men saw Wu-Jiang. They may be judged to be biased but maybe their testimony will carry some weight. D'you think that any of Wu-Jiang's comrades would speak out, or would they be afraid of offending Colonel Chen?"

"We'll have to see, and hope they will."

CHAPTER 19

The day of the hearing arrives. Marcus is led into the Great Hall which is not full as it was before. In fact it is cavernously empty. This is not a public hearing, but one held in camera by Gan who acts in the capacity of a magistrate. Colonel Chen, and four senior officers are there too. The Protector-General alone will make the decision, but he's astute enough to know that he should have the support of the others, or if not, at least not their active opposition.

Gan and his colleagues are sitting cross-legged on the wooden dais, passive and pyramidal in their draping silks. Gan is in the middle, not on the rostrum this time. A spectral silence heightens the anxiety Marcus can't help feeling. These men are so remote, so obdurate, that making a positive impression on them seems virtually impossible. His advocate is the only hope. He and Kang take a chair in front, at a lower level, facing the tribunal. Gan opens the proceedings.

"Marcus Velinius Agricola," his pronunciation is incomprehensible, "we are here to consider your actions on the day of the victory celebration. Since we were all there and know what you did, a prosecutor will not be required.

"It has been alleged that your behaviour, in that it directly challenged in public the authority of a senior officer of the army, amounted to treason in the third degree".

Kang whispers to Marcus, "Third degree treason's not very serious. If there's a prison sentence it'll be short and you've already served time."

"Kang Guiren, I understand you will represent the accused. Is that right?"

"Yes Protector-General."

"Then proceed with your opening remarks. Let us have an outline of your case."

"As you say, Protector-General, we were all present on that occasion. But we may have different appreciations of what the accused intended when he said what he did. His actual intention is vital and should be tested here by the tribunal. It should be accepted as a guide to interpreting his words. Their plain meaning is not enough; what lies behind is critical.

"It is one thing to challenge authority wilfully, quite another to give that impression without meaning it. If it is the latter, no challenge in reality occurred; the appearance of it would be an illusion. As Confucius advises, we must be vigilant in separating reality from illusion.

"I can assure you, Protector-General, the accused had no intention of insulting Colonel Chen, or impugning his authority. He is from a radically different culture than ours, one where rude manners are common, untuned to the sensibilities that we take for granted. His sole motivation was to help correct a situation that was not right and in that sense actually enhance Colonel Chen's authority. As we are taught, authority is augmented when it is seen to act on the basis of rightness.

"I will call a witness to give evidence proving that the charge against Wu-Jiang was false, and the accused will state his benevolent intention. Of course it is up to you to judge whether he is sincere but I am confident you will find he is.

"Admittedly he went about it in a clumsy way, but his purpose was commendable. In doing so he was following one of the fundamental precepts of Confucius – that one, in good conscience, should confront a superior when he is wrong. In the absence of that how can righteousness be assured? All the more remarkable that he did it, as he is a foreigner. True, he failed to follow the rituals, but that should be forgiven as he is not schooled in them.

"With your permission, I would like to call Huang Bo as a witness."

"Yes, go ahead."

An usher brings Huang Bo in by the side door. Face impassive, he's guided towards the dais. He stands in front, a few paces away from Kang.

"Huang Bo, you are the commanding officer of the platoon in which Wu-Jiang served in the recent battle with the Hsiung-nu, is that right?"

"Yes sir."

"I want you to describe to the Protector- General the actions of Wu-Jiang in the battle. I remind you that you must tell the truth or you will be severely punished."

"Yes sir, I know. I was leading my men forward in the attack when four Hsiung-nu surrounded Sun Chonglin and knocked him down. Before they could finish him off, Wu-Jiang rushed forward and chased them away, killing one of them and saving Sun Chonglin's life. It was a brave act and should have been rewarded. I made a recommendation but it was never acted on. Someone higher up stopped it."

"We heard later that Wu-Jiang was accused of cowardice and was to the punished. I understand he was thrown into prison. The accusation may have been based on an earlier event in the battle, which was misunderstood. In the thick of the fighting Wu-Jiang pulled back with four men to entice the Hsiung-nu to overextend. The tactic was sensible; it was not cowardly. Anyway it had the desired effect."

"Are there other men in your platoon who are willing to corroborate your story? Was the accused there to your knowledge?"

"All the men in my platoon will back up what I said. Three of them are waiting outside to testify if your Lordship wants them. I saw the Roman contingent fighting next to us. I don't remember seeing the accused specifically but I assume he was there because the other foreigners were."

Kang calls Marcus to testify: "Marcus Velinius Agricola, please tell the Protector-General what you saw on the day of the battle. You are expected to strictly tell the truth. Is that understood?

"Yes it is. I saw what Huang Bo described. I was fighting with my cohort next to Wu-Jiang's platoon. I was concentrating on what I was doing since the action was heavy at the time, but I could easily observe Wu-Jiang driving off the Hsiung-nu soldiers, also saving his comrade. It only took a second to see."

"Tell the Protector-General why you spoke up that day."

"It seemed to me that a brave man was being falsely accused. I knew very well what happened in the battle. Where I come from, saving a comrade in battle at the risk of one's own life produces the highest medal the army can give to a soldier below a general. There's nothing higher.

"What was alleged was absolutely untrue. I felt I had to speak up. I didn't mean to be undiplomatic. If I gave offence I apologise for it. I acknowledge that I could've got the point across in a better way. But I can assure you that I had no intention of insulting Colonel Chen. He's in a position of high authority and I respect that. I know now that an indirect approach to superiors is required in the Han culture. But I didn't know that at the time. In Rome we are usually direct. It's a big difference."

"Thank you, Marcus Velinius. Protector-General, you see what the facts of the Wu-Jiang case are. No one has come forward to dispute them. I submit that the only conclusion that can be reasonably drawn is that the army staff made a mistake. Let us accept that it was unintentional and that nobody needs to be blamed.

"As for the accused, he was acting reasonably, out of a desire to correct that mistake. He has apologised for speaking in too importunate a manner. I ask Colonel Chen to accept the apology and forgive him. He was only trying to help someone falsely accused, who I remind you is a member of our own armed forces. In that he was acting as a comrade, something for which we should pleased. Besides, as we all know he performed well on the battlefield.

"These facts show that he committed no treason, only a breach of etiquette which, because of his different background, should be considered minor. He has received sufficient punishment for that already."

Gan says, "Colonel Chen, what do you think?"

"Protector-General, I consider what the accused said and his manner of saying it were wrong. He shouldn't have done it. We cannot have foreigners opposing our authority, no matter what the reason is. I'm pleased however that the record has been set straight on the Wu-Jiang affair by Huang Bo. He'll be released immediately. I'll award him the Order of Merit, first degree. He can go back to his unit.

"As for the accused, he deserved punishment. However, taking into account the fact that he's served over two months in prison and has apologised, I consider he's received enough."

"I agree with your wisdom Colonel Chen," Gan says." I order the accused to be released. He can now rejoin his comrades. Let this be a lesson to him that the Han are fair minded but will not brook any disrespect. I thank you all for coming here, especially Kang Guiren for shedding light on this difficult matter. A deviation in the right order of things has been corrected and a useful ally has been rehabilitated. The proceedings are terminated."

Marcus receives the verdict with an impassive face. Among the Han, it's not considered dignified to show emotion, nor in Rome either. He feels it deeply though and has to fight to keep it hidden. Most of all it is gratitude to Kang, a man who has crossed the valley of difference to be a true friend, his allegiance duly tried. That fact is almost as important as being released from prison; it proves that it's possible to make the sort of connection that must be made if he's to find a sense of home in this alien culture where he'll undoubtedly spend the rest of his life. That link and what it leads to can't occur without a process. It has started with Kang.

Now that he has his freedom, to make it worthwhile he must gain the consent of Meilin's father. That issue must come to a head without delay.

CHAPTER 20

Meilin and Gan arc in the family suite which has several rooms. Meilin is in hers, thinking about how she should approach her father, desperately worried that he'll refuse and what she should do if he does. The sun is streaming through her small casement window lighting up the blue silk which covers the roughness of the mud brick walls. She paces up and down, treading heedlessly on the intricately designed silk rugs woven with the famous blind stitch. Each stitch, closely applied to give the surface its sheen, is so tiny that many of the weavers eventually lose their sight. She's in two minds; should she go to see him now or wait. Maybe something will happen to put him in a particularly good mood. That's procrastination. She must go now and face the consequences.

With a burst of determination she leaves the room and walks through the stone corridor up to the top of the southern tower where he has his office. It looks over a stand of poplars past the hot cobblestone quadrangle.

On her way, she sees them through the window and stops for a second in thought. The local tradition comes to mind where a newly married couple is given a young poplar tree as a wedding present. Might she and Marcus be given one and might its symbol ensure, as it's supposed to, that they'll have a long life and be fruitful? Tense and anxious, she goes through the door her father always leaves open. He's at his desk signing some papers.

Too impatient to give the usual polite greeting, she blurts out,

"Father, I want to tell you something very important, but I'm nervous you won't like it. I implore you to be understanding. You've always been kind to me. Please be kind now."

"What is it my dearest child?"

"I'm in love with the Roman officer, the one on trial who you released from prison today. He says he's in love with me and I know he is. We want to get married."

"Oh dear", Gan says, exhaling wearily. His shoulders slump.

"How did this happen. How could you even have met him?"

"I saw him at the victory celebrations where he spoke out and was sent to prison. I thought that was a terrible thing to do to someone who was only trying to help. You've always taught me how important righteousness is. What Colonel Chen did was not right.

"I went to see him to say we're not all like Colonel Chen. He seemed like a good man, wrongly treated. I came to see him often in prison and we got to know each other. I thought he was interesting, not like the young men out here, superficial and barely educated – really boring.

"What d'you think father? I know this looks odd. But it wouldn't be the first time for a marriage between us and foreigners. The Court often sends daughters of high born officials, even princesses, to be married to Hsiung-nu chieftains. They're completely different from us, much more barbaric than Romans, judging by Marcus. Those girls have to marry against their will, to men they can't even carry on a decent conversation with. They smell and are always drunk on that horrid mare's milk. The girls are unhappy for the rest of their lives. But it happens. At least I would be happy."

"I don't know Meilin. This is very unusual – never happened before. It's different with the Hsiung-nu – at least they look like us. Besides there's a diplomatic reason. None here. It's different, different.

"Your mother and I have always thought you would marry an official and live in genteel society one day. I know it's a bleak place out here to bring up a daughter, but we won't always live in Gaochang. Perhaps, now I'm a marquis, I can get a posting in Chang-an, or at least in Lanzhou. There you'll find more interesting people. They're much more cultivated. Can't you wait for that?"

"I don't want to meet anyone else. I love Marcus. Don't you see?"

"Yes, yes, I suppose. Anyway, this is all very sudden, very sudden. You'll have to let me have time to think about it. I'll speak to your mother. In the meantime I think it best you don't see the Roman."

"Father, I don't want to go to a big city. I want to live in a place where the air is free and I can hear the birds. Why can't I see Marcus. We're not doing anything wrong."

"I just think it's better. We don't want gossip to start. You know what rumour mongers people are out here. It would be very damaging to our family if word got out about this. Now, I have some more papers to sign. We'll speak about this later."

He lowers his head into the papers and she leaves. It could have been worse. At least she has a chance to work on her mother, who's a bit of a romantic and could be sympathetic. But the task is going to be difficult. Her father doesn't like confrontations, so his leaving the issue open may not mean much. Besides, while he's a benign man he's very conservative.

She goes straight to her mother's chamber and tells her about Marcus and the conversation she's just had.

"Mother, what d'you think? Will you help me persuade Father?"

"Oh my goodness, Meilin, I don't know what to say. Your father's right to take time to think about it. Something like this has never happened before. People will be shocked. I suppose you must listen to your heart. But be patient – don't push too hard.

"I don't know what to say. I'm sympathetic of course- I want you to be happy. But after all we live among traditions. You know how strong they are. We have to mind what people think, especially in our position. If your father loses face we'll all be finished."

"Can't you be stronger than that Mother? I need real support. It's going to be hard to persuade him. Your help will be crucial. To be any use at all you'll have to take a stand. Tell him interracial marriages have been allowed in the past– with the Hsiung-nu. Why not here? Please Mother."

"It's hard for me too Meilin. This is all very stressful. Oh, why did it have to happen? Couldn't you just not see the Roman for a while? Maybe you'll feel differently after a bit."

"Mother."

"No, I suppose not. All right, I'll do what I can. But don't be impatient. This'll take time. You know how cautious your father is. He's always afraid of making the wrong decision. It's a good thing not to take risks."

છ

That night Marcus is back in his tent a free man, with a pillow filled with salt as is the custom. Cool air slips through the entrance, its flap folded back. Relief at his release leads him into a deep and dream-free slumber. The Eumenides are off bothering someone else. At the end of his bed Ting Ting snores, a feature of the compromised breathing of his breed.

Around midnight he's awakened by furious barking, louder and more insistent than ever before. It takes a couple of seconds to register. He rolls over to take a look – just in time to see an arm and a knife in the air. Instinctively he lurches upwards towards the shadowy figure and tumbles with it onto the ground. Ting Ting has locked his jaws onto the intruder's pant leg and is violently shaking it from side to side, growling fiercely. As Marcus tries to grab the knife arm, the man breaks free, kicks Ting Ting off, and runs out of the tent. Shaken but angry, Marcus looks outside but sees nothing. He goes back into the tent to find Ting Ting.

"Good dog, Ting Ting, very good dog. You saved my life", he says, still breathless and heart racing, as he pats his little friend. "You deserve a reward."

He rummages around for the dried meat he always keeps for a treat. Enough starlight comes through the entrance to find it. Ting Ting sits up on his haunches, tight with anticipation, bulging eyes gleaming in the partial light. He's capable of supernatural concentration whenever food is the object – a role model in the art of focussing. Marcus gives him several morsels which he gulps down, too eager to chew.

In the early morning he takes Ting Ting for his usual walk. As soon as they're outside the tent, Ting Ting zooms off at top speed in a figure of two interlocking loops, his short legs working at furious pace. The pattern ends at Marcus, with the little dog panting and wagging his tail. He often does this when he's happy.

Leaving Ting Ting in the tent to sleep – he loves to sleep whenever he can, no matter whether it's night or day, Marcus goes to see Kang.

"Guiren, last night someone tried to kill me while I was sleeping. My dog woke me up just in time. An intruder was about to stab me with a knife. I was able to knock him down but he fled before I could hold him. I couldn't see his face so I wouldn't recognize him. Have you any idea who it might be?"

"No I don't. This is serious. I'll investigate. Colonel Chen is devious enough to be behind it. He really had no choice but to let you go. Maybe he's feeling vengeful. I'll see what I can find out."

"I wonder", Marcus says," whether the Protector- General had something to do with it. Meilin told him we wish to get married and he didn't like it. I'd be surprised though since he and I've always gotten along well, unlike Chen."

"No I'm certain it wouldn't be him. He's a good-natured man, a bit indecisive at times but not murderous. He's incapable of doing something like this. He's too attuned to Confucian ideals. It has to be someone else. Just go about your normal duties while I investigate. Don't tell anyone."

As soon as Marcus goes back to his tent he speaks to Gaius and a few of his officers in confidence, ignoring Kang's advice not to tell anybody – he probably meant only the Han anyway. The Romans organize a watch at night to prevent further attempts.

⊂⟨

Three days have passed since Meilin spoke to her father. It seems he's avoiding her, or maybe he's just too busy. In the meantime her mother has approached him several times. She's tried to press the case, but despite a desire to help, the edge of her advocacy is blunted by the grinding mill of tradition. It's the father's decision in the end and in her heart she's content to let him take the blame.

Meilin can't wait any longer. She bursts into her father's office. He's alone, reading a scroll of parchment, a cup of tea on his desk.

"Father, have you made up your mind? I must know."

He looks up, surprised by the suddenness. His daughter is usually more circumspect.

"Meilin, this is something that can't be decided quickly. There's a lot to consider, more than you probably appreciate. You must be patient. I'm thinking about it."

"If you don't give your consent I'll be unhappy for the rest of my life. I'll never marry another man. Please, father. Marcus is a brave soldier and a good man. You've said so yourself."

"You know your happiness is important to me Meilin. But you must understand this is highly irregular. What would people in polite society think? Or people around here, even. I can accept that Marcus is a good man, but it's so irregular, so irregular. It's not the same as a marriage made to secure a treaty. There's no diplomatic reason here. Love is important but not the only thing where marriage is concerned. I don't want to disappoint you but I can't give my consent yet. Give me more time. I must consult with people."

Meilin leaves the room silently seething. It's best not to push the issue further today. She's never confronted her father before, respects his authority too much for that. But she's reached the point where her love for Marcus is the diving force in her life. It's clashing with her filial duty and threatens to overwhelm it.

She silently weeps as she walks down the corridor to her suite, relieved that Ping isn't there. The view from the window overlooking the oasis, which she has always loved, seems barren of beauty. She can't see anything good in it. Even the snow lotuses below she brought from the mountains and tends herself are no better than weeds. As she enters the privacy of her bed chamber, a turbulence of guilt and anger overwhelms her. All she can do is throw herself onto the bed and grab the pillow, squeezing it in two and sob uncontrollably.

☙

The next day, calmer now, Meilin slips away from her governess to meet Marcus in the privacy of a well on the outskirts of Goachang where the desert becomes a land of fire. Since ancient times the people in this region have tapped the runoff from the mountains through a system of under-

239

ground channels, linked by wells. Earth dug from them is piled up in circles which are set in straight lines. They look like sunken pots with their rims exposed.

She climbs down the friable slope where a small poplar tree gives assistance. Marcus is there already, sitting beside the slowly flowing water. They embrace – a long kiss, and sit down together. He's decided not to tell her about the intrusion until Kang has completed his investigation – no need to worry her until all the facts are known, for until they catch the culprit it could happen again. Knowing the prospect of that would just create needless anxiety. Once he's caught he can tell her and it'll just be history. It seems sensible to take the risk that another attack will occur and she'd be furious he didn't say anything.

She's brought a Hami melon, famous for its sweet and delicious taste. Its skin is so thin the juice leaks through. She cuts up a couple of slices and gives him one and says,

"I love this shelter – it's so intimate, like a secret room – those little lizards over there always keep confidences. Here we can feel the wonder of nature – live in harmony and enjoy beauty. But at home it's different. Why do people always have to wreck things? I wish we could just be here forever.

"I had another session with him yesterday. I have to say it doesn't look good. He won't make up his mind. I know he doesn't like it – too worried what the reaction will be. Mother seems willing, thank goodness, and may have some influence, although even she's not totally convinced. But, you know in our culture it's the father that makes the decision."

"What do you think we should do?"

"All we can do is wait and hope he comes around. Maybe Kang Guiren can help. I know he likes you. And he's more broad-minded than most of the people Father listens to. He says I'm not supposed to see you."

"That's terrible. Will you obey him?"

"Certainly not. What a question to ask. But we have to be discreet. If he finds out we're seeing each other he may harden up and never give consent."

They go back to the fortress gloomy, by separate paths. They're at a stumbling block. Any thought of eloping would be a fantasy. Marcus would be ostracised and have no employment. Gan would dismiss him from his command and disown Meilin. They would have nowhere to live. The brutal reality is that without paternal consent they would have to spend their lives in secret love, lurking in the shadows and terrified of discovery.

The walk through the oasis is melancholy. Is there something in him that prevents fulfilling his capacity for love? First Aurelia, then Meilin have come within his orbit and spun out of it. It would've been possible to marry either, different though they are. Aurelia is more of an extrovert, Meilin more modest, but both have strength of character and are beautiful in their own way. It's no good comparing them. The only hope of course is that one day the obstacle to marrying Meilin will be removed. It's frustrating to be so powerless; not even to be able to assist in the process. All that can be done is to be patient, as Meilin says – hard for a man of action.

Back at the fortress a messenger comes to the Roman quarters outside the walls and says Kang wants to see him. He goes over immediately.

"Marcus, I've discovered who was behind the attempt on your life. It was a conspiracy led by a fanatical Han nationalist. He was the one who attacked you. One of my servants overheard him talking with other soldiers about the attack – said he would have succeeded if it hadn't been for your dog. They were the ones who accused Wu-Jiang. I had them arrested and interrogated.

"The culprit has confessed. He admitted he and his friends were upset at the decision to free Wu-Jiang and furious that he was decorated. He blames you for the whole affair – thinks if you're out of the way, the conspirators would have a chance of persuading Colonel Chen to take a different line. There's deep prejudice here against Wu-Jiang's minority group, going back for years. That's the motivation, plus the fact that he and Wu-Jiang had a few arguments in the past. They hate each other.

"I'm satisfied that Colonel Chen had nothing to do with it. He can be intemperate at times but when he heard the evidence at the trial he was convinced. He doesn't bear you a grudge."

"Thank you Guiren. I'm grateful for your efforts. It's a good result. What'll happen to the fellow?"

"He'll be punished and so will his co-conspirators. There'll be a military trial of course but they'll be convicted. They're in prison now. It'll be up to the Protector-General to impose sentence. He can't afford to be lenient since it's necessary to keep the minorities from rebelling. It's a constant problem for us. I imagine the attacker will be executed. The others will be discharged from the army and receive long prison sentences.

"There's been a new development. The Protector-General's decided to take his family and five hundred troops, me included, to Lanzhou. It's the capital of this region – much bigger than Gaochang, a proper city. He'll head up the Commanderie there. It's a major promotion for him. You and your Romans are to go with him as part of the escort. You'll represent a quarter of the force so you'll play an important role. The Han are placing a lot of confidence in you. It's based on what you did in the battle against the Hsiung-nu."

"That's interesting. I would have thought that maybe he would not want me to come. As you know, he isn't keen on Meilin and me being together."

"You're right. He wanted you to stay here but the Court at Chang – an ordered him to take you and your Romans. That's why you're to go. The mandarins are curious about you and want you closer to the Capital so that one day they'll see you. Colonel Chen will be left in charge of Gaochang."

"Where's Lanzhou?"

"It's further east, not far from the capital at Chang – an where the Emperor lives. It's a couple of month's march away from here, along the Caravan Road. I suppose you're willing?"

"There's no choice. Besides I imagine Lanzhou's more civilized than this place."

"Yes it is – a good deal. It's a main hub for the Caravan Road – the gateway to the West. But it's still in touch with Chang-an, and is a centre for Confucian learning. Now that you can speak our language pretty well, you'll fit in there. "

It's pleasing to hear Kang speak of fitting in. He's worked hard at the language. On one level he's beginning to be accepted. People are getting used to him and it doesn't seem an exaggeration to say that Kang has become a real friend – extraordinary with their backgrounds being so different. Until recently neither knew the race of the other even existed.

Maybe Confucius was right when he said people are close to each other by nature and only diverge as a result of repeated practice.

Marcus has written down some of the Master's analects. It's amazing how close they are to the wisdom in the Graeco-Roman tradition. But not identical; it's perplexing to see how low the social rank of the soldier is. Notwithstanding that, the Han soldiers seem competent, certainly enough to hold the wild Hsiung-nu at bay.

It's a given that the Han people will never fully accept a newcomer. Perhaps some may, but not most, not at that level where social acceptance excludes people with a foreign accent, even when race is not an issue. But of course it is an issue – that makes it harder. After all, Romans are xenophobic too; how could he expect others to be different?

But there're many levels of acceptance and he feels the first has been achieved through his friendship with Kang and his relationship with Meilin. It's a cultural breakthrough which he never thought possible. Reaching other levels could follow. It's clear that performing well at something useful helps to overcome barriers. Probably it's the essential thing. He can count on his military prowess to accomplish that. The reaction to his success against the Hsiung-nu proves it.

Gan is pleasant, even cordial at times, although of late he's more reserved – quite understandable. Other senior officers are friendly and always willing to talk. Even Chen deigns to offer a smile sometimes now. The benefits of tolerance are clearly apparent, something Marcus never had to consider before, when he was in the comfort of power.

"Guiren, do you think we'll stay in Lanzhou permanently?"

"Yes it's possible. But nothing is guaranteed. You'll have to be where the Protector-General needs you. You and your comrades really belong to him in a way because he pays you."

"I'm starting to think about what my comrades and I'll do when we retire. My childhood background is farming and many of my comrades come from the land too. We enjoy the regime in Gaochang – working the land when we're not required for military service. But it's always just as labourers, working under someone, not owning anything.

"Do you think we could make an arrangement with the Protector-General to have some land outside Lanzhou to work ourselves, and spend more time at it? We've saved our salaries and could pay if it's not too much. We'd still be available for call up when we're needed to fight. I know that would mean we wouldn't do as much guard duty, but we could still do some. Anyway our greatest use is in battle."

"I don't see why he wouldn't consider it. There's plenty of good farm land about a week's march west from Lanzhou. The area's sparsely populated so it should be easy to acquire some. I'll ask him. Though, I'll have to separate that from what he's considering about you and Meilin. That may be hard to do, so don't count on it."

"Thanks Kang. You're a good friend."

ଔ

The first thing to do in preparation for the journey is to check on Ting Ting, make sure he's ready to travel. The little friend rushes up, wagging his curly tail and making squeaking sounds, trotting around in circles. As usual, he picks up something in his mouth, this time a sandal. Marcus settles him down with a treat and says what they're planning to do. The words don't communicate semantic content but there's no doubt a certain understanding exists. Expressive changes in his wrinkly black face, a twitch in his silky ears, a cocking of his head, show he's paying attention.

Marcus comes out of the tent, Ting Ting trotting behind, and asks Gaius to call the cohort out in formation. Ting Ting sits patiently beside him, head imperiously high, while Marcus addresses the troops.

"The Protector – General has ordered us to go with him along the Caravan Road – east. His family is going too. Get ready to march tomorrow at sunrise.

"We'll be heading to the biggest city in the Region. It's the local Han capital. About eight week's march through rough country – mostly desert. A lot of it's Hsiung-nu territory; so we have to be on our guard.

"Tribes assemble in these parts to raid caravans. If they hear the Protector-General is travelling with us, we can count on an attack – a big one. Even with the Han escort, we could be up against some pretty stiff odds. The Protector – General should have requisitioned more men but Colonel Chen fears another attack on Gaochang. We make up about a quarter of

244

the escort so a lot will depend on us. It shows that the Han have confidence in Roman ability – a good thing if we're going to continue to do well out here.

"I'm sure you all will welcome a chance for more action – pretty boring waiting around here. But make no mistake about it, we'll probably have to earn our keep."

It's a relief to know that Meilin will be coming. The thought though drives home how uncertain their relationship is. It's out of their control, like a falling leaf in the wind. At any time Marcus could be ordered away to another place, never to see her again, maybe lose his life. Perhaps that's what Gan has in mind instead of outright refusing his consent

ଓଷ

The morning mist lies low on the motley oasis floor and begins to burn off as the Flaming Mountains ignite. With some apprehension, the party marches out of the fortress onto the Road. The hundred and forty-five Romans are in front of the turtle-roofed chariots which carry the Protector-General and his family. Behind them is the baggage train with Ting Ting safely installed in a wagon. The Han troops bring up the rear.

As they reach the outskirts of the oasis, Marcus says to one of the guides, "What are those people doing over there?"

There're hundreds of men and women sitting with sand piled up around their legs, sometimes up to their waists. Children are playing nearby, tumbling down the dunes and shrieking with delight. People take shelter under colourful fabric lean-tos supported by thin wooden poles. Reds, yellows, and pinks are dotted over the dunes which are scalloped in sine waves. Others are sitting in the harsh sun. It's a complete desert, not like the steppe which, although dry, supports a threadbare cover of vegetation. There's none of that here to disturb the perfect smoothness of the sandscape.

"They're taking the sand cure. People with sore joints come here from all around. The heat from the sand gives them relief. It's a traditional method."

Meilin and Marcus have furtive meetings when the expedition stops for the night, but they have to be careful. Meilin is afraid of her father and doesn't want to jeopardize the chance he'll approve. He's forbidden contact and that has to be respected, at least ostensibly.

The Road leads through the desert into oases and more desert, sometimes carrying twin humped camel caravans heading in the opposite direction. At times it encounters towns and villages, entirely dependant on water gleaned from mountain run off which leaks into the land. It's tapped by wells linked by underground aquifers – like the one Marcus and Meilin met in.

Strange shapes are carved into the landscape by the ferocious winds that can blow a man down and transport fine grained soils over endless distances in eye-stinging blizzards. Marcus can't help but think that they're going through terrain that harbours more dangers the further east they go. But the biggest danger lies in what the Protector General may decide. Will the Road help in some mysterious way now that he's in its power? Marcus thinks of it as a companion these days, not always benign, but sometimes so. It's such an influential presence that possibly it has a mind of its own; certainly it has a consequence.

CHAPTER 21

The caravan lumbers along slowly and is now in country vegetated only by wind -blasted shrubs. It's enough for flocks of goats though. At times they block the Road like swelling clouds, dirty white against the beige steppe. Kang says they're prized for their fine hair. Expensive garments are made from it – in high fashion at Court.

Fierce winds are blowing up every day now, tossing dust in gritty swirls and reducing men to crouching. They have to close their eyes to thin slits and breathe in short gasps through scarves made from scraps of fabric torn from their clothing. The caravan refuses to stop, forcing its way on in blind determination.

Outside a walled oasis town two weeks from Gaochang, the terrain loses its vegetation entirely and subsides into a black and barren horror of coarse gravel that sometimes rises in hillocks, sharp and ominous, harsh on the soft leather boots the men wear. It's as lifeless as the mouth of hell. An ugly gaseous smell rises from the black shards. Marcus takes comfort that his Han comrades know the place and don't feel the danger he's inclined to sense. They spend two weeks in its melancholy grip. Then the land builds quickly to a commanding height. Kang tells him it's the Jiayuguan pass. On the other side is an amazing sight.

A huge mud brick wall, the height of three men, snakes over the desert like a mighty dragon, slinking off into the distance and vanishing into a hazy horizon. From the top of the pass it's possible to get an impression of its width – sufficient to allow two chariots to pass each other. At the height he's on he can see across a distance as far as Rome is from the sea and still the wall continues. Marcus can't imagine how people could engineer such a structure anywhere in the world let alone in this remote place. Even the Titans would have trouble. Just the challenge of keeping the wild Hsiung-nu at bay during construction would be daunting.

"This is the wall which emperors have built over the centuries to keep the Hsiung-nu out – or it's supposed to," Kang says. "Chin Shi Huang di started it a long time ago so he could unite our country. Later emperors extended it in stages over the years. Now it goes all the way to the Imperial capital.

"Soon we'll be in Jiuquan, the headquarters of the local prefecture. It's an important garrison town.

"The name means 'wine spring'. People say that a general who defeated the Hsiung-nu in a great battle was given some special wine by the Emperor. Instead of drinking it himself, he poured it into a pool nearby so his troops could celebrate the victory with him. The men loved him for it – ha ha ha.

"Locals mine jade from the mountains here, different colours – black, white and green. The stone is sacred to us. Drinking cups made from it are so fine they glow in the moonlight."

They stay in Jiuquan for a few days to resupply the caravan. Meilin is unable to bear the suspense any longer and goes to see her father. He's in his suite in the small fortress where they're staying.

"Father it's a long time since I asked for your consent. We're well on the way to Lanzhou and I need to know before we get there. May I have your answer please, please."

"I know I've taken a long time Meilin. But it's a very difficult thing. I've thought about it a lot. I also know it's unfair to keep you waiting my dear girl. Unfortunately I have to say no. I cannot grant my consent. I'm very sorry to disappoint you, but they're just too many cultural barriers. It'll be better in the long run. You'll see."

While his answer is not unexpected, until now hope has massaged the anxiety of waiting. Those words have destroyed it, swallowed it up in a devastating certainty. It's useless to argue. That's been done to no avail; even her mother has tried.

She buries her head in her hands and breaks into shaking sobs. Gan is shocked to see his daughter like this and doesn't know what to say. He moves over and tries to comfort her but she pushes him away and rushes out of the room.

ↀ

The caravan starts up again and passes through a grassland corridor. Kang says;

> "It's where Emperor Wu bred horses from the heavenly herds of Fergana. He's the famous emperor who opened up the Caravan Road – beat back the Hsiung-nu to do it. Over there on the right are the Qilian Mountains; the Stony Desert is on the left, past the grass."

Word filters through they're now in the danger zone. Everyone is on full alert, scouring the horizon for tell-tale signs of Hsiung-nu horsemen. Someone claims the first hint will be the smell – the Hsiung-nu never bathe. Marcus knows it well. Han common soldiers curse their leaders for not bringing more troops. Romans check their swords. Marcus puts his hand on Owl's Head. Gan's family particularly feels the tension; Meilin stays close to her mother. The women try to quell their temptation to imagine the horror the desert raiders are capable of, and nobody speaks.

The waiting is intolerable, aggravated by the slow pace of the caravan. The Road is in its treacherous mood, hankering after violence again. It's inevitable here, a natural occurrence in this part of the world. The stories Marcus heard from the Sogdian merchants in Margiana come to mind. They seemed fanciful at the time, but not now. Even the landscape is threatening. The heat haze on the mountains causes shapes to appear and slowly move – like monstrous sentinels signalling a coming attack.

Everyone has their eyes fixed on the horizon, fearing the time they will see the clear sky dirtied with the signal of doom. So far no beacon tower has released its smoke. But two weeks out of Jiuquan, one day in the morning the dreaded black plume rises ahead of them. They can see its origin in the direction they're heading, standing tall and lonely on the steppe, breathing out its dark smoke straight up into the still air.

Marcus knows they're in for the fight of their lives. Shiung-nu scouts must have been shadowing them, taking cover behind the slight rises in the land. They'll be salivating at the tortoise shaped chariots because they would know a rich party is there for the taking, coming into their territory with a relatively small escort, easy to overwhelm.

Gan orders a halt and his military Commander calls the officers together, including Marcus. As they discuss strategy a dust cloud soils the horizon.

> "It's the Hsiung-nu," says the Commander, "Take up the emergency positions. They'll be here in a few minutes."

In a rush, the wagons and chariots are collected and overturned. Gan and his family take refuge in the centre, huddled in a group. Soldiers dash to put on their armour and grab their weapons. Han cavalry mount their horses. Their infantry forms up around the vehicles. Shouts and frantic movement startle the air.

The Romans have to go to the wagons to get their arms. They run as fast as they can back to the front of the caravan. They arrive as the first wave of horse archers appears, riding hard towards them at right angles to the Road. The raiders are yelling ferociously, their recurved bows stretched for action. Yak tail standards with vertical banners announce their identity – not from Jir-Jir's tribe. Marcus is relieved. A burden is removed that might have weighed him down. Now nothing can stand in the way of utter determination to kill.

He gives the command "Form the Testudo". The men raise their shields as one, drawing the scales across their heads and torsos. Arrows bounce off in pings and nobody is hurt. The quantity is nothing like the inexhaustible arsenal at Carrhae. The archers look perplexed, uncertain. The Testudo is new to them. To anyone who has not seen it before it would look invulnerable to attack. It might be capable of something devastating, imbued with the hidden power of the unknown. They flinch and withdraw.

After regrouping they charge again. This time they avoid the Testudo and go straight for the Han on the left, shooting a cloud of arrows that covers the sun. Despite being heavily outnumbered, the Han cavalry ride out and halt the assault temporarily. They're soon overwhelmed but manage to change the form of battle. The Hsiung-nu, still on horseback, sling their bows and fight hand to hand with their long swords. The Han infantry now enter the fray. They wield hook – tipped halberds to pull the riders off their horses. It's a difficult task as the centaurs of the steppes are at one with their beasts. Frenzied fighting engulfs the Road and blood saddens its dust.

Marcus orders a collapse of the Testudo and yells out,

"Fight like you've never fought before. They'll kill us all if we lose."

He leads a charge from the side into the battle storm. Thoughts of Meilin, vulnerable among the wagons, animate him more than ever before. Gaius has never seen him so fierce. He's berserk, a state unusual for Roman soldiers. They're trained to be steady, methodical. He's like Achilles leading his Myrmidons at Troy. He feels like him, invulnerable. He's faster than the fastest, more skilful than the most skilful, destined by the gods to conquer. In a flurry of upward thrusts he dispatches three horsemen. He sees an opening in their ranks. Instinctively, he orders his men to crash through behind him. Nothing can stop him.

The ferocity of the Roman attack unnerves the Hsiung-nu and they retreat – but not for long. Soon they attack again, with renewed vigour and their superior numbers begin to tell. They surround the defenders, both Roman and Han, and squeeze them into a smaller and smaller ball around the wagons and their precious cargo. Confusion, of men charging and retreating, horses rearing up and neighing, shouts of triumph and cries of death, envelopes the Road in a chaos that would make even Mars shudder. It's hard to see through the swirling dust, often only weird shapes can be made out, like the ones the Sogdian merchants recounted.

The Hsiung-nu fight in a disorderly mob, without pattern or predict-ability, but they're fierce and determined, wielding their long swords with tremendous agility, so at one are they with their horses. And they have numbers on their side. Inevitably they start to overwhelm the defenders. Soon they'll cut them to pieces and all will be lost. It seems only a matter of a few more minutes. The caravan is doomed to be another trophy for the Road.

In the melee, Marcus notices something that gives him an idea. It's a man with armour highlighted in gold, furiously urging his men on. A comrade is carrying a vertical banner by his side. It must be their leader.

Marcus yells out: "Gaius, our only hope is to get that commander."

Standing back from the fight momentarily, he quickly points to ten men:

"Back up Gaius and me. Follow me."

They charge in a wedge, led by Marcus, through the Hsiung-nu horse-men, bashing with their shields. Gaius is slowed down, wounded, but keeps fighting like a Homeric hero. Marcus reaches the commander who rears his horse up and gives him a mighty swipe with his sword, hitting his shield and knocking him down. Rolling just in time to avoid the stamping hooves, Marcus gets on his feet, drops his shield and sword. He rushes at the man before he brings his sword into play again and grabs his clothing, pulling him off his horse with a sudden shout from the pit of his stomach, contracted into a ferocious concentration of will.

The wounded Gaius and the rest of the Romans hold back the Hsiung-nu as they move in to protect their leader. Dust and confusion swirl around the lethal combat. No quarter can be given – there's no time; the blood is too hot, the stakes too high. The pressure on the Romans is intense; pushed back and taking casualties they can't hold out for long. Marcus knows he has very little time to do his job.

He picks up his shield just in time to parry a vicious slash by the Hsiung-nu commander, now on his feet. The strength of the man is prodigious. Marcus is forced onto his knees. Holding his shield up, he scrambles over to his sword, grabs it and stands up. He must get in close where his short weapon has the advantage, but try as he might he can't get past the man's defence. The Hsiung-nu is too agile, keeping his distance. He's like Jir-Jir, moves like him, on the balls of his feet, which are always a little apart just under his shoulders, keeping him on balance at all times. With a sudden movement too quick to see, he flips Marcus' sword out of his hand.

Marcus retreats and pulls out Owl's Head, holding his shield out in front. The commander circles him. Then, again in a sudden move, he swings his sword at Marcus' head. This time the Roman sees it in time and raises his shield. The blow glances off and wounds him in the shoulder, penetrating his armour. The sight of his own blood infuriates him, propels him with new energy.

He rushes at his opponent in a charge of desperation and feints to the left with his shield. As the Hsiung-nu reacts, he manages to get close enough to plunge Owl's Head upwards into the bottom of the man's chest, underneath his breast plate. The commander goes down, sword falling from his hand, shock twisting his stony face in the last sign of life. For an instant, a breathless Marcus stands looking at him lying flat on his back. He assumes he's dead.

"Get back to the wagons – on the double."

It all happened so fast that the Hsiung-nu troops couldn't react in time – or at least not enough of them. And those who were close to the commander the Roman contingent were able to keep at bay, just long enough. A few minutes more and it would have been overwhelmed.

When word spreads that the leader is lost, energy goes out of the Hsiung-nu, like air from a blown up bladder punctured by a dagger. Without him, doubt, the subverter of courage, infects their minds and they decide it's better to save their own skins than continuing to fight. It's too difficult, too costly. They break off, intent only on retrieving their dead and departing as fast as possible. The defenders stand by, too tired and relieved to fight any more. They watch like condemned men given reprieve, as the scourges of the steppe ride away into the dusty haze, limp bodies hanging over their horses.

CHAPTER 21

Marcus checks for casualties – fortunately the wounds suffered, while in some cases serious, are not mortal. Except for Gaius. Everyone knew he was hurt but no one realised how seriously. He's lying down, shoulders propped up by a colleague and one knee slightly raised. His huge frame is covered with wounds. The worst one is in the side, where the breast-plate fails to protect. Someone has taken off his armour, revealing the gash, the width of a sword. His breath is laboured and low.

"Marcus, we've come a long way. Sorry I can't go on."

Before Marcus can respond, Gaius' head flops. All are stunned, especially Marcus. He can't speak, can only kneel down and pick up his friend's hand and hold it. Not only was Gaius a lifelong friend, he was the last personal link with home. Now that is broken. The loss is crushing; it breaks his heart. Suddenly Kang realises the situation, and dropping his voice in sympathy, says;

"Marcus! Come to the main chariot. Meilin's been wounded. A stray arrow hit her."

In a fog Marcus runs over. Meilin is lying in her mother's arms, pale and quiet, the arrow still in her shoulder. Gan is standing by, frozen. Sensing something, she half opens her eyes. A glance of recognition flashes across the space, and fills it with love. Gan catches the look, a touch of sympathy crinkling his impassive face for an instant. Marcus can only stand apart, silent, staring. In a few moments he feels able to ask the Han physician who's standing by: "How bad is it?"

"Not too bad. The arrow hasn't touched anything vital. It isn't in very deep – must have glanced off something which slowed it down. I'll be able to remove it easily. I'll give her some healing herbs now and some others when I've taken the arrow out. She'll make a full recovery. She needs rest though."

Gan says, "We'll stay here for a while. It's best she's not bumped around on the Road. Anyway there're others who also need a few days to recover."

They can't remain long though; there's not enough water. But they must bury the dead. Small parties of Han and Roman soldiers carry their fallen to separate locations in the desert within eye distance of the Road. The full Roman cohort is there, even the wounded, some hobbling with the support of their comrades. All is quiet and the sun has just slipped behind a line of dark clouds high on the horizon.

Each group conducts its own ceremony a hundred paces apart. They're close enough for the prayers of each to be heard by the other, connected as it were by the solemnity of death in a common cause. The sympathy each feels for their own fallen reaches across the distance and forms a silent bond.

Dressed in full uniform, Gaius is lowered into a hastily dug hole. With the Romans standing in formation, Marcus stoops over him in tears and places his last denarius in his mouth, payment for the grim boatman who'll ferry his soul across the Stygian river into eternity. He stands up slowly, his eyes fixed on the grave.

> "We'll miss you Gaius Fulvius. You were the Ajax of the Roman army. Like that mighty hero of the Achaeans, no enemy could stand up to the battering of your shield. It was a shield which no man but you was strong enough to wield like you did. You were a bulwark, an inspiration to your comrades to the end. May your spirit find happiness in your life to come. I'm sure it'll be in the Elysian Fields. If anyone deserves to be there it's you. From this time on you'll live in two places, there and here in our hearts."

They spend a few moments in silence and with a different tone of voice Marcus says

> "We battered the Hsiung-nu so hard they won't come back. This'll be the last raid we'll have to beat off. Well done. You all fought at the top of your form –never better. We saved the Protector General and his family. Sometimes I'm not sure which side the Caravan Road is on but there's no doubt it was on our side today. Our wounds will heal – only a matter of time. Gaius Fulvius would have appreciated your effort in coming to bid him farewell. It's fitting it was at a time of victory."

Back at the caravan, Marcus runs into Kang.

> "Kang, would it be possible for me to visit Meilin?"

> "I know it's hard, but for the moment I think it best for you to stay away. The parents want to be with her alone, and the issue of marriage would be embarrassing to them, especially as the Protector-General has forbidden contact. Her prognosis is favourable so she'll get better soon".

"Unpleasant advice Kang but I suppose you're right. I would risk a confrontation, the last thing Meilin needs now. All right I'll stay away, be with my comrades."

ɑ

After three days, the caravan starts up and moves on to the next oasis, a day's march away. The beacon tower on its border is thankfully free of the dreaded plume. The Hsiung-nu have departed this area – for now.

Past the oasis the Road moves into a wide expanse of fertile land, studded with rivers and small lakes, green and agricultural. They stop beside one of the lakes for the night.

Meilin's mother goes to her husband,

"I'm worried about Meilin. She's not recovering as well as the doctor predicted – seems depressed; she's given up. It's because you won't give your consent. That's certain. I know it's difficult and I was in two minds about it myself. But things are different now.

"We can't stand by and let our daughter die of a broken heart. Besides, even I know that Marcus and his Romans saved our lives. Yen-xu, you must change your mind. If you don't, you'll be responsible for her death. I'll never forgive you."

"Liling, I understand what you say. But her condition isn't as bad as you say – the doctor says she'll recover eventually. The wound's not serious. Maybe it'll take a little longer to heal if she's depressed but she won't die. Let me think about it some more. It's not an easy thing; I made my decision after a lot of thought. Changing it would be difficult.

"I agree that circumstances are different now, but the fundamental problem remains. How would it be received in Lanzou, particularly now that I'm a marquis? We have the position of our whole family to consider, not just one member. Liling, don't think I'm a heartless man – just give me more time."

"This is a real crisis Yen-xu. You must change your mind. I don't care what you say; she'll die, our daughter will die. And you'll be responsible. You will, you absolutely will."

Gan has never seen her like this before and doesn't know what to say. So he says nothing and just walks away. He takes a long stroll by the side of the lake, and doesn't get back to the wagons until the sun is beginning to fall behind the trees.

ᴄꙅ

The next day, the caravan continues its journey through the fertile country; Kang says they're about ten days from Lanzou. He remarks to Marcus that the Protector-General seems particularly distracted, not like himself – aloof and uncommunicative.

Two days later, after the tents are pitched, a Han soldier comes up to Marcus and says the Protector General wants to see him.

Gan is alone when he arrives.

"Marcus", he's never called him that before, "I would like to speak to you about the subject I know is on your mind.

"I assume Meilin has told you that I've felt unable to give my consent to marriage between you. My decision was not from any misgivings about your character; it was purely because of the cultural barriers. However, the battle out here has changed things.

"I love my daughter and came very close to losing her to that arrow. It's forced me to think more deeply about the consequences of my decision – put greater weight on her happiness. Besides, I am grateful to you and your Romans for what you did. You were the main reason the Hsiung-nu were beaten off and we're alive. I know it.

"In a sense we're in a second life, where the constraints of the first don't apply. The decision I made belongs to the former life so I am free to make a new one without having to change my mind. I'm now willing to give my consent to you marrying my daughter. May good fortune follow you both."

He extends his hand and Marcus shakes it warmly, putting his left hand on Gan's arm.

"Thank you sir for your understanding; I'm very appreciative. Have you told Meilin?"

"Not yet. I'll wait till the physician is finished with his treatment. Now, let's talk about practical matters. Kang Guiren tells me that you and your comrades would like to have some land for farming. That's good. It'll give you a higher social status. You should know it's above the soldiers' and just below the scholar's.

"In view of your service in the battle I'll give you an estate of land – enough to afford you an appropriate standing. It'll also be a dowry."

He points to the right of the Road, to flat green land interspersed with forested hills running towards the mountains.

"That land over there is good for all kinds of crops – wheat, soy, millet, beans, onions fruit too – melons, peaches. You can farm there and build houses. There're no people in the immediate area, although some a little way off. This is a sparsely populated part of our country.

"Thank you very much Sir. We'll always be at your service. You can count on it. Your generosity is appreciated very much. My comrades too will be delighted. They've been wanting to settle down to farm and make a new life in your country. Like me, they'll be grateful."

Gan is pleased – he's reached a felicitous solution. Marcus and Meilin will live in the country, far enough from Lanzhou for society not to realizes he has a daughter married to a foreigner. There may be rumours but the situation won't be confronting. He'll have time to prepare the way for an eventual coming out if that ever becomes necessary. It probably won't.

They go back to Meilin who's asleep. The doctor has extracted the arrow and given her a potion of sedating herbs. Marcus walks off the Road alone into the grassy wilderness, happily waving in the breeze. It's green all the way to an unblemished lake set at the foot of the Qilian Mountains. The suddenness of it all is like a thunderclap releasing a cleansing shower into energy-sapping humidity. In an instant the stifling air is washed away and the day is clear.

It's just as well he can be by himself for a while; he needs to collect his thoughts. There're practicalities flowing from the breakthrough he must take care of. As he strolls on the grass, lost in thought and imagination, he strays close to the Road. There seems to be an old man in local peasant clothing walking slowly by with a pitchfork over his shoulder, a cloth bundle hanging from it. His head is bent over with effort, obscuring his face. He moves quickly to catch up to him. As he passes him from behind he looks at his face. It's his father. In a flash, the image of the man disappears and nothing is left on the Road.

He dismisses the event as a function of the strain he's under and sees Ting Ting trotting up with a sandal in his mouth; the faithful dog must have followed him from the wagon area. He holds a strategy meeting with his little counsellor who sits patiently on the grass, cocking his black face from time to time to show he's paying attention.

CHAPTER 22

He goes to the wagons with Ting Ting toddling along behind. Meilin is awake with her mother and Ping sitting beside her. In times to come he can barely remember the happy haze he was in let alone the events than ensued over the next days and weeks. As in a dream he tells Meilin about the consent, sees her leap out of bed into his arms, and hears the whoops of joy from her mother and Ping.

Any fear he had that Meilin wouldn't want to live in this remote place with no great fortress or even a mansion, evaporates when she speaks of its beauty and peacefulness. They'll be together in a home they'll build within the shadow of the mountains, far away from stultifying society. Her parents will visit sometimes; it's only a week's journey along the Road from Lanzhou. They might even go there themselves at some point. And caravans will pass by bringing news of the outside world. They'll be in an idyllic universe of their own, untroubled by the pressures of conventional life.

He walks over to his comrades who are lounging around their tents and calls them together. Rather shyly he tells them of the marriage and with a gleam in his eye points out that it could be a precedent for all of them to follow if they wish. Gan has said there are plenty of marriageable women in the environs.

"We have the opportunity to stay here and make a new life for ourselves. The Protector General has given us all the land you see around here – a whole lot more than we could ever have hoped for back home. You can see how fertile it is. Many of you come from a farming background and all of us did farming in Parthia. We can build houses here, marry local women and create a new home. Of course we have to stand ready for military call up whenever the Protector General needs us."

He can tell by the murmuring that the men are pleased with the prospect. Most of them have talked about it before, agreeing it would be the best outcome, even though it didn't seem to be a real possibility at the time.

Marcus informs Gan of his comrades' reaction and asks him to speak to them direct. The next day he assembles them and introduces their benefactor. Kang is also there. Marcus has told him the news and he's delighted, sees it as a wise decision.

"Romans, you have fought well for the Emperor and deserve to be rewarded. By the authority vested in me by the Emperor I hereby grant you through Marcus Velinius sufficient land around here to support you and any families you may have in the future. I will settle on the boundaries later. There are young women in the region who may be willing to come here to live. You must be aware that this will not relieve you of your duty as soldiers if I call upon you. That could be at any time.

"I'll establish this place as an official village and appoint a commissioner. He and his staff will look after the administration. Your village needs a name. Marcus do you have a suggestion?"

"Yes Sir I do. Alexander was the greatest adventurer in the world where we Romans come from. He founded many towns which he called Alexandria, some in Asia. Let's call our new village that."

"All right, I agree. But that word is too difficult to pronounce. Besides, we don't like a name with more than two syllables. We'll delete the first and last one and call it Liqian." He pronounces it 'Leechan.'

"I'll make sure everybody knows it's founded by Romans. Even the Court at Chang- an will be told."

Marcus says,

"Your version doesn't sound much like Alexandria but that's all right; we'll all know what it means."

"Yes, good. It's just very difficult for us to pronounce your words – ha ha ha.

"That's settled then. I wish you good fortune in Liqian and long lasting prosperity. The Hsiung-nu aren't usually active in this region, but sometimes they are. You'll need to be aware of that. I'll leave it to you to set up the appropriate defences."

The first task is to build houses. Marcus and Meilin decide it would be best to do this before the wedding. Fortunately the winter is still some time off. Gan sends emissaries into the countryside to hire workers skilled in construction, offering good pay in cash. People in this part of the Empire are poor, barely able to eke out a hard scrabble living because their plots are so small, unlike what Gan has given to the Romans. As expected, the response is positive. They love cash.

The emissaries are instructed to make it clear to everyone that Liqian is a new village established personally by the Protector General. He'll guarantee it'll receive whatever financial support is necessary. The new inhabitants are promoted as fearless soldiers of the Emperor who come from an exotic background. Young women who could work in the fields for good wages are invited to come, even before farming commences. They'll be looked after by the Protector General until then. Temporary quarters will be set up near the caravan for the influx of workers. The glamour of the offer attracts more women than required so the emissaries have to make choices. Many applicants are disappointed.

Construction of the houses begins. The Romans participate but only as semi skilled labourers. They don't know how to build houses in the Han style, but at least they can make the mud bricks for the walls. Local skills are required for, among other tasks, thatching roofs and erecting wooden pillars to hold them up. The house for Marcus and Meilin is the largest, a substantial two storey oblong building with a majestic view of the mountains from the second floor bedrooms. It has a tiled roof with gracefully curved eves projecting outward to keep rain water from running down the walls.

Gan and Kang go on to Lanzou with the caravan which is now guarded only by the Han troops. They assume that if the Hsiung –nu attack, they won't have the numbers to cause a problem. Anyway, after their mauling such a short time ago it's unlikely they'll venture forth again so soon. Meilin's mother, along with Ping and the maids stay behind.

In six weeks, Gan and Kang are back and at least the bride and groom's house is sufficiently complete to move in, even though much still needs to be done. The wedding can be held. By this time other liaisons have sprung up. Almost all of the Romans have found women. They intend to be married, but later, at the homes of their fiancées.

It's a simple wedding, with only the father and mother, Kang and Ping attending the bride. Meilin appears in the traditional red veil and the ceremony is brief but happy. The banquet will be the high point of the day.

Tables and benches, made especially for the occasion, are set up outside near the wagons. The guests include all the Romans and the senior officers of the Han escort. Although approaching winter the weather is still warm. As the sun goes to bed with the mountains, stars pop into view in spurts. When darkness falls, a shooting star in the West curves across the heavens like the stroke of a master calligrapher. Suddenly bangs, as if from small explosions, spring up behind the guests. The Romans are startled, stop talking and lurch around to see, but the Han seem to take little notice. Marcus asks Kang what they are.

> "They're bamboo sticks. We use them for celebrations. You know that bamboo grows in hollow sections divided by nodes. Short bamboo branches are heated and that expands the air inside. When the pressure builds up enough it suddenly bursts the nodes, making a loud noise. It's a very old tradition."

The banquet floats with bonhomie. The drinks flow; the music from the rain-drop shaped lute and soft drums is romantic and the speeches complimentary. Ting Ting sits under the head table hoping for scraps. Kang explains in a speech the Confucian view that marriage is the basic unit of society. And Meilin is happy. Marcus is too, but a little distracted in his happiness. He can't help thinking of the Road, which he imagines is smiling tonight, like a friend might. It's nearby, close enough to see.

The great Connector has brought him such a long way, through testing times and agonies of the soul and delivered him to his final destination – a place he's not chosen but one where it's possible to feel at home, to feel at a personal level the connectedness that is its essence. The Road has been a subtle teacher, introducing wisdoms of which he had no idea when he started his journey over three years ago with such a different outcome in mind. Maybe one day he'll go to its beginning in the grand capital of his adopted country. But that won't be until he's settled down in Liqian with his new wife and his comrades, sadly one short of the hundred and forty-five who fought to save the caravan.

Now that they have the Protector-General's blessing, not only he but his comrades too can have wives and produce children who will learn about their heritage and pass the knowledge down the line, forever bringing a touch of Rome to the Qilian Mountains.

The points of light in the sky allow him to see the outlines of the majestic range in the distance whose transcendent beauty will enhance his home. It invites thoughts of Platonic perfection – a realm where the spiritual dimension can be as free as the air of the early dawn. Today he saw an eagle bank high in the sky, with the sun on its back, slowly glide out of sight, in peace.

With the clarity of truth, Gan's consent announces acceptance into the culture where he'll spend the rest of his life. If Meilin at the deepest level, and her father to a degree, can grant that acceptance, others might follow, not everyone to be sure, but some, and that would be enough. He's not required to abandon his own culture; he can remain proud of it so long as it's consistent with the values of his new home, and it is. He just needs to broaden the space he lives in, something which the Road has taught him to do. As a mist covers his eyes, he thinks that Socrates was right after all, and Confucius. He has crossed a threshold. In a moment he stands up, lifts his glass and proposes a toast to his friend Kang, holding Meilin's hand.

EPILOGUE

Today, tourists crowd the little village of Liquian, for it's time for the much talked about Roman parade. Villagers, dressed up in full Roman uniform, complete with shining helmet, breastplate and rectangular shield, are beginning their march through the main street towards a little round temple on a hill. Built by local artisans, it has an open roof and columns but no walls. It looks Roman. The procession is like the ancient triumphal pageant that ended at the Capitoline Hill in the Forum. As in Rome, the street is lined with enthusiastic spectators.

The tourists, who are all Chinese, have come from long distances to see the strange sight of men with partial Caucasian features, clothed in period costume never seen in China. Their blue or green eyes, long noses, and fair hair stand out in the area, one of the remotest in China.

The legend of the lost Roman legionnaires is being kept alive with the aid of commerce but it has substance, if not proof, behind it. In the Chinese History of the Former Han Dynasty, mention is made of eight paintings (now lost) depicting the battle of the Talass River. The author speaks of more than a hundred soldiers arranged in a "fish scale" formation in front of the town gate, a pattern scholars are convinced refers to the Testudo. Chinese and Hsiung-nu armies never employed this technique. Also, the account refers to a double palisade of wood on an earthen wall that encircled the town. Again, this Roman device was never used that far east – except for this one time.

Professor Homer Dubs, an English historian at Oxford, wrote a seminal paper on the subject in the 1950's, specifying the number of Roman soldiers who got this far east – a hundred and forty – five. Parents from Liqian have been teaching their children for as long as can be remembered that their ancestors were Roman legionnaires who came along the Silk Road after a great battle, settled in what became their village and married local women. Liqian (pronounced 'Leechan') was the original Chinese name for Rome before it was changed to Daqin. Some scholars think it is a contraction of Alexandria, the city many people associated with Rome. The first syllable 'A' and the last 'dria' were dropped.

As would be expected, DNA samples have been taken of the villagers – but only recently. The analysis shows that nearly sixty per cent of the villagers' genetic structure is of Caucasian origin. While this does not mean the people are Roman descendents, it lends support to the theory. The proof must come from cultural evidence which at this stage is only suggestive. One day it might be supplemented by archaeological excavation, which up to now has not been permitted as the authorities have been uncomfortable with the implications of the legend. That may change.

Archaeologists at the recently set up Italian Studies Centre at Lanzou (capital of Gansu province) hope to conduct digs to find objects left by the Roman immigrants. It seems likely though that even if they find nothing supportive, the cultural memory of the people of Liqian will keep the legend alive, demonstrating the inspiring role the Silk Road has played throughout history in bringing people together from different ends of the world.

HISTORICAL NOTES

BATTLE OF CARRHAE 53 BCE

Battle fought near a small town in south eastern Turkey (now called Harran) between the invading Roman army and the Parthians in 53 BCE. Although outnumbering their enemy four to one, the Romans suffered a catastrophic defeat at the hands of the Parthian horse archers who used high velocity composite bows. The invaders lost 20,000 men killed and 10,000 captured. The remaining 10,000 escaped. Their commander Marcus Licinius Crassus was killed after the battle.

CASSIUS 85 BCE–42 BCE

Gaius Cassius Longinus was a Roman senator and military figure. Having studied philosophy at Rhodes, he was considered a competent philosopher of the Epicurean school. When Crassus invaded Parthia, Cassius was his quaestor, a role responsible for logistics. Later he became the main instigator in the plot to assassinate Julius Caesar. While Brutus actually led the conspirators, it was Cassius who was the intellectual force behind the coup. In Julius Caesar, Shakespeare has the dictator say, "Yon Cassius has a lean and hungry look. He thinks too much. Such men are dangerous."

In the civil war that followed Caesar's assassination, Cassius and Brutus fought Antony and Octavius at the battle of Philippi in Macedonia, and lost. Hearing of Cassius' death by suicide after the battle, Shakespeare has Brutus say of him "The last of all the Romans."

CRASSUS 115?–53 BCE

Marcus Licinius Crassus was known for his extreme wealth, acquired in some cases by unconscionable means. When Sulla seized Rome and confiscated the goods of those who had opposed him, Crassus purchased much of them at a fraction of their worth. Later, he made a fortune buying up houses in Rome which were destroyed by fire and rebuilt them with slaves bought for the purpose and skilled in architecture and building. He owned and operated extensive silver mines. One of the vestal virgins had a desirable property in the suburbs of Rome that Crassus wanted to buy. Seeking to get it at a cheap price he befriended her, an action that led to accusations of seduction.

He was, however hospitable and charming, always courteous and friendly. He was one of the best speakers in Rome, well read in history and schooled in Aristotle. He often lent money without interest to friends (at one time guaranteeing Caesar's debts) but was hard and unsympathetic in collecting it. Of him Plutarch says "the many virtues of Crassus were darkened by the one vice of avarice."

After defeating Spartacus, a Thracian gladiator who fomented a revolt among his fellows, Crassus joined Pompey and Caesar in the First Triumvirate in 55 BCE. He became pro consul of Syria and obtained the command of seven legions for the invasion of Parthia. He died at the battle of Carrhae.

GAN YEN-XU AND CHEN TANG

They were the Protector General of the West and military commander respectively. Their headquarters were at Gaochang in the Turfan depression situated in Xinjiang. By forging the Emperor's signature (a criminal offence) and with the eventual co-operation of Gan, Chen called up military forces, crossed the Pamir Mountains and defeated Jir-Jir at the battle of the Talass River. The victory secured for both of them significant rewards and a pardon.

HAN DYNASTY

Founded in 206 BCE after the collapse of the Qin empire which had united China, the Han dynasty lasted 400 years and represented one of the greatest periods in Chinese history. Even today the ethnic majority in China call themselves "Han". Under Emperor Wu di (141-87 BCE) China became a Confucian state (replacing Taoism) and pushed back the Xiungnu, opening up the Silk Road and gaining access to the heavenly horses of Sogdian Fergana.

JIR-JIR

Having led his people to the Talass River, Jir-Jir conquered various tribes, including the Wusun, and brought the Sogdian kingdom, centred in Samarkand, under vassalage. His rise threatened to cut the Silk Road off from international trade, alarming the Han. In 41 BCE he built a fortified town in the Talass valley and made it his capital. The empire he founded collapsed when an invading Han army defeated him in a major battle. Chinese sources claim Roman soldiers fought with his army.

LEGEND OF THE ROMAN LEGIONARIES

People in the village of Zhelaizhai (formerly called Liqan) near Yong-chang in China's far western province of Gansu have believed for years that they are the descendants of Roman legionaries who migrated across the Silk Road and settled there, marrying local women. Their features bear certain Caucasian characteristics- light coloured and sometimes curly hair, large straight noses, blue or green eyes. The remains of a rammed earth wall said to be part of Roman fortifications stand at the edge of the village.

Testing has confirmed that 56 per cent of their DNA is of Caucasian origin. While this doesn't prove they are of Roman descent, it adds some credibility to the local peoples' belief, particularly when supplemented by Chinese historical evidence.

Currently the local Buddhist monk says prayers for the souls of the Romans who, he says, visit his temple. The people of Yongchang have erected a statue of a Roman on the main street, for the area is being developed as a tourist attraction. Parades of residents dressed up in Roman uniforms are held periodically. They march up a hill to a small Roman-like temple built of concrete, with tourists lining the way.

Support for the legend lies in an account contained in the Chinese History of the Former Han Dynasty written by Ban Gu (32 BCE–220 CE). It inspired an article in 1955 by Homer Dubs, an Oxford history professor. Recounting the battle of Carrhae and Pliny's statement that Roman prisoners were taken to guard the eastern frontier of Parthia, Dubs cites the passage in the Chinese text that speaks of paintings depicting the battle at the Talass River.

The first scene is of "More than a hundred foot-soldiers, lined up on either side of the gate in a fish-scale formation." Dubbs concludes that this most probably refers to theTestudo. In the third scene, the account states "Outside the earthen wall was a double palisade of wood." This was a standard Roman defensive structure and was not used by others, certainly not in Central Asia.

While painting was common in Han China, Dubbs points out there was no precedent for it to record a contemporary event, except this one. He says "The use of pictures in a Roman *triunphus* is well known."

MAGI

The term (singular, magus) was used by the Greeks in the Hellenistic period to denote followers of Zoroaster, who they thought had the ability to read the stars. Because the magi were noted for not only astrology but also various other forms of wisdom (which some Greeks thought was trickery) the word meant the practitioner of magic as well. From magi we get magic in English. It is thought possible that one or more of the Three Wise Men in the Bible were Sogdian magi.

ORODES 11

King of the Parthian Empire from 57 BCE to 37 BCE. He deposed his brother, Mithridates, who fled to Syria and later returned to Parthia with an army. The civil war thus caused ended with Orodes' general, Surena, defeating him at Seleucia in Southern Mesopotamia.

Orodes invaded Armenia while Surena fought the Romans at Carrhae. His purpose of dividing his army in two was, on the one hand, to force the Armenian king to abandon his Roman alliance and submit to him, and on the other, as Plutarch says, to let Surena "first run the risk of battle and draw the enemy on".

He was eventually murdered by his second son, Phraates, who first had him poisoned.

PARTHIAN EMPIRE 247 BCE–224 CE

Founded by an ancient Central Asian tribe of Iranian nomads it extended from what is now south eastern Turkey to eastern Iran. Located on the Silk Road, Parthia was a centre of trade and commerce between Rome and the Han Empire. Its army consisted largely of horse archers with composite bows which were capable of greater thrust than those common further west. Their troops were famous for feigning retreat, shooting while they rode away – the "Parthian shot".

SILK ROAD

This was a complex network of trade routes stretching 6500 km from Rome to Chang an, the capital of the Han Empire (near modern Xian). From the Mediterranean it went through Turkey, Iran, Turkmenistan, Uzbekistan, over the Pamir Mountains and across Xinjiang, and Gansu to Shaanxi province. The term was coined by Ferdinand von

Richthhofen, the uncle of the Red Baron, who was a frequent traveller to China in the latter part of the 19th century.

No one knows when it began to carry traders, but nephrite jade is known to have been traded along it from the 2nd millennium BCE. Around 130 BCE the Han emperor Wu di opened a route across the Tarim Basin (encompassing the Taklamakan desert) and Gansu province of China, which had been interdicted by the Xiung nu for years. The emperor wanted secure access to the so called heavenly horses of Fergana, a Sogdian region (called Dayuan by the Han). These steeds were bigger than the Han variety and ideal for war, a near constant state at the time.

SOGDIANS

They were an ancient Iranian people inhabiting Central Asian lands roughly where Uzbekistan and western Tajikistan are today (known in literature as Transoxiana). Sogdiana lay between the Oxus (Amu Darya) and Jaxartes (Syr Darya) rivers. Samarkand and Bukhara were its major cities. A province of Achaemid Persia, it was conquered by Alexander the Great and subsequently incorporated into the Hellenistic Graeco-Bactrian kingdom. The Fergana valley lies in it east of Samarkand.

The Sogdian language, of eastern Iranian origin, was the linga franca of the Silk Road. Sogdian merchants played a key role in the movement of culture – philosophy and religion, as well as goods. Their religion was Zoroastrian, based on the teachings of Zoroaster (born in either North Eastern Iran or South Western Afghanistan in the 5th century BCE) which essentially postulated a single god and the eternal battle between Good and Evil. Archaeologists have uncovered impressive examples of Sogdian architecture and painting, suggesting a thriving cosmopolitan civilization of high sophistication.

SURENA

Surena, of a noble family, was considered the second most prominent figure in Parthia, after the King. He was a courageous and gifted military commander who conquered Seleucia and defeated Crassus in the battle of Carrhae. Plutarch says "for bodily stature and beauty no man like him." Orodes, the Parthian King, had him executed out of envy. The King himself was ultimately assassinated by his son, Phraates.

XIUNG NU

The Xiung nu, of Turkic origin, were nomadic people who ranged across the steppes of Central Asia, including Xinjiang and Mongolia. They are known in the West as Huns. Constantly raiding China from the north, it was to defend against them that the Chinese built the Great Wall (beginning near Jiayuguan in the western province of Gansu). While of the same race as the Han, their language is entirely separate. Their encounters with the Han over the centuries exemplify the classic clashes between nomadic and sedentary peoples. In 54 BCE the Xiung nu empire split in two. The western part migrated to Sogdiana and established a new empire at the Talass River.

FU CHEU FU oder
FO KYEN.
A. Vorstad
B. Brücke v
C. Fluß vo
D. Wasser